SORCERY AND STARDUST

BOOK ONE

SORCERY AND STARDUST

SAMANTHA STORMFURY

Stardust Empire Publishing

SORCERY AND STARDUST - BOOK ONE

SORCERY
AND
STARDUST

A sorceress.
A warrior.
A space deer.

SAMANTHA
STORMFURY

|| BESTSELLING AUTHOR ||

GLOSSARY OF TERMS

Want to know more about a specific character? You've come to the right place!

I keep a working Character Glossary for each of my worlds on my website.

Check it out here:

www.sliceofsammy.com/character-glossary/

For anyone who looked at the stars and wished.

CHAPTER
ONE

Arcana drew in a lungful of sharp morning air, expanding her chest to capacity and savouring the chill. Long tendrils of curling gold edged a mauve and crimson sky, promising another clear day. She tightened slender fingers around her steaming mug and exhaled in a gust, the bitter essence of the frozen landscape tingling through her veins and out between her lips. The beacon of warmth in her hands abruptly disappeared.

"Ugh." Arcana looked down. The amber liquid had frozen at an odd angle, partially sloshed up the rim of the mug as though in preparation for a sip.

"Did you freeze your tea again?" A great drift of snow shot up into the air as Caelum stood, shaking himself off in a show of fur and slush.

Arcana tipped the mug upside down in demonstration. "Yeah."

"What is that, the third one so far?" Caelum lowered his shaggy head and scratched at one ice-speckled foreleg. Arcana watched in silence, admiring the elegance of his antler rack, each dip and whorl carrying remnants of the snow which had piled up as he slept. Long, sleek fur cascaded like silk from his muscular frame, a silver grey which darkened to black down his spine and mottled across his hindquarters. Caelum turned towards her, his black eyes bottomless and filled with thousands of tiny, swirling stars. "Well, is it?"

"I haven't been counting." Arcana stared into the mug, where her reflection stared back from the mirror-like surface of the tea. White skin -

1

whiter than snow, starker than salt - and midnight hair which tumbled straight and glossy to the base of her spine. She bore the slightly ovular face and button nose of a classic beauty but her eyes, a deep black without iris, pupil or white, ruined the effect. Without the signature features of most normal eyes they seemed too large in her face, emphasised by long black lashes which further unbalanced her cuter, canvas-worthy assets. Slender, not particularly muscular - no sorceress was - with middling to small breasts and a basic hourglass shape, there was nothing much to distract an onlooker from the full impact of her unusual face. Aware that Caelum was watching her self-assessment with an impatient, if not reproachful air, Arcana raised an ebony brow and leant back against the frigid weatherboard of the shack in which she had spent the night. "Did you regret your decision to sleep outside so much that you spent the entire night dreaming of hot beverages?"

Caelum snorted, pawing at the snow. "I already told you, I won't fit inside the wayhut. Doorway's too narrow."

"Yeah, I know." Arcana shivered, and not from the cold. "I would've felt better with you inside. The warg were howling all night."

"I noticed. If it helps, they're not particularly close - it's just the sound carries so easily over the ice." Caelum yawned, his majestic profile thrown into silhouette by the rising sun.

Arcana rolled to her feet, staring over Caelum's broad shoulders to the icy wasteland beyond. "Say what you like, but this trek is taking us steadily closer to their godawful wailing - or are you going to tell me that's a trick of the tundra?"

"No, you're right," he allowed. "If you're worried, we can go back -"

"Don't be silly. I'm just grouchy after trying to sleep on that frozen bed." Arcana tucked her long, ink-black hair into the collar of her jacket and dragged a knit hat into place atop it. "The wayhut is woefully ill-equipped for this icy hellhole - anyone who wasn't me would freeze to death in a couple of hours."

Caelum turned his head south, where barren drifts of unmarked snow were gilt with morning light. A green tinted mountain loomed in the distance and Arcana knew without seeing that his eyes were trained upon it. "Ice princess status notwithstanding, if we don't get a move on the day will be wasted."

"Suits me – the sooner we get started, the sooner we leave this ill-begotten iceberg." Arcana lifted her leather satchel from the porch and shouldered it in one swift movement, clumping down the steps to halt before a bank of waist deep snow. "South?"

2

"Yes." Caelum pushed through the drifts towards her, leaving a deep furrow in his wake. "I can hear that mountain singing."

Arcana buried her hands in the fur of his shoulder and swung astride, settling the leather satchel comfortably in her lap. Her legs tucked around Caelum's ribs with the familiarity of long practice and his antler rack rose in two enormous, elegant silhouettes on either side of her field of vision. She brushed a finger along one velvety edge, entranced by the whorled pattern which was unique as any fingerprint. The surface began to smooth and change as she watched, velvet receding and curved edges sharpening until Caelum wore an antler rack of glittering, coffee-black blades. Arcana withdrew her hand from the scimitar curves and said; "Getting the weaponry out already?"

"All that howling set me on edge. Also, I visited the dreambank while you slept," Caelum answered, turning south and pushing into the snow.

"The dreambank?" Arcana sat up straight, fingers clenched to fists in his long, silky coat. "But... here? There's an access point here?"

"Yes." Caelum's voice turned dreamy as he left the drifted snow surrounding the wayhut and began to pick his way across the hard-packed ice of the tundra. "It was fragile and fractured, like trying to catch falling water. Either way, the fact I saw anything at all - and the singing coming from that mountain - means we're on the right planet."

"I never doubted your instincts in the first place." Arcana reached out to flick playfully at a black-tipped ear. "Did you see anything useful?"

"Fragments. Enough to point us in the right direction. It's like looking into a kaleidoscope and makes about as much sense." His ears flickered thoughtfully. "You were right, though. We're going towards the warg, rather than away from them."

Arcana shivered. "We never do anything the easy way, do we?"

"Where would the fun be in that? You never know, we could get lucky and find the temple before we find the warg. It might even be in one piece." Caelum turned his head slightly to regard her, the swirling stars in his black eyes a sharp contrast to the silver-grey fur of his face.

"Oh please. Look at this place - if the warg are here, whatever we find will be a ruin. Even if all they're doing is hiding from the weather, they'll have found the temple by now. It's how they work," Arcana muttered, shielding her eyes with one hand and glaring off into the stark white distance. "I just don't see why there'd be a temple on this miserable haemorrhoid of a world in the first place."

Caelum chuckled. "This planet wasn't always covered in ice, you know."

"Don't be ridiculous." Arcana waved a hand upwards, where the sun winked weakly above them. "It's too far from the sun for anything else."

"It used to be closer. And there was a moon... maybe even a different sun," said Caelum. The amusement was gone from his voice, replaced by the sombre, distant tone that often coloured his memories of the dreambank.

"Wait... you're saying this wobbly hunk of rock used to be in a *different place*?" Arcana demanded. Caelum was silent for so long that she yanked on the arm-length fur at the back of his head, earning herself a sharp snort and a threatening shake of his shoulders.

"I told you, the dreambank is fractured." Caelum's ribs expanded beneath her for a moment, then he sighed. "I saw green, and life, and a bigger sun, and a very large planet off the port side. Some sort of ferrying system, like that ridiculous setup that runs between Jupiter's moons. So yes, I think it used to be somewhere else."

Arcana turned her eyes upwards, where the sky remained a strange shade of after-dawn grey and would for the rest of the day. There was certainly no large planet on the horizon and hadn't been since they landed two days ago. "A different location would certainly explain why the wayhut was so badly provisioned, but who... *what* could move a moon? What happened to the planet?"

Caelum's shoulders rolled in an elegant shrug. "If I knew that, I would tell you." Calm words, but the hackles at the base of his neck were stiff with frustration. Arcana stroked her fingers though his fur until it began to relax, glaring out at the landscape. There was nothing to see beyond the flat, solid ice of the tundra, nothing to hear beyond the stinging wind. For want of anything better to do, she began braiding the long hair that grew down the ridge of Caelum's spine, trusting his instincts to take them wherever it was they needed to go. The sun was well overhead when his steady progress abruptly halted, jerking a complicated braid out of her fingers. Arcana looked up through the swirl of his antlers to see that the landscape ahead rose into a short, stubby hill at the foot of the green tinged mountain.

"It's here," Caelum said.

"It... that?" Arcana frowned. "It looks like a half-built sandcastle."

"Illogical construction or not, somewhere up there is the reason we came." He was silent a moment and then sighed, a great rumbling of his chest. "This place... I feel strange. Edgy. As though there's something I should be doing, or something I should know, but I can't do it because I don't know it."

4

"That's why we're here, isn't it? To unlock the secrets hidden inside you." Arcana jumped down from his back, her booted feet sliding across the ice. Caelum's head snaked out, his teeth fastening over her coat and steadying Arcana when she would have fallen. "Thanks."

"Welcome." Caelum waited while she regained her balance then turned to look at the mountain, his posture cramped with lines of tension. "I feel like we need to hurry."

Arcana glanced around them nervously. "Warg?"

"No. Something else." Caelum tilted his head, starry eyes roving over the almost sheer ascent. "In the interest of haste, I think a staircase would be handy."

"Only you would ask for a staircase up a mountainside," Arcana grinned, crouching to flatten her hands against the snow-flecked ice beneath them. She called her magic, savouring the chill heartbeat of the landscape that flowed in her veins. Caelum moved closer until his legs almost brushed her shoulder, cloven hooves weaving an intricate dance as the ground beneath them began to reform. The ice buckled and cracked, the inch-deep covering of snow sloughing sideways as first one step, then another, rose gracefully from the tundra's frozen surface.

"Halfway up for now," Caelum murmured and Arcana obliged, continuing to shape the shallow ice stairs until they connected with the hillside where he indicated. Caelum regarded her work in silence, his twitching tail the only sign of life. "That never gets old."

"I'll take that as a compliment." Arcana pushed to her feet, shaking the last few snowflakes free of her clothing.

"You should." He tossed a rogue's grin at her but it was short lived, falling into a frown. "The singing is getting more urgent. Let's go."

"All right." Arcana twisted one hand in his fur, dragging herself onto his back. "But for the record, following the directions of a singing mountain might be misconstrued as crazy."

"It's never stopped us before." Caelum flowed over the hardened ground without fear of slipping, picking up speed until he may as well have been flying. Moments later they stood at the top of the stairs, eyeing the wall of snow and ice before them. "Although I'll admit it's never been this strong before. Are you sure you can't hear it?"

"Not a thing." Arcana clutched at Caelum's fur as he stepped fearlessly onto a narrow ledge, navigating footholds that should have been impossible for his size.

"Here," he said at last, motioning to a section of the hillside that looked like any other. Arcana waved a hand and the snow slithered aside, revealing solid ice. Caelum's ears flickered. "We need to go in."

"I figured." Arcana slid carefully off his back and flattened her hands against the mountainside. She called her magic and pushed, walking forwards. The wall gave way beneath her touch, retreating and widening to form a tunnel big enough for even Caelum to follow easily. It should have become darker as they progressed but the ice projected a soft blue light that filled the tunnel.

"How did you do the light?" Caelum asked.

Arcana paused, looking back over one shoulder. "I didn't." She removed her hands from the ice and the light winked out.

"It's not... that's not your magic?" He sounded uncertain for the first time since their arrival.

"No." Arcana touched the wall again and the light returned, soft and blue and constant. "Should I stop? We can go back if you're worried."

"The blue light is creepy, but..." Caelum frowned, scuffing at the floor of the tunnel with one neat, cloven hoof. "We need to keep going. Just be alert."

"Okay." Arcana pushed further into the mountainside, Caelum so close behind his breath tickled her ear. They walked in silence, save for the rasp of Arcana's lungs and the soft slither of her feet along the icy flooring. All of a sudden her magic cut off, the feeling akin to that of a solid slap. Arcana gasped and stumbled face first into the wall ahead, rebounding into Caelum and plunging the tunnel into darkness.

"Arcana?" Caelum's voice echoed through the inky black.

"I'm fine." Arcana leant against the side wall and the blue glow returned, revealing an imposing stone slab in front of them. "Whatever that is, it rejected my magic."

Caelum leant over her shoulder, his fur tickling one cheek as he squinted at the door. "I guess that means it's not for you to open. Can you increase the light?"

"I don't know." As if hearing her words, the tunnel brightened, throwing the carving on the door into focus. Arcana gasped and took a half step back. "Caelum – is that your face?"

"Not my face, but one like mine. And look; a keyhole." He jerked his chin and Arcana saw at once that the deerlike face on the door had a soft indentation where the nose should be, and two long, narrow slits at the outer edge of the antler rack.

Arcana frowned. "Are you sure about this?"

"Not at all." Caelum slid past her, placing his nose in the indentation and the tips of his antlers into the stone slits. A moment passed, then another, and then the door began to glow, a gentle green light that emanated from the places Caelum touched and spread until the entire carving's face was illuminated. The slab swung aside with a huge groan, leaving Caelum standing alone in the blackened maw of a doorway. He turned to regard Arcana with gently swirling eyes. "Shall we?"

"Wait - there's no light," Arcana protested. "I can't see in the dark."

"Hmmm." Caelum poked his head through the door and swung it from side to side. "Nothing. What about that magic ice?"

Arcana looked at the glowing wall with a degree of uncertainty. In her experience, it was unwise to trust an unknown source of magic, much less meddle with it - but without a fire handy, what choice did they have? Frowning, she bladed her hand and made a scooping motion against the wall, using her magic to carve out a fist-sized ball of ice. The tunnel immediately darkened but the globe in Arcana's palm retained its eerie blue luminescence, shedding a soft glow around her for several feet. She held her breath a long moment - but nothing happened, save for Caelum to stare at her inquiringly.

"Okay. Here we go." Arcana twined her fingers into the fur at Caelum's shoulder and lifted the orb higher, widening the circle of light. The glowing ice was no match for a proper torch but it alleviated the worst of the gloom, revealing a vast rectangular chamber whose far wall had collapsed in a tumble of rubble and snow. A stone dais stood in the centre of the space, the back end partially covered by debris. As they approached, Arcana made out the crumbling remains of a tall, circular structure with a shorn-off stone pedestal to one side.

"Do you see that?" Caelum's steady, hypnotic pace faltered for a moment and then he shot forward with his nose outstretched, jerking free of Arcana's grip. She stumbled on the uneven floor, the light in her hand zagging crazily across the stone walls.

"Great Gods of Sorcen, what are you-"

"Here!" Caelum's voice bore an urgency which had Arcana hurrying forward. He stood at the base of the dais, head lowered to the armoured figure slumped on the floor.

"What in the name of magic?" Arcana dropped to one knee beside the figure, reaching out to carefully tug the dented helmet free. The face inside was male and bloody, his soft teal skin and high cheekbones framed by a tumble of dark curls. "A knight?"

"Is he-?" Caelum broke off.

Arcana laid two fingers against the knight's throat, pressing down, searching. His skin was cold to the touch, sticky with sweat and blood, but beneath it all Arcana felt the unmistakable flutter of a pulse. "Alive, but barely." Arcana moved her hand over his plated chest, where the metal had been slashed diagonally from pectoral to hip. Dark blood flowed readily from the gash, pooling on the floor and coating her fingers. "We need to get him out of here."

"Put him on my back." Caelum dropped to the ground, silver fur spilling across the stone floor and immediately staining dark with the warrior's blood.

"Yeah, sure. Hoist a knight in full plate armour onto your back," Arcana growled, levering her arm behind the warrior. His eyes flew open at the touch and she gasped as jade fire spilled down his cheeks, mingling with the blue glow of the ice orb and casting eerie shadows over the planes of his angular face. Though the knight's eyes appeared featureless, Arcana knew without doubt the moment he focussed on her.

"Run," he grunted.

"Shhhh. I need you to get onto Caelum's back." Arcana grabbed the knight's chin as his head began to list. "Can you do it?"

"No... leave. Run..." The knight groaned, trying to pull away until his gaze fell on Caelum, kneeling patiently on the floor. His jaw dropped open.

"Please listen to her," said Caelum quietly.

"A deerken," he breathed, and just when Arcana feared he wouldn't move, the knight gripped her arm tightly and pushed himself upright. Even doubled over it was impossible to miss the fact that he was almost seven feet tall, his frame wiry but powerful underneath what remained of the armour.

"Of course. Don't move for me, no, but a big hairy goat? No worries," Arcana drawled. She inserted herself under his arm, doing her best to provide support as the knight slung a leg over Caelum's back.

"My sword..." He gestured to a long, wide blade on the floor, revealed by the absence of his body.

Arcana bent to heft it and staggered under the weight. The giant sword - it had to be at least as tall as she was - barely shifted an inch. "No way am I going to be able to carry that. We'll have to ditch it."

"No!"

"Put it in the bag," Caelum jerked upright, ears swivelling towards the tunnel. "And hurry. I have a bad feeling."

"A bad feeling? Great." Arcana slid her satchel off and crouched on the bloodied stones. The knight's brilliant green eyes widened as she slipped the mouth of the bag over the tip of the blade and tugged, inch by slow inch, until the entire sword had disappeared. Arcana flipped the satchel shut and repositioned it over her shoulder. "Much better."

"Mage," the knight whispered.

"Sorceress," she corrected, stepping beside him and hefting the glowing ice. "And slave to the first rule of adventuring: always have a magic bag. Now, let's get you out of here."

"Warg!" Caelum's shout echoed through the crumbling cavern, his stardust eyes wide in the pale blue light. A shadow hurtled across the room towards them, claws rasping on stone. Arcana dropped to one knee, flattening her hand against the floor and calling her magic. It rose through her veins, dragging the energy of the stone and the earth along with it. The warg leapt, no more than flashing fangs and whirling claws in the half-dark. Arcana raised her arm and great pillars of stone shot out of the ground, huge and ancient teeth more than twice her height. The warg yelped as the stone skewered his body and the room fell silent.

Arcana stood and dusted her hands. "That was close. I thought you said they were further away?"

"Yeah, and you said they'd be here. One of us had to be wrong," Caelum murmured, ears flickering as he listened to the dripping silence. "This place must be connected to their den. Probably a side effect of the cave in."

"Hmm." Arcana stepped over the gritty rubble, the blue light in her hand spilling across the furred face of a creature who was neither human nor animal, but some bizarre blend of both. The warg's tongue lolled out at an angle, eyes wide and lifeless. "He was only young."

"That's why he was so easy to kill." Caelum high-stepped past the body, nose wrinkled in disgust. "The scent of his blood will call the others. We need to move."

Arcana reached inside the neckline of her top, where a tooth hung on a length of leather. She closed a fist around the necklace and prodded it with her magic. "Whatever energy stopped me opening that door is thick through the whole place. I've got a basic trickle of power, but not enough to charge the tooth. We need to get outside to jump."

Caelum grunted, already moving for the tunnel. "I figured as much. Come on."

Warg. Always warg. Arcana waved a hand and watched as the stone spikes returned to the earth. The dead warg now lay at her feet, his chest a gaping hole. Looking much like the classic bipedal werewolf out of a Terran horror story, the warg were a force to be reckoned with. They bred incessantly, fought without mercy and possessed an innate cunning surpassed only by their physical abilities and natural weaponry. But how did they get out here, to this misbegotten lump of ice and snow? Arcana stepped around the corpse and made for the tunnel, placing her feet carefully to minimise the sound of their passing. It was no use; a terrible howl echoed through the vast room and moments later warg began boiling out of a crack in the corner.

"Run!" She shouted, leaping between Caelum and the slavering, racing bodies. He bounded away and Arcana threw her arm skywards, sending their tiny orb of light up and up and up. In her experience, it was always a bad idea to meddle with strange, wild magic - unless, of course, there were worse things chasing you. So Arcana poured her own magic into the globe, feeling for the spark inside, grabbing it, twisting... Until the orb exploded in a blinding ball of brilliance. The warg howled in pain, falling away from the bright light that spun and shimmered in the air above.

Arcana leapt for the tunnel, blinking the radiance from her own vision as she raced along it, dragging her fingers down the wall for balance. A pool of daylight called her on, Caelum's silhouette framed in the entrance. Together they crept along the tiny goat track, back towards the icy staircase. Arcana forced herself to take deep, steadying breaths, absorbing the cold into her lungs, changing the magic from the earthy interior of the temple to the chill of the frigid outdoors.

"They're still coming," Caelum warned.

Arcana looked over her shoulder, where the tunnel had come alive with the sound of snapping teeth. "Be ready. This could go badly." She closed her hand to a fist, collapsing the icy entrance. The mountain groaned, the warg howled and for a long, terrible moment everything was still. She flicked a glance at Caelum, watched his ears swivel until they were trained on the mountain.

"Get on," he commanded. An ominous crack punctuated the words, followed swiftly by sloughing, swishing and rumbling. Arcana hauled herself up behind the knight as a great wall of snow came crashing down the mountain towards them, dotted with boulders and fuelled by crumbling masonry. Caelum leapt down the icy stairs and Arcana leant over his neck, using her body weight to hold the knight's limp body in place.

The ground bucked and heaved but Caelum didn't miss a beat, his cloven hooves cleaving thin air as often as they did the ice. "Did you have to bring down the whole mountain?" He shouted, his voice snatched by the wind and muted by the roar of the earth.

"I didn't mean to!" Arcana cast a glance over her shoulder to see the avalanche rapidly gaining speed, spitting rock and ice and warg into the air behind them.

"We need to jump! I can't outrun it." Caelum reached the bottom of the stairs and threw himself across the ice, a desperate race to buy them time. Arcana reached inside her furred coat and yanked the leather thong from around her neck. Clenching the tooth in her fist, she crushed herself against the knight's plate armour, wrapped her legs tightly around Caelum's ribs and focussed her attention on the tiny talisman in her hand.

At first, nothing. No more than the roar of the icy doom behind them and the undulation of Caelum's body as he raced over the bucking ground. Arcana closed her eyes and held her breath, anything to shut out the world and focus. She probed the tooth with her magic, finding a crack through which she could gain entry. The inside was a tranquil dream that spoke of lazy summer days, softly swaying flowers and gentle breezes. Arcana melded with the energy and dragged the sensation over them like a blanket, forcing it into Caelum's flesh, into his bones, suffusing their combined essences with an otherworldly presence until the ice, the snow, the land around them shimmered as if in a heat haze.

And Caelum jumped.

For moments that lasted lifetimes, they hung between realms and realities, bound together only by physical contact and shared determination. Then with a gut-wrenching lurch the universe realigned itself and they were no longer speeding across an iced landscape but standing in a carpeted room, face to face with a deerken skull.

"Made it," Caelum wheezed, his head between his knees.

"Are you okay?" Arcana slid off his back, dragging the armoured knight with her in an awkward tangle of clattering limbs.

"I will be. That was close." Caelum shook himself thoroughly and turned towards their guest. "How is - wait, is he *green*?"

"I don't think his skin is green so much as teal." Arcana laid her hands against the knight's chilled cheeks and frowned. "And yes, he's still alive. Help me get this armour off, would you? I need to see his wounds."

"Hang on." Caelum set the sharpened edges of his antlers against the edge of the breastplate and heaved. The leather ties shredded and the entire thing rolled off, thumping onto the floor on the knight's opposite side. "There."

"Thanks." Arcana peeled back the remains of the linen shirt underneath to reveal the great, bloody gash that stretched from the knight's right hip and ended just below his left armpit. "Wow."

"He's lucky he wasn't disembowelled."

Arcana narrowed her eyes at the wound, still steadily pumping dark burgundy blood all over the place. "Actually, I think whoever did this was aiming for heart, then guts - you know what? Rescind that. They were trying to cut him in half." She pressed her lips together. "This is more than a first aid kit job. I'll need fire."

"On it." He moved away, and Arcana busied herself soaking up some of the excess blood with a nearby blanket while she waited. Less than a minute later, Caelum dropped an old-fashioned lantern onto the ground beside her. "Here."

"My bedside lamp?" Arcana stared down at the tiny flame, barely taller than that of a lit candle. "Is that really the only fire we've got?"

"On short notice, yeah." He rolled his shoulders in the deerken equivalent of a shrug. "Everything in the kitchen's powered by the engines – no open fire."

"Frigging spaceships." Arcana flipped the lantern's latch and opened the tiny glass door. She placed one hand above the flame, letting it lick across her palm and between her fingers, filling her with heat and light. It wasn't much, but it would have to do. She set her other hand on the warrior's hip, covering the edge of the gash. The smell of burning flesh filled the air and Caelum snorted, prancing away. Arcana ignored him, drawing on the flame and focussing the heat, cauterising the knight's wound one slow inch at a time. Sweat trickled into one eye and she blinked it away, wishing vainly for a blazing furnace rather than the cheery, tickling flamelet of her bedside lamp.

"Almost there," Caelum encouraged.

Arcana grunted, dragging the magic now, forcing it through sluggish arms, determined not to falter. Too fast, and the flame would go out. Too slow, and it wouldn't be enough to melt that teal flesh back together. She leant forward, pressing her palm against the knight's chest to seal the last part of his wound. "He's lucky he's unconscious." Arcana pulled her hand from the lantern and scrubbed at her face, equal parts relieved and exhausted.

"Will he live?" Caelum asked, taking the lantern's handle between his teeth and lifting it out of the way.

"He bloody better," Arcana snapped, resisting the urge to sag forwards onto the carpet. Instead, she fumbled with the fastenings of her coat, now far too warm for the controlled climate of the ship. She dragged it off, dropping it onto the carpet beside her, and allowed a moment to appraise her strange guest.

His skin was indeed a soft shade of teal; not too light, not too dark.

Pleasant, Arcana thought, a pleasant complement to the jade eyes she'd seen inside the temple. His dark curls were stuck with sweat and blood to his face but it was possible to see they were a shade of teal also; almost black, not quite. High cheekbones and long lashes lent him an other-worldly elegance, enhanced by a slender, wiry frame sheathed in muscle rather than overburdened by it. Dirty and bleeding, he was one of the most handsome creatures Arcana had ever seen; she had no doubt that clean and animated, he'd be breathtaking.

Caelum appeared with a blanket and together they drew it over the knight's body, now branded with a livid burgundy burn. Arcana folded her coat and slid it underneath his head, then pushed to her feet to find Caelum watching her, the stars in his eyes swirling gently. "He'd be better in a bed," the deerken remarked.

Arcana shook her head. "I'm not game to move him, not when it might reopen that wound." She sucked on her teeth for a moment. "The carpet will do for now and when he wakes – if he wakes – we can move him into one of the beds. Is our orbit stable? Shields up?"

"Of course. You don't want to leave?" Caelum looked surprised.

"I do, but I'd like to talk to Captain Slashy before we go too far."

"He *is* the reason we were called," Caelum said, his tone flat.

Arcana waved a dismissive hand. "I'm not doubting your instincts - but why? How did he get here? Where is he from? Who tried to cut him in half? What in the name of a thousand suns has he got to do with us?"

"I don't know, but he's ours," Caelum insisted, his voice suddenly petulant. "We were sent to him."

"Do you have any idea how crazy that sounds?" Arcana buried her hands in her hair, tugged in frustration. "We've spent fifty years following your instincts across space and this is the first time we've ended up with a third wheel."

"That alone should show you how important he is," Caelum replied.

Arcana rolled her shoulders in a vain attempt to ease their tension. She wasn't going to win the battle - wasn't even sure exactly what the battle *was*. And yet - "Look, I just want to talk to him, okay? I don't know where to take him, what to do with him, until we at least answer some of those questions."

"All right," Caelum agreed. Then, "He's rather beautiful, don't you think?"

"Exquisite." Arcana regarded the knight through narrowed eyes. "But I don't always trust beautiful. Slashy could also be vain, or cruel, or, you know, a bad guy who wants to kill us."

"He's got laugh lines in the corners of his eyes and my instincts don't lead us to bad guys." Caelum's voice was tart. "You worry too much. Also... Slashy?"

She shrugged. "Gotta call him something."

"Huh. I guess so. Well, whoever he is, he's not going anywhere for now. I'll watch him," Caelum said.

"Thanks." Arcana stood on tiptoe and planted a kiss on the side of his furry nose. "Now, if you'll excuse me, I have warg to wash off."

CHAPTER
TWO

"He's awake."

Arcana groaned and pulled the quilt over her head, only to have Caelum catch the edge in his teeth and whisk it off her with surgical precision. "I hate you," she grunted, throwing one arm over her eyes and curling both knees to her chest.

"You do not," Caelum answered evenly. Arcana set her jaw and remained silent. Caelum's breath gusted over her as he sighed, and a moment later she felt the insistent jab of his antlers down the length of her spine. "If you don't move, I'll carry you in there in your underwear. Who knows, Slashy might even like that."

"I've only slept for an hour!" Arcana caught the base of his antlers in one hand and dragged herself into a sitting position, rubbing sleep from her eyes.

"Five, more like, and you could've slept longer but you were too busy drinking tea and frowning at our friend."

"Frowning at his armour," Arcana grumbled, scrubbing her hands through tangled hair. "Whatever caused that injury sliced the metal clean through."

"So I've heard you say - at least a dozen times already," Caelum drawled. Irritation rode high in his tone, the line of his shoulders. "You really are a pain when you wake up, you know that?"

"Sorry." Arcana pushed herself upright and stretched stiffened limbs. "Let me find something to wear and I'll be right there."

"Better. Apology accepted." Caelum tossed the last over his shoulder as he disappeared out of the door.

"Ugh." Arcana padded into the bathroom and splashed water on her face, eyeing her unkempt reflection in the mirror. Black eyes stared back, startlingly dark in her china white face and ringed by sleep circles. Added to her wayward, ink-black hair, Arcana could for all the world have crawled out of a grave rather than her own bed. She grimaced, dragging bedraggled tresses into a haphazard ponytail, and returned to her room.

So, he was awake. Arcana flicked a glance at her bedside clock. Twelve hours since she'd sealed his wound, and he was cracking an eyelid? *Impressive*, she thought, grabbing faded jeans and a baggy knit jumper from her dresser. She dragged them on over her bra and panties, jumped up and down on the spot to try and clear the cobwebs from her brain, and then padded barefoot across the hall.

The door swished open at her touch to reveal Caelum curled up on a large, backless lounge with his eyes half closed. Their guest lay on the floor as he had the day before, only now his eyes were open, his head turned towards her as she entered. Arcana had thought animation would enhance the ethereal quality of his features and she was right; he exuded an aura of effortless grace and coiled energy that was obvious even lying down.

"Good morning," Arcana said, forcing a bright smile onto her face. Dried blood crusted the edge of his jaw and one cheek, marring the breath-taking elegance of Slashy's face as he stared back at her. Jade flame still flickered within his eyes, though with far less intensity than in the ruined temple. She searched them again for signs of pupil or iris, but there was nothing - only the fathomless jade light. Still, Arcana knew he was looking at her, sizing her up as she had done with him hours earlier. She choked back the urge to laugh. Bed hair and last week's jeans - hardly an impressive introduction. "My name's Arcana. This is Caelum, and you're on our ship."

Slashy stared at her impassively, arms draped across his chest, fingertips clenching the edge of the blanket. Now that the sweat had dried, his dark hair curled loosely about his head, accenting the pale teal hue of his skin far better than before. A muscle in his jaw worked as Arcana approached, kneeling beside him just out of arm's reach. A waiting game, was it? She curled her hands in her lap and returned his stoic expression in silence.

"We saved your life, you know," Caelum said finally. Slashy flicked a glance across the room and Arcana saw a flicker of uncertainty dancing in his eyes.

"Deerken do not talk," he said. Now that his voice was clear of pain and exhaustion it had a gentle, velvety resonance, but the words themselves were clipped.

"*Don't* they?" Caelum blinked owlishly. "I assure you, Arcana's no ventriloquist. This is definitely my voice."

"I have never met a deerken who could talk," Slashy amended, his brows twitching as though Caelum were an inexplicable puzzle.

"Well now you have," Caelum returned equably. The knight lapsed back into silence, his gaze lingering on Caelum for a long moment before turning back to Arcana. His carefully blank expression tensed, as though he was about to speak and thought better of it.

"So, have you got a name?" Arcana asked, tilting her head to one side.

"Captain of the Apollo guard, Betelgeuse wing. Designation Zerytto, number six five five thirty-two," he said, his eyes never straying from her face.

Arcana snorted and shook her head. "Now that is a load of bullshit if I ever heard it. What are you, five?"

His cheeks flushed a darker shade of teal, which if possible, made him more attractive than before. "I am not in the habit of giving my true name to captors."

"What makes you think you're a prisoner?" Caelum's face furrowed in confusion.

Slashy's eyes swivelled slowly, purposefully upwards, to the grinning skull on the wall above them. The movement caused an elegant tilt of his chin, muscles shifting down his throat and upper chest. Arcana watched the delicate grace of his body, narrowing her eyes. There was a certain strict control to his actions that belied pain underneath. "You have a poached deerken skull mounted on the wall. You invaded a portal chamber and carry a magic bag which has conveniently swallowed my only possession. You bypassed all manner of protections to stand upon sacred ground, yet claim not to know who I am. Why else would you be in that place if not to seek the Timeless Kingdom?" he was panting by the end of his speech, sweat beading on his brow.

Arcana stood and crossed the room to where her satchel lay on the table. She returned to Slashy's side and flipped the bag open, tipping it up until the point of the oversized sword thumped on the carpet. It was huge, stained dark with blood and required both hands and all her strength to get it out of the satchel. Runes trailed down the blade's spine and several notches were cut into it near the hilt, leaving four wicked looking spikes at the topmost corner. Arcana tossed the satchel aside and stepped back to lean against the table. "There. I'd tell you that I only put it in the bag to bring it back here safely, but you've clearly formulated your own opinion. I'd also tell you that we've been searching for information to help us and that's how we ended up in the temple, but you've formulated your own opinion on that too. I don't know where or what the Timeless Kingdom is, but there's no point me explaining that either because – wait for it – you've already drawn your own conclusions."

"You forgot the part where we're poachers," Caelum said. His body hadn't moved, but he was quivering with tension.

"Oh yes. My favourite part. This one, I *will* correct you on – that, up there, is the skull of Caelum's mother. And you know what? I tried to save her life, but I couldn't. She's on that wall for a whole lot of reasons, none of which are your business. So screw you. All I did was save your life and ask your name but you know what? I called you Captain Slashy before and I can continue to live with that." Arcana got to her feet and jabbed a finger in his direction. "You go on right ahead making your own assumptions. Meanwhile, I'm going to have some breakfast and after that, I'm going to send you back to that shitty ruin where we found you." Angry sparks fizzed and popped in the air around her head. Slashy's eyes tracked the tiny flares for a few seconds, then sought her face, but he didn't speak. Fine. If that's the way he wanted to play it, fine. Arcana turned for the door, her hands clenching into fists to cut off the tiny fireworks still skittering in the air around her.

"Wait."

"Forget it." She placed her palm on the sensor plate and the door swished open, revealing the slavering snout of the warg on the other side.

Time stood still as Arcana stared into the creature's dull amber eyes, her surprised expression reflected in his pupils. Thin lips pulled back from razor sharp teeth as the warg lunged, a growl rumbling in his throat - but he was too slow. Arcana placed her hand on his chest and pulsed her anger outwards, drawing on the thrumming energy of the ship. The warg's growl cut off and the creature slumped to the floor with a steaming hole where his heart used to beat.

"Arcana!" Caelum shouted. He was between Slashy and a warg, his velvety antlers sharpening into blades. A second creature materialised in the air above, dropping onto Caelum's back with a howl.

"What in the - They're wearing teleporters!" Arcana slapped the heels of both palms together, blasting a beam of white hot energy at the warg on Caelum's rump. The creature fell off with a shriek, his furred legs charred and one arm disintegrated. Dancing away from the slashing claws of the second beast, Caelum buried one cloven hoof deep in the warg's skull, silencing him permanently. Growling low in his throat, the remaining warg launched himself at Caelum's exposed withers. The deerken twisted, entangling the beast in his antler rack and throwing it on the floor at Arcana's feet.

The warg hit the carpet and rolled upright, flinging itself at her face with dripping jaws wide. Arcana threw herself backwards, one arm outstretched, fingers brushing the length of a slippery fang as they fell in a tangle of limbs and fur. Magic surged and the warg's howl of victory cut short as his head disappeared in a shower of sparks. Arcana hit the floor with a bone-jarring thud and skidded on her shoulders, gore splattering the front of her body.

Caelum appeared overhead. "Are you okay?"

"Fine." Arcana coughed and sat up, shaking her hand and spraying blood across the carpet. "Oh, ugh. Yuck."

"They sure made a mess." Caelum wrinkled his nose in disgust.

"Actually, I think you'll find *we* were the ones who made the mess." Arcana picked a gobbet of flesh from her jumper and dropped it on the floor with a grimace. Rather than focus too closely on exactly what she was covered in, she turned her attention instead to their reluctant guest, still reclining on the carpet over the other side of the room. "You okay?"

Slashy opened his mouth as if to speak, the sound disappearing on a gasp as the air shimmered and another warg appeared, dropping several feet to straddle the knight's chest. Arcana leapt to her feet, calling her magic - but Slashy was faster. With a great yell, he caught up the sword beside him, driving it through the warg's abdomen and out the other side. The warg roared with fury, claws outstretched and body bearing down in spite of the enormous blade. Slashy twitched his shoulders and threw the creature sideways, rolling with the sword until it was he who straddled the warg's chest, pinning the creature to the floor.

"Kill it!" Slashy's features twisted in agony as he fought to keep his attacker subdued. Arcana vaporised the warg's head and shoulders with an energy blast, rushing forward to catch the knight as he slumped over the hilt of his sword.

"Caelum! Get us out of here," she cried. Slashy's skin was slick with blood, his face set in a torturous mask. He motioned to his sword and Arcana reached out, grasping the hilt with both hands. It was stuck fast. She set her foot against the warg and tried again. No luck.

"Here." Slashy's hand closed over hers and together they wrenched the blade free.

"Thanks. Caelum, how much longer?"

The deerken stood in front of a wall panel whose screen rolled with lines of red text. "I've mapped a course, but you sapped the star drive during that battle – we're stuck."

"Oh, for Sorcen's sake." Arcana splayed her hands flat on the sticky carpet, sending questioning tendrils of magic through the bowels of the ship. The star drive fluttered weakly at her touch, mere glowing embers where there should have been a furnace. Arcana cradled the flagging energy with her magic, absorbing and multiplying until it was huge and hot and deadly. She fed the thrumming power back into the star drive, filling the wheezing shell until it creaked an ominous protest.

"We're out." Caelum's voice was full of relief as Arcana sagged back onto her knees, rubbing a bloodied wrist across her forehead. When she raised her eyes, Slashy was propped up on his elbows, luminous eyes filled with astonishment.

"Did you just recharge the ship with *magic*?" He demanded.

"Yes. I used the energy from the star drive to vape the warg, and then I put it back so we could get out of here - and if that didn't convince you we mean no harm, then nothing will." Arcana moved to cross her arms over her chest, remembered the gore, and put her hands on her hips instead. "Now, seriously, who the hell are you? What is going on?"

"My name is Fenris, Guardian to the Weaver and Warden to the deerken." Dark lashes rested briefly on soft, teal cheeks. "Please forgive my trespass on your honour - I appear to have misunderstood your intention."

"Fenris, huh?" Arcana drummed her fingers restlessly on one thigh. Fenris' eyes were tight with pain, one hand clutching convulsively at his ribs, body sheened with sweat. She sighed and shook her head, the last of her temper sliding away. "Okay, Fenris. Apology accepted."

"Thank you," he managed, jaw clenched tight.

"Looks like you overdid it lifting that ridiculous sword. Lie down and let me see." Arcana pushed Fenris back against the carpet, wiping blood off his chest with her sleeve. The edges of his wound remained sealed but dark stains bloomed beneath the skin, curling tendrils of burgundy that grew even as she watched.

"He's bleeding internally," Caelum murmured, his breath warm in her ear.

"Probably all that leaping around." Arcana frowned, her fingers moving gently over the planes of his chest.

Fenris flinched and grabbed her wrist, the grip strong for all his arm shook. "Don't," he managed, his face even paler. "I can't-"

"If you won't let me look, then you need to tell me where the pain is. I can't help you otherwise," she said, transferring her gaze to his.

"Pain everywhere." Fenris' fingers tightened convulsively on her wrist, eyelids fluttering. "I feel… tired."

"I need you to be more specific," Arcana urged, patting his cheek with her free hand. Her only answer was a sigh as Fenris' eyes rolled back and his body relaxed. "Damn."

"This is more than you can handle." Caelum lowered his head to sniff the knight's shoulder. "He's out cold."

"Yeah." Arcana grimaced, carefully removing Fenris' long fingers from around her wrist. "We're going to need help."

"He said he was Warden to the deerken, which sounded like a title. He said it as if… as if there might be more of me," Caelum whispered.

"I know you have questions, but we really don't know anything about him - and yes, I know, your instincts don't lead us to bad guys. You said that already." Arcana sighed, tucking Fenris' hand down by his side. "I wish I had your faith."

"It's less faith and more desperation at this point. He *recognised* me, Arcana. He knows what I am. It took thirty years before even *we* knew what I am." Caelum's eyes were shining, his nostrils quivering with anticipation. "Think what else he might be able to tell us."

"I get it, and I'm happy for you to ask - but right now we need to save his life. Again," Arcana added. She offered Caelum a rueful smile she didn't quite believe.

"That much is obvious. I already set a course for Sorcen."

Arcana scrubbed at her face with one hand, peering through her fingers at the unconscious man on the floor. "Sorcen?"

"Don't sound so traumatised." Caelum lipped at her hair. "This is way beyond us - beyond most healers. We need Lesce and you know it."

"Ugh. Fine, take us home." Arcana got to her feet, dusting bloodied hands uselessly on her ruined jeans. With the star drive pushing them through the galaxy at a speed beyond imagining, there was no longer any danger of ambush - which meant there was nothing left to do but clean up the mess. She and Caelum dragged the corpses into the centre of the room and Arcana used the last of her borrowed star drive energy to vaporise the grisly remains.

"Carpet's ruined," Caelum mourned, scuffing the once fluffy flooring with his hoof.

"Yeah. Don't worry, I'll get it replaced once we land." She reached out to pat his shoulder but he danced away from her bloody fingers.

"No offence, but hug me when you're clean." Caelum's ears flickered. "I wonder what those warg were after? Teleporting into a confined space is pretty risky."

"Him, obviously." Arcana gestured at Fenris. His breathing was shallow with pain, even in unconsciousness, but she could do nothing more.

Caelum hummed an agreement. "I've never seen warg with teleporters before. I didn't think they had the sense to understand them. Is someone controlling the packs?"

"That's a question only Fenris can answer - but someone *really* wanted him dead, that's for sure," Arcana mused. "His body was almost cleft in two and the warg were still chasing him."

"Judging from the way he handled that sword, being cut in half wasn't nearly dead enough - and the warg knew it." Caelum shook himself all over, his silvery fur shimmering under the artificial light. "It's a carpet ruining mystery."

"You and your carpet! I told you, I'm going to replace it." Arcana waved a hand at the macabre mural of blood and grime splattered around the room. "I notice you're not complaining about the walls."

"I don't cuddle into the walls," Caelum replied, ears twitching. "They lack a certain fluffy appeal."

"Well you're going to have to curb your floor-loving tendencies until we land, okay? You know the Council. If they think it'll buy them more leverage over us, they'll find you carpet so fluffy it's knee deep. Hell, they'll even weave it for you out of their own hair," Arcana growled.

"Gross. I don't even want to think about hair carpet. That's just wrong." Caelum looked horrified, the hackles standing up straight down his spine.

"You get my point. Although I still have my reservations about taking Fenris to Sorcen when he's clearly being pursued." Arcana ran a hand through her hair and it immediately tangled in a mess of knots and drying warg bits. "Oh, yuck. I need to shower before I spew."

"You do. But to address your concerns, there's no way to get a teleportation lock after we engage the star drive - it's too fast. You know that. And even if there was, anyone stupid enough to attack a planet full of sorcerers is going to learn a very quick and nasty lesson," Caelum answered.

"Oh yes, let's drag the whole planet into this. Excellent idea."

"Stop it. You're just grumpy because you're covered in brains." Caelum jerked his chin at her, eyes dancing with laughter. "There's nothing else you can do for Slashy right now. Go and wash."

"Fenris," she corrected, allowing him to usher her out of the room. The hallway was clean and fresh, the lingering scent of blood and magic swept away by the ship's cooling system.

"I like Slashy." Caelum stepped neatly around her, moving up the passage towards the bridge. "Fenris sounds too serious."

"Excuse me, did you meet the guy? He's got serious written all over him. I bet he even pisses frowning," Arcana snorted. She paused outside her room, narrowing one eye in thought. "How long until we reach Sorcen?"

"Only a couple of hours. More than long enough to eat and shower, if that's what you're wondering." Caelum nosed the access plate outside her room and the door swished open.

"Good. Call me if anything happens." Arcana tiptoed across the carpet lest she drip blood on her clean floor, ignoring Caelum's snort of laughter as the door swished closed. She gained the bathroom without incident and stripped her ruined clothing straight into the garbage disposal, mourning the loss of her favourite comfortable jeans. Disappointment turned rapidly to shock as she caught sight of her own reflection, face and hands painted entirely red with drying blood and her hair flecked with Sorcen knew what. She hurried for the shower and the water activated as soon as she stepped inside, sluicing over her body and steaming up the glass. Arcana grabbed the soap and scrubbed herself raw, meticulously washing her hair and standing under the pressurised spray until the water ran clean.

Blasted warg. Arcana grimaced, stepping out of the shower amidst a cloud of steam. Had those warg in the temple really been natives? It seemed an awful coincidence for their chance encounter to then be followed up by a boarding - and she'd never been inclined to believe in coincidence. Particularly when it had sharp teeth. Fenris' face rose in her mind, his muscles tensed as he sagged over his sword. Who was he, to garner such attention from the warg? Arcana snatched a towel from the railing and dried herself vigorously. First breakfast, then Lesce. *Then* answers. She dropped the towel into the laundry chute and returned to her room, dressing in warm leggings and a blue knee-length dress with stars embroidered at the hem. After a quick moment to brush and style her hair, Arcana slid her feet into a pair of comfortable calf-high boots, pushed all thoughts of Fenris from her mind and went in search of something to eat.

The original silver décor of the ship's galley had long been overhauled and boasted mismatched chairs, a wooden table and a warm, hand woven rug. Arcana and Caelum had collected the pieces throughout their travels, each one with a unique story that transformed the kitchen into the hub of their spacefaring home. Arcana felt immediately better once she entered, sauntering over to the chiller unit and squinting at the contents. How long had it been since they stopped for supplies? Judging by the bare shelves staring back at her, too long. She shut the door and slapped the controls on the stove, where an old-fashioned iron kettle was already waiting. At least she could make a cup of tea - proper tea, not that awful herbal stuff that had been vac-packed at the cabin. Above the stove, a set of inlaid wooden doors opened to reveal the shiny surface of the freezer, which popped open at her touch. A slow smile spread across Arcana's face as she withdrew a container filled with traditional Sorcen pastries. Perfect.

The kettle began to whistle and she turned the heat off with one hand, while sticking the container of pastries into the ship's cooker with the other. By the time she had finished brewing her tea, the cooker beeped to announce the pastries were ready and moments later Arcana plunked her breakfast down on the wooden dining table, relaxing into her favourite chair with a sigh.

"Eaten yet?" Caelum's disembodied voice caused her to gasp and jump, gripping her mug with both hands.

"Great Gods of Sorcen! I almost spilt my tea," Arcana spluttered, lifting her eyes to the comm screen on the wall opposite.

Caelum's face stared back at her, black eyes glittering with amusement. "Totally worth it."

"What do you want?" Arcana demanded, grabbing the nearest pastry and biting into it. Warm berry jam dissolved her irritation and she closed her eyes, savouring the sweetness.

"Ship just alerted me we're fifteen minutes out of Sorcen. Thought I'd let you know."

"Fifteen minutes?" Arcana's eyes flew open and she stared at the cuckoo clock on the wall. "I thought you said a couple of hours?"

The deerken shrugged. "Looks like you overcharged the drive. We're going to be almost forty minutes earlier than the original estimate."

"Forty minutes... how fast are we going? Can the ship take it?"

"Of course it can. Systems show mild strain but nothing extreme." Caelum tilted his head to the side. "Feel free to check for yourself, though."

Shoving the pastry into her mouth, Arcana rolled out of her chair and onto the floor, flattening the palms of her hands against the rug. Closing her eyes, she sent her magic into the bowels of the ship, assessing first the crystal engines and then the star drive, thumping hard under the strain of an overcharge - but holding. She sighed in relief. "Remind me to be more careful next time."

"Careful? It was an emergency. You can siphon some of the energy off if you're worried, but it would probably blast a hole in the side of the ship." Caelum's ears flickered. "Actually, you know what? Don't do that. Let's pretend I never spoke."

Arcana snorted a laugh, crawling back into her chair. "I do that a fair bit. Now if you don't mind, I need to stuff my face. I am absolutely not turning up at Lesce's door without having eaten breakfast - or have you forgotten what happened the last time I did that?"

"I don't think *anybody* could forget that. Better eat quick then, because I'm going to need your help with Fenris." Caelum tilted his head in consideration. "Unless you want to go in officially?"

"No! No, we don't have time for all that. Just get me landing clearance and we'll manage Fenris ourselves. I'll deal with the Council later." Arcana shuddered.

"I thought you might say that. We're coming in at night so that'll make things a lot easier. I'll meet you down by Fenris in five." Caelum touched his nose to the screen and the comm went dark. Arcana snatched another pastry and crammed it into her mouth. Her tea was still steaming, so she poured it into a travel mug and fitted the watertight lid. With tea and pastries in hand, Arcana palmed open the door and went to meet her sister.

CHAPTER
THREE

THE DOOR OPENED AS ARCANA RAISED HER FIST TO KNOCK; WARM LANTERN light flowed out into the darkness. A young woman stood in the doorway, dark red hair shimmering in the light. A baby perched on her hip, clinging to a loose tunic with one hand and a half-eaten biscuit with the other. "It's you!" the woman cried, her face suffused with joy.

Arcana lowered her hand and smiled. "Hello, Ember."

"Ma, Aunt Arcana's here!" Ember called over her shoulder.

"Well let her in," laughed a voice from inside.

"Here! Come in, come in." Ember thrust the baby into Arcana's arms as she slipped through the door, Caelum close behind. The baby cooed up at her, a sweet mixture of pale skin, white hair and golden crumbs. Her pale eyes glittered with joy and her face split in a gap-toothed grin which Arcana couldn't help but return.

"To what do we – good heavens above, who is that?" A sensible looking woman with plum coloured hair rushed to Caelum's side, where Fenris lay draped across the deerken's back.

"Hi, Lesce. This is Fenris, and he's the reason we're here. He needs your help," Arcana said.

Lesce bent to peer into Fenris' unconscious face, wiping carefully at the beads of sweat upon his brow. "Flare! Salve! Get out here!"

Two men appeared immediately, falling over one another as they responded to Lesce's no-nonsense command. "Arcana?" The taller of the two - though not by much at just shy of six feet - stopped dead in his tracks. Broad shouldered with a muscular chest to match, he was clothed in the traditional crossover robes of a sorcerer and bore a head of shockingly bright orange hair that stuck off his head in great, thick spikes. Blinking carnelian eyes as though to clear a mirage, he spluttered; "Great heavenly fires, it *is* you!"

"Hello Flare." Arcana couldn't help but grin as her older brother bounded across the room to enfold her in a bone creaking hug. "Careful, you brute! I've got the baby."

Flare peppered her face with kisses - and then the baby's. "As if I'd ever squish my grand-niece," he scoffed. Up close, his softly tanned face was marked with a smattering of freckles that had been known to drive women wild. In fact, Arcana reflected, everything about Flare drove women - and men, for that matter - out of their minds. On the tail of that thought was her brother's smile, turned up to full, knee-melting wattage. "By Firius, it's good to see you."

"Greetings later," Lesce barked, slapping Flare across the shoulder. "Get this poor creature off Caelum's back and lie him down by the fire."

"All right, keep your socks on." Flare pressed a final kiss to Arcana's cheek and crossed the room to thread both arms beneath Fenris' shoulders. Lesce's husband Salve, a short, stocky man with iron grey hair and a capable air, supported Fenris' lower body and together they laid the wounded knight on the floor. Salve flipped back the blanket, revealing Fenris' ruined tunic and the insidious purple bruising across his torso.

Even Lesce gasped as she dropped to her knees, laying one hand over the knight's heart and the other on his navel. "By all the gods, Arcana, what did you do to him?"

"I tried to save him," Arcana answered, wincing as the baby pulled her hair.

"Really?" Flare flicked a horrified look in her direction. "Remind me not to call you next time I need saving." The effect of his words were ruined by the laughing twinkle in those bright orange eyes, and Arcana found herself making a rude gesture at him.

"Stop joking around and boil me some water," Lesce snapped. Her gaze was fixed off in the middle distance and when she next spoke, it was to her husband. "He's bleeding internally. Can you keep his pulse steady while I work?"

"Of course." Salve settled down opposite his wife and pressed both hands over Fenris' heart, allowing Lesce the freedom to send her healing skills where they were most needed. "I have him."

"Good." Lesce looked up briefly. "Ember, make Arcana and Caelum comfortable, will you? Let your father and I see if we can't save this poor man's life."

Ember slung an arm around Arcana's waist and led her through an archway into a cozy sitting room. A jumble of mismatched couches and side tables filled most of the space, with a low circular table in the middle of the floor. The younger woman moved to a sideboard and began preparing a pot and several cups. "Don't worry about mother - she'll be glad to see you later."

"I know. I'm more interested in Fenris than her manners, anyway," Arcana forced herself to answer Ember's smile with one of her own. The baby gooed and giggled, fisting a hand in Arcana's hair and yanking hard. "Ouch! Is this adorable creature really yours?"

Ember beamed with pride. "Yes."

"She's beautiful. What's her name?"

"Lizelle." Ember tucked her sleeve over her fist and used it to wipe the baby's soggy chin. Lizelle burbled in delight, snatching clumsily at the bright fabric.

"Is she your first?" Arcana asked, watching the little limbs in fascination.

"Oh really, Aunt Arcana, it hasn't been *that* long since you last visited!" Ember giggled, her cheerful expression mirroring that of the baby's. "You were here for the wedding and that was only five years ago."

"Was it?" Arcana glanced back at the fire in the main room, but it was impossible to see beyond Lesce's no-nonsense bun and the knotted strings of her apron. "I can't remember."

Ember chuckled again and went back to making tea, leaving Arcana free to watch as Flare deposited a steaming bowl of water on the floor beside his youngest sister, murmured something in her ear which received a curt nod in return, and then straightened to saunter in Arcana's direction. He walked with an ease she'd always admired, as though the burdens of life were a joy upon his shoulders - though as the commander of Sorcen's armies, Flare was both piercingly intelligent and deadly when he wished to be.

"So who's our mystery guest?" Flare breezed through the archway, teasing a laugh out of Ember with a well-placed peck on the cheek. He turned to waggle his eyebrows suggestively at Arcana. "Your latest, sis?"

"Are you kidding?" Caelum snorted loudly. "I'd have to flush myself out the airlock of the ship."

"True... the idea of Arcana actually getting it on with someone is pretty shocking. We all know her panties are laced far too tight for that." Flare grinned and gave Caelum's shoulder a playful shove. "Still, he's unfairly handsome, sis. Don't tell me that even you are immune to a man who looks like *that*."

"Are you serious? Fenris is in mortal danger," Arcana said, glaring at her older brother.

Flare waved a dismissive hand. "Pffft, Lesce does mortal danger ten times a day on her own, let alone with sturdy old Salve there to help out."

"That's why we're here." Arcana smiled, sinking onto one of the couches and settling Lizelle in her lap. Flare flung himself down beside her, tucking one leg under Arcana's thigh and wiggling his toes in a move calculated to infuriate. Arcana narrowed her eyes, swatting one ankle. "Don't start me, Flare. There's nothing going on. We just met."

Flare tipped his head back dramatically. "Always so suspicious, sister dear. I only care about your wellbeing." Again, that mischievous twinkle. "Now tell me everything before I have to trounce it out of you."

"Honestly, Uncle, is gossip *all* you care about?" Ember plunked the teapot into Flare's lap, grinning good naturedly. "Heat, please."

"It's not gossip if it involves the emotional welfare of my favourite sister," Flare protested. He laid the flat of one hand against the teapot and drew lazy circles in the air with the other. Spitting orange runes appeared over the teapot, glowing bright for a fraction of a second before they jumbled together and swirled down inside the spout. "First water, now tea. You know I'm a Class One fire sorcerer, right?"

"Of course you are." Ember patted his cheek, retrieved the now steaming teapot and wandered back to the sideboard.

"Well?" Flare turned his gaze back to Arcana.

"For Sorcen's sake! You never let up, do you?"

"It's one of my more endearing qualities." Flare's grin was unrepentant and so warm, Arcana couldn't help but return it.

"Fine. His name is Fenris. Guardian to the Weaver, Warden to the deerken." Arcana glanced through the archway, where Fenris' dark green mop of curls was barely visible behind Lesce's crouching body. She thought of Ember, patting Flare's cheek without a second thought, and wondered if Fenris would welcome such a gesture.

"Guardian to the who?" Flare frowned, the expression enhancing the naturally flawless contours of his face. "What does that mean?"

"I don't really know," Arcana answered, blinking herself back to the present. What in the name of Sorcen was she thinking?

"You, the grandest and most amazing sorceress in the universe, don't know who or what he actually is?" Flare asked, twitching an immaculate eyebrow.

Arcana sighed, shaking her head. "Please tell me you're still single."

"Ouch!" Flare pouted at her, his cheeks dimpling. "Low blow."

"He is," Ember said from the sideboard.

"You both know that's by choice." This time Flare's voice was edged with steel, and Arcana was surprised to see something haunted shifting behind her brother's eyes. She opened her mouth but he shook his head imperceptibly. When he spoke, his voice carried nothing more than a good-natured tease. "I'm just waiting for the right person to come along. There's no rush, dear niece."

Ember snorted. "Oh please. At seventy-five, Gramma and Grampa have long given up hope." With her attention on the tea cups in front of her, she failed to see the tightening around Flare's jaw. "I mean, it's never too late, of course, but most of us are well married by fifty."

"Speaking of Ma and Pa, where are they?" Arcana asked, seizing the change of subject.

"Who knows? They left a couple weeks ago to go hug trees or some shit." Flare waved a hand dismissively. The grit she had seen in his gaze disappeared, replaced once again by the familiar, breezy Flare she'd known all her life. Arcana stared a moment, then turned to accept a cup of tea from Ember in exchange for the sweet weight of Lizelle.

"They went to check the far-reaching orchards before winter hits," Ember supplied.

"Thank you," Arcana answered. She sipped her tea, closing her eyes to relish the breadth of delicate flavours.

"Think quick!" Flare quipped. Arcana's eyes flew open as the rim of her cup caught fire, tiny delicate flames that danced ever closer to her face. She blew them out as candles on a cake and raised an eyebrow at her older brother.

"Really?" Ember laughed and tried to smother the sound, struggling to look serious. "Honestly, Uncle. She's been here five minutes and you're already trying to set her on fire?"

Arcana merely raised a brow at her older brother. "You never tire of that game, do you?"

"Nope. Now that I have your attention, though, back to your friend Fenris." Flare accepted his own cup from Ember with a nod of thanks, gulping it down without bothering to check the temperature. "What else do we know about him?"

She shrugged. "Precious little, save he was being pursued by the warg and recognised Caelum as a deerken."

"So, what - based on that alone you've crossed the universe to save his life?" Flare twitched an eyebrow, twisting to peer through the archway. Lesce and Salve still murmured over Fenris' prone body, their heads close together and their hands weaving an intricate dance in the air above his chest. "I don't buy it."

"Caelum's inner radar led us to an abandoned temple. Fenris was inside, wearing a full suit of plate armour and bleeding all over the floor. I couldn't just leave him," Arcana added, blushing as Flare continued to stare at her. "Caelum assures me his instincts would never lead us to someone unsavoury."

"No." Flare's voice was quiet. "Just a knight in shining armour, it seems."

"Don't be -" Arcana paused. Well. When he put it like *that*; "I couldn't just leave him to die, Flare."

Her brother adopted a lopsided smile. "I wasn't suggesting you should - only that it's kind of weird."

"There's clearly more to this than meets the eye, but you didn't hear Fenris talking on the ship – he knew what a deerken was and claimed to be a protector of some sort." Caelum shook himself thoroughly. "We've spent fifty years searching for clues about my heritage and I'll bet my left antler he's got the answers."

"Only the left one? Doesn't seem that confident to me." Flare's expression was deadpan as he drained his cup and set it on the floor beside the couch.

Caelum's ear flickered. "I'd bet the right one too, but I've become attached to it over time."

"I feel you, brother." Flare nodded sagely. "I'm rather partial to my right one myself."

Arcana burst out laughing. "I've missed you."

"And I you," her brother returned. "Any enemy to the warg is a friend of mine, that's for sure. Nasty bastards, the lot of them. Were you injured?"

"No." Arcana took another sip of her tea, pushing away memories of fetid breath and sticky blood. "Just Fenris. I did what I could, but I won't feel better until I hear-"

"He'll be fine," Lesce interrupted from the doorway. She leant heavily against her husband, brow studded with sweat. "He's sleeping now."

"Come, sit." Salve ushered Lesce into the room, where she collapsed onto one of the free couches.

"You look like shit," Flare said, bounding out of his chair. He poured a cup of tea and offered it to Lesce, flicking the side of the cup as she reached to accept. Steam rose from the amber liquid, filling the room with the scent of cinnamon.

"I feel it, too." Lesce accepted the steaming cup with a nod, her eyes fastened on Arcana. "Those injuries were very serious - he wouldn't have lived another hour. What happened?"

"I only know part of it, but I'll tell you what I can." Arcana took another sip of her tea and launched into an explanation of what had happened since she and Caelum had landed on the strange ice planet.

"The warg teleported into the ship itself?" Ember's face was pale.

"That part's unusual. The warg are cunning in the same way a wolf is cunning, but their bloodlust takes precedence above all else. Programming and activating a personal teleporter requires presence of mind at the very least." Flare's eyes narrowed in thought. "If you put that aside, however, the actual teleporters are not a difficult thing to reason out. All they need is something of Fenris' to get a lock with."

"He didn't leave any possessions behind but he had bled on the temple floor," Arcana offered.

"Bio matter is temperamental at best but if there was enough of it, then yeah, blood would work. How long did you say you were in orbit?" Flare asked.

Caelum rolled his shoulders in a shrug. "Twelve hours at least."

"Anyone with a passing knowledge of biological science or gene splicing could easily extract a teleport lock from a blood sample in that time - but that's not a skill I'd attribute to the warg." Flare nodded in Arcana's direction. "You're right in your suspicion that someone else is behind the attack."

"Gene splicing? That's illegal," Lesce protested.

"Oh, well, excuse me," Flare drawled, turning a lazy glare on his youngest sister. "Maybe you should've been on hand to inform the pack of murderous half-men the error of their ways. I'm sure they wouldn't have bothered if they knew it was *illegal*."

"Flare," Salve warned, shaking his head.

"Come on, Salve, even you aren't that naive." Flare turned his eyes skyward and subsided with a snort.

"It doesn't matter - the only thing of note is that there's more to this than even I thought at first." Arcana sucked on her teeth. "I probably should have moved Fenris sooner, but I wanted more information."

"For what it's worth, I would've done the same thing." Flare nodded in her direction, his good humour restored as quickly as it had disappeared. "You don't know Fenris, and let's face it - the likelihood of pursuit was pretty slim."

"Thanks, but I still wonder if I was gambling with his life unnecessarily. I'm no healer, and that gash he had was nasty. I assumed it was superficial, but..." Arcana trailed off and shrugged, looking to Lesce for confirmation.

"You did well with what you had - the original wound is cleanly sealed and free from infection. It sounds as though Fenris' battle with the warg was the problem, not your ministrations." Lesce finished her tea and set the cup down, leaning back against Salve.

Arcana nodded, releasing a breath she hadn't realised had been trapped in her lungs. "Thanks."

"Lifting that giant sword and a warg at the same time would tear apart anyone's insides - I still don't quite believe it and I was there," Caelum snorted.

"You know what they say about guys with big swords, right?" Flare grinned, waggling his eyebrows.

"Do women actually hear the words that come out of your mouth? Or do you just set fire to them until they agree to sleep with you?" Arcana asked, shaking her head with a laugh.

"I'll have you know I'm a well-respected member of the community and I don't need to set fire to anyone. My natural charm speaks for itself." Flare winked and the room was silent, because they all knew it was true. "Besides, I know warg are tough, but lifting a sword isn't that big of a deal - even injured."

"You don't understand." Arcana pushed off the couch and moved to Caelum's side, flipping open the satchel bag she'd slung around his neck before leaving the ship. She reached inside, wrapping both hands around the hilt of the enormous blade and slowly drawing it free.

"Great heavenly fires." Flare stared wide-eyed as the sword slipped from Arcana's grasp and landed on the floor with a dull thud.

Arcana spread her fingers to encompass the full width of the blade. "*This* is Fenris' sword."

"That thing is as tall as you are, and at least half as wide," Lesce noted, her eyes round.

"I've never seen a sword like that." Flare rolled off the couch, wrapped both hands around the hilt and heaved. The blade slid a bare half inch across the floor before he released it, red-faced and sweating. "Holy. Shit."

"Fenris can lift this with one hand," Arcana said quietly, savouring the silence that followed her statement.

Flare grunted, wiping at his forehead. "Now I feel like a weakling."

"What were you saying about compensating?" Arcana asked, her tone dripping sugar.

Flare growled something unintelligible at her but his eyes sparkled with mischief. "You'll keep, sis. You know you will. Seriously, though, this guy is some kind of special." Flare shoved at the blade with his foot and winced. "Nobody normal carries that sort of thing around."

"What an interesting puzzle. Fenris is muscular, but not abnormally so. I examined him thoroughly and found nothing unusual," Lesce said, frowning at the sword. "Flare is easily his superior in muscle mass."

Flare snorted. "Wow Lesce, only you could say that and make it sound like a turn off."

"Gods above us, Flare, will you be serious for once?" Lesce snapped, her hands clenching to fists in her lap.

"Sorry. You're right." Flare took Arcana's hand, his face twisted into an expression of concern. "Arcana, this dude must be seriously sexy if even Lesce's noticed his muscles. Are you feeling unwell, or have you just not boned a guy in so long that your vagina's closed over? Whatever the problem, I know a world class healer who can help."

Arcana stared at her brother for a heartbeat, then another, the room suffused in shocked silence. Laughter bubbled in her chest and a moment later she let it out: a loud, braying laugh that drained all the tension from her. She laughed until her eyes watered and her stomach hurt, and then she draped herself on Flare and squeezed him tightly. He returned the embrace fiercely, burying his face in her hair. "Great gods of Sorcen but I love you," Arcana managed, her body still wracked with giggles.

"Welcome home." His words were no more than the softest breath in her ear.

"You. Are. Ridiculous," Lesce hissed, clutching her tea cup with white-knuckled fingers.

"Flare, you made her blush," Arcana whispered loudly.

"*Both* of you are ridiculous!" Lesce shrieked. She stood abruptly and flung her teacup at them.

Flare uttered a word and the porcelain exploded in a tiny ball of fire. "Too slow, healer girl," he chuckled. Lesce shrieked again and stormed from the room. Moments later, a door slammed heavily enough to rattle the pictures on the walls.

"How many cups do you guys go through?" Arcana asked.

"That'll be the fourth this month. Don't ask about the plates; I've lost count." Salve fixed Flare with an expression somewhere between resigned amusement and irritation. "I really wish you'd bait her less."

"So do I." The corner of Flare's lip twitched into a self-deprecating smile. "I just can't help it, brother. She's so... so... *stuffy*."

"Sounds like you and Lesce are the same as ever, then." Arcana patted Flare on the arm. "I'm surprised you still live here."

"Actually, I don't. I have an apartment in the city, where I spend most of my time - I'm only here tonight because I had some official business to discuss with Salve," Flare admitted, running a hand through his hair. It stuck up at all angles in a way that would have been ridiculous on anyone else, but made Flare look endearing. "That and I wanted to make sure there wasn't a surplus of tea cups."

Salve chuckled quietly. "Lesce wanted to turn Flare's old bedroom into a music room, but your parents refused. It's still Flare's, and he uses it from time to time."

"When Lesce's not trying to kill you, I'll bet." Arcana grinned at Flare, reaching for her cup of tea. "So you're saying that if I'd arrived any other time, you'd be off wooing some poor young thing in the city?"

"Something like that, although I haven't had much extra time lately. I've been pulling double shifts at the Fire Tower the last few weeks. There are some things nobody needs to see, and me after sixteen hours' Tower duty is one of them," Flare replied, reaching out to flick the side of her cup. Steam immediately rose from the liquid within and Arcana sipped appreciatively.

"Getting old?" she teased.

"Never," Flare grinned. "There's been some piracy in our system lately and we haven't been able to catch the ships responsible. The incidents were isolated at first but have become quite regular, so we've been running double surveillance shifts. Poor Shard's been there almost twelve hours now."

"Shard's in charge of the Tower defence system," Ember supplied, her face filled with pride at her husband's achievement.

"Nobody more unshakeable than an earth sorcerer," Flare said. "His insight is invaluable and he's a solid Class Two."

"I always said he'd be good up there." Arcana glanced out the doorway to where Fenris slept on the floor by the fire. Flames flickered over his teal skin, burnishing it with copper and emphasising the angle of his cheekbones. "Any idea which pirate owns the ships?"

"No, which has been bothering me for a while. Most pirates wield egos large enough that they spray them all over the front of their ships, but these are unmarked. They flit in and out for a week or so, raiding whatever trade ships are nearby, then disappear for a few days. All in the outer edges of the system, but frequent enough to keep the Towers on full alert. If it goes on too long, our economy will start to show damage through loss of trade." Flare scrubbed at his hair, frowning. "I want to investigate but the Council thinks it's unwise."

Arcana snorted. "Too many stuff-nosed aristocrats hiding in their comfort zones."

"I might remind you that your sister is one of those stuff-nosed aristocrats," Salve said dryly, crossing his arms over his chest.

"Oh, yes. I forgot Lesce was the Healing Elder." Arcana frowned, tapping one finger against her lip. "Sorry, Salve."

"Don't worry sis, it only serves to back up your comment - and Lesce's one of the flexible ones." Flare screwed up his nose in disgust. "I've been recommending action for months but the Council thinks the outer reaches of the system are beyond our immediate concern."

"That's never stopped you before." Arcana gave her brother a searching look, got the confirming wink she was looking for. "Right. So what have you found?"

"Shard noticed a pattern to the raids and began mapping them," Ember supplied. "He even predicted the latest appearance – but the Council remain unimpressed."

"Pirates travel randomly, not in a repeated pattern." Arcana raised an eyebrow in Flare's direction. "At least, no pirate I've ever met."

He shrugged. "You'd know that better than I."

"I was a mercenary, Flare, not a pirate," Arcana growled. "It's different."

"Meh. A roseapple still tastes the same, whether it's pink or green." Flare shrugged again but his lazy smile said he didn't mean the words. "If you have some ideas, I'm sure the Council would love to hear them - and I'd love the backup."

"No. Oh, no. If I have it my way, the rest of the Council won't even know I've set foot planetside." Arcana sliced one hand through the air in front of her.

"Are you kidding? Forgetting the fact that Lesce will rat you out in an instant, that crystal cruiser you rock around in is almost as famous as your face. The only reason nobody's banging on the door right now is because it's the middle of the night. Tomorrow will be a whole new story," Flare warned.

Arcana clenched her hands into fists and ground her teeth. "Great."

"Speaking of tomorrow, it's fast approaching. Will you be sleeping here?" Salve asked.

"No. I mean yes, eventually, but not now. I've only just had breakfast," Arcana admitted.

"Well I've had a long day and I think it's time for a solid rest." Salve rolled to his feet with a hefty sigh. "After I console my wife, of course."

"Is that what the young kids are calling it these days?" Flare asked, arching a perfect eyebrow. "Consolation. I like it."

"Ugh!" Salve threw his hands up in disgust and marched out of the room, shaking his head as he went. Arcana covered her smile behind one hand lest he look back but he didn't, and a moment later she heard the distinct sound of a door opening and shutting again.

"I might bunk here too. It's a little late to head back to the city." Flare yawned and stretched. "Besides, Lesce will love it when she sees me in the morning."

"No sense me lying in bed and staring at the roof. Caelum, you want to go visit the shrine?" Arcana asked, glancing over her shoulder.

"Always," he answered, starry eyes whirling quicker in anticipation.

"Not to mention, it's the place you're least likely to be disturbed. Smart." Flare tapped one finger to the side of his head and then saluted with it.

"Don't you forget it," Arcana grinned, then hesitated, her eyes drawn once again to Fenris' prone form on the floor. "What about Fenris?"

"I'll watch him from behind my eyelids," Flare promised solemnly.

Arcana snorted and gave him a playful shove. "That's not what I meant."

"I know. But seriously, he'll be fine. Lesce and Salve put him back together - he just needs to sleep and recover. Go on. I'll see you tomorrow." He smiled, but she caught the faintest hint of a question in the lilt of his voice.

"I'll be here." Confused by the uncertainty and unabashed relief in Flare's expression, Arcana wrapped her arms around him and squeezed.

"Good." Flare breathed deep of her hair and then stepped back, waved her a lazy salute, and ducked out. Arcana stammered a hasty goodbye to Ember and Lizelle, chasing Flare into the kitchen, but the door to his bedroom was already closed.

"Let him go. We'll ask later." Caelum nosed at her shoulder and Arcana nodded in mute agreement. She glanced down at Fenris, so close she could have touched him if she stretched out her foot. He looked peaceful and pain free, his body relaxed in sleep, one hand curled across his chest and the other lost beneath his tangle of dark curls.

"I'm relieved he's going to live." Arcana tore her eyes from the knight on the floor and made for the front door, stepping out into the cool night air. "Whatever he did drained an enormous amount of strength."

Caelum appeared in her periphery vision, his pale grey fur dappled with shadow in the vague moonlight. "You doubted Lesce?"

"No, of course not - but do the maths. Lesce said he wouldn't have survived another hour. If I hadn't accidentally overcharged the star drive... Anyway, I guess it doesn't matter. He's alive, which means you'll get to question him to your heart's content once he wakes." Arcana looked up, using the stars for guidance. There were no signs to the shrine, no pathway to follow, only the memory retained in her bones and the map sparkling above. She adjusted her course slightly and then focussed ahead, her family home quickly disappearing from sight as they entered a band of close growing trees.

"You really think he'll answer?" Caelum asked.

"I don't know. It's the least he can do in return for his life," Arcana replied. Caelum moved closer and she swung onto his back, leaning into the warmth of his body as he picked up speed, moving across the ground with effortless grace. Trees flowed past them as shadows, the air heavy with the scent of late autumn and the song of night-time insects. Arcana took it all in, filling her lungs, absorbing the unique essence of the forest until she thought her chest would burst.

"You miss it," Caelum said, his whisper so soft it almost didn't exist.

"So do you," she breathed, rubbing her face against his silken coat.

The drumbeat of the wild thundered in Caelum's chest as he raced across the darkened terrain and Arcana knew her own heart fluttered in synch. All too soon he began to slow, skirting the edge of an overgrown cleft and splashing through a tiny stream. Through another copse of trees, they entered a clearing large enough for a small house and perfectly round. The ground dipped slowly, forming a large, shallow bowl. In the exact centre the grass was a little too green, a little too soft. Arcana slid from Caelum's back as they approached, each step causing the hairs on the back of her neck to stand on end. Magic crackled in the air around her, whispering almost-heard nothings as she stepped onto the too-perfect grass. Caelum dropped to his knees just short of the epicentre and Arcana joined him, one arm around his shoulders.

"Hello, mother." Caelum's voice carried the rustle of fallen leaves and his starry eyes whirled and dipped in a pattern unique to this one place, rearranging themselves to show a different constellation. There was no answer – there never was. But there, in that moment, Arcana looked into Caelum's face and saw the eyes of another, heard the echo of her almost-voice in his altered tone.

"Even death cannot truly claim her," Arcana murmured. Caelum leant forward to rub his face along her dampened cheek, brushing aside tears she hadn't realised were shed, and then laid down on the grass and closed his eyes. Arcana curled up in the lee of his body, staring up at the starred sky above. Magic moved around her, through her, as strong now as the day she had first encountered it. Sleep was an impossibility here but so was true wakefulness, as though the moments hung suspended like dewdrops between time. Arcana succumbed to the pull of a reality beyond her own comprehension, closing her eyes whilst the magic scoured her soul clean.

CHAPTER
FOUR

When Arcana blinked next, dawn's grey blanket had begun to lift and birds chirruped in the surrounding trees, promising a bright, clear day. She sat up, dew rolling off her hair and trickling uncomfortably into her damp clothes.

"Good morning." Caelum raised his head in unison with hers, his voice still tinted with the susurrus of fallen leaves.

"I guess so." Arcana ran a hand through her hair and shook the residual dew from her fingers. "I don't remember sleeping."

"I don't think we did," Caelum answered, his gaze far off.

"I remember lying back to look at the stars, and now this." Arcana waved a hand at the ever-lightening morning. "If I didn't sleep, what else would you call several missing hours?"

Caelum's ears flickered. "You lent your strength to me. I dreamt many things."

"The dreambank?" Arcana rolled onto her knees, heart leaping.

"Yes. No. I don't know." Caelum shook his head. "It felt different to anything I've seen in the dreambank. Those are fractured, mashed images and snatches of sound. This was a lot more intense. Like a holovid message."

"What did you see?"

"I saw a place... a castle." Caelum's voice rolled in a hypnotic rhythm, his body trembling. "Bright and dark, like a shadow in the light. Too colourful and too grey. The vines are growing, then brittle, then fresh with the warmth of eternal spring. Statues broken and made whole, covered in lichen then clean. Swept halls, footprints in the dust. Blood, long dried, and a waterfall made of tears. A secret is waiting behind your face and the warg are everywhere."

"Woah." Arcana rubbed one hand across her forehead, replaying his words in her mind. "That's intense. Are you certain it wasn't the dreambank?"

"I've never had a connection to the dreambank like that - not even here, with mother's energy and your infinite power battery. It was a message, but I'm not sure who for." Caelum found his feet, showering Arcana in a fresh round of dew.

"What I wouldn't give for a fire sorcerer about now," she muttered, shaking the moisture off her arms.

Caelum blinked down at her. "Sorry."

"Forget it. Did the message give you anything?" Arcana tested stiffened limbs before standing. "A sense of time, or direction?"

"No. But whatever the message is, I have the feeling I'm supposed to deliver it." Caelum frowned, pawing in frustration at the grass beneath them.

"Vandalising your mother's grave isn't going to help," Arcana pointed out. He didn't answer, so she grabbed the closest antler and tugged his head around to face her. Caelum's eyes were very wide and round, the stars floating within almost completely gone. "We need to get you out of this energy. Come on."

"I…"

"*Move.*" Arcana called her magic, clenching her free hand into a fist. A gust of frigid air buffeted the deerken from behind and he stumbled forward. Walking through the invisible barrier surrounding the shrine was like walking through a curtain of iced water and Arcana released Caelum to hug her arms to her body, breathing out a cloud. "It *would* have to frost this morning."

Caelum dropped his head between his knees and shook it fiercely. "Sorry. How can someone deceased still hold so much power?"

"It's just an echo." Arcana smoothed the fur along his cheek. "She's not going to open the ground and climb out."

"You're right." Caelum raked his gaze along her body and wrinkled his nose. "You look uncomfortable."

"I am." Arcana picked at a sodden sleeve but it was no use; the dew had sunk through her dress and slicked it to her skin like glue. Summoning her magic, she ignored the organic energy of the forest and focussed instead on the softly shimmering sound of the water clinging to her body. A moment's concentration and a finger flick later, she was dry - though still shivering with the cold. Water droplets hung suspended in the air around her, glistening in the dappled sunlight and returning hundreds of distorted versions of Arcana's unkempt reflection. She snorted. "I'm not sure if that was worth the effort or not."

Caelum tilted his head to one side, watching the droplets as they pattered to the forest floor in a tiny shower of rain. His fur began to lengthen in response to the chill, winter flowers budding and blooming across his antler rack. "Oh, I don't know," he said. "It's pretty, and at least you're dry."

"Still cold, though." Arcana started up the gentle slope of the bowl, boots crunching through the frost. "Let's head back. I could use a cup of tea." She crested the lip and paused at the sound of someone crashing their way through the undergrowth.

"I think it's Flare," Caelum whispered.

A familiar voice swore loudly and Arcana choked back a laugh. "Sure is. He always gets lost out here - let's show him the way." She raised both hands, sweeping them apart as though opening curtains. The forest buckled in response, undergrowth flattening and trees curving into a long, straight tunnel carpeted by fallen leaves.

"Arcana?" Flare stepped slowly into view, his hair full of twigs and a fireball crackling in the palm of one hand. "Is that you?"

"Of course." Arcana snapped her fingers and one of the trees beside Flare leant down to slap the fireball in his hand with a wet branch. The flames extinguished with a hiss, leaving the fire sorcerer coughing through a haze of smoke.

"Heathen," Flare yelped, waving his hand as though stung.

Arcana grinned. "Think quick, remember?"

Flare fisted both hands on his hips. "You're supposed to say that *before* you ambush me," he grumbled, forcing Arcana's grin even wider. Then a tall figure stepped into view beside her brother and she froze.

"Is that *Fenris*?" Caelum whispered.

"I... holy shit," Arcana managed. Fenris lent heavily on a staff for support, but even hunched over, he dwarfed the fire sorcerer beside him. Where Flare was roped in lengths of golden muscle and armed with a charming smile, Fenris' frame was sheathed in paler splendour, his body built for speed and manoeuvrability. Flare's flame orange hair stuck off the side of his head in an adorably rumpled way, while Fenris' dark teal curls tumbled over his forehead and around delicately pointed ears. Both men wore confidence, but each in their own way; Flare with a casual swagger, and Fenris - well, even pallid and limping, it was impossible to miss the predator stalking beneath the surface of his skin.

"His eyes are glowing," Caelum hissed.

"They glowed before," Arcana replied, swallowing the lump in her throat. Those burning, jade eyes, devoid as they were of feature, were undeniably focussed on her. "I don't know why you're surprised."

Flare and Fenris started along the tunnel together, the fire sorcerer matching the wounded knight's slower pace. Fenris navigated the forest with a dangerous fluidity, the only sound of his passing the soft thud of the staff he lent upon. As they drew closer Arcana realised it was not a staff at all - it was his sword, turned point down and used as a walking stick. Flare pulled up a few paces short of Arcana, flashing the sort of smile that disarmed anyone on the other end of it - except, of course, that he was her brother, and she was immune.

"Hey, sis. I believe you two have already met but this is Fenris, your knight in shining armour." Flare swept a flourishing bow, his eyes glittering with mischief. "Fenris, this is my little sister Arcana, greatest sorceress in the known universe. That there is her furry soul-sharer, Caelum."

Arcana gaped as Flare regarded her intently from underneath his lashes, lips quirked in challenge. "Right. Yes. Hi," she managed, turning back to Fenris. He stood head, shoulders and half a chest above her, limbs long and graceful as an assassin's. Arcana pasted a smile on her face, desperately seeking her equilibrium. "I'm surprised to see you awake so soon. Welcome back."

"Thank you. I believe I owe you my life… again." Fenris' lips curled upwards, the ghost of a smile which echoed in Arcana's bones.

Great gods of Sorcen, she thought, her heart thumping erratically. *Is this how people feel when they look at Flare?*

"Don't worry about it." Caelum stepped in when it was clear she couldn't. "How did you get past Lesce?"

"She was reluctant to let me out, but Flare is very convincing." Fenris' voice was like warm velvet, his tone carrying a dark amusement that was echoed in Flare's unrepentant grin.

"You know Lesce - anything to get rid of me," Flare snickered, and Arcana could only imagine what he'd said to get his own way. "You look half frozen, sister dear. Did you sleep out here again?"

"By accident," Arcana admitted.

Flare rolled his eyes and reached out to flick a finger against her shoulder, muttering under his breath. Warmth spread over Arcana's body in a wave, erasing the lingering chill left by the frosted morning. "There - although I don't understand why you insist on camping out in a crater."

"We all have our flaws." Arcana shrugged, her smile easy. "Besides, what does it matter when I have my big brother to look after me?"

"Hah!" Flare waved a dismissive hand but Arcana could see he was pleased. "Much as I'd like to hang around and indulge in your flattery, I'm late for the Tower. Swing by later? Lesce said the Council will want to see you."

"Ugh. Maybe." Arcana screwed up her face, glancing towards Fenris - but he was staring down into the shrine's shallow bowl, his expression far off.

Flare followed her gaze and stepped closer, lowering his voice. "Take care of your knight in shining armour, okay? Lesce said his wounds are healed, but he'll be weak for a while." The fire sorcerer waggled his brows suggestively. "Don't do anything that might wear him out."

"Get out of here," Arcana growled, flipping her older brother off. He went with a mischievous wink, jogging down the tunnel she'd created without looking back.

Fenris watched Flare go, his eyes roving over the moulded foliage. "Your skill with the forest is incredible."

"Thank you." Arcana tugged softly on a lock of hair. "So... how are you feeling?"

"Honestly?" Fenris chuckled, a warm sound at odds with his drawn expression. "Like I have been trampled by a herd of heavy creatures. I didn't tell your sister that, however."

Arcana felt the corners of her lips tug upward. "Wise - she'd never have let you out of the house if she'd known, no matter what Flare said."

"So your brother warned me when I woke and expressed a desire to see you." Fenris held out one arm, and it took Arcana a long moment to realise he was offering a warrior's forearm grip. "I believe we got off on the wrong foot during our original introductions and I would like to rectify that. Shall we start again?"

"I'm still not sure why I should trust you," Arcana admitted, narrowing her eyes at his outstretched hand.

"Be assured I feel the same way - yet here we are." Fenris' gaze burned into the side of her face but if he worried, it was impossible to tell.

"Ah, what the hell." Arcana laid her palm over his forearm and Fenris smiled as he followed suit. "I guess that's as good a plan as any. Should I go first and say we mean you no harm?"

"Considering you've already gone to the trouble of saving my life, I am inclined to believe you." Fenris smiled, leaving unspoken that he hadn't moved to harm her, either.

"Twice," Caelum said.

Fenris' smile widened as he removed his hand from Arcana's arm. "Twice indeed. I am in your debt."

"Forget it." Arcana waved a hand. "I don't like owing or being owed. There's no need to be so formal."

He blinked. "I am accustomed to a certain degree of formality."

"Wow, what did you think of Flare, then?" Arcana snorted a laugh, quickly covering her mouth with her hand. *Elegant,* she thought, but Fenris appeared to be considering her question rather than paying attention to her manners.

"Your brother is an immense well of power and wisdom, tempered by an inane sense of humour and catastrophic good looks," Fenris said eventually.

"Uh… yup. Got it in one." Arcana shook her head. "You sure you've never met him before?"

"No, I have not." Fenris sounded almost apologetic, the hint of a smile tugging his lips again. "Tell me, are there other deerken nearby? I would like to speak with them."

"What? No. We've never met another one," Caelum said.

"Never?" Fenris' voice hitched in astonishment.

"No." Caelum shifted restlessly. "Only my mother, whom I don't remember."

"How unusual." Fenris hesitated, knuckles whitening around the hilt of his sword. "If there are no other deerken here, might I ask the circumstances of your birth?"

"Hang on a second." Arcana frowned, holding up a hand when Caelum would have answered. "Caelum's birth story is no real secret, but first I want to know your motives. You accused us of poaching on the ship."

"An insensitive remark," Fenris agreed, his face pinched with remorse. "Perhaps an exchange of information, then? If you don't mind, I'd like to sit down first."

"An exchange seems fair." Arcana flicked a finger and thick roots thrust upwards out of the ground, twisting into a simple bench. Fenris stared in amazement so she sat down, waiting until he collected his wits enough to sit beside her.

"Incredible." Fenris leant forward, muscles slithering under soft teal skin as he examined the impromptu furniture. After a long moment, he shook his head and set the enormous sword on the ground by his feet. "I will be better placed to offer information if I understand your story first - if that suits, of course?"

"Like I said, it's no real secret. Short or long version?" Arcana asked.

"Long," he responded, leaning back on his hands.

"Okay." She worried her lip a moment, casting her mind back fifty-two years to an entirely different life. "I was out collecting berries in the forest with Lesce. Out of the blue, the ground started to shake and there was a terrible ripping noise. Lesce tripped and I threw myself on top of her. When the quake finally stopped, we saw this... well, I guess it's a crater," Arcana gestured at the sloping grass bowl beside them.

"Had there been forest here?" Fenris asked, his eyes following the line of her fingers.

"Dense forest. But it was gone and lying in the centre of the crater was a deer. She had a great gaping hole in her chest and blood was running everywhere." Arcana pressed her hands to her heart. "The doe asked for our help - she was pregnant and labouring to deliver a fawn. I remember trying to pack her wounds with the cloth from our baskets and sending Lesce for help."

Fenris blinked. "She didn't try to heal the doe?"

"She couldn't - Lesce was young then and hadn't imprinted." Seeing his look of confusion, Arcana sighed. "We're born as blanks and gain our magic after we hit adulthood. Think of it as nature's safety measure."

"It would be catastrophic to have powers like Flare's in the hands of a baby," Fenris agreed. "So Lesce was unable to assist - but you had your own powers?"

Arcana favoured him with a bitter smile. "Not like what you've seen - I was a water sorceress of mediocre skill. I tried to make the doe more comfortable but it was impossible." Arcana shivered, wrapping her arms around her body. "She cried out for my help and I saw a tiny head being birthed. The fawn's eyes were closed and I could see right through it."

Fenris' lips pressed into a thin line. "And what did you do?"

"I went to catch the fawn but every time I tried, my fingers passed right through. When I thought to give up he opened his eyes - black, empty pits of eyes that seemed bottomless. The moment we looked at each other, my hands found sticky fur and he was solid. Those eyes terrified me but I couldn't look away. I stared and stared and stared..." Arcana caught her breath and broke off. Even now, with the length of years behind her, the memory was sharp and nauseating. "I felt like I was falling. Everything went black. My body was on fire, then it was numb. I thought I must be dead."

"I have that effect on people," Caelum said, so solemnly that she smiled.

"Stars began to wink, tiny pinpoints of white that flickered on and off. Floating in the nothing was a tiny fawn. He was a suggestion of a thing, the stars burning around and through his little body. I reached out to touch his cheek and there was... something. A pulling, a pushing, I don't know, but it got steadily worse, taking me apart at the seams. I remember thinking it should have hurt, being shredded like that." Arcana raised her eyes to Fenris' and saw his expression fused into one of horror.

Caelum knelt and laid his head in her lap. "I don't remember it at all."

"Be grateful - nobody should have to remember a thing like that."

Fenris steepled his fingers, tapped them against his chin. "How long did it last?"

"I don't know. I remember sitting up in the grass, aching all over and holding the newborn fawn. He was solid and real and he bleated at me. The doe nosed at him and whispered 'Caelum.' Magic rose around us, thick and heavy - it felt like being dragged down a drain. I remember clinging to Caelum while the ground twisted and bucked... and then I must have fainted. When the rescue party arrived, Lesce said my hair had turned black and my skin a stark white. The healers found a pulse but couldn't wake either of us. Even unconscious I wouldn't let Caelum go, so we were transported together. When I eventually woke and looked in the mirror, my eyes were as black as the empty wells Caelum had first shown me. When Caelum opened *his* eyes, they had the stars inside them." Arcana's lips curled and she stroked a hand down Caelum's cheek. "And so were we bound together, a life for a life."

"I imagine your healers would have been mystified," Fenris mused, his gaze far off.

"They were." Arcana frowned. "The Council wanted to run tests, millions of tests. I was young, frightened and confused, so I let them. In addition to changing my looks, the magic flux altered my powers. I went from a Class Five water sorcerer to something so strong it could no longer be classified, with all the elements at my disposal."

"I would not believe it, save that I am sitting here in front of you," Fenris admitted at last, his face grave. "I have never heard nor witnessed such a thing as you describe. Never."

"I wish I could say I was surprised, but I'm not. Once I tired of the Council's ever-pressing need to study me, Caelum and I determined to set

47

out on our own to see if we could find out more information." Arcana shrugged, skin prickling as his gaze fastened on her face. "We've wandered the galaxy for half a century, following Caelum's inner voice, and discovered precious little... until you."

Fenris swept her body with assessing eyes. "Forgive my forward statement, but you do not look over half a century old."

"I'll take that as a compliment." Arcana chuckled. "The average lifespan on Sorcen is three centuries, so I'm still classified as young."

He nodded. "That makes more sense - so you're about a quarter of the way through?"

"Give or take."

"And what about you?" Caelum raised his head, the blossoms on his antlers swaying. "You claimed on the ship you were a protector of my kind. That's what Warden means, doesn't it?"

"Yes, I am a protector of your kind." Fenris reached out tentative fingers, brushing the silver fur along Caelum's jawline. When the deerken didn't protest he repeated the movement, lips curving in the ghost of a smile. "A Warden's duty is to the deerken first. A Guardian serves and fights for the Weaver. I am fortunate enough to claim both titles, though Guardian is the one I use most often."

"Why is that?" Arcana asked.

"Guardian is a title most people understand without need of further explanation." Fenris turned to face her, his gaze travelling slowly up Arcana's throat and across her cheeks before settling - as though reluctantly - upon her eyes. Warmth swept her skin in a wave, followed by the intimate brush of a thousand feathers. Arcana's heart thudded unusually loud in her ears, her neck and cheeks darkening with a blush that, for all her efforts, she could not control. Something moved in the flickering depths of those jade eyes but Fenris blinked rapidly before she had a chance to look closer. "Forgive me," he murmured, shaking his head as if to clear it. "I am still trying to get my thoughts in order. Perhaps the best place to start is with a brief history lesson?"

Caelum lifted his head, starry eyes whirling in anticipation. "Please." The deerken's posture was casual but it was impossible to miss the enthusiasm in his voice - if he had noticed the strange moment which had passed between Fenris and Arcana, he gave no sign. "I know nothing of my ancestry."

"Very well." Fenris braced both forearms on his knees and steepled his fingers. "I am from a place called the Timeless Kingdom."

"It sounds like something out of a fairy tale." Arcana frowned, searching her memory. "I don't think I've ever heard of it before."

Fenris nodded. "Most never have - and that is by design. The kingdom inhabits a space between other spaces, outside of the grip of time and all the realities that move along with it. There is no way in or out, save for the portals - at the foot of one such structure is where you found me."

Arcana cast her mind back to the darkened temple and the crumbling circular structure inside. Trying to keep the sharp edge of skepticism out of her voice, she said; "So you live in an imaginary world accessible only by magic doors?"

"Is that truly so difficult a concept?" Fenris raised an eyebrow. "I find it difficult to imagine a sorceress who has never seen a magic door."

Arcana waved a dismissive hand. "We have portals here. But they lead to somewhere real."

"The Timeless Kingdom is real." Fenris' jaw clenched, a muscle working up near his throat. After a long moment he sighed and continued; "We are ruled by the Weaver, a queen of immense power and limitless love. The deerken are her children - or so she calls them - and live there with her. It is the job of a Guardian to keep the Weaver's balance, and the job of a Warden to look after the deerken, particularly when they need to leave the Kingdom."

Caelum's ears flickered. "No offence, but I don't need a lot of looking after. I'm fully toilet trained, eat all my vegetables and know how to stick the pointy end of my antlers into the bad guys. What need would I have for a Warden?"

"You appear to be different," Fenris said. "Within the Timeless Kingdom the deerken are as normal as you or I but once they step outside, they walk between time and reality. Every future, every past, every possibility rains down around them. They are the Weaver's eyes and ears, existing beyond the veil of normality. Those who see one do not *really* see it." Fenris passed a hand in front of his face as though to dispel an illusion. "Deerken are the sort of thing you would blink twice at and not see again. There is a price for that ability, though - the sweet-natured creatures are easily consumed by the confusion of what they see. Outside the Kingdom, they need guidance and protection, which is why a Guardian and Warden pair work in partnership with every deerken."

Caelum looked down at himself. "I'm solid and real and not in the least confused."

"So was your mother," Arcana added, frowning at Fenris. "Surely there must be a loophole somewhere."

Fenris shook his head. "Not in my experience. When a deerken births, the fawn is in a state of flux. Other deerken gather nearby to stabilise the energy created by a birthing - if left to run rampant, it could tear a hole in the weave." The Guardian worried his lower lip for a moment. "I have never heard of a fawn born outside of the Kingdom. Deerken cannot stabilise their own energies outside, let alone that of another. What you are saying should be impossible."

"I've learnt that impossible is a malleable concept." Arcana sighed, turning the information over in her mind. "What is the weave? Would tearing a hole in it be something people would notice?"

"Oh yes." Fenris' smile became edged. "The Weaver creates the fabric of time, space and reality - we call it the weave. Threatening the integrity of the weave can collapse worlds or render entire realities obsolete."

"Oh," Arcana managed.

"Indeed. Another fact of note is that a deerken requires the same support upon their deathbed as they do when birthing. The energies expelled by a deerken in their final moments are just as volatile." Fenris tapped a finger on his chin. "There *is* record of deerken dying outside the Timeless Kingdom but the results were catastrophic."

Caelum flexed his shoulders and looked down at his mother's grave. "I'm assuming you mean more catastrophic than a crater in the forest."

"Very much so." Fenris hesitated, then shrugged and said; "Before I became a Warden, there was an incident in which two deerken were poached. The energy fallout from their deaths tore a hole in the weave - the planet disappeared and the people on it were destroyed. The rift expanded ever outward and wreaked havoc before it was finally closed at great cost to my people. No deerken have fallen pregnant in the two centuries following this event."

"What?" Arcana shot upright, her mouth agape. "How can that be? Caelum's only fifty-two."

"Now you understand, perhaps, why I am thrown by your existence." Fenris reached out with gentle fingers and stroked the fur along Caelum's flank. "To make things more interesting, deerken cannot speak. They communicate through a series of images and memories which they project outwards at will, or leave in sub-space for other deerken to discover. It takes many years of training for a Warden to understand, and even then, with room for error. Only the Weaver can speak with them fluently."

Caelum glared down at the Guardian. "I've always been able to talk. My mother could talk. How do we know you're not just feeding us a steaming heap of bullshit?"

Fenris stared up at the canopy of the forest above them, the dappled sunlight playing across the soft planes of his face and highlighting the arch of his throat. Arcana found herself drawn to the thumping pulse in his neck, a steady beat that counted out the moments he was lost in his own thoughts. "You do not," Fenris said at last, his voice carrying a bone-deep weariness. "We do not truly know or trust one another. Every word I speak could be a falsehood."

Arcana narrowed her eyes. "You could say the same of us."

"No." The ghost of a smile teased his lips, that burning gaze still focussed on the canopy above. "You have spoken only truth. I can smell it."

"Truth has a smell?" Arcana considered Fenris anew, looking beyond borrowed clothing and heavy injury to the lean musculature of him. A knight - a Guardian, yes - but now that she watched his movements, Arcana revised that summation to predator. The quiet she had mistaken for lethargy was in fact a conservation of energy, each movement executed with a warrior's grace and the silent air of a man who knew how to handle himself. If he possessed a heightened sense of smell, it was likely he had other abilities - meaning to turn her back or even blink too slowly might be a fatal mistake.

Oblivious to her thoughts, Fenris dipped his chin in assent. "So do lies. Everything has a unique scent." He turned to look at her then, the weight of his burning gaze wrapping Arcana in a velvety cloak of heat. "In the spirit of goodwill, I will tell you that my kingdom has been invaded and my people betrayed."

"Betrayed? That's how you got injured," Arcana realised.

Fenris' knuckles whitened where they gripped the wooden bench. "Yes. I had no choice but to flee and once I am healed, I must return. In the interim, I am grateful for your hospitality."

"This is my planet of birth, but I don't live here." Arcana waved his gratitude away with a lazy hand. "Thank Lesce."

"Very well. I will thank Lesce upon our return." Fenris shifted his gaze to Caelum. "May I visit the place where your mother fell?"

Caelum turned to the lip of the bowl, ears pricked forward. "Sure. Just watch out for the whammy."

"Whammy?" One dark eyebrow winged skyward.

"When Caelum's mother died, she left some sort of magical residue behind. Once you step inside that circle of funny looking grass, you'll see what we mean." Arcana gestured at the lush circle of green in the epicentre of the bowl. "We call it the shrine."

"A respectful title." Fenris nodded in approval, snatching his sword from the ground. He dug it point down into the earth and hauled himself upright, graceful in spite of the obvious effort required. After a moment's pause, he moved to the rim of the bowl and began a tedious descent down the slope.

Caelum sidled close enough that Arcana could feel the heat of his body through her clothes. "Aren't you going to help him?"

"No," Arcana returned. "You might be feeling gooey but I'm keeping Fenris firmly where I can see him."

"Good idea," Fenris said over his shoulder. Arcana blinked and he grinned, the expression showing the briefest flash of elongated canines. "I should warn you, I have excellent hearing."

"Just keep walking, Slashy." Arcana crossed both arms over her chest and hoped he couldn't hear the way her breath caught when that devil's smile had curled his lips. Fenris chuckled and turned away, moving steadily towards the edge of the shrine. Arcana heard him muttering rhythmically under his breath before he took a tentative step inside the circle; his gasp was sharp and he fell to his knees, face twisted with shock. The enormous sword slid through his fingers, flattening the grass with a satisfying thump.

"I don't think he was expecting that," Caelum said.

"Nope," Arcana answered, and it was her turn to grin. Her expression faltered when she saw Fenris close his eyes, a shimmering silver tear sliding down one cheek. "Do you remember the first time we stepped inside?"

"I think I cried for a week." Caelum lipped at her hair in thought. "At least."

Arcana said nothing as Fenris got to his feet, reclaiming the fallen sword. He bowed long and low to the shrine and turned to begin a laborious climb back up to the top of the bowl. "I have never experienced something as profound as that," he declared, chest heaving like a bellows as he arrived beside them.

"I know what you mean." Arcana stepped closer, eyes narrowed. Beneath the disguise of his borrowed coat, the Guardian was trembling. "Are you all right?"

"I will be... I might sit down again." Fenris nodded towards the bench. Arcana slipped beneath his arm, ignoring his look of surprise as she offered the strength of her body. He moved slowly, letting her take only a fraction of his weight at first, then more when it became apparent she wasn't made of glass. A few shaky steps later, Fenris slithered fluidly onto the bench and sighed, flashing an exhausted smile at Arcana. "Thank you."

"Welcome." Arcana's skin tingled where his fingers had slid across hers and she bunched them into a fist to banish the sensation. "If I don't take proper care of you, Lesce will skin me alive."

Caelum lowered his head, sniffing at the dark curls which had been plastered to Fenris' forehead by sweat. "He smells okay. Just tired."

"I may have over extended myself, but I wished to visit your mother's shrine. It is a mysterious place." Fenris leant into Caelum's nose, one hand reaching up to stroke along the deerken's jaw. "It would have taken an enormous power to contain the energies of both a birth and a death."

"Don't look at me." Arcana shook her head, both hands raised as though to ward him off. "I told you, I was a Class Five water sorcerer. Less than average."

"Perhaps in the beginning. Are you a water sorceress now?"

"No, of course not. I can absorb and reproduce whatever energy is most dominant in my surrounds - or something less dominant if I concentrate. Except healing," she added, pointing to his chest. "I can't heal."

"You also said that after you successfully birthed Caelum - something which should have killed you and potentially destroyed your entire planet - there was a great surge of energy and you passed out," Fenris continued, his face serene. He flicked her a long, amused look. "Twice your people were saved from certain death and there was, by your own admission, nobody else here."

"You think I did it. You really do." Arcana shook her head. "You don't understand. I spent *months* learning to use my new abilities. I'm still learning. I know I talked about malleability before, but what you're suggesting is truly impossible."

"*You* are impossible," Fenris said firmly. "You and Caelum. What you have, what you are - a soulmerge, two halves of a whole - should be impossible. The tale you told me should have ended in death and destruction for millions upon billions of people - and yet here you stand, smiling and healthy, and the earth with only a tiny pockmark to show that enormous, rending power was ever here." The Guardian shook his head slowly. "Forget impossible. It is miraculous."

Arcana could only stare at him, mouth open. Her fingers itched, her body trembled, and against all rationality, her magic surged and roiled, barely contained beneath the surface of her skin. She took a deep, shaky breath and forced it down, along with the denial that bubbled against her lips. "Even if you're right - and I'm not saying you are - it doesn't matter now." Her lips twisted into a crooked grin. "I assure you, I'm no miracle."

"Oh?" Fenris raised an eyebrow and turned to Caelum. "How did you know to find me in that temple?"

Caelum's ears laid flat against his head and he shifted restlessly from hoof to hoof. The fat blossoms on his antlers seemed to pinch and pucker, reacting to the hesitation visible in every line of his body. Arcana laid a soothing hand against the pulse thumping in his neck. "It's all right. Tell him."

"I hear whispers," Caelum said at last, craning his head back to look up at the canopy as Fenris had done earlier. "Inside my mind. Sometimes a snatch of sound, sometimes an impression, a feeling. We've followed them for fifty years now but never found anything." The deerken's chest expanded in a great sigh. "A week ago, I woke to hear singing. Beautiful, barely there - it dragged us halfway across the galaxy, gaining strength and volume, all the way to that tiny hunk of ice." Caelum turned to look at Fenris, his eyes whirling. "And last night, I had a vision. I've never seen anything like it before."

Fenris listened patiently while Caelum recounted what he had seen. "You saw the Timeless Kingdom," the Guardian said afterwards. "That vision was a message - to you and perhaps to me."

"But why?" Caelum asked, ears pricked forward.

"I believe the Weaver wishes me to know she is alive. Scattered, but alive." Fenris blew out slowly between his teeth. "It seems she guided you across space and then passed the vision down through your mother's energy."

"I imagine all deerken talk to her like that," Arcana ventured into the silence that followed.

"No," said Fenris quietly. "They do not."

Arcana chewed her lip a long moment. "All right, ignoring the fact that all the hairs on my neck are now standing on end - how did *you* end up in that temple?"

"As I said before, I was betrayed. Ambushed and sliced open with my own greatsword." Fenris' hand moved to his chest, his flickering gaze distant. "I managed to recover the blade before I fell through the portal, and -" He paused, shook his head. "Forgive me, but the rest is a long story I am not comfortable telling just yet."

Arcana followed his eyes to where the greatsword gleamed in the morning sunlight. She'd never heard the word before, but it seemed an apt description for such a blade. "Ambushed. That would explain why your greatsword has no scabbard," she said.

"Yes. The scabbard was left behind - cut from my body when I was attacked." Fenris sighed, gaze lingering on the sharp edge of the blade. "Better to lose the scabbard, however, than the blade itself."

"I know someone who can help you out with a new one," Arcana offered.

"You would do such a thing?" Fenris looked surprised. "I would be eternally grateful."

Arcana shrugged, jamming her hands into her armpits to stave off the morning chill. "No need for gratitude - I just don't want you accidentally cutting my arm off during your convalescence."

Fenris' eyes crinkled with amusement, jade fire dancing. "That would be inconvenient."

"Exactly." Arcana felt the corners of her lips tug out, pulling into a smile of their own accord. "We'll make a stop then, when you're up to it."

"And once you're healed - you're going home?" There was an edge to Caelum's voice, a feverish spark in his eyes. "We can take you back to the portal."

"I would that you could, but I destroyed the portal to avoid pursuit." Fenris sighed, his fists clenching and unclenching. His expression remained blank but something haunted shifted behind his eyes. "Only the Weaver can repair it now."

"Then we'll take you somewhere else," Caelum insisted.

"No!" Fenris and Arcana spoke in sharp unison, exchanging a look of surprise in the silence that followed.

Caelum bristled, the blossoms on his antlers curling. "Why not?"

"Because it's foolish." Arcana took a deep breath, reaching out to pluck one of the withering blooms. "I'm not risking our necks for someone else's problem." She flicked a glance at Fenris. "No offence, of course, but this isn't anything to do with us."

"But it *is* to do with us!" Caelum's eyes rounded. "The call *led* us to Fenris, Arcana. It dragged us halfway across the known universe to save his life, and now we've had a vision aimed specifically at him. How can you think-"

"Listen to her, Caelum." Fenris' voice was cool and soothing. "I still don't know who I can and cannot trust - and I am forced to include you in that number, despite the fact that you saved my life. You could be a trap set just for me."

"A *trap*?" Caelum turned his starry gaze on Arcana, the constellations whirling in distress. "How would we possibly be a trap?"

"The point of a trap is to be attractively packaged," Fenris pointed out, his tone reasonable. "For all I believe your story, you must admit it is convenient for a heretofore unknown deerken to appear before me, calling for a Warden's knowledge, just when everything else in my world falls to ruin."

"Unless we're *meant* to help you," Caelum insisted. His ears flickered rapidly in agitation, then froze. Furry eyebrows drew together. "Everything? Everything in your world?"

Fenris' jaw worked silently, then he sighed. "I suppose there is no harm admitting it; if you are a trap, you would already know. Yes. Everything."

"Arcana..."

"No. I said we'd save his life and you could ask questions - and that's it." Arcana took Caelum's great head in both hands and leant over to kiss his nose. "Don't look at me like that. We're not going to abandon Fenris and he's not well enough to leave, even if he wished to. For now, we're companions whether we like it or not."

Caelum narrowed his eyes at her, stars glittering in a rare display of temper. "And then?"

"Then Fenris can do whatever he needs to do, and you and I will follow the siren song in your heart to our next destination." She tried to sound glib but Caelum's spine stiffened.

The leaves on his antlers shrivelled, the blossoms browning as if burned. "This is not a relationship where you own me. I am not a pet."

Arcana's fingers tensed in his fur, her heart thumping arrhythmically. "Caelum -"

"We *are* where we need to be," he growled, cutting her off. "This is where my siren song has led us. There's nothing else - it's quiet now."

"Peace, brother," Fenris put in, his voice pitched to soothe. "Your sister is wise. You should listen to her."

"You two are ridiculous. And blind." Caelum tore his head from Arcana's grasp in a flurry of withering petals and stomped off into the forest, legs quivering with impact but hooves silent in the underbrush. Arcana covered her face with one hand, her throat tight.

"He makes no noise," Fenris noted.

Arcana peered between two fingers. The Guardian's gaze was half lidded and turned in the direction Caelum had flounced. "No. He can't." She sighed. "It's hard to see, but Caelum actually floats half an inch above the ground. Most times, it's useful - but it takes the heat out of a tantrum, which only makes him angrier."

"So I see."

"You said before we had a soulmerge. What does that mean?" Arcana asked, more to distract herself from Caelum's bad mood than from a real desire to know. Fenris was quiet a long moment, his gaze still on the trees where the deerken had disappeared.

"I think you understand the concept," he said at last, turning his flickering gaze on her. "You fell into the flux of Caelum's birth and became his anchor. The flux rewrote you, moulded you into something else – both of you – something new."

"My mother used to call us the two headed monster." Arcana smiled in spite of herself.

"She was more accurate than she realised. You have anchored Caelum into a single reality and given him the power of speech - and doubtless many other things. I wager that more has changed for you than simply a reforging of your magical abilities, also. I called you brother and sister, but it is a paltry terminology. You are two halves of a single entity, each with their own body and mind. A concept I cannot possibly verbalise." he shrugged, spreading long fingers in a helpless gesture. They were trembling.

"You're tired. We should get you home," Arcana said, jerking her chin at his hands.

"I am not ready for the walk." Fenris shook his head with a sigh. "This sojourn has taken more energy than I care to admit."

Arcana chewed on the inside of her cheek. "I've got an idea. Caelum?"

Fenris raised an eyebrow. "I thought he left."

"He can't go far, trust me." Arcana cleared her throat and raised her voice another notch. *"Caelum!"*

"What?" The deerken's peevish voice threaded between the trees, followed swiftly by the appearance of his head and shoulders.

"Fenris is pooped. Can you help?"

"Yeah, sure. Why not? It's not like I have anything better to do." Caelum high-stepped over to Fenris, temper written in the lines of his body. He shook his coat to rid it of twigs and leaves and dropped to the ground, debris raining down around them.

"You would allow me to ride?" Fenris stared down at Caelum's silver-furred back with a mixture of awe and reluctance.

"Let me guess," Caelum snorted a cloud of leaf litter up into the air. "People don't ride deerken in the Timeless Kingdom."

"No." Fenris' lip twitched ever so slightly.

"Well, I tote Arcana around all the time and sometimes I'll allow a couple extra passengers." Caelum tossed his head impatiently. "Ride, or don't ride - it's up to you."

"Thank you." Fenris pushed to his feet, swaying unsteadily. Arcana rushed to grab his arm, fingers tight as he slung a leg over Caelum's back. She stepped aside as he drew the greatsword into his lap, settling it flat across his knees.

"Is that going to be safe there?" she asked, eyeing the naked blade.

"I would slice myself apart before I allowed it to trim even a single hair on Caelum's body," Fenris promised.

"Let's not cut you open again so soon." Arcana rolled her eyes as she swung into place behind him, looping her arms around his back to grasp Caelum's thick fur.

"You will not ride in front?" Fenris chanced a glanced over his shoulder. "It makes sense, seeing as I am taller."

"Right now, a stiff breeze would send you flying. Until you're stronger, it's safer if I ride behind you," Arcana pointed out.

Dark brows furrowed. "Oh. I suppose that makes sense."

"It does. I do what I can, but I don't have any hands so if you pass out, you'd probably fall without Arcana in place to hold you." In spite of his ire, Caelum rose carefully to his feet. "Ready?"

"Lean forward over his neck and hold on tight. Caelum's gait is smooth but he's quick," Arcana warned. Fenris immediately did as he was told and she draped herself over the hard length of his spine, resting her face against his shoulder. His heart thumped beneath her cheek, swift and sure and oddly comforting. She cleared her throat. "Okay, Caelum. Take us home."

CHAPTER
FIVE

ARCANA SAT IN THE WINDOW SEAT OF THE COMMON ROOM, A STEAMING TEAPOT on the sill beside her. Frost spangled the glass and beyond it, a heavy fog obscured everything from view. Only the timepiece on the wall hinted that dawn was close.

"Have you slept yet?" Lesce's no-nonsense tone preceded her cool hand on Arcana's shoulder.

"You can read my vitals. You already know the answer," Arcana snorted, unblinking. Her sister sighed and plopped down next to her on the plush window seat.

"Is it just your body clock?" Lesce asked.

"I think so. Don't you?" Arcana dragged her attention away from the foggy landscape and eyed Lesce over the rim of her teacup. The other woman's plum coloured hair was drawn into a sensible bun, her burgundy eyes serene as she produced a travel cup from inside her apron.

"I suppose so." Lesce reached for the teapot Arcana had set on the window sill. Her hands were compact and calloused, nails filed short. Practical, like everything else about her. Lesce filled her travel mug and replaced the pot on the sill, looking up at Arcana with a steady, almost businesslike expression. "It's hard to tell with you sometimes."

"I thought you were the best," Arcana teased.

Lesce froze with the cup midway to her mouth. "So I'm told," she said, her voice clipped.

"Come on, Lesce, lighten up a little. It's me." Arcana prodded her sister in the arm and received a grimace in return.

"Sorry. Since I took over as the Healing Elder I've heard that sentence a lot, and not always in a nice way." Lesce smiled, but the expression did not reach her eyes.

Arcana returned the smile with an equally empty one of her own. "It's not so fun to be the best sometimes, is it?"

"Flare seems to like it," Lesce snorted.

"Do I look like Flare to you?" Arcana raised an eyebrow.

Lesce remained sombre, burgundy eyes exploring Arcana's face. "No," She agreed at last. "You don't look like Flare." The words *any more* hung unspoken between them.

"You guys never did get along. Is it really that bad?" Arcana asked, her fingers tightening involuntarily around her cup.

"Yes," said Lesce simply. She held up a hand to forestall Arcana's next comment, a sad smile playing across her lips. "You were our bridge, Arcana. Flare and I are too opposite to co-exist peacefully. Once you left..."

"There was no longer a bridge?"

"Exactly. Don't feel bad - we still love each other. We just don't get along. The best solution is to stay away from each other as much as possible, though that can be difficult with our Tower duties." Lesce offered a watery smile. "Speaking of Tower duties, the Council is waiting for you to visit. Are you going to town today?"

Arcana nodded, transferring her gaze to the closed doorway of the guest room. "As soon as Fenris is awake."

"He's an interesting creature, that man. His sleep is deep and recuperative, something beyond what I'm used to seeing. I believe he'll return to full strength quickly," Lesce said, her eyes distant.

"You can check vitals from afar?"

"If I try hard enough." Lesce winked. "Don't tell anyone - I wouldn't want Salve to think he's out of a job."

"I doubt that, there's too big a need for mid-level healers – unless that's changed since I was here last?" Arcana asked.

"No, it hasn't. There are, in fact, fewer healers ranking Class Two and above than when you were last here. We rely heavily on the middle classes to keep us afloat but they simply cannot handle the most difficult tasks." Lesce's brows drew together and her mouth puckered. "It's exhausting."

"Higher classes are rare no matter what school of magic you imprint into," Arcana said.

Lesce worried her knuckles for a moment and then said; "True, but not so many people die from a lack of high ranking earth sorcerers."

"Good point."

"Can you heal yet?" her sister asked, narrowing her eyes suddenly.

"No. Oh, no." Arcana sliced the air with both hands. "Come on Lesce, you already know the answer to that."

"You healed Fenris."

"I *sealed* his wound. With a candle!"

"I still can't comprehend how that was even possible, but nevertheless he lives entirely because of your efforts," Lesce insisted.

"Don't lie to me. I watched you heal him myself," Arcana scoffed.

"He would never have made it here if you hadn't stepped in first," Lesce said firmly, sipping at her tea. "Using the candle inside your lantern was a brilliant idea."

"You say that, but I had no way to sense what was going on inside his body. I didn't heal, I melted his flesh!" Arcana grimaced, plucking at the velvet seat with one hand. "Fenris wouldn't have that enormous scar if you'd been there and we both know it. Face it, Lesce - even my magic has limitations and healing is definitely one of them."

"If you think so. Fenris said you and Caelum were an enigma," Lesce pointed out.

"He also thought we were deerken poachers," Arcana said, shaking her head.

"An understandable mistake." Lesce's eyes were focussed on her face, looking *into* her rather than at her. "Why are you so suspicious of him?"

"Why are you all so quick to trust him?" Arcana demanded, clutching at her teacup until her knuckles whitened.

"Hmm. Instinct," Lesce answered, rolling one shoulder. "That and I like his accent."

"Oh, please." Arcana gave her sister a lopsided grin. "You like his *accent*?"

"I'm married. Further appreciation would be inappropriate," Lesce's tone carried an edge which said marriage hadn't prevented her from appreciation, only verbalisation of it.

"And you think you're not like Flare," Arcana chided.

"Tell me you haven't noticed - I've seen you watching him," Lesce said quickly, one eyebrow raised.

"I've noticed," Arcana allowed, the words dragging out against her will. "He's..."

"A weapon," Lesce agreed, her sigh completely feminine.

"Lesce!"

"Don't worry, he's still asleep. Besides, he was looking at you too, you know," Lesce said, and this time the glitter in her eyes was unmistakable.

"Lots of people look at me, Lesce. I've grown used to it." Arcana's voice was carefully dry; her palms were sweating around the cup.

"That's not what I meant and you know it. Arcana, have you looked at anyone since-"

"No," said Arcana coldly, "I haven't. That part of me is dead."

"Really? Then why are you blushing?"

"I hate you," Arcana whispered, but her heart wasn't in it and Lesce knew; she chuckled, a sound startlingly like Flare. "Honestly, Lesce, I *can't*. He looked at me and I thought I was going to be swallowed alive." Arcana shook her head. "I don't even know him."

"If you give him a chance-"

"I said no." Arcana pushed to her feet, draining her tea in one gulp and setting the cup aside. She'd dressed simply in thick black leggings and an oversized burgundy knit jumper which hung almost to her knees. Movements jerky with temper, Arcana picked up the plaited leather belt that had been resting beside her and used it to cinch the jumper in at her hips.

"Nice," Lesce commented, eyeing her figure. Unlike Flare, she knew better than to push her siblings when they were uncomfortable. "Nothing like that in town."

"I've given up trying to keep track of Sorcen fashion. I dress how I like." Arcana tugged on her boots and looped a warm, fringed scarf around her neck.

"I thought you were waiting for Fenris?"

"I am, but I hate being idle. I think I'll go and see about the fog." Arcana peered through the frost spangled window, wondering if Caelum was outside. He'd barely spoken to her since returning from the shrine the day before. "Are you leaving soon?"

"Not for an hour or so," Lesce said.

"Would you send Fenris out when he wakes? Something tells me he'll be up by true dawn." Arcana shook her head. "Those warrior types always are."

Lesce raised an eyebrow. "Says you, who's been up most of the night baking pastries."

"I was hungry!" Reminded of her hard work, Arcana grabbed one of the berry-filled delicacies and stuffed it into her mouth as she disappeared out the door, fleeing her sister's laughter. The outside air was crisp and Arcana shrugged further into her scarf as she strode away from the house, wolfing down her breakfast before the frost could ruin it. Fog lay heavy across the ground, camouflaging the property's waist-high fence and the decorative gate by the roadside. Caelum was nowhere to be seen but Arcana wasn't worried. When the deerken needed space, he liked to spend his time snuggled down with the chickens in the family's barn, where magic kept the environment warm and dry. She smiled, wondering how many eggs would be hidden beneath his long fur come dawn.

Thoughts of Caelum led to thoughts of Fenris, and her disconcerting conversation with Lesce. Since finding Fenris at the base of his ruined portal, Arcana felt as though she were being dragged backwards through a hedge, thorns and all. She shivered. The sooner Fenris was on his way, the sooner she could reclaim control of her own life. For now, though, better to stick with what she *could* control - such as the fog, which she'd promised Lesce she was going to move.

Arcana began to draw in slow, purposeful breaths, inviting the fog into her lungs and spreading it through her body. The damp clouds began coiling around her feet and ankles, begging to be petted. Arcana raised both hands and the living cloud rose too, dipping and swirling and forming into barely-seen faces and complex shapes upon command. She smiled. Just because she'd decided to move the fog didn't mean she couldn't have a little fun with it first.

"Incredible." Fenris' voice was so close his breath tickled her ear.

Arcana jumped, biting her tongue to keep from crying out, her concentration dissipating - and with it, the fog creatures. "What in the name of boiling water is wrong with you?" she growled, spinning on one heel. The Guardian stood so close he was almost on top of her, once again leaning on the greatsword. Fog swirled around and over them, a boiling, restless cloud that blocked out the rest of the world.

"I surprised you. My apologies." He inclined his head and shoulders in her direction. "Lesce said I would find you here. I did not mean to interrupt but I have never seen such a thing as that."

"Fog?" Arcana eased a clenched fist over her still thumping heart, not bothering to disguise the tart edge to her voice.

"Cats made of fog. Faces, waves, trees. Birds," Fenris replied, smiling. "A rare talent."

"So I'm told," Arcana answered, eyeing him critically. He seemed straighter than the day before, his face less gaunt.

"I feel much better," Fenris agreed.

Arcana blinked. "I didn't…"

"I could see the analytical expression on your face." The corner of his mouth twitched.

"Just like I can see the smug one on yours?"

Fenris smiled properly then, the expression lighting his whole face and stealing the breath from Arcana's lungs. "Something like that." He reached a hand out to the fog, watched it curl around his wrist like a living thing. "Would you mind if I asked how your magic works? I queried your sister last night but she said it was impossible to explain."

"Hah!" Arcana grinned at the thought of her officious sister. "She palmed you off because she was examining you."

"An interesting turn of phrase. Yes, I believe you are correct - she was looking at me in a way that made me feel as though I was being turned inside out. I tried to distract her with small talk," Fenris admitted. Arcana chuckled, imagining the scene in her mind's eye: Fenris, shirtless on the edge of the bed and Lesce studiously ignoring his polite questions while she prodded and poked at his long scar, checking that all was as it should be.

"Lesce isn't very good at small talk. Too serious," she said, blinking to banish the image.

"Indeed." Fenris traced his foggy arm through the air, the corners of his eyes creasing in delight as the gesture left a discernible trail of vapour. "I surmised that the best person to ask about your particular talents was you."

"I don't understand it completely, but it's no real secret." Arcana shrugged. "People often ask me how I do it."

"And what do you tell them?"

"I tell them it's magic." Arcana grinned and he laughed, a short, joyous sound. "If I were trying to be more specific, though, I'd say it changes depending on my environment. Right now, the predominant thing in my environment is the fog. I breathe it in and my body absorbs the properties of it, which is then reflected in my magic. Yesterday in the forest, I bent the trees because I took on the nature magic. On the planet where I met you I had ice magic, but inside the temple there was no ice so I commanded the earth instead."

"Lesce said you healed me with a candle – surely that is not the predominant energy aboard a spaceship." Fenris frowned, his hand fluttering involuntarily towards his chest.

"No, it's not. I've learnt with time that exerting my focus allows me to reject the energy I'm absorbing passively and instead take on what I choose, so long as it's in my immediate vicinity. That's a lot harder and requires me being in contact with the item. For example, out here if I wanted earth magic I could have it, but I would need to get down on my knees and bury my hands in the mud." Arcana grimaced at the thought.

"And the candle?"

"Caelum brought me a lantern because it was the only open flame I have on the ship. He knew I'd need fire to seal your wound. A candle only puts out a small energy, so I used my abilities to magnify that energy until I could melt flesh together - and even then, there are limits to how much an energy can be amplified. It was a slow and tedious job." Arcana shivered at the memory. "You were lucky to be unconscious."

Fenris nodded, his eyes narrowed in thought. "I think I understand. And Caelum? Are his powers similar to yours?"

"His abilities depend on the environment and involve only himself. On the planet where we found you, he had a winter length coat. Out in the forest yesterday, his antlers bloomed with life." Arcana shrugged. "I had several thousand years of sorcery lore to base my studies on but nobody here had ever met a deerken, so Caelum's been going it alone. He can exert some will over his body, but not a lot."

"A normal deerken fades into the environment. It seems as though Caelum's body is reversing that, enabling him to alter his appearance instead," Fenris mused, tapping his chin. "I would imagine your soul anchoring him to this plane is what allows a physical manifestation."

"Lucky him." Arcana's words were dry, but they bought Fenris' gaze to her face. His eyes roved restlessly across her cheeks before locking with her own. The air warmed immediately, as though someone had wrapped a blanket around her shoulders and was tickling her with the softened edges. Arcana's heartbeat thumped overloud in her ears, cheeks heating of their own volition. Fenris stared her down. Bent as he was over his sword, his face was only inches higher than hers. She blinked slowly, owlishly, earning a moment's reprieve before the feeling crashed back in again; velvet and feathers and glorious heat. Arcana's breath hitched and she was seized with an irrational urge to lean in closer, to breathe deeply of Fenris' scent - evergreens with an overtone of cinnamon.

"Arcana?" His voice came from far away. His accent was lovely, as Lesce had pointed out; it seemed to thrum inside her chest.

"Stop it," she whispered, reaching up with a trembling hand to brush a lock of hair back from his forehead. His skin was cool and soft. "Stop doing that." The sensation disappeared immediately, leaving her short of breath and mildly dizzy. Fenris caught her elbow as she stumbled; Arcana leapt back as though his touch would burn her and fixed him with an icy glare. Tendrils of fog curled between them, wrapping her legs and waist in a belated suit of misty armour. "What the hell was *that*?"

"It didn't work." Fenris sounded dazed, astonished, confused.

"What didn't work?"

"My glamour. It didn't work." His careful formality had dropped away and the fire in his eyes flickered with uncertainty. "It always works."

"You tried to put a glamour on me?" Rage sparked in the pit of her gut. Magic was one thing, but *mind control*?

"No, you don't understand - it's involuntary." He held up both hands as though to ward off a blow. "I - I can't look anyone in the eye or I snare them by accident."

"You did it yesterday, too, didn't you? I thought it was a trick of the shrine," Arcana recalled, crossing her arms to hide their trembling.

"I did. At first it was an accident. Your eyes are..." Fenris trailed off and cleared his throat. "But you didn't respond the way people normally do. I thought it was because I had been injured and was too weak, but I feel a lot better this morning."

"So you thought you'd try it again?" Arcana wondered what would happen if she punched him. A flush rode high on her cheeks; all she could think about was the soft feel of his skin beneath her fingers. It made her want to hit him all the more.

"Yes." Fenris' voice was meek. "I had to be sure."

"Why?"

"Because nobody is immune," he said softly.

"I'd hardly say I was immune. I -" She waved a hand in the direction of his face. "I wouldn't normally do that."

"I was commanding you to turn and walk away from me," Fenris said, his voice so soft she could barely hear it. "I was commanding you to tell me if this was a trap. But it didn't work - your actions were your own."

"That feeling, though, that... warmth. I felt the energy." Arcana swallowed through her embarrassment. "What are you? Glamour is an old word - we don't even use it here." Her eyes narrowed. "Are you fey?"

"I am part fey," Fenris admitted after a long moment. "I've never had someone pick that up before."

"I'm not a fey fanatic - I just know a lot about magic. The fey always know exactly what they're doing; everything is calculated and strictly controlled. Involuntary isn't in their lexicon. My mother used to say 'only a fool trusts a fairy.'" She sneered the last, hooking her fingers around the words.

"I'm *part* fey," Fenris repeated, sounding injured. "A half-blood. My glamour is involuntary."

"Explain." Arcana tapped a foot impatiently, setting the fog dipping and swirling across the ground between them. "Most specifically, the part where you -"

"It's my eyes," Fenris said, closing them for a long moment. "The glamour happens on eye contact. I usually spend my time looking at people's left ears."

"Don't they notice?" Arcana raised an eyebrow; his eyelids flew open and he regarded her in astonishment.

"Of course not," Fenris spluttered. "My eyes are full of fire. Nobody can tell where I'm looking."

"I can."

"You cannot!"

"Try me." Arcana fisted both hands on her hips. His uncertainty was going a long way towards salving her embarrassment; the longer it continued, the better.

"All right." Fenris took a deep breath. "Tell me where I'm looking, then."

Arcana tipped her face upwards so that she could follow his gaze. "Forehead. Ear. Nose. Cheek. Lips. Shoulder. Throat. Hey," she put a finger under his chin and pushed upwards. "I'm up here, asshole."

"Incredible," he breathed. "You really *can* see where I'm looking."

"Yes. Your eyes are like an open book, but I'm not interested in reading," she growled.

The ghost of a smile flitted across his lips. "My apologies. I was trying to test you."

"Well, you succeeded in pissing me off instead," Arcana answered.

"Why? Is it so terrible for a man to appreciate a beautiful woman?" Fenris' voice took on a velvety quality which curled around the edges of his accent, lending a dark and delicate depth to his words.

"I'm not beautiful." Arcana snatched her hand back and turned away. "I'm an anomaly. A science project gone wrong. No need to be cruel about it."

"Arcana-"

"The sun is starting to rise. Time to get Caelum out of bed." Arcana stalked across the yard, the fog parting to allow her through. She watched the barn closely, counting paces, whilst Fenris looked on with a puzzled expression. Just before she reached the property's fence line, the air beside her puckered and Caelum appeared with a barely audible popping sound.

The deerken snorted in surprise, shedding several chicken feathers and blinking sleepy eyes in a desperate attempt to take in his surroundings. "Was that necessary?"

"Yes," Arcana whispered, throwing her arms around his neck and burying her face in his fur. She didn't care if he was still angry at her - right now, his strength was all that kept her standing.

"What's the matter?" Caelum's irritation evaporated and he curled his head around her shoulders in the deerken equivalent of an embrace.

Silver-grey fur spilled through Arcana's fingers as his coat lengthened in response to the cold, the ridge down his back tipped with black. "Fenris -"

"What magic was that?" Fenris arrived behind her, sounding slightly breathless.

"Arcana and I are quite literally bonded. If we're too far away from one another, the link snaps into effect and I jump to her side. Involuntarily," Caelum added. "We have about a thirty-pace maximum range. Anything more and pop! There I am."

"How unusual," Fenris murmured, and Arcana could imagine the frown furrowing his brows.

"Yeah, we're full of surprises. Too bad I can't do it on purpose," Caelum grumbled.

"I'm sorry?"

"I can't jump on purpose. Only like this," the deerken repeated. "Now, you want to tell me what you did to Arcana?"

"I... I looked at her," Fenris' voice was coloured with embarrassment.

"You *looked* at her? What, like, naked through the window or some-thing?" Caelum's voice was tinted with astonishment and the beginnings of anger.

"No!" Fenris and Arcana exclaimed in unison. She leant back from Caelum's fur long enough to shake her head. "No, Caelum, nothing like that."

"I have a natural glamour. I noticed yesterday that it was not working, so I tested it to determine if that was due to my exhaustion. But Arcana is immune." Fenris' face was creased with uncertainty, the muscles in his neck working as he swallowed. His eyes brushed across Arcana's fore-head, skittered down her cheeks. "I apologise for upsetting you but I acted from necessity. I told you before I was betrayed and I meant it; comrades I counted as brothers sought an end to my life and the lives of others I care for. I am cast from my home and suddenly here you are, a charming enigma full of power and potential. So conveniently placed – perhaps coincidence, perhaps not. Until I know the length and breadth of the plot, I cannot say for sure. Please understand."

Arcana watched him silently, watched the way his hands clenched to fists, watched the way the muscles corded with tension in his shoulders. He was genuinely upset, she realised, and yet... she shivered. No. "I understand but I don't like it."

"The feeling is mutual," Fenris replied fervently. "But I had to know."

"Hmph." Arcana channelled her temper into the fog, raising a hand towards the sky. The thick mist around them coiled and surged upwards as though powered by a great spring. Higher and higher it went until the first morning rays splashed across the billowing clouds, burnishing them with golden light and evaporating the fog into a soft, misting moisture. She wanted to shout at Fenris, to slap him - and had the strangest feeling he'd allow it, which took the wind out of her sails. Arcana sighed. "Forget it. Let's go, before the streets get too crowded."

Caelum crouched without protest; Fenris climbed aboard with the greatsword in his lap and Arcana slipped in behind him, reaching around the Guardian to curl her hands in Caelum's long fur. She leant forward as Caelum swung himself upright, pushing Fenris down with the combined weight of momentum and her body. He went boneless beneath her, his flesh warm even through their clothes, his body forgiving. Arcana shoved the scent of him from her mind as Caelum set off down the road.

Sorca City's outskirts rose around them, a jumbled mixture of traditional domed houses and squarer, functionally shaped shops. The few residents out and about had all turned their faces up to the clearing sky, wonder and sunlight reflected in their eyes. Caelum's haunches bunched and suddenly those shocked faces were behind them, the city's wide, cobbled streets passing in a blur. Arcana prodded Fenris in warning as Caelum propped, spun on a moment and sidestepped neatly through the open double doors of the blacksmith's forge.

"Earthmother save me!" the burly man by the forge leapt back in fright, his bare chest glistening with sweat.

"Good morning, Wright." Arcana smiled as she slid down from Caelum's back.

Wright squinted through the light of his furnace. "Arcana? Is that you?"

"Of course." Arcana bounded across the floor to enfold the smith in a sooty hug. He returned the embrace with a laugh, squeezing until her ribs creaked.

"For the love of melted iron, girl, you sure know how to make an entrance!" Wright leant back to grin down at her. Everything about the smith was broad and muscular, from his shoulders to the tips of his fingers. His skin was the colour of coffee, lit by ochre eyes and framed by sweat darkened brown hair. Soot clung to him like a second skin and despite the chill autumn morning, he wore only a pair of loose cotton trousers and a leather apron.

"I didn't ruin anything, did I?" Arcana leant around him to look at the forge.

"Oh no, I was just tidying and prepping. Who's your friend?" He nodded over her shoulder. Arcana turned to see Fenris slithering to the floor, gripping the greatsword with white knuckles. Caelum sniffed him all over, nudging at limp arms until Fenris raised a hand to stroke the deerken in reassurance.

"This is Fenris. Apparently he doesn't ride well," Arcana added, eyeing the Guardian critically.

"Well, I don't know anyone who rides Caelum well except for you." Wright's grin was crooked. "I didn't even hear you coming."

"Of course not. You imply I run on the ground rather than over it," Caelum scoffed.

"You'd be responsible for all that fancy weather magic, then." Wright jerked his chin towards the doorway. "Nobody else strong enough in town right now."

Arcana grinned, wiggling her fingers. "People looking at the sky don't see me whizzing by."

"Huh. Clever," Wright guffawed. "Now what do I owe this unexpected visit to? Unless you finally decided that Caelum needs shoeing."

"In your dreams, blacksmith." Caelum danced soundlessly across the stone floor of the smithy.

"Fenris has a sword that needs scabbarding. I was hoping you and Briolette could help." Arcana gestured at the greatsword.

Wright whistled between his teeth. "That's a big one you got there, friend. No wonder you want Briolette in on this," he added, nodding his head. "Yes, I think we can help you."

"Will you need the blade?" Arcana frowned. "He's a little attached to it."

Wright raised an eyebrow in Fenris' direction. "Is he mute?"

"No, good sir. My apologies - I was merely shocked by the manner of our arrival." Fenris stepped forward with a pale face and a dry smile, leaning the sword point down against the stone edge of the furnace. "I believe my breakfast might still be out on the street, along with a few of my vital organs." He offered his freed hand to the smith and they exchanged a firm forearm grip, nodding politely to one another.

"Fair enough." Wright's broad smile showed white, even teeth. "I've not been on Caelum's back since I were a lad but some memories never fade."

"Were you friends as children?" Fenris enquired politely.

The smith barked a laugh. "Are you serious? She's almost double my age! Or hasn't she told you?" Wright looked from Arcana to Fenris, his face split with mirth. "Don't let her fool you with those youthful looks, young man. Arcana's always looked exactly as you see her now – well to me, at least. Once upon a time, she and Caelum used to visit the spring carnival and Caelum'd give rides to the little ones. I had my turn a good thirty odd years ago now."

Fenris' burning jade eyes swept Arcana from head to foot, the hint of a smile tugging at his lips. "Is that so?"

"Sure is. You honestly didn't tell him?" Wright raised both eyebrows at Arcana. "If you're going to tote about someone so young, at least do him the favour of letting him know." Turning back to Fenris, he dropped his voice to a stage whisper. "She's in her seventies, you know."

"*Wright!*"

Fenris stepped into the silence, one hand held up for peace and his smile broad enough to show definite fangs inside his mouth. "Fear not, honourable smith, I am aware. In fact, if it eases you, I am older than your lovely Arcana."

"You are?" Wright and Arcana spoke in unison, but if Fenris was bothered by their shock, it didn't show. He simply nodded.

"Much older," the Guardian said, flashing his fangs again. Arcana couldn't help herself; she ran her eyes down the length of his body and back. He looked a man full grown, dangerous and sleek, but she wouldn't have pegged him as much more than thirty. If that. However, if he was half fey - well, the fey lived five or six centuries, sometimes far longer. And though Wright's comments had been meant in jest, Arcana now found herself wondering exactly how old he was. Catching her astonished appraisal of his body, Fenris' grin took on a wicked edge and though he appeared not to move, he was suddenly far more masculine than before.

Arcana growled and turned to Wright. "We've not known each other long enough to exchange life stories. How soon can you have the scabbard ready?"

Wright eyed the greatsword, sucking the inside of his teeth. "Couple of days I suppose, maybe less if Bri's involved." He glanced at Fenris. "Can I take a tracing?"

"Of course," Fenris nodded. Wright moved to the sword and grunted, muscles bulging as he struggled to lift it off the ground with both hands. Fenris leant over and took the blade from the smith, hefting it with ease in only one hand.

"Shit a brick," Wright blustered, taking a step back in surprise. "You're stronger than you look."

"So I've been told. Where would you like it?" Fenris asked, his lip twitching in amusement.

"Over there." Wright waved a hand vaguely, staring at the greatsword with great puzzlement. "Would you mind giving me a hand with the blade?"

Fenris laid the greatsword on the smith's long bench. "It would be my pleasure."

"Thanks. Bri's inside, Arcana, if you want to see her," Wright tossed over his shoulder.

"Of course I do." Arcana smiled and stepped through the leather curtain separating the smithy from the house beyond. In contrast to the smoky forge, the house was clean and simply furnished, utilising the same circular layout common to Sorcen residences. In addition to the firepit in the centre of the room, cushioned benches lined a long table and a kitchenette took up most of the eastern wall. The dining table was piled high with scraps of leather and buckets of rough gemstones. A woman with khaki coloured hair was bent over a wooden workbench which took up most of the available floor space on the western side of the fire pit - it too, was covered in baskets of gems, leather and tools. She straightened as Arcana cleared her throat, turning to reveal a belly heavy with child.

Briolette's deep brown eyes widened in delight. "Arcana!"

"Briolette, look at you!" Arcana stepped forward to embrace the younger woman.

"Time flies, eh? Only a couple of months to go now," Briolette grinned, her freckled face flushed beneath a fine layer of grease and dirt.

"It's barely breakfast time and you're already filthy," Arcana laughed. Briolette crossed her eyes in an attempt to see down her own nose, using the back of one wrist to push thick-rimmed glasses into place.

"Am I? I've been setting stones this morning and I clean them as I go, that's probably why," she said, shrugging her long plait back over her shoulder. "I'm so glad to see you!"

"It's been a few years," Arcana acknowledged.

"Is this a scheduled visit? Lesce didn't say anything at my last check-up. I always ask," Briolette added, grinning again. "Oh, I'm so rude! Tea? I'm sure the kettle's here somewhere."

"I'm fine, thanks. I actually came by with a challenge for you," Arcana smiled. The younger woman's joy in her work was always infectious.

"A challenge!"

"Yes. Remember that beautiful bag you made me?" Arcana asked.

"Your adventure pack! Of course, how could I forget?" Briolette nodded enthusiastically.

"Right. Well, it's great! I use it all the time. It's at home in my room right now. I was actually hoping you could work some similar magic for a… friend of mine. He's got a really big sword." Arcana waved her arms in a vague indication of the greatsword's height.

"A friend with a large sword?" Briolette tittered and winked.

Arcana rolled her eyes. "Does everyone on this planet have Flare's sense of humour?"

"Maybe time away has made you too stuffy," Briolette suggested with another giggle.

"Probably." Arcana's lips pulled into a smile. "Well, what do you think? Wright's taking the blade's measurements now. Can you give it a try?"

"Sure! You know I love a challenge," Briolette laughed. "I'm just putting the finishing touches on my latest commission and then I'll be all yours. By the time Wright's finished his half of the work it should be no problem."

Arcana took the other woman's hand in her own and squeezed gently. "Thank you."

"Always welcome!" Briolette's grin turned cheeky and the younger woman cut a glance towards the blacksmith. "So, who is he?"

"Nobody," Arcana replied curtly. Rather than take offence at her tone, Briolette laughed in open delight, shoving playfully at Arcana's shoulder until she sighed and held up both hands in defeat. "Fine! His name is Fenris. I haven't known him long. He's recovering from some serious injuries under Lesce's guidance and I thought I'd help him out."

Briolette pursed her lips, considering. "Is he cute?"

"Briolette!"

"What? A girl can't do a little window shopping now and then? Ooooh you're blushing," Briolette grinned. "He must be cute."

Arcana rubbed both hands over her heating face. "Bri, please."

A loud chuckle. "Fine, fine. I'll check Wright's drawing later and start designing-" Briolette cut off as the front door to the residence swung open, setting a long chain of bells jangling loudly.

"Briolette, baby, you in here?" A slick male drawl, accompanied by the sound of a shuffling swagger. The newcomer's head was a silhouette in the morning sunshine, but Arcana would have known that voice anywhere - it still haunted her nightmares.

Briolette's lips pressed into a thin line. "What are you doing here, Algae?"

"Just coming to check on Mama's pres- whoa, Arcana! Sweet lips of heaven, is that you?" the drawl changed from suave to surprised, then back again in the blink of an eye.

Arcana didn't even bother attempting to smile. "Hello, Algae."

He hadn't changed much. Same ocean blue hair, same dimpled cheeks and cocky smile. A multi-layered navy cloak cascaded fashionably from a gold-embroidered shoulder pad, secured across the front of a sheer turquoise tunic with a golden chain. Black leather pants and boots completed the ensemble, oiled to a sheen and adorned with a multitude of bright golden buckles. Algae whistled appreciatively, his eyes sweeping Arcana's body with ill-disguised hunger. "Baby girl, you are luscious! Have you been working out? Because you are only ripening with age."

"If you're here about your mother's gift," Briolette said loudly, "It will be ready in a fortnight, as I promised you last week." She crossed her arms over her chest, then uncrossed them as Algae's gaze raked across her plumped-up bosom.

"I know what you said, sweet cheeks, I just thought you might have put a little rush on it for me." Algae winked. "I'm sure it's not every day a sorcerer of my calibre places an order."

"I don't put a rush on my work for anyone, ever, and I certainly don't arrange my schedule based upon sorcerer classification. I only produce the best," Briolette snapped, her face red with outrage. "I'll have it ready in two weeks."

"Oh come on now, I'm sure you can squeeze it out sooner. For me?" Algae's smile widened to display perfect white teeth and he stepped forward, leaning in until Briolette backed away.

"She said no." Arcana slid between them and held up a hand to fore-stall his advance. Algae blinked slowly, looking up from beneath long blue lashes, sapphire eyes filled with smoke and promise. Arcana swallowed heavily, forcing her lungs to obey and her nose to ignore the offensive punch of his cologne. "Back off, Algae."

"No need to get cranky, angel," he purred. "If you wanna get close you just have to ask. Heavenly waters but it's good to hear my name on your lips again."

"I think it's time for you to leave."

Algae leered and leant closer, placing his chest against the palm of her open hand, his warmth seeping into her skin through the barely-there fabric of his tunic. He lowered his head until it was moments from her face, lips curling into a secretive smile. "You can try to hide it if you like, but I know the truth. You miss me. Your body misses me. And *I* have missed you."

"Blinded by your ego, as always." Arcana gave his chest a firm shove. Algae jerked back a step, eyes dark with desire as he laid a hand over the spot she'd touched. Arcana swallowed bile and hardened her expression. "I'm pretty sure I asked you to leave."

"Leave? But this is the fun part, sweet lips." His lips curled and Algae stepped close again. "Agree to dinner with me."

"No. For the thousandth time, no. Never." Arcana called her magic, dragging it through the confusing mixture of elements in the room. The fog was no use to her here, but perhaps the gemstones - her thoughts cut off as Algae suddenly disappeared, leaving Arcana staring at her own reflection in a wall of shining silver.

Algae leapt backwards with a startled shout as the greatsword turned sideways, the sharp edge of the blade now facing the other sorcerer. Arcana stared over the top of it, first at Algae's reddened face and then, barely daring to believe it, at Fenris. His body was stiff, his face a thundercloud. "The ladies asked you to leave," Fenris said quietly. His words carried an edge that raised the hairs on Arcana's arms.

"Who in the name of holy water are you?" Algae puffed out his padded shoulders, looking for all the world like an indignant tailor's mannequin - glittering and empty.

"I am Fenris, Guardian to the Weaver and Warden to the deerken," Fenris responded evenly. Beyond him, Caelum and Wright stepped out of the shadowy blacksmith and took up positions slightly behind the Guardian. "And you, it seems, are unwelcome."

"Unwelcome?" Algae flicked a glance towards Arcana, licked his lips, and turned back to Fenris with a sneer. "I am Algae Enrien, Class Three water sorcerer and Captain at Arms for the Water Tower - you have no right to speak to me that way."

"I have no interest in your name or your title," Fenris replied coolly. "True warriors do not seek to intimidate others with their position. Now get out, before I abandon my manners and throw you out."

Algae's jaw dropped, his eyes wide and hurt as he turned his gaze on Arcana. "*This* is your new plaything? Does it even wield magic?"

"Fenris is not my plaything, just as I'm not yours." Arcana raised her hands and the gemstones on the bench answered the call, rising out of their basket like a snake with a thousand glittering eyes. "You've worn out your welcome, Algae. Go back to the Tower."

The stones dipped and swirled through the air, wrapping Algae's shoulders in a spangled blanket. Arcana twitched her fingers and the water sorcerer stumbled, the gemstone cloak all-but dragging him towards the door. "Shining river of - Arcana! Stop it!" Algae threw a disbelieving look over one shoulder as he was dumped unceremoniously on the front doorstep, the gemstones sweeping back inside the workshop as the door clanged shut. On the other side, Algae's indignant silhouette scrambled upright, straightened its cloak - and stormed away.

Arcana returned the gemstones to their basket and sagged against the table. "He went easier than I thought."

"That only means he'll be back." Caelum sounded darkly amused. "You really should let me disembowel him one of these days."

Arcana grunted noncommittally. Briolette appeared beside her, wrapping one thin arm around Arcana's waist. "Are you okay?"

"Yeah." Arcana hugged the younger woman gently. She glanced at Fenris, who had lowered the sword point down onto the floor and was once again leaning on the hilt. "Thanks. You didn't hurt yourself, did you?"

"No, I am past that point - it is my energy that flags, not my body." Fenris crinkled his nose in distaste. "Who was that odious man?"

"Exactly who he said he was. He and I... Well, a long time ago, we... Er... We..." Arcana trailed off, her cheeks heating.

"Arcana and Algae have a history." Briolette's face was sympathetic.

Fenris' eyes rounded and his jaw dropped open. "Are you trying to tell me you were once in a relationship with *that*?" he demanded, jerking a thumb towards the door.

"It was a long time ago," Arcana muttered. "I was young. I didn't know any better."

Fenris crossed his arms over his chest, brows drawn together in a frown. "He didn't behave like it was a long time ago."

"Algae never does." Caelum made a sound of disgust in the back of his throat. "He's a bilge rat."

"Look, we all make mistakes, okay?" Arcana passed a hand over her face, grimacing when she realised they were all still looking at her. "Can we just drop it? Please?"

"You should at least tell Fenris something," Wright said, his tone reproachful.

"Why? We're not - oh, whatever. Fine." Arcana sighed, clutching the edge of the table tight enough that it hurt. "I met Algae at a social function when I was eighteen. We had a steady relationship for a year or so, then I fell into the flux and everything changed. Our relationship ended about a year after that because I caught him in bed with several other women." Arcana narrowed her eyes at the memory. "I called Flare from the neighbour's house and he arrived almost instantly. He chased the women away, tossed Algae into the street, burned the house to the ground and carried me home like the broken doll I was. I vowed then and there never to be that stupid again." She regarded the collection of astonished faces and frowned. "The End."

Fenris was the quickest to recover. "Flare burnt a house down? Is that not a crime?"

"Not," said Arcana shortly, "For Flare. He was a decorated war hero before I was old enough to imprint - and there are only a few years between us. Everyone loves him. Nothing he ever says or does is judged unacceptable." Arcana drummed her fingers on the table, answering the question she saw forming on Fenris' lips. "After Flare took me home, he called the Water Tower and explained the situation - including what he'd done. The Water Elder apologised for allowing Algae to inconvenience his day." Arcana scooped a large gemstone off the floor and set it on the table with a satisfying thump. "There. Now you know. Happy?"

"Hmmm." Fenris narrowed his eyes until nothing more was visible than a faint green glow beneath his lashes. "Happy isn't the term I would use."

"Good point - it would imply that I'm interested in your feelings on this subject. Which, incidentally, I'm not." Arcana pushed away from the table, dusting her hands on her pants. "Well then, now that's seen to, shall we go? We still need to stop in at the Council."

"Are you sure you're okay?" Briolette asked breathlessly. She flicked a glance at Fenris, licked her lips as though she were about to speak, and didn't.

"Yeah. Thanks for agreeing to help me out," Arcana said. The other woman's face went blank for a moment and then she laughed.

"Oh yes, the scabbard! With all that commotion I'd forgotten. Come back in... two days?" She looked to Wright for confirmation and he nodded.

"Perfect. Thank you." Arcana embraced them both, heading for the front door before anyone else decided to ask pointy questions. "See you in two days."

"Thank you both." Fenris bowed stiffly from the hips as Arcana yanked the door open, setting the bells jangling again. "I look forward to seeing you again soon."

Arcana ducked through the open door, holding it wide for her companions. Wright slung an arm casually around his wife's shoulders and, as soon as Fenris had turned his back, gave Arcana a large thumbs up and a broad wink. *I like him*, the blacksmith mouthed across the empty space. *Go for it.*

Arcana flipped him off, earnt a laugh in response - then the door closed and they were gone.

CHAPTER
SIX

THE SUN OUTSIDE WAS WELL UP AND ARCANA BREATHED IN THE WARMTH AS IT fell over her face. The sounds of a bustling street were only steps away but Briolette had nurtured a thick-branched hedge around the front entry, granting Arcana a much-appreciated bubble of peace.

"How are we going to do this?" Caelum asked.

"Fenris can ride. I'll walk," Arcana answered, eyes closed. After the confrontation with Algae she felt a distinct need for her own personal space, and just as distinct a need not to explain that to the men alongside her.

Caelum, ever perceptive, nudged her shoulder with his nose. "Are you sure?"

"It's only a short way. We'll be fine."

"Is there danger?" Fenris asked.

Arcana opened her eyes to find him watching her beneath knitted brows, his expression so fierce she laughed. "No, there's no danger." When his scowl remained firmly in place, Arcana shook her head. "You'll see. Mount up and prepare to experience the life of an unclassified sorceress." Fenris' eyes narrowed but he climbed aboard Caelum's back without protest, knuckles turning white as the deerken regained his feet. Arcana stepped into the street with her head high, raven hair fluttering in the slight breeze. Caelum made no sound but she could feel him close behind, knew without seeing that his nose was above her left shoulder.

Sorca City's streets were a mix of colour and sound, houses and shops piled atop one another and bordered by wooden market stalls with coloured fabric shades. People thronged atop the swept cobblestones, chattering and laughing in loud voices, their bright hair and loose clothing shimmering in the morning sunlight. Arcana counted five steps before the woman nearest her blinked and looked twice, stepping back in shock. Her companions turned to see and they, too, fell silent. Slowly, slowly, the swathes of people parted and the sound in the street dropped from a cacophony to a whisper. Arcana forced a smile onto her face and met the eyes of all who looked her way, daring little waves for the children who peeped between their mothers' skirts.

Ahead of her, a great clearing in the centre of the city housed a circle of five towers. The Earth Tower, tall and straight and built of sandy yellow stone. The Water Tower, soft and curved in shades of blue. The Fire Tower, jagged and edgy and blood orange. The Nature Tower, a spiralling edifice of living trees and finally the Healing Tower, a slick black obsidian marked intermittently with glistening white stones. A spiderweb of bridges connected the towers at irregular intervals, each one decorated with flapping pennants and covered in bold, coloured shade cloth as on the market stalls in the streets below.

Arcana stepped onto the manicured lawns and headed towards the softly curved Water Tower. A sorcerer in blue livery pulled the door open as she approached, nodding respectfully and murmuring a soft greeting. Arcana returned the nod and stepped into the open, airy foyer, pausing a moment for Caelum and Fenris to join her. Barely had they crossed the threshold when the hundreds of people outside began talking loudly, all at once; the sound echoed through the tower's lobby like the dull roar of an indignant beast.

"Greetings, my lady." An older man in long, formal blue robes shut the door firmly, cutting off the noise.

"Pool, is that you?" Arcana grinned, exchanging a warm forearm grip in greeting.

"It is indeed. Greetings to you too, Caelum. I see the years are treating you both well." Pool softened the formal exchange with a hearty laugh. He was a thick set man, barely taller than Arcana's five and a half feet, with a friendly, open face and hair the colour of a stormy sea.

"And you! This is my companion, Fenris. Pool was one of my first instructors at the Water Tower," Arcana added, bopping the sorcerer affectionately on the shoulder.

"Pleased to meet you." Fenris slithered down from Caelum's back, his knuckles tight on the greatsword as he bowed politely and offered his arm.

"And you, honoured warrior. I heard you were gravely injured and am glad to see you healing well," Pool returned the forearm grip with enthusiasm, the gold-trimmed edges of his robes swishing across the floor as he moved.

"Thank you," Fenris answered.

"I take it you're here to see the Council?" Pool asked, retreating to a polite distance.

Arcana sighed. "You know it."

"Allow me to escort you, then. This way." The older man swept a draping sleeve, turning to follow the gesture.

Fenris caught at her elbow as they fell in behind. "Out there in the street... was that normal?"

"Yes," Caelum answered, his nose appearing between them. Arcana reached up to scratch behind his ear, narrowing her eyes as she saw Fenris doing the same on the other side. He caught her looking and smiled.

"Once upon a time I was part of the crowd. Now I part it," Arcana said, shrugging away the gentle ache in her chest.

"A difficult scenario. Do all higher classification sorcerers receive such treatment?" Fenris asked, limping along beside her. Arcana opened her mouth to ask if he was all right, noted his ghost of a head shake, and reconsidered.

"Most higher classification sorcerers blend in, with a couple of notable exceptions. Flare, for example," Caelum chuckled.

Fenris raised an eyebrow. "Oh?"

"Flare is an interesting case in his own right. Common belief is that he was born to sorcery. He imprinted early - there's still a tree in my mother's back garden which bears the marks of his firestorm. A lot of people describe imprinting as a growth, or an evolution. Flare described it as having his blindfold taken off and seeing the world through eyes that already knew it." Arcana wished, not for the first time, that she had Flare's unique perception. "Most sorcerers spend at least two years studying and perfecting their craft before they're ready for anything, but Flare flew threw his trials in a matter of months and was in charge of the military within a year. He's constantly fronting magazines and appearing on holo-casts - everyone loves him."

"You must be very proud," Fenris said.

"Proud and jealous. Sometimes both, at the same time," Arcana admitted with a laugh.

"I can understand that. He seems as though he has managed to keep a cool head, regardless of said popularity." Fenris paused and for a moment, there was only the sound of their footsteps, and of Pool's swishing robe ahead. Arcana waited, sensing the question on his tongue - and was not disappointed when Fenris said; "If the people have such opposing reactions, what happens if you walk the street together?"

"Flare's popularity outweighs the spectacle of Arcana and I," Caelum replied, his chest rumbling with laughter. "But it's irritating having to untangle lingerie from my antlers. Hysterical men and women have terrible aim."

Arcana rolled her eyes. "That only happened once."

"Twice," Caelum returned, shaking his huge head in mock irritation.

"… untangle lingerie from your antlers…" Fenris repeated, half to himself.

"Yeah. You have to see it to believe it," Arcana said. "Flare loves everybody, and everybody loves Flare."

"Here we are," Pool announced suddenly, drawing to a halt. He turned in a theatrical swirl of sapphire velvet, revealing a set of shallow steps. At the top, an elaborate stone panel graced the wall of the tower. The relief stretched twice Arcana's height and was carved with swirls and runes, inset with semi-precious stones. At the very centre a sunburst surrounded a robed figure, one hand stretched towards the sky.

"This is a door?" Fenris asked.

"Of sorts. The Elders meet in a secret location, only accessible through here. Each of the five Towers has one and they can only be activated by class one sorcerers who know the correct spell." Pool waved an expansive hand at the carving. "It is the duty of each Tower to maintain and protect these sacred doorways. Arcana, would you like to do the honours?"

"Of course." Arcana stepped up to the panel and placed her hands inside two small recesses set at chest height. The stone immediately hummed to life, the carved swirls and runes illuminated by a vivid rainbow of light that glowed from beneath her palms. The illumination trickled through the carved channels and joined, at last, in the central figure. With a soft hiss, the stone panel dissolved away and a soft blue light stood in place.

"A portal." Fenris nodded in appreciation, then looked over at Arcana. "You didn't look like you said a spell."

Pool looked somewhat disappointed. "You've seen a portal before?"

"He has." Arcana reached out to pat the deflated sorcerer on the shoulder. "And to answer your question, I don't need to perform the spells any more. The door knows me."

"It *knows* you?" Fenris repeated, his eyebrows lifting. They were long, slender and delicate, a perfect match for the sweeping planes of his face. Arcana wondered idly if he plucked them into perfection.

"Arcana's magic is hard to explain. The Council are expecting you, so I will leave you here," Pool announced, straightening his robes.

"Of course. Wouldn't want to keep them waiting." Arcana gripped her former teacher's arm. "Thanks, Pool. Good to see you again."

"And you." Pool nodded once and turned away, bunching his robes in one fist as he descended the shallow stairs.

"Ready?" Arcana asked. Fenris nodded so she turned into the blue light, relishing the cool, tingling feel of the magic as the portal washed over her skin and the Water Tower faded from sight.

A heartbeat later, sunlight bombarded her from all directions and Arcana blinked to reduce the glare. She stood in a large, round room sporting over a dozen high windows, each with the curtains drawn back to allow the autumn sunlight inside. Five panels were set at regular intervals around the room's circumference, each leading to a tower back in Sorca City. Caelum stepped through the portal behind her, followed by Fenris, who had one fist clenched in the deerken's fur. He blinked in surprise as his body rematerialised, checking himself over with an odd, throaty sound.

"Are you all right?" Arcana asked.

"Yes. I - yes." His lips thinned and he looked up from beneath long lashes. "The last time I travelled via portal was far less enjoyable."

"Ah, I see we have visitors. Welcome!" A wiry man with a ready smile loped forward to clasp Arcana's forearm. His sparkling green eyes were almost completely hidden behind a mop of chaotic emerald hair, which draped around an equally epic beard. He wore a short set of robes that seemed little more than rags tied together with rope at the waist, and a woven circlet of branches set into his hair. His arms and legs were as gnarled as tree branches but his voice was filled with warmth.

"Your grace, may I present to you my companion, Fenris?" Arcana inclined her head, gesturing to the Guardian beside her.

"But of course, my girl! I am Vino, the Nature Elder. Welcome to Sorcen," Vino clasped Fenris' forearm.

"Thank you, your grace." Fenris executed a short bow over their clasped arms, his expression schooled into a mask of serenity.

"Come, come, we have been looking forward to your arrival. This way." Vino beckoned, turning towards an enormous rectangular table in the centre of the room. Another man and three women awaited them, inclining their heads towards Arcana as she approached.

"Your esteemed graces." Arcana inclined her head in return. "Allow me to present to you my companion: Fenris, Guardian to the Weaver and Warden of the deerken."

"It is an honour to meet your graces." Fenris stepped forward, tucking the greatsword under one arm to execute a flourishing bow. In spite of herself, Arcana was impressed. Fenris had said he was used to a more formal setting, and he had certainly meant it - his bow was both grand and smooth, performed with the ease of long practise.

"The pleasure is ours. Anyone who brings Arcana back to Sorcen is a welcome sight! I am Brook, the Elder of Water." A middle-aged woman stepped forward, her sapphire hair streaked with paler blue. She wore a shimmering set of turquoise robes and was crowned with a silver circlet inlaid with sapphires. Brook offered her arm and Fenris returned the forearm grip with a solemn expression.

"About time you showed up." A portly, middle aged man with a luxuriant beard crossed his arms over his chest. "It's been two days since you landed."

"Blaze!" Brook shot him a quelling look but he merely shrugged, brushing a chair aside to lean one hip against the large table.

"Well, it has," Blaze said. Enormous copper brows beetled, all but eclipsing the reddish eyes beneath. "I don't like to wait."

"Fenris, this is Blaze, the Elder of the Fire tower. I apologise for the delay, your grace. Fenris was badly injured and required Elder Lesce's urgent attention." Arcana nodded in the direction of her sister, who looked a stark contrast from her usual self wearing the heavy black robes of a healer, her hair crowned with an elegant twist of obsidian and silver.

"I am most grateful for your efforts, Elder Lesce." Fenris bowed low to Lesce, shooting Arcana a sideways glance from beneath his lashes. "I was unaware you were part of the ruling Council."

"It's a sacred duty but not one that was relevant at the time of your injury. Being an Elder makes me no less of a healer," Lesce responded, smiling.

"I imagine it only makes things worse," a stocky woman with ochre hair grunted.

"In my case, yes," Lesce agreed. "We're imprinting fewer healers by the day."

"A cause for concern, but certainly not one that our unique and most talented Arcana need worry herself over." The other woman smiled, a flat expression that did not reach her sandy eyes.

Arcana turned to Fenris and forced a smile onto her face. "This is Gravella, the Earth Elder. We went to school together as children."

Fenris offered his arm to the other woman, who swept forward in a flurry of golden robes to accept the formal gesture. "Pleased to meet you. Together we are the ruling Council of Sorcen," said Gravella.

As though prompted by the announcement, the Elders returned to their side of the long table and dropped into a collection of high backed chairs, robes rustling and swishing around them. There was no other furniture in the room, leaving guests no option but to stand before the Council on the bare stone floor.

"Are there only five schools of magic, then?" Fenris asked. If he was bothered by the lack of seating it did not show in his politely interested expression, nor the relaxed set of his shoulders. Arcana envied him that ease; whenever she stood in front of the Council, facing down five pairs of eyes and all those sweeping folds of formal fabric, she felt as though she were on trial for an indefinable set of wrongdoings.

"Yes and no, dear boy. We like to think we cover the majority, but there is a vast range of skills across our people. However, even those of us with more unique abilities find it convenient to pledge to one of the major Towers," Vino answered, his smile so wide it disappeared behind his bush of a beard.

"As interesting as discussion of our people is, we should not become distracted." Brook steepled her fingers beneath her chin. "Arcana - we have not seen you for several years. I presume you have a report?"

"Of course, your Grace. As per our arrangement, Caelum and I have been scouring the galaxy for information which may help us understand our origin and the finer workings of our abilities. Caelum's instincts led us to a small, ice covered planet at the outer edge of the Viridian system, from which we rescued Fenris." Arcana gestured to the Guardian beside her.

"Interesting." Blaze rocked back in his chair, fingers laced atop his paunch. "After all this time, I didn't think your search would turn up any tangible results. So, the warg were waiting for you, I take it?"

"I'm not sure, your grace. At first I assumed they were natives - then they ambushed us later, aboard the cruiser. We were able to repel them, of course, but..." Arcana hesitated, biting her lower lip. "There is quite a mess."

"Never mind the mess. I will have it seen to." Vino waved an impatient hand. "I'm more concerned about the motives of these warg."

"The warg were chasing Fenris, your grace. They had personal tele-porting devices with a blood lock," Caelum said. Arcana shot him a quelling look, which he ignored. "We've done our utmost to protect him since that time."

"Indeed?" Vino turned his emerald eyes on Fenris. "I believe that means you'd best tell us a bit about yourself, young man."

"My name is Fenris. I am a Guardian to the Weaver and Warden of the deerken, citizen of the Timeless Kingdom." Fenris straightened perceptibly, the sleeves and ankles of his borrowed clothing sliding further up his arms and legs, enhancing his extra height. His words carried an odd formality which made his accent thicker and lent him an air of almost medieval mystery. "The Weaver rules the Timeless Kingdom and her children are the deerken, who look as Caelum does but walk between time and reality. The Wardens are those who nurture, train and guard the deerken. The Guardians are the personal bodyguard of the Weaver and carry out her bidding."

"I have never heard of this... Weaver. Is she a Queen, then, to rule a kingdom?" Brook asked.

"Yes, your grace, you might say so," Fenris answered.

"A Queen who bears the title of an artisan. What exactly does she weave?" Gravella asked.

"A complex question to answer, your grace." Fenris' grip tightened on the greatsword, the muscles in his jaw doing an intricate dance as he considered the question. "She weaves the fabric of time, space and reality. Everything that ever was, could be, or will be. All possibilities, all lives, all dimensions are birthed and nurtured within the warp and weft of her work."

"Are you trying to say she creates... The universe?" Lesce gasped, her eyes round.

"Everything," Fenris confirmed. There was a long and profound silence, during which the Elders looked around, muttering under their breath as though a previously invisible being might appear at any moment.

"I am nobody's puppet," Blaze said at last, puffing out his chest.

"Of course not, your grace." Fenris smiled wide enough to display his fangs. "The Weaver only creates. Your world, your reality, your time and space - everything you have is created by her. It is your choice how you utilise it, and my job to police it."

"I'm not sure I grasp the enormity of this concept," Brook admitted, her face pale. "It is difficult to believe such a being could truly exist."

"Your grace, I have served the Weaver for many years and I still do not comprehend the enormity of her person, let alone her work. Suffice it to say she is the singular most precious being that will ever exist." Fenris paused, and in the silence Arcana could hear her own heart, thumping overloud in her ears. "The deerken come a close but necessary second. They monitor the weave and, in turn, the Wardens monitor them, ensuring their safety. If there is a discrepancy in the weave, the Guardians are dispatched to put it right."

"Warden and Guardian. You claimed both of those titles," Gravella said, her eyes narrowed.

"Yes, your grace. I did." There was a short, tense silence in which all five of the Elders stared expectantly, and Fenris stood immobile.

Blaze barked a laugh, thumping one pudgy fist down on the table. "Well, boy, you are a breath of fresh air. Do we have to drag the information out of you?"

Fenris raised a single, perfect eyebrow. "I have already given you information, your grace. I apologise if it seems inadequate. Unfortunately, such is the import of my mission that I must remain reticent."

"Bit hard for us to help if you're determined to keep your mouth shut," Blaze grunted, watching Fenris through narrowed eyes.

The Guardian interlaced his fingers around the hilt of the greatsword, face impassive. "Begging your pardon, your grace, but I came here at Arcana's request because she and Elder Lesce saved my life - I did not come to ask for your assistance."

Arcana stared, wondering where the man she had come to know in such a short time had gone. It was as though that Fenris had vanished, replaced by this cold, smooth talking stranger. His manners were impeccable, shrugged on over an absolute belief in his own superiority. Arcana thought it gave him an edge that bordered on disrespectful - the Elders, however, seemed impressed; they were murmuring and nodding to each other behind steepled fingers and glittering glances.

"Perhaps in a show of good faith, Guardian, you could be persuaded to indulge us just a moment," Vino said finally, leaning forward on knobbly elbows. "Surely if you're on a mission, you must have a leader to which you wish to return, or a destination where you are intending to travel. If, indeed, you do not need our help, then how are you proposing to get there?"

Fenris didn't move, but Arcana noted the lines of tension appearing in the set of his shoulders. The look he gave the Council was openly assessing, a man used to being in charge, used to weighing the trustworthiness of those in front of him - and the Council were, each and every one of them, leaning forward, eager for his approval. When had the weight of authority swung in his favour? Arcana wondered. Before she had a chance to ponder further, Caelum pushed forward.

"We'll take him," he said. Arcana narrowed her eyes, but Caelum was deliberately looking elsewhere. "Arcana and I found him. We're responsible for him."

"Is that an offer you are permitted to make?" Vino levelled a gimlet stare on Caelum, lips quirking ever so slightly. "I believe you need the blessing of this Council to undertake such an action, Caelum - and if you think we're inclined to lend out Sorcen's single greatest resource to a warrior we know next to nothing about, then you are sorely mistaken."

"I am not a *resource*," Arcana snapped, her reluctance forgotten in a sudden spurt of temper. She shoved her way to Fenris' side. "How dare you?"

"Easy," Fenris murmured. His fingers were cool on her arm and for a moment, Arcana could only stare at the place where his hand gripped. "They are right to be suspicious of my motives."

"It doesn't matter. They have no right to speak about me that way," she growled, jabbing a finger at Vino. "You don't own me."

"Arcana - peace." Fenris tightened his grip on her arm, the gesture soothing rather than painful. He took a half step forward, as though to shield her with his body, but did not relinquish his hold. "Your esteemed graces. If I were to answer some of your questions - bearing in mind I might not be able to answer them all - may we perhaps reach some common ground?"

The Council turned inwards again, murmuring to one another and making impatient gestures half hidden in the folds of their formal robes. The faintest glimmer of a smile tugged at Fenris' mouth and Arcana's heart lurched sideways as his voice carried to her on the winds of memory. *I should warn you, I have excellent hearing.*

"Very well, Fenris." It was Gravella who spoke, her clipped tone and interlaced fingers at odds with the hungry glint in her eyes. "Our first question is this; if your people have Guardians for the Weaver and Wardens for the deerken, surely they themselves have a leader, a representative to the Weaver?"

Fenris tilted his head to one side, considering. "I suppose such a question is innocent enough. The Warden's leader is bestowed the title of Keeper. The Guardians look to the Walker and there is a third, the Weaver's personal blade, who is known as the Overlord. It is the Overlord's job to hear the Weaver's wishes and carry out her will, acting as a bridge between Wardens and Guardians and helping to guide the Kingdom as a whole."

"A ruling monarch, with a triumvirate of advisors. That makes a certain sense." Gravella's eyes narrowed, her hands flattening on the table. "So tell me, how many of your people claim the title of both Guardian and Warden?"

"Only one, your grace. The Overlord, in order to properly bridge the people, must be both Guardian and Warden," Fenris replied quietly. Arcana felt her breath catch in her throat; was he saying...?

"But *you* laid claim to both titles," Blaze sounded almost accusatory.

"I did." Fenris remained outwardly calm, but Arcana couldn't help but think he looked like the cat who'd just gotten all the milk. The Elders were silent as his words sank in, as their collective minds reached the conclusion that Arcana had already arrived at.

Fenris was the Weaver's Overlord.

"If you're so important, what in the name of soaked kindling are you doing *here*?" Blaze demanded.

Fenris' face twisted, his free hand curling into a fist. "We were betrayed by one of our own and invaded by the warg. The Weaver handed a mission of utmost secrecy down to me but I was wounded during the battle." He laid a hand flat against his chest, dragging ever so slightly at his borrowed shirt to reveal the leading edge of the thick scar Arcana had given him. "I leapt into a portal as it collapsed and remember nothing else until Arcana discovered me."

"You jumped into a collapsing portal?" Brook's face was horrified. "You'd risk being torn apart!"

Fenris looked up at her from beneath his lashes, the fingers of his right hand tapping idly along the hilt of the greatsword. "There was no other way," he said at last. "The Weaver ordered me to close the portals to prevent the warg abusing them - I closed all but one before I was attacked by our betrayer. He drew my sword from the scabbard I carried upon my own back and struck me with it." The Guardian's lips pressed into a thin line and Arcana wondered who he was angrier at - the person who had struck him, or at himself, for getting struck at all. "Though the decision to flee is heavy on my heart, I could not fulfil my duty to the Weaver from beyond the veil of death. So I took my chances and leapt into the portal as it collapsed. It was... an unpleasant journey."

He didn't know the outcome of the battle, Arcana realised. It was evident in the hunch of his shoulders; the guilty exhalation of breath. Seized with a strange impulse to offer comfort, she brushed her fingers against his spine, taking care the Elders didn't notice. Though his posture didn't change, Fenris flicked her a grateful glance which, she knew, he was now aware that only she could see.

"So the warg who chased you aboard the ship… they were hired by the traitor?" Brook asked. Her blue brows were bent together, pale fingers rapping a restless pattern on the tabletop.

"I wish I knew the answer, your grace. They were all despatched and their devices destroyed." Fenris lowered his head as if in thought. It was only Arcana who saw his eyes slide over the Council, sizing up each member. "I can only assume so."

"Hmm. A troubling story you have shared, Overlord. Troubling indeed," Vino murmured. "You are most lucky to be alive. Please know that you are welcome to rest here as long as you need."

"Thank you, Nature Elder." Fenris clicked his heels together and bowed deeply. "I will not trouble you or your people long. I must find an active portal and return home as soon as possible."

"As well you should. It sounds as though your people have need of you. If there is anything we can do to offer our assistance, please…" Brook left the sentence hanging, her voice warm.

"There is one thing, your graces," Fenris said carefully. "Is there a portal here on Sorcen I may examine?"

"Young man, we are sorcerers. There are portals aplenty on Sorcen," Vino chuckled, waving a lazy hand toward the carved panels lining the walls.

"Of course. My apologies. I meant specifically a portal that was not of your making. It would be twice your height, a circular structure on a plinth, with a pedestal to one side. Inactive, of course," Fenris added. The Council shared a long, collective look and then finally Vino shook his head.

"I know of nothing like you have described." The Nature Elder spoke slowly, his brow furrowed. "We are a well-established civilisation; surely if such a thing existed, we would know about it."

"Perhaps. Would it displease you if I checked? My people often work in the shadows - it is more convenient that way." Fenris shifted restlessly on his feet and Arcana wondered if he was beginning to tire, standing and talking for so long. The Council seemed to notice too; Lesce's eyes narrowed on Fenris, her gaze focussing on a point somewhere in the middle of his abdomen.

"I thought you said there was only one portal remaining that was active?" Gravella demanded, eyes narrowing to slits. "It seems an almost impossible chance that it would be here."

"My apologies, your grace." Fenris inclined his head in her direction. "The seven gates within the Timeless Kingdom are our master gates and each connect to a number of minor ones in the weave at large. While one master gate remains open, it means there are a handful of minor gates which also retain their functionality. Were I to find one of those, I would be able to return home."

Apparently satisfied he wasn't going to drop at their feet, Lesce blinked rapidly and turned her eyes to Fenris' face. "Still a slim chance of success."

"Yes," he agreed. "And yet, I must try."

"While you are a guest of Sorcen, you may do as you wish, so long as it does not disrupt our people. Arcana and Caelum will guide you and see to your safety," Brook said, her smile broad and gentle.

"What?" Arcana blinked, looking from Fenris to the Council and back again. "You can't be serious."

"Is there a problem?" Gravella raised an eyebrow, her face cold and haughty.

Arcana clenched her fists lest she give the Earth Elder the sharp side of her tongue, and took a deep, steadying breath. "I don't see how we can help. Caelum's instincts have led us all around the Galaxy. We've seen all sorts of interesting and strange things, and we've been back on Sorcen many times. If there was a portal here, he would've sensed it by now."

"Not necessarily - Caelum may have never been close enough to receive a signal." Fenris turned so that he could look Arcana fully in the face. "It is a simple matter to check. We do not even have to leave this room."

"Really? How so?" Brook leant forward eagerly.

"I believe that Caelum has been passively sensing the residual energy of the Timeless Kingdom when he passes near a portal or temple. With focus and direction, he should be able to seek out the energy instead of waiting for it." Fenris stroked Caelum's shoulder and smiled, ever so slightly. "As long as Caelum is willing, of course."

"No," said Arcana, at exactly the same moment that Caelum said "Yes," his body quivering with sudden excitement.

"It will not endanger him," Fenris promised, barely glancing at Arcana. "It is a simple mental exercise, nothing more."

Caelum looked hurt. "Arcana?"

"This is *not* our battle," she hissed, her words low enough that the Elders strained forward. It was clear from the frustration on all five of their faces that they were unable to catch her words. Fenris, she knew, would hear her clearly - but he said nothing, only looked to Caelum.

"It is," said Caelum finally. "You just don't want to admit it. Besides, this isn't your decision - it's mine, and I'm going to do it." He angled his body towards Fenris, dismissing Arcana with the rounded weight of his shoulder. "Show me how."

Arcana took a step back, her stomach knotting in horror. In all their time together, she and Caelum had never disagreed; not like this. What was wrong with him? Fenris set the greatsword on the floor and extended his long fingers, placing them carefully around the base of Caelum's jaw. He smoothed his palms along the deerken's chin and angled Caelum's furry face upwards, looking for all the world as if he intended to kiss him. Caelum stood peaceably, his star spangled eyes whirling slowly, his body relaxed and content. Arcana's chest tightened as she watched, so much so that she laid a hand over her thumping heart. Perhaps there was nothing wrong with Caelum - perhaps *she* was the problem. But why?

"You need to find the dreambank first. That will allow you to connect to the energy of the portal." Fenris' body curved towards Caelum, his face lowering until they were both at the same level - and for the first time Arcana realised the Guardian was the taller of the two, though not by much.

Caelum's ears flickered back and forth nervously. "I can only get into the dreambank when I'm asleep."

"When you sleep, your mind relaxes and becomes more receptive. You can create that state whilst awake, if you work at it." Fenris' long fingers massaged the edge of Caelum's jaw and the deerken's eyes drifted shut. "Push away your conscious thoughts. Ignore the world around you and turn your focus inwards. Concentrate on the peace inside of yourself and allow it to drift towards you. Quietly, slowly, invite it in. If you have accessed the dreambank before, then you can do so again."

Silence, save for the gentle swish of a breeze outside, and the sound of Arcana's teeth as she ground them together. The Council of Elders watched with varying degrees of interest and skepticism while Fenris continued to gently smooth down the fur along the sides of Caelum's face, his fingers nimble as a musician.

"Got it!" Caelum exclaimed, his body trembling with excitement.

"Excellent. The key thing now is not to look, but to feel. Feel the energy of the portal. Imagine it, wonder about it." Fenris still spoke softly but his shoulders had set with anticipation. "The dreambank cannot be commanded but you can find things if you know the way to ask."

Caelum's ears flickered. "I don't know the feeling."

"Yes you do," Fenris replied. "You opened the sealed door to the temple where we met. You've felt the energy that flows in those places and followed their siren call for decades. You know."

Arcana opened her mouth but Fenris gave her such an intense look that she closed it again. Their gazes locked and she felt the pull of his glamour, wrapping her in velvet warmth and inviting her to fall into the depths of his soul. She forced the energy aside and raised her chin in silent challenge. His eyebrow arched, a tiny smile tugging at the corner of his lips - then Caelum squealed in excitement and Fenris looked away, leaving Arcana's heart thumping as though she'd been running.

"I found it! I have it!" Caelum's eyes flew open, the stars in their depths swirling an intricate dance of exultation.

"Well done." Fenris leant in to scrub enthusiastically at the ruff of charcoal and silver fur between the deerken's shoulder blades. "What did you see?"

"Not much. Grass. Rocks. Nothing concrete but I've got a lock on the energy. It was like you said, the feeling. I didn't think I knew what you meant but I did. Arcana, I can't believe it! The dreambank, during the day!" Caelum exclaimed, dancing across to her on silent hooves.

"You're incredible." Squashing the squirming feeling in her gut, Arcana opened her arms. Caelum swayed into her embrace, rubbing his cheek against her shoulder. She returned his caress, relieved that he seemed to have forgotten their disagreement in light of his success. Arcana looked over the curve of his neck to see Fenris watching her, that same secret smile shadowing his mouth. She narrowed her eyes at him but the smile only spread, lighting his whole face and giving her another glimpse of his fangs.

"So that's it, then? It didn't look like much," Blaze grunted.

"It was more difficult than it appeared, your grace." Fenris turned and accorded Blaze a short bow. "Caelum is lucky he already had some association with the dreambank and knew what to expect."

"You intend to investigate this portal, then?" Brook asked.

"As long as your graces do not object, of course. There is no telling the condition of the portal without seeing it." Fenris bent to scoop up the greatsword, leaning heavily against it. "If I were to visit this portal, I would need Caelum's guidance and it may take us far afield of your city. Does your offer of his company extend to such an excursion, given the information I have shared?"

"Allow us a moment to discuss it." Vino held up a hand and the

Council turned towards each other, their voices lowered beyond Arcana's ability to decipher. Freed from the weight of their gazes, Fenris turned to Arcana, his expression distinctly smug. He'd planned the entire exchange from the beginning, she realised. Even her protests - which, to her, had felt entirely spontaneous - had only served to weight the mysterious import of Fenris' mission to the Council.

"You." Arcana put her hands on her hips and tapped one foot, her voice low enough the Council wouldn't hear it. "Caelum can't go anywhere without me, you know."

"Best you stop being deliberately obtuse then, because I'm going with Fenris." Caelum spoke breezily, but his eyes glinted with barely disguised temper.

"Caelum -"

"We discussed this yesterday. I want to go. I *need* to go." Caelum shoved angrily with his nose, forcing her to clutch at his fur for balance. Arcana opened her mouth to reply, but at that moment the Council of Elders turned back to face them, hands collectively folded in their laps.

"We've reached a decision. You may visit the portal on Sorcen with Arcana and Caelum as escort, as long as we receive a full report upon your return." Vino leant forward, bracing his forearms on the table. "It is those terms or none at all, Overlord. What say you?"

Fenris executed another flourishing bow, this one far fancier than the first. "I am honoured by your confidence in me, your graces. I thank you for your generosity and look forward to speaking upon our return from the portal."

"As do we," Brook smiled. Arcana ground her teeth, hands clenched to fists. Could she punch Fenris in front of the Council? Probably not, judging by the way they were looking at him with shining faces and forward leaning shoulders.

"Well then, if all our business is concluded, I think it's time we take our leave, your graces," Arcana said, drawing herself up to her full height. "I have fulfilled my end of the bargain and reported as required."

Vino held up a hand. "I would ask one more thing before you go."

"Your grace?" Arcana raised an eyebrow.

"I'm sure Flare told you about the visitors to our star system?" Vino's voice was polite and though it had the cadence of a question, Arcana sensed it was more of a statement and smiled coldly.

"He did," she affirmed.

Gravella snorted. "Breaching security as he sees fit - as usual."

"Arcana is far from a breach; she has as high a security clearance as you and I," Vino returned amiably. "In fact, I would be curious to hear your opinion on these matters, my dear."

"Flare said there are regular incursions into the system. Unknown ships following the same path each time and raiding traders, though they are yet to pay the planet any attention. Is that still the case?" Arcana asked.

Vino nodded. "It is."

"In that case, I would increase Sorcen's defences and order an investigation into the matter, your grace." Arcana spread her hands. "Even on the outer rim of the system, pirates are not to be trifled with."

"Blast them out of the sky and they'll pose no further threat," Blaze growled, punching a fist into his open palm.

"An unnecessary display of force will only draw their attention and we're ill-equipped for an invasion. Reconnaissance gives us a better understanding of their intentions," Brook responded.

Gravella crossed her arms over her chest. "They haven't even glanced in our direction so far. Let them be."

"And wait around for a nasty surprise?" Lesce pinched the bridge of her nose. "Sticking our heads in the sand isn't the answer."

"Says the healer who complains she's lacking recruits," Gravella retorted.

"As you can see, we are divided," Vino broke in, raising a hand to forestall Lesce's response.

"You appear to have the deciding vote, your grace. What do you think?" Arcana asked, her eyes on the Nature Elder.

"I am reluctant to commit to an attack without understanding motive, but I am equally reluctant to put our people at risk unnecessarily. I have meditated long on the matter and reached no satisfactory conclusion. Your brother believes that refusing to arm ourselves with knowledge puts us at a greater risk than that which we would incur by being... How did you put it, Gravella? Nosy," Vino chuckled, but his gaze was sharp.

"So he said the other night." Arcana nodded, setting her hands on her hips. "What's the problem with a little reconnaissance?"

"Many of the attacks have been on intergalactic trading vessels, not just our own ships. If we were to begin investigating, the Galactic Alliance would need to be informed and even invited to work alongside us." Vino frowned at the tabletop, tracing the whorls in the wood with a restless finger. "We've fought hard to maintain Sorcen's independence from the Alliance and I fear asking for their support would require us to acquiesce to a request of theirs in return. They've been attempting to establish an Alliance Outpost here on Sorcen but we've avoided it thus far by being more useful to the Alliance than they are to us. In this instance, it would at last be the other way around."

Arcana narrowed her eyes. "Let me get this straight - you're hesitant to investigate a potential threat to the entire planet because of *politics*?"

"Indeed," the Elder returned, without a shred of guilt. "The entire universe is built on politics, Arcana. There would be much more at stake than first impressions implicate."

"And if the pirates do decide to turn on us, what then? You have no idea of the size or strength of their operation - what if it's an entire fleet?" She stared out at the Council in disbelief; only Lesce met her eyes, with a small nod of encouragement. "I urge you to contact the Galactic Alliance as soon as possible. If nothing else, they may have information they can offer. Even if the price is high, the lives of our people are worth far more."

"Thank you, Arcana. I will meditate on the advice you have given us and come to a conclusion as soon as I am able." Vino pressed his palms together and inclined his head.

"I pray for the sake of the people that you do, your grace." Arcana managed a stiff bow, looking up from under her lashes. "Will that be all?"

"Yes, quite." Vino turned a firm, almost fatherly expression on Fenris. "It has been a pleasure to meet you, Overlord. We look forward to a report upon your return."

"The pleasure was mine, your grace." Fenris bowed low to the Council, his formal flourish receiving murmurs of approval from more than one member. Arcana turned on her heel before they saw her face, stalking over to the portal and shoving her hands into the recesses of the stone carving. The panel flushed with energy and dissolved, revealing the portal behind it. Arcana ushered Caelum and Fenris through and then followed, breathing a sigh of relief as she rematerialised in the Water Tower.

"Thank the stars that's over," Caelum grunted. "I always feel like they're sizing me up for a roast dinner."

"They're a pack of fools. I can't believe Vino's risking lives because he's worried about Sorcen's reputation," Arcana growled. She shook her head to clear it, caught Fenris watching her. "As for you... I don't know if you're terrifying, arrogant, clever, or all of the above. How did you do that?"

"I have a lot of experience handling governments. I do what I need to." The corners of his eyes crinkled in sudden amusement. "You disapprove of my actions?"

"Damn right I disapprove. That was..." Arcana waved a frustrated hand, searching for the words to best describe her feelings.

The Guardian's amusement spread, pulling those full lips into a broad smile. "Neatly done?" He suggested.

Arcana stepped in to poke him in the chest. "Did you glamour them?"

Fenris blinked in surprise, humour fading. "Of course not. I do not make a habit of caging others against their will - and even if I had, you would have noticed. Anyone caught in my glamour becomes stupefied." Fenris crossed his arms over his chest, jaw twitching with barely disguised temper. "What I did in there is merely the result of years of practice."

"You better be telling me the truth," Arcana growled, narrowing her eyes.

"Allow me to demonstrate something." Fenris took a large step back-wards and then locked his gaze to Arcana's. "You may be immune, but you can feel the energy. Does it seek you now?"

She frowned. "No."

"Because I am too far away." Face set in harsh lines, Fenris swept closer, stopping just within arm's reach. "And now?"

A slight tug; the softest, barely there whisper of a feather. Arcana's nose crinkled. "A little."

Before she'd drawn the next breath Fenris was in front of her, his chest pressing against her own and both hands locked around Arcana's biceps. He yanked at her body until she was forced to tip her head back, to stare into the burning depths of his eyes. "And how about now?" He growled. Tension hummed through his body until they both shook, Arcana unable to think beyond the crushing scent of evergreen and cinnamon that wrapped around her soul. Heat swamped her body, a thousand soft feathers murmuring across her flesh. Fenris' accent was midnight velvet, his voice having dropped an octave until it vibrated in her bones. "*This* is how close I need to be to successfully steal someone's will. I can assure you I do not make a habit of it."

Arcana's breath came in gasps, her fingers itching with the need to stroke him, to tug him closer. Fenris' grip tightened on her arms, the pres-sure almost painful, and a long shudder rolled up his body, as though he were fighting the urge to pull her closer - or shove her violently away. Arcana flinched, the thought a bucket of cold water over her psyche. "I believe you. Let me go."

Fenris released her immediately, retreating beyond arm's reach before Arcana had the chance to blink. She turned and swept down the dais steps, making her way to the door and slipping gratefully outside into the afternoon sunlight. What was the matter with her? The two sorcerers stationed by the door snapped to attention and Arcana acknowledged

SAMANTHA STORMFURY

them with a nod, striding out onto the grass. She heard Caelum murmur
to the guards and then Fenris appeared by her side, maintaining a
respectful distance. Arcana clenched her teeth. He'd felt so good pressed
up against her, his voice in her head and his scent in her nose - and that
never happened to her. Ever. If not for his astonishment the first time and
now his anger this second time, Arcana might have thought Fenris had
intended the reaction, but instinct told her that he was just as thrown by it
as she was.

"Arcana! Hey!" Flare's shout echoed across the lawns, and Arcana
looked up to see him jogging towards her.

"Flare." Arcana grinned in relief and raced to meet her brother. They
crashed together in a tangle of arms and legs, Flare spinning her around in
a tight, dizzying embrace. Arcana clutched at the front of his robes as he
set her back on her feet. "Where are you off to in such a hurry?"

"Nowhere, really. I was just finishing off a few errands and spotted
you. Been to visit the Council?" Flare's grin was lopsided.

"How can you tell?" Fenris asked.

"Arcana has that sort of look about her that I get when I visit the Council. The sort of frustration that comes from being gifted permission to wipe
your own asshole. Or worse, having to ask permission yourself." Flare
winked conspiratorially. Fenris burst out laughing, leaning heavily on the
greatsword for support. The sound was light and pure and totally at odds
with the serious nature he'd displayed thus far.

"Flare spends a lot of time answering to the Council," Arcana said,
smiling in spite of her determination otherwise.

"Answering! *Advising* is the correct term." Flare puffed his chest out
and clicked his heels together, buffing his nails mockingly on his robes.
"So, it seems like you escaped with your life?"

"Barely," Arcana grunted.

"It seemed a fairly normal sort of meeting to me," Fenris said, wiping
tears of laughter from his cheeks.

"Spoken like a man who regularly attends formal, faffy meetings,"
Arcana muttered, clenching her fists lest she thump him. "You played
them like a violin-harp. They never knew what hit them."

"True enough," Fenris grinned, his expression unrepentant. It made her
want to hit him all the more.

"Sounds like you put on a good show, sis." Flare reached out to tousle
Arcana's hair with brotherly affection. "I'm pretty much done for today.
What's say we kick it back to Ma and Pa's place and I'll make you a
mulled cider?"

"Mulled cider? I just survived the Council and all you can offer me is a *mulled cider*?" Arcana demanded, screwing up her face.

Flare blinked and laughed. "Okay fine! If you're happy to drop past my city residence I've got some firewhiskey I can bring along instead."

"You've got firewhiskey?" Fenris' face perked up at once.

"Right this way, noble warrior." Flare swept an arm towards Sorca City's skyline. "Let's get this party started."

"Your city residence, huh?" Arcana narrowed her eyes. "Am I going to get hit by flying panties again?"

Flare grinned. "I hope so."

"Mature." She rolled her eyes and linked her arm through his. "Whatever. Better than the standard weird looks, I guess."

"I like to think so." Flare laughed and together they set out across the lawns, heading for the outskirts of town.

CHAPTER
SEVEN

ARCANA WHIPPED THE HEAVY TARPAULIN OFF THE GRAV SLED, COUGHING through the cloud of dust that swirled around her. Caelum sneezed, his nose wrinkling in disgust as the fine particles settled on his fur.

"That sled doesn't look like it's been used in years," he muttered.

"Lesce was serious when she said Ma and Pa like to travel by foot," Arcana agreed, tilting her head to one side. The sled itself was intact, but the windscreen was covered in grime and splashes of mud camouflaged large sections of the hull.

"It looks as if it went mud wrestling," Caelum laughed.

"I'd say Flare borrowed it for a joyride with one of his lady friends and didn't hose it off afterwards," Arcana guessed, tapping one finger on her chin.

Caelum took a half step back, his lip curling. "Please tell me the inside is going to be clean."

"Hah! I hope so - and if not, may I remind you that we're only doing this because you wanted to?" Arcana smiled through gritted teeth.

The deerken shook his head. "I really don't see what your problem is. First you grump at me by the shrine, next you're a pain at the Council meeting, then you glower at the boys over the rim of your firewhiskey, and now I'm copping snide remarks about Flare's flagrant love life. Honestly, what is going on?"

"I don't know." Arcana crossed her arms over her chest and glared at the filthy sled.

"Liar." Caelum snorted a great cloud of dust into the air and promptly sneezed again. "We don't have long before drunk and drunker notice we're gone, you know - so unless you want to have this conversation in front of them, I'd start talking."

Arcana tapped a restless finger on her elbow, caught between the temptation of sharing her thoughts and the terrible direction they would lead her. "Fenris makes me uncomfortable," she said at last.

"He... how? Has he been rude? Inappropriate?" Caelum looked bewildered.

"No. He's been..." Charming, in spite of the circumstances. Clever. Kind. Arcana bunched her fists in the sleeves of her jumper and growled low in her throat. "I don't know. I don't trust him."

Caelum regarded her for a long moment, the silence drawing out until it was razor thin and Arcana felt the heat creeping up her cheeks. She heard the sharp intake of his breath, then; "You *like* him. Don't you?"

"Don't be ridiculous. I've known him two days," Arcana snapped, but the blush was creeping higher, betraying her.

"Two days is more than long enough to ascertain that he's tall, dark, handsome, witty, intelligent, strong, brave-"

"Enough," Arcana begged, holding up a trembling hand. She couldn't look at Caelum, couldn't stand to see her own reflection in the starry expanse of his gaze. "I can't explain it, okay? For all his virtues, I feel like I can't trust him. And that makes me uncomfortable."

"Arcana... is it possible you don't trust him because you don't trust yourself? After what happened with Algae - "

"Don't!"

"Stop interrupting me, dammit!" Caelum stamped his hoof, sending up an even bigger cloud of dust than before. "You're uncomfortable because Fenris' proximity is bringing up baggage you've never addressed. Tell me I'm wrong. Go on."

"I don't think I want to give you the satisfaction." Arcana narrowed her eyes at the sled's dented access hatch.

"Right. Well, for the record, I can't find anything wrong with him, myself." Caelum's voice was dry, and Arcana could sense his eye roll without having to look at him. "Out of the two of you, one is being a bitch, and it's not Fenris."

"Caelum..."

"Look, just give the guy a chance, okay? He's been through hell and somehow, we're connected to all this - and you know it. I know you do. Besides, you know almost nothing about him. He might be married. Or gay." Caelum tilted his head to one side, considering. "Or, you know, anatomically incorrect or something. Maybe he's got tentacles, or a third nipple."

"And maybe he's the Prince of Darkness, with a thousand moaning concubines in every port," Arcana muttered - but her heart wasn't in it, and a smile was tugging her lips out of their determinedly sour countenance. "I'm sorry, Caelum. I am. I can't help it."

"I know. Just try to lighten up, okay?" He crossed the room at last and nuzzled her cheek.

Arcana sighed and leant into him, closing her eyes. "Fine. But only for you."

"I can deal with that. Now, can we use this thing or what?" Caelum poked gingerly at the grounded sled with one hoof.

"Dunno. Have to see if it's got power." Arcana crouched in front of the maintenance panel, wiping away a layer of crumbling grime so that she could palm it open. The sled's mechanical insides were in considerably better condition than the outer shell, gleaming silver in the late afternoon sunlight. Arcana slipped her hands between rods and tubing, feeling her way across greased metal until she was buried up to the elbows. Then she closed her eyes, leant her forehead against the rim of the access hatch and let the world fall away.

The core of the sled, as with all craft produced on Sorcen, was based around an array of crystals that absorbed sunlight and stored it for future use. When the engine was powered, the crystals fed energy not only into the ship's systems but also back into each other, allowing the array to function for a good deal longer than the original charge should have allowed.

Arcana's magic brushed the crystal array and it tinkled in response. There wasn't enough power to turn the unit over but a spark of life remained, buried deep. She inhaled, filling her lungs with dust and the pungent scent of grease, threading her magic through the crystals and merging with the essence of the sled. Magic hummed through the craft and Arcana shaped the tide of energy with her will, refilling exhausted power reserves and prodding sleeping systems. When she was certain the sled was in working order, she gave the crystal array a solid magical shove. The grav sled gave a rattling cough and hummed to life, lifting off the ground to float arm's length above the floor. Arcana withdrew from the access panel with a sigh of relief, wiping her forehead with the back of one wrist.

"Incredible." Fenris' tone was filled with awe. Arcana jumped at the sound of his voice, grabbing convulsively at the side of the sled lest she topple sideways onto the dusty floor.

"Great gods of Sorcen," Arcana managed, one hand over her thumping heart. She turned to find Fenris leaning against an old workbench, his eyes luminous in the gloom. The greatsword was slung across his back, held in place with a length of frayed rope that Flare had gifted him earlier for just such a purpose. "You nearly gave me a heart attack."

"Perhaps you need to become more aware of your surroundings," he suggested, one eyebrow arching.

"Easier said than done when I'm communing with inanimate objects," Arcana answered.

"That seems inconvenient. Who guards your body during a battle?"

"Caelum, of course. Thanks for the warning, by the way," she added, cutting the deerken a glance.

Caelum rolled his eyes. "Oh please, he was just looking."

"Flare said I would find you here," Fenris continued as if Caelum hadn't spoken. His eyes flickered unnaturally bright and Arcana wondered how much firewhiskey was burning through his veins. "I am most impressed by your ability to recharge the sled. How long would it have taken in the sunlight?"

"To be useful to us? A couple of days, I guess." Arcana shrugged. "It was pretty flat."

"Are there many sorcerers who have such an ability?" Fenris asked.

"What, recharging a crystal array? 'Course not." Flare appeared, a slightly wobbly silhouette in the doorway. "Otherwise she wouldn't be so freaking awesome, would she?"

"Don't be ridiculous. There are plenty of talented sorcerers who work with the crystals to create and enchant the arrays," Arcana said.

"But none who can imitate the full power of a sun," Flare replied, shaping a large circle with his arms and winking at Fenris.

"I don't imitate the sun. I take the energy of the sled, amplify it and give it back," Arcana answered. Flare was silent a long moment, his brows drawn together.

"So it wasn't fire magic? More like... Sled magic?" He asked, wiggling his fingers. Caelum sniggered, bending his head to rub it on one foreleg.

"Something like that," Arcana agreed, narrowing her eyes at first Flare, then Fenris. "Have you two finished playing boy's club, then?"

"Indeed. We decided to stop at four glasses of firewhiskey. It is surprisingly potent," Fenris thumped his chest in appreciation.

"Yeah, I'd say four glasses is more than enough, especially if it's Flare's brew," Arcana agreed. Flare coughed behind his hand, then straightened comically when Arcana levelled an accusatory finger at him. "You've had more than four, young man. I can tell."

"Maybe." Flare gave an exaggerated shrug. "I wasn't counting - Fenris was. He likes my vintage, though."

"Flare's work is exceptional. I was unaware that firewhiskey was the creation of fire sorcerers, although now I say it aloud it makes a certain sense." Fenris grinned lopsidedly.

"Indeed. It's one of Sorcen's biggest exports." Arcana nodded towards the sled. "Don't forget we have a trip to plan though."

"Oh yes, to find the portal. Fenris told me all about it while we were clinking glasses. Need an extra set of hands?" Flare turned both his hands palm up, as if to shrug, and fist sized fireballs crackled to life within the cradle of his fingers. "I roast a mean marshmallow."

Arcana raised an eyebrow at her brother. "You want to come with us?"

"What, were you planning a tryst? Someone's gotta keep you focussed on the task at hand." Flare winked, closing his fists and extinguishing the fireballs with a puff of smoke.

"Oh come on, Flare! If you like Fenris so much, *you* take him to bed." Arcana glared at her brother from beneath lowered brows, hoping the shadowed interior of the shed hid her blushing face.

"Me? Sleep with Fenris?" Flare blinked in surprise, then turned to give Fenris a speculative look. "I mean, I'm not denying his sexiness, but it seems unfair to cut your lunch like that, sis."

"Hey, hang on a minute." Fenris stood bolt upright, his face blanched in astonishment. "You can't be serious."

"Deadly serious." Flare leered at Fenris, his orange eyes darkening with wicked invitation. "Men, women, that weird fluffy llama creature from Gordax IV - it's all just part of the fun, really. Seems a shame to choose just one side, don't you think?"

Fenris stared at the fire sorcerer, his mouth flapping like a fish. "I'm... flattered, but I prefer the company of women," he managed.

"Women in general, or one in particular?" Flare tilted his head to one side, eyes slitted. "I mean, are we talking hitched here, or not?"

"Er..." Fenris looked helplessly at Arcana, his teal skin darkening with what she had to admit was a rather attractive blush.

"He's asking if you're married, or otherwise attached," Arcana clarified, shooting Flare what she hoped was a warning look. He was grinning wildly, his orange hair stuck out in all directions, the haze of firewhiskey softening the sharp edges of his face.

Fenris cleared his throat a couple of times, looking for all the world like a caged animal. After a long moment, he visibly gathered himself and said; "No, I am unattached. No significant other." Then he turned his eyes on Arcana. "Is he always like this?"

"Only when he's drunk," she grinned. "Don't worry - Flare's a tease, but he's not a sleaze. He is, however, trying to distract me from the original question, which is why in the name of rotten fruit you'd be interested in coming to find the portal with us?"

Flare looked up at the roof, examining the supporting beams. "You know, I think this shed could really use a skylight."

"Flare! I'm still charged with the grav sled energy and I *will* blast you to the other side of the yard if I have to." Arcana raised a menacing hand and Flare took a half step back.

"Okay, okay already! Look, I don't want to get in the way or anything but Lesce sent me a memo." Flare spread his hands helplessly. "She asked me to tag along."

"The Council really don't trust me, do they? After all this time." Arcana clenched her teeth and growled, tiny sparks of energy fizzing and popping in the air around her head. "So, what are you, their guard dog now? That does it! I'm going back there and-"

"Arcana." Fenris jerked forward, both hands palm out. "Stop."

She did - but only because it seemed a better alternative than storming into the solid wall of his chest. "What?"

"Flare's not here to watch you. He's here to watch me." The Guardian's voice was so smooth it was almost a purr, softened by firewhiskey and the half-light. "Think for a moment. You are this planet's most unique treasure and I am an unknown quantity. If you were the Council, would you let us wander off into the wilds alone?"

"I..." Arcana cleared her throat and frowned. Fenris took another half step forward and placed a gentle hand on her forearm. She stared at the contrast of his soft teal fingers against the stark white of her own skin and swallowed heavily.

Taking her silence as encouragement, Fenris ducked his head to catch her eye. "Flare is the best warrior on Sorcen - you told me so yourself. He is also your brother and will defend you no matter the cost. What better choice for your personal guard?"

She turned to her brother. "Flare?"

The fire sorcerer let out an explosive sigh, running one hand through his orange hair. "He's right, Arcana. The Council are very much aware that Fenris is a seasoned warrior with an unknown set of skills. They believe his story but you are... well, you. Lesce asked me to tag along and watch your back." Flare looked to Fenris, his hands spread in apology. "Sorry, brother."

"I am not offended." Fenris shrugged. "In the Council's position, I would do the same."

"I... This is ridiculous." Arcana rubbed at her forehead to ease the dull ache building there.

"It's a precaution. Besides, I'll bring the firewhiskey," Flare grinned.

"No. If this is really going to happen, there will be no firewhiskey," Arcana snapped, waving a finger at him.

"Okay, okay! I was just kidding. Come on, sis, don't tell me you're still mad?" Flare asked, his brows pinching.

"A little," Arcana grunted. "I love you but I can take care of myself."

"You do not know the extent of my skills. It is a prudent action," Fenris said again.

"A prudent - you don't know the extent of my skills, either," Arcana mimicked his tone and pitch, and earnt herself a start of surprise in response. After a long moment, Fenris withdrew his hand from her arm, bowed and retreated to his former position against the bench.

"Come on, sis. Is it really that big a deal to spend time with your bro?" Flare put on his best pout, fluttering his lashes dramatically. "I missed you."

Arcana ground her teeth, feeling, not for the first time that day, as though her life were bumping swiftly down a steep slope and she had no choice but to hang on and hope. "Fine. Since we've established I cannot wipe my own nose on Sorcen without the Council getting involved, let's move on." She took a deep, steadying breath and gestured behind her. "The grav sled's charged so there's no real reason to hang about. When do we get this show on the road?"

"If we leave under cover of darkness we are less likely to attract curious witnesses," Fenris said.

"Good idea. I only need a few hours to whip back to my place and grab some things. We can leave tonight, if you want - but I won't be sober enough to drive," Flare added.

"I can drive." Arcana looked to Caelum, the stars swirling softly in the depths of his eyes. He nodded slightly. "Okay... let's do this. Flare, go and get your stuff. I'll sort out something to eat and we'll leave as soon as you get back."

"Can I eat too?" Flare adopted his best plaintive expression.

Arcana sighed. "Sure, why not? We'll leave after you've returned and scabbed the leftovers. Better?"

Flare's mouth twitched and he nodded. "I can live with that."

"If you're quick, you can eat with us," Arcana added, giving him a stern look.

"Okay, okay, I'm going!" he laughed, flicked a lazy salute her way and then disappeared out of sight. Arcana laid a hand against the grav sled and powered it down, stepping away as the craft settled gently onto the shed floor.

"I am sorry this has caused you such inconvenience," Fenris murmured, his face half hidden in the shadows of the doorway.

"Do you always apologise when you don't actually mean it?" Arcana asked, dusting one hand on her thigh.

He blinked a moment, then inclined his head in acknowledgement. "It is a habit of serving the Weaver so long. Manners, as it were."

"Right, well, cut it out." Arcana made a slicing motion in the air with one hand. "Empty apologies mean nothing to me. I'd appreciate it if you just speak your mind."

"Many people ask for honesty, then find they do not truly appreciate it." Fenris tilted his head to one side, the green fire in his eyes casting sharp shadows over the planes of his face. "I should hate to offend you by accident."

"I've run the gauntlet of pretty lies before. I'd rather an ugly truth any time." Arcana rapped her knuckles a final time on the now dormant sled, listening to the metallic echo. "Truth is always better. Always."

"I'll keep that in mind. You still seem agitated," Fenris observed, pushing away from the bench as she approached.

"I am." Arcana stepped out of the shed and into the chill afternoon air, shielding her eyes with one hand as she looked towards the sun. It had already begun to lower, extending the first tentative tendrils of bronze across the landscape. She could feel Fenris watching her from the doorway, expecting her to elaborate. "Flare's assignment has reminded me that I don't trust you."

Fenris fell into step beside her, thumbs jammed casually into his belt. "But you like me, which is at odds with your instincts."

"How do you know that?" Arcana paused a moment to look up at him.

He smiled, revealing his pointed incisors again. "I can smell it."

"You can smell it," she repeated.

"You did ask for my honesty," Fenris reminded her, his smile widening. "Have you changed your mind already?"

"No, I just... why have you been sniffing me?"

At that, he laughed, an easy, pleasant sound that swept her arms in a wave of warm goosebumps. "I have not been sniffing you," Fenris promised. "You would have noticed. Certain strong emotions have a scent. Happiness, sadness, anger, lust, fear - and the subtler feelings, too, if you know someone well enough."

"I'm not sure I completely understand," Arcana confessed.

"I do," Caelum said, assuming his normal position over her shoulder.

"Oh, well, in that case." Arcana rolled her eyes and started walking again. "So tell me why you think I like you against my better judgement."

Fenris rolled into motion beside her, considering the question. Arcana watched him out of the corner of her eye, the way his gaze internalised and his shoulders hunched slightly. Somehow, he had vocalised exactly how she *did* feel, and far better than she could have done herself. When Fenris finally spoke, his voice was almost hesitant, as though he genuinely worried about displeasing her with his answer.

"You do not smell afraid, so that is the first and most important thing. I have no wish to instil fear in you, and many people become afraid when they learn the truth of my glamour." He paused, worrying at one lip with a pointed canine. "As for my deduction - Your scent sways between sharp tones I would normally associate with mild hostility or distrust and the sweeter notes of friendship, or affability. I cannot be any clearer than that," Fenris shrugged.

Arcana thought over his words, her boots crunching across grass that had already begun to frost. "I've heard Caelum talk about the stench of fear before, so I guess it makes a certain sense. Although I don't like to think that I smell."

"You smell pleasant through all ranges of emotion," Fenris assured her, his luminous eyes intent on her face.

"Well thanks, I guess." Arcana felt herself flushing and looked away towards the gate. A figure was moving down the drive towards them, the open gate partially hidden behind him. "Who the hell is that?"

"Algae," Caelum and Fenris said in unison.

"Algae?!" Arcana repeated, stunned. "What in the name of rotten meat is *he* doing here?"

"I don't know but I'd hazard a guess he waited for Flare to leave before he made his appearance," Caelum said, his words clipped.

Fenris nodded. "The timing is incredibly coincidental."

"Great. First you and Flare get into the firewhiskey and torment me, now Algae twice in one day. It's great to be home," Arcana growled.

"I assure you I am sober enough to be in my right mind," Fenris protested.

Arcana didn't answer - she stalked towards Algae's silhouette, her frayed temper flaring. Algae stopped, waiting for her to approach with his arms crossed. The afternoon sun caught at his pale blue hair, burnishing it with strands of rose gold and reflecting brilliantly off the metallic accents on his clothing. Arcana stopped several paces short, hands on her hips. "What are you doing here?"

"Good afternoon, my dear. The sullen look becomes you." Algae's eyes swept her body, leaving a slimy feeling wherever they lingered. "Now how about a smile? I know you're secretly glad to see me."

"Why. Are. You. Here?" Arcana repeated.

"I have come on official business from the Water Tower," Algae announced. He performed a deep, flourishing bow and Arcana could not help but reflect how ridiculous the gesture looked on him, whereas Fenris could deliver the same thing with an air of masculine grace. Then Algae straightened and his supercilious expression stalled her thoughts. He extended a ribboned scroll towards her. "For you, my love."

Arcana snatched the scroll from his hand and shook the ribbon off. "I'm not your love."

"You have always been my love," Algae responded, watching her through half lidded eyes.

"Whatever," Arcana muttered, pulling the scroll open. "An invitation to a formal banquet in our honour. What a surprise."

Caelum snorted. "Haven't we ignored enough of those by now?"

"Apparently not. You know how the higher ups like to fuss." Arcana squinted at the finer writing along the bottom. "They want to commemorate my long-term involvement with the Water Tower."

"They just sanctioned a mission. Why host a banquet?" Fenris' murmur was so faint Arcana had to strain to hear him; the thunderous expression on Algae's face said he'd tried and failed to catch the words.

"The officials who dream up these invites aren't privy to Council business - they belong to the faffy, boot licking side of politics," Arcana replied. She let the scroll curl closed of its' own accord and offered it back to Algae. "Unfortunately I have other business to attend to. Pass on my regrets to the Tower."

Algae's eyes rounded and he took a half step backwards, away from the scroll. "You can't decline a banquet held in your own honour!"

"I can and I will. The Water Tower has a yearly banquet to celebrate those who've served for certain lengths of time and whilst I appreciate the wording, this party isn't specifically for me." Arcana flicked her wrist, eliciting a satis-fying crackle from the paper in her hand. "According to this, the banquet takes place tomorrow night - the Water Tower doesn't throw together a formal occasion that quickly, merely an invitation to one that was already organised with a little fancy wording to suit. I'm flattered, but I'm going to be elsewhere."

"But I had planned to escort you." Algae opened his arms, rolling one shoulder dramatically. "Together, we will shine brighter than all the jewels upon Sorcen."

"No." Arcana crossed the two steps between them and slapped the scroll against his chest. "Not going to happen."

Too late she realised her mistake - Algae dragged her body against the length of his, humming appreciatively. "Perhaps I can change your mind?" He offered, dipping his head towards her.

"Let go." Arcana shoved at his chest but Algae tightened his grip, fingertips digging painfully into her skin.

"You used to like it when I nibbled on your ear," he continued as though she'd never spoken, sliding his lips along the edge of her ear lobe. "I want to hear you screaming my name."

Arcana went cold all over. She flattened her hands over Algae's chest and expelled the last of the sled's energy directly into his sternum. There was a great flash of light and the water sorcerer flew backwards, crashing to the dirt ten paces away in a confusion of chiffon and velvet, tiny pieces of burnt parchment fluttering down around him. "I told you never to touch me again and I meant it," Arcana snarled, her heart thumping. "You make me sick."

Algae sat up, clutching at his blackened chest with a wounded expression. "My love, I-"

"Shut up." Arcana dragged her magic through the earth, freeing a clump of rocky debris and hurling it in Algae's direction. He rolled aside, the projectile narrowly missing his shoulder.

"I came in good will!" Algae shouted, scrambling to his feet.

"Then leave while you still have the chance, or I'll blow your balls off like I should have fifty years ago." Arcana clenched her extended hand into a fist and a pillar of stone shot out of the ground by Algae's feet. He danced aside, his eyes wild.

"What is going on here?" Salve's voice boomed from the front door of the house. A few moments later, the sturdy healer materialised out of the sunset, his brows drawn into a frown. "Arcana, why are you demolishing the driveway?"

"I was just seeing Algae off the property."

"Oh?" Salve peered at Algae with all the enthusiasm of someone preparing to clean their shoes. "Algae Enrien, I almost didn't recognise you, so covered in earth and muck. Do you need me to assist you through the gate?"

"No thank you, Healer." Algae dusted at the charred remains of his shirt and cloak. "I'm afraid our beloved Arcana is having a moment of hysteria. I fear she is unwell."

"*Unwell?*" Arcana raised her arm. "I'll show you unwell."

Suddenly Fenris was in front of her, his hands on her shoulders, his face filling her vision. "Leave it. He's not worth it," the Guardian murmured, his voice soft.

"Get out of the way. I'm going to rip his useless arms off and shove them in his puckered ring hole," Arcana snapped.

Fenris' lips twitched, the corners of his eyes creasing with barely contained laughter. "As much as I appreciate that image, I say again: he is not worth your time or energy." He touched her cheek for a fraction of a second, diverting the gesture to tuck a stray lock of hair behind her ear. "Giving in to the whim of temper will only give more power to Algae. Believe me."

"He's caused me a lot of trouble over the years. Surely better to just teach him a lesson," Arcana growled.

Fenris arched a brow, his fingers moving in soothing circles on her shoulder. "If you perform the grisly acts your rage dictates, you will surely end up in prison. How, then, are we supposed to eat dinner and go on our way? I'd have to come and break you out and that would be tedious indeed."

"You're saying I should leave Algae intact because you can't be bothered busting me out of jail?" Arcana bit the inside of her cheek, fighting the sudden urge to laugh.

"Well, he did try appealing to your common sense, but that didn't work." Caelum nudged her shoulder with his nose. "Come on. Fenris is right and you know it."

"All right," Arcana sighed. Fenris squeezed her shoulders a final time and let go, stepping aside to reveal a perplexed Algae posturing among a pile of grit and dust halfway down the drive. She waved a dismissive hand at him. "We're done here. Go home, Algae."

"Absolutely not." Algae puffed up his chest indignantly. "I came here on official business."

"Your Tower business has been concluded," Salve pointed out, but Algae was already shaking his head.

"Not to my satisfaction, it hasn't. Arcana is mine and I will *not* be diverted." Algae glowered at Fenris. "I don't know what manner of creature you are, stranger, but you have no right to interfere with the courtship of my woman."

Arcana's breath caught; Fenris looked amused. "Do women normally shoot you when you court them?"

"Only Arcana." The words tumbled out reluctantly and drew Algae's hands into fists.

"Then I would take a hint, if I were you," Fenris said. Arcana shot him a sharp look - he was still smiling, but there was no mistaking the sinister edge to his tone.

Algae spluttered and choked, his face darkening with rage. "You really want to test me? I hope you're prepared, stranger." He raised a shaking finger and began drawing a rune in the air before him. It shimmered with blue light, spinning slowly in place. "In the time-honoured fashion of our people, I, Algae Enrien, issue due challenge to you, Fenris, visitor from the stars."

Arcana's mouth dropped open. "Salve-"

"An honour challenge has been issued. I stand witness," Salve announced.

"What? You can't be serious," Arcana managed, certain the betrayal she felt was painted over her face.

"You can see the rune as well as I." Salve tilted his head in the direction of the magic. "The spell is already cast. I'm sorry, Arcana - only Fenris can answer now."

"What is he asking of me?" Fenris' eyes were fastened firmly on the shimmering blue rune, his face carefully blank.

"Trial by combat," Salve said, his face apologetic. "If you accept, you will fight until one of you either yields or is unable to retaliate. The rune is a spell which, when activated, will place both of you inside a protective barrier until the duel is finished. It is an ancient and honoured practice in our culture."

"And if I refuse?"

"The rune will be branded into your flesh for all eternity, where it will burn with the fire of a thousand shames," Algae responded, his grin malicious.

Fenris crooked a brow. "I see."

"If you accept the challenge, you're on your own. The barrier prevents outside interference." Arcana shook her head. "I'm sorry, Fenris. I didn't mean for this to happen."

"It is no matter - I will fight him. This will still be quicker than breaking you out of prison." Fenris winked and Arcana realised with a start that he wasn't worried - in fact, if anything, he seemed amused.

She sidled closer and lowered her voice. "Your injuries -"

"Are mostly healed. I will survive." Fenris' voice was dry - the look he flicked down at her anything but. "Don't tell me you are concerned for my welfare?"

Arcana was saved from having to respond by Salve, who cleared his throat loudly and gestured towards the glowing challenge. "If you wish to accept, you must walk through the rune. That will activate the barrier and signal the start of the battle. I will serve witness," Salve added, with a pointed look at Arcana.

"So will Caelum and I," she muttered, crossing her arms over her chest.

"Very well. Guardian?" Salve interlaced his fingers behind his back.

Fenris reached over his shoulder to tug on the greatsword's hilt. The blade sliced through the rope with a soft hiss, the makeshift harness falling in tatters to the ground. Fenris hefted the sword in his hand and strode towards Algae, passing through the floating blue rune without hesitation. The sigil exploded into a shower of tiny blue sparks that flew high in the air, forming a transparent dome about forty paces wide.

"Prepare to pay for your interference, warrior. I will accept no less than your humiliating defeat." Algae unclasped the remains of his cape and it slithered down his arm to flop gracelessly onto the dirt. "Arcana is mine."

"Arcana's will is her own, as is her body," Fenris said softly. "No-one holds the right to claim her."

Algae barked a short, incredulous laugh. "That alone shows how little you truly know about her." He began to move, fingers weaving and legs sliding, an intricate combination as graceful as falling water. Arcana shivered, wrapping her arms around herself as the spell evoked memories of a rolling green hill, a swift rushing river and a much younger Algae, wearing a rakish grin as he showed off what he'd learnt at the Tower that morning. Memory Algae fissured as actual Algae shouted aloud; a short incantation to complete the spell. A gout of water shot from his palm, crossing the distance between the two men in an instant.

"Don't." It was Salve, and Arcana blinked to find his strong arm thrust out across her body. She'd taken three steps toward the arena, her feet following the lump in her throat. "You must wait and watch."

"Yes. Sorry. I'm fine, I promise." She forced herself to back up against

Caelum. Where was Fenris? Algae's spell was powerful - Water sheeted out across the magical barrier in a confusion of bubbles and foam. Had it connected? Arcana bit her lip as the water began to subside, pooling ankle deep inside the dome of energy. Algae's triumphant smile faltered as he realised what Arcana had - the space in front of him was empty.

"You missed," Fenris said. Algae spun with a shout to find the Guardian less than a pace behind him without so much as a hair out of place, the greatsword point down in the water. Arcana grinned in relief.

Algae made to step away but Fenris became a blur of movement, driving the hilt of his sword up into the sorcerer's stomach and then knocking him flat with a blow to the head. Algae landed with a terrific splash, coughing and choking as he pushed to his knees. Mud caked his arms and trousers but his eyes were focussed on Fenris, his lips already moving, followed by swift undulations of his hands and forearms.

"That's Greater Geyser," Arcana muttered, digging her hands into Caelum's fur as the ground began to rumble.

Fenris leant backwards as a geyser erupted out of the earth a hair's breadth in front of him, showering the battlefield in water and debris. Another emerged, then a third, each as strong as the last. Arcana had a brief view of the vicious expression on Algae's face before yet another eruption of water blew up between them. Shadows flickered in the half light, a suggestion of motion drawing her gaze upwards. Arcana gasped as she realised it was Fenris, hopping and jumping across the top of the geysers, visible only for a moment before disappearing again and again.

"Is he teleporting?" Arcana whispered.

"No." Caelum's ears flickered once. "He's just very, *very* fast."

"You can see him moving?"

"Yes," Caelum answered, his eyes trained on the arena. "It's... incredible."

Fenris appeared suddenly in mid-air, his body stretched out like an arrow, the greatsword's weight clutched to his chest. He fell straight downwards, into the flying foam and mist. Arcana caught her breath as the geysers abruptly eased, leaving the arena chest deep in choppy water. All manner of debris floated on the surface, turning the impromptu pool a murky brown and rendering it impossible to see what lurked beneath.

Fenris and Algae surfaced simultaneously, dripping and dirty, five paces apart. Algae wiped blood from his nose with the back of one wrist, smearing scarlet across the lower half of his face. He caught sight of the mess on his hand and snarled a quick command, wrenching both arms upwards as though pulling up a particularly insolent blanket. The water lurched in response and Fenris was dragged under, leaving an unnatural stillness behind. Arcana's heart thumped uncomfortably in her chest, a mixture of fear and anticipation.

Algae began to chant again, swaying in the water - which began to swirl and churn in response. He was barely half way through the spell when Fenris erupted out of the water in front of him, the greatsword clenched firmly in one hand and eyes ablaze behind a curtain of sodden teal hair. The two men stood nose to nose for a single, frozen moment, Algae's fingers hesitating in their intricate dance. Then Fenris' arm shot out, teal fingers closing around Algae's throat and cutting off his incantation. Algae gurgled in surprise, abandoning his sorcerer's grace to flail ineffectually at Fenris with desperate hands. The Guardian dodged the blows without blinking, the muscles across his shoulders cording as he lifted his opponent into the air.

"Yield," Fenris commanded.

"No!" Algae's hands began to move, the trembling start of a spell - but Fenris shook him like a doll, sending a spray of filthy water across the arena and leaving the other man bedraggled and gasping.

"If you pass out, your defeat will be most undignified. Yield," Fenris repeated. Water had slicked his clothing to his body, revealing every inch of his chest and shoulders, the long arms - and the muscles in his forearms as they tightened, pushing his fingers more heavily into the flesh of Algae's neck.

"*No.*" Algae gasped for air, his face beginning to turn an unusual shade of red.

Fenris rolled his eyes, hefted the greatsword in his left hand and placed the naked edge beneath Algae's chin. "Don't make me cut you open, sorcerer. Yield. Be it the blade or the black maw of unconsciousness - You have lost." Fenris pressed the blade closer, drawing a single, shining drop of blood.

Algae glared down at him, legs kicking weakly, face darkening to plum. "I... Yield," he managed. Fenris released him immediately and Algae slid bonelessly into the murky water, disappearing beneath the surface with barely a splash. The magical barrier dissipated, releasing the pool in a tide of brown muck. Arcana dragged herself onto Caelum's back as a muddy wave surged towards them, spreading across the yard until there was nothing more than soaked earth to show the battle had ever taken place.

Caelum chuckled as she slid back down again. "Don't want to get your feet wet?"

"Not particularly. These are my favourite boots," she answered absently. Her eyes were trained on the battlefield, where Fenris was once again leaning on the greatsword, catching his breath whilst Algae lay face down in the mud, coughing and spitting out water.

"Algae Enrien, you have admitted defeat." Salve sloshed over to the other sorcerer and fisted a hand in his sodden cerulean hair, hauling Algae upright. "I declare Fenris the victor of this honour battle."

"I...he..." Algae spluttered. Salve released the back of his tunic and shoved, none too gently, in the direction of the gate.

"It is done. You are not seriously injured - except, perhaps, for your pride. Go home," Salve commanded.

Algae turned towards the road, his legs unsteady and his gaze filled with hatred as he looked back at Fenris. "This is not finished."

Fenris merely arched a soggy eyebrow. Algae growled inarticulately and stormed away, muttering under his breath as he disappeared out the gate and around the corner. Arcana heaved a sigh of relief, staring at the empty space until she was certain he had really gone.

"Do you need medical attention?" Without waiting for an answer, Salve placed one hand against Fenris' chest, his eyes narrowing in concentration.

"No, thank you," Fenris replied, but his gaze was over Salve's head, focussed on Arcana. A smattering of twigs and leaves adorned his hair, which in turn was plastered to his face. Water rolled down his cheeks and beaded in his eyelashes, dripping intermittently onto Salve's outstretched arm. Arcana returned his gaze steadily, and after a long moment Fenris' face split into a mischievous grin which she couldn't help but return.

"Huh. Nothing but fatigue - I'm impressed." Salve stepped back, drawing a communicator from his pocket and flipping it open. "Feel free to avail yourself of the showers; Arcana can show you where to leave your wet things. If you'll excuse me, I will see to this mess and ensure that Algae returns safely home." He turned away, tapping the communicator's screen as he strode toward the front gate.

Arcana tiptoed over the soggy part of the yard to where Fenris waited, Caelum hard on her heels. "I guess this means congratulations are in order. Well done."

"Thank you. That was a peculiar battle." Fenris rolled his shoulder, falling into step beside her as they moved towards the house. "I have never fought in a magic dome before."

"You were amazing. I think that takes the record for the quickest honour battle I've ever seen," Caelum chuckled.

"I had no wish to entertain Algae's ego for longer than necessary." Fenris shrugged. "In truth I could have ended it sooner but I had no wish to maim or kill him."

"Didn't want to waste time waiting for me to break you out of prison?" Arcana joked, leading him around the side of the house.

"Indeed. I didn't realise I'd be getting wet, either." Fenris' chest rumbled with laughter and he raised one arm to squeeze a dripping sleeve. "At least it's done with. Perhaps now he will leave you alone."

"Oh, no. You don't know Algae. His ego is second to none." Arcana smiled bitterly. "That battle will convince him that whatever strange story he's concocted in his head was true. You may have beaten him, but he will be angrier now than he was before - and more determined to prove his point. Whatever that is." She ascended a set of well-worn steps, opening a weathered door in the side of the house. *Whatever that is?* Her inner voice mocked. *You know what Algae wants.* Arcana shivered and stepped inside the house, flipping the lights on to reveal a tiled laundry room.

"Do you think Algae will challenge me again?" Fenris stepped up behind her, trailing water and leaf litter. He had to duck to fit beneath the eaves and once inside, his lithe frame seemed to fill the tiny room, eclipsing even the greatsword as he leant it against one wall.

"No - According to Sorcen lore, he can't. You beat him fairly, so he has to wait a minimum of three months. Even then, he can't challenge you for the same reason." Arcana yanked open one of the overhead cupboards and began dragging out a collection of large, fluffy towels.

"So he has three months to make up something new?" Fenris grinned as he drew his shirt off over his head, accepting her proffered towel with the other hand. Arcana's breath caught at the sight of all that soft, teal skin drawn taut over sliding muscle. She'd seen his chest when he'd been injured of course - but now he was standing in front of her, dripping mud and water, watching her from curious green eyes. Expecting her to say something after that gasp, she realised.

"Um. That looks much better." Arcana waved a wobbly hand at the long, finger-width scar which cut from left pectoral to right hip, narrowly missing his navel and disappearing beyond the waistband of his trousers. The scar tissue was smooth and supple and if she had not been responsible for placing it there herself, Arcana would have guessed it to be a few years old. She cleared her throat, acutely aware of the pulse thumping below her jaw. "Sorry you got wet on my account. Algae doesn't like taking no for an answer."

"He is that sort of character. If not me, he would have taken out his inability to control you on someone else." Fenris stepped closer, heat radiating off him as though he were a banked furnace. "Given you've already said you don't trust me, I am once again touched by your concern."

"I..." Arcana looked up to find him looming over her, burning green gaze intense. She swallowed, her cheeks flushing. "There's a basket there for your wet things. Through that door is the wash room you used yesterday. I'll find some clothes for you."

"Thank you," Fenris said quietly, his lips curling at the corners. Arcana took a half step back and found herself against the washing machine, the cool metal biting into her spine. Fenris followed as if they were dancing, leaning around her to drop his sodden tunic into the basket she'd indicated. He went suddenly and completely still, and Arcana flushed anew as she recalled not only his excellent hearing, but his heightened sense of smell. At this angle the curve of his shoulder was so close as to almost brush her arm, affording - inviting - a sweeping view of the planes of his shoulders, his back, the dimple at the end of his spine. If she so much as inhaled too deeply she'd be pressed against him, against the furious heat of his flesh. Freezing water dripped from the ends of his hair, plopping onto her collarbone and making Arcana jump in fright. Just like that the spell was broken and Fenris straightened.

"I'll go find you something to wear." Arcana slipped sideways and raced from the room, her breath slicing at her lungs. Caelum waited outside, grazing on some tufted grass at the base of a tree.

"Smooth," he said, looking up as she scurried down the steps.

"Shut up," Arcana hissed. Caelum snorted and returned to his grazing, one ear flickering towards the open door. Arcana looked back to find Fenris watching her, still leaning on the basket. Wet hair hung down across his eyes, his slight smile at odds with his coiled muscles and predatory air.

"Go and wash!" Arcana commanded, slamming the outer door shut. She turned and fled towards the front entrance of the house, followed by the sound of his laughter.

CHAPTER
EIGHT

Arcana drummed her fingers on the smooth exterior of the grav sled, squinting uselessly into the darkness outside of the shed. She exhaled in a frustrated gust, watching the cloud formed by her breath billow up towards the ceiling where a few intrepid moths danced around the single hanging lamp.

"Sorry I'm late!" Flare jogged into the shed with his hair tousled and a bag slung hastily over one shoulder.

"I was starting to think you weren't coming," Arcana said, pushing away from the side of the sled.

"I know, I know. I got distracted." Flare grinned. "A couple of times."

"A couple of times?" Caelum echoed.

"Well if I'm going to get distracted, I figured I'd better do a good job of it." Flare's grin widened and he winked.

"Sometimes I'm sure you're adopted." Arcana shook her head, amusement warring with irritation. She reached out to slap the exterior controls for the grav sled, the door sliding open with a soft hiss. "Just get in already."

"Why the serious face? Don't tell me you're still mad at me, five hours later? And why is Fenris wearing my old clothes?" Flare added as he clambered into the sled. Arcana climbed in behind him, giving her brother a firm shove when he would have stopped. Fenris was curled up on one of the couches at the back of the sled, his eyes closed and the greatsword on the floor in front of him. He was dressed in a sturdy pair of trousers

119

and a long-sleeved tunic which were both a few fingers too short, leaving his ankles and forearms exposed. Even with a belt, the tunic hung off his lithe frame like a sack. Flare eyed him critically. "I thought he was wearing Pa's old shirt before? Not that I mind sharing, of course, but look at him - he'd have been better off keeping his own pants on, at the very least."

"We had a visit from Algae," Arcana said, dropping into the pilot's chair. "I saved you some dinner, by the way. Container's in the warmer."

Flare slid into the passenger seat beside her, his brows drawn. "Algae?"

"Yeah. Fenris' clothes got wet and Pa had nothing else spare. You're the next tallest person in the family so..." She trailed off, gesturing to the warrior resting in the back.

"Whoa, just wait a second. Did they *fight*?" Flare demanded, sliding open the lid on the warmer and dragging out a sealed container.

Arcana nodded. "Honour duel."

The heady aroma of winter stew filled the cabin but Flare stared at her, suddenly oblivious to the food in his hand. "I'm sorry, you did not just say honour duel."

"She did," Caelum snorted, his enormous antler rack appearing between them. "Excuse me a moment. Just having some logistical issues getting my giant arse into the sled."

"You used to ride in the sled all the time." Arcana leant backwards to watch him awkwardly reversing his body into the empty space normally reserved for cargo.

"Apparently I've grown," Caelum grumbled. Arcana bit her lip, stifling a laugh as his antlers clattered against the roof and his tail whisked over Fenris' cheek. The Guardian's eyes flew open and he sat bolt upright, shimmying aside to allow Caelum more room.

"Good morning," Arcana greeted. "Welcome to the circus. Would you mind closing the door so we can get going?"

"Of course." Fenris leant over to palm the sled door shut. "Do you need assistance, Caelum?"

"Does it look like I need assistance to you?" Caelum snapped, wriggling his hips until they slid, at long last, down into the space beside the seats.

"Not at all," Fenris returned, his lips twitching.

Arcana bit the inside of her cheek to keep from laughing. "Next time I'll open the cargo door for you."

"Shut up," Caelum grumbled, leaning his head on a vacant chair. "Let's just get this over with."

"You got it." Arcana turned back to the sled's controls, her hands fluttering over a variety of switches and flashing lights.

"Where are we headed?" Flare asked.

"Wherever Caelum points us," Arcana answered, swiping her hand across the sled's main screen to dismiss the automated programming. A hatch opened in the middle of the dash and the steering yoke rose into view. She fitted her hands into the controls, kicked the engine over and guided the sled out into the darkness.

"So back to the part where there was an honour duel," Flare said, turning to Fenris. "Explain."

"Algae appears to have taken exception to me. He and Arcana were arguing and I stepped in. Then we fought." Fenris shrugged, setting his overly large shirt rippling.

Flare waved his fork impatiently. "And?"

"I won. Although I got a little damp in the process." Fenris made a face, tugging at his borrowed clothing.

"You won?" Flare grinned. "Excellent! Bet captain slimeface loved that."

"Of course I won," Fenris returned, his face stiff.

"Hey man, no offense intended - I've never seen you move. Shame I missed the action," Flare grunted, spooning stew into his mouth.

"It was amazing. I've never seen such a quick, clean victory. Watch the replay as soon as you get the chance," Caelum urged, craning his head to see out of the front windscreen.

Fenris blinked. "Replay?"

"The rune Algae drew in the air officiated the battle as an honour duel. Part of that spell means that once you accept the challenge, the battle is recorded magically into a... Well, for all intents and purposes, a spell book. Every honour duel ever fought is kept inside, and any sorcerer can request to watch a duel at any time," Arcana answered, bringing the sled up above the tree line. "Caelum?"

"East," the deerken replied. Arcana nodded, turning the snub-nosed craft in the direction he'd indicated.

"Magically recorded duels," Fenris repeated, half to himself.

"Comes in handy if someone's accused of cheating, or for educational purposes. But mostly it's just entertainment," Flare chuckled.

Fenris shifted in his chair, his brow furrowed. "So the whole planet will see Algae's defeat?"

"There's an entire holo channel dedicated to it," Flare affirmed. "Why the face? Don't fancy the idea of being famous? It's great for the ladies."

"I have no need for a multitude of women." Fenris frowned, shaking his head. "It is the secrecy of my mission which concerns me."

"Honour duels are a large part of Sorcen lore. It's important to keep a record of them but if it makes you feel better, the footage stays planetside," Arcana reassured him. "A business type wanted to make an intergalactic holocast once - turn the honour duels into a sport - but the Council forbade it."

"Thank you." Fenris' brow smoothed and he relaxed back into his chair. "I do not regret the battle, but I feel better knowing the evidence of it will be contained."

Arcana turned her eyes forward again, tapping the sled's display to bring up a nightmap of the terrain. Flare and Fenris fell to chatting about the finer points of the duel but their voices quickly faded into the background of Arcana's own thoughts. Seeing Algae again - how long had it been? Ten years? And he hadn't changed, hadn't acknowledged that half a century and a great, gaping divide stood between them. She remembered his painful grip on her body and shuddered; two showers and it hadn't been enough to bring her peace. Eternity would never be enough. Arcana sighed, reaching into the neckline of her dress and gripping the leather thong which hung there. The tooth from Caelum's mother was a familiar weight which bought both comfort and a gentle ache.

"How many are left?" Caelum murmured, his head appearing on her left side. She glanced over at him, chuckling to see his antler rack jammed between the seats and the outer hull of the craft.

"Two - and you know that. You don't look comfortable," she added.

"I'm not. We didn't really think this through," he admitted, his eyes swirling with annoyance. "I suppose it was a bit of a desperate topic choice. I was trying to distract you."

"From?" Arcana asked, but Caelum only stared her down. She sighed again. "You know me too well."

"That and your self-flagellation face could only be confused with constipation, and I highly doubt you are taking a dump in the pilot's chair," said Caelum cheerfully.

Arcana choked out a laugh and elbowed him firmly in the side. "Caelum!"

"What? It's true. Besides, it made you laugh." His face twisted into the deerken equivalent of a grin. "Look, Arcana, you can't change the past. What's done is behind us - behind you, more to the point. But you *can* focus on the future. You can choose to leave it all behind."

"Not when it comes back to bite me every time I visit." Arcana flicked a measured glance towards Fenris and hoped Caelum understood. Whilst the Guardian was still laughing with Flare, she had no doubt his excellent hearing allowed him to hear every word they said.

"You know, it occurs to me that we've spent my entire life trying to sort my issues out - and never once have we stopped to think about you." Caelum's eyes sparked with a contrary light which said he was well aware Fenris may be listening and didn't care in the least. "We should."

Arcana blinked up at him in surprise. "We should?"

"Of course. I've dragged you unwittingly down a very bumpy road and you've never once complained. You went from being part of a community to being a singular, spotlighted entity. I imagine it would be lonely inside your heart, inside your head. It wasn't until the Council meeting that I started to think about it, and realised that we've been searching the stars for my answers, without pausing to address your reality." Caelum wriggled his head awkwardly, scraping his antlers along the bulkhead until he could press his nose to the side of her face. "I'm sorry."

Arcana removed one hand from the steering yoke and brought it up to stroke his chin, brushing her own cheek in the process. Her hand came away wet; she rubbed at her tears in astonishment. What in the name of Sorcen was wrong with her? Caelum turned his face in and licked her cheek, his broad tongue clearing the tears in a single stroke. She leant gratefully against him and after a long moment of silence, she picked up his mother's tooth, holding it where they could both see the soft ridges of bone and the long roots where it had once been embedded in her jawline. "Wearing this reminds me not only of what I was before but how lucky I am now, to have you in my life," she said firmly. "I wish there was a way to do the jump spell without destroying the teeth - I'll be sad when they're gone."

"If Fenris can teach me how to jump on my own, we won't need to burn them," Caelum said.

Arcana clenched her fist around the tooth in her palm. "Yes. I'm sure you can do it, with Fenris to help you - what you achieved in the Council room alone shows his knowledge is worth our time. Maybe you'll get an opportunity to practise while we search for the portal." She smiled and hoped it looked more genuine than it felt.

"You want me to try jumping in and out of the sled?" Caelum laughed, his fur tickling her cheek.

"Of course not, but I envisage we'll be away at least a day or so." Arcana prodded him under the chin. "There might be time to try it down on the ground."

"True. We're quite a way away yet - which means you're going to have to make peace with yourself, at least temporarily." Caelum huffed at her cheek gently.

Arcana shook her head, staring out the windscreen at the fathomless black sky. "You never let up, do you?" She murmured. "I don't like feeling out of control, Caelum - and you have to admit we're being driven by the situation rather than our own conscious will. We have absolutely no idea what dangers lie around the corner." Arcana flicked him a glance out of the corner of her eye. "I also worry you'll be disappointed if we don't get the answers you're searching for."

"Considering I don't know the questions to ask, I'd say that's pretty unlikely. It's wise to be cautious but if we don't take a little risk we might not find anything more - and without risk, there's no true reward. For either of us." Caelum wriggled his head backwards until his antlers came free of the bulkhead with a loud clatter.

"Whoa there big guy, you okay?" Flare laughed, reaching out a steadying hand.

"Fine, apart from this was the stupidest idea ever," Caelum grumbled, squeezing past the seats. "In fact, getting my head stuck in the side of the ship is so much fun I might take a nap." The deerken settled back down in the cargo area with an inelegant thump and buried his head under his forelegs.

"That's not such a bad idea." Flare yawned and stretched. "If nobody minds, I might get some sleep too. It's been a long day and my firewhiskey's worn off."

"Go for it." Arcana waved him away. "I'm only flying in a straight line."

"Awesome." Flare patted her on the shoulder and made his way towards the back of the sled. "Wake me if anything interesting happens," he added, then curled up on one of the unused bench seats, dragged his robes around him like a blanket and closed his eyes.

Fenris gestured to the seat Flare had vacated. "May I?"

"Sure. Not that you can see much." Arcana nodded at the darkened landscape outside. They were far enough off the ground that the sled's spotlights were more hindrance than help, so she'd elected to turn them off and navigate via the on-board nightmap. It left only the violet dark beyond the windscreen, broken here and there by the shimmer of moonlight on water or the occasional wink of a star in the clouded sky.

"I can see," Fenris said, his luminous eyes focussed outwards.

"You can see in the dark? Of course you can." Arcana shook her head, huffing a laugh. "I'm not sure, at this point, why I'm even surprised."

"Both of my parents are naturally nocturnal, so the cloak of night is a comforting one for me." Fenris leant back in his chair and crossed his feet at the ankles, Flare's ill-fitting pants rucking up to mid-calf. He'd kept his own boots, a sturdy leather pair with heavy buckles that had seen better days - and by the look, were still slightly damp.

"So... nocturnal by nature," Arcana said, more to fill the silence than out of real curiosity. "What about the exceptional hearing, the heightened sense of smell, the super speed - and whatever other secret talents you've got stashed up your sleeve?"

Fenris laughed; a sharp, surprised bark that he smothered quickly with one hand. "I was born this way," he chuckled, shoulders shaking with mirth.

Arcana raised an eyebrow. "So the Weaver's got a race of super-dudes just awaiting her discretion?"

"Oh no, not at all." Fenris shook his head for emphasis. "Becoming a Guardian doesn't award extra powers - a candidate must be talented to begin with. The Weaver is very particular about who she chooses."

"So how did you get picked?" Arcana asked, glancing down at the nightmap. They had left the forest and were gliding smoothly over a vast inland lake, with no shore in the immediate vicinity. She flipped a switch to keep the sled on course, then removed her hands from the yoke and turned to face Fenris. "Aside from the aforementioned super powers, of course."

Fenris snorted. "I am an unusual case," he said at last, glancing down at his hands and then back up again.

"You're saying that to *me*?"

Fenris grinned, and Arcana suspected he may have laughed again, but for the guilty glance he shot towards Flare. "Good point. Well, the short version is simple enough - my mother is a Warden. She met and fell in love with my father and eventually I was the result," he gestured along his body with a fine boned hand.

"Ta daaa," Arcana supplied.

"Something like that. I was born and raised among my father's people. My mother lived with us, but her duties as a Warden often took her away for weeks at a time. As a young child I never asked where she was going but as I grew older I struggled to fit in amongst my peers, and her absences were painful." Fenris squinted into the middle distance, lost in the pain of an old memory.

"Halfbreed." Arcana crinkled her nose. "I'm a full-blooded sorcerer, but ever since I bonded Caelum - I get it."

"So I have seen." Fenris inclined his head in acknowledgement. "I inherited my father's physical abilities to a point but I lack the muscular stature that his culture prized. Despite my finer build, I was able to match my peers in strength - and in fact, I am faster than they - but it didn't matter. I was different and notably so. Even my skin is the wrong colour," he raised one arm, his mouth a sour twist.

"They picked on you for the colour of your skin?" Arcana frowned. On Sorcen, sorcerers came in a veritable rainbow of skin tones. Even after bonding with Caelum had blanched Arcana's skin salt white, she'd never received so much as a second glance - not for that, anyway. She opened her mouth to say she thought Fenris' skin tone was beautiful, and then thought better of it. "So what happened?" She asked instead.

"I learnt to fight early, and well." Fenris grinned viciously, a baring of teeth which showed the full length of his fangs. "One afternoon in my mid-teens, while I lay abed, I heard my mother saying she was needed urgently and had to leave at once. I decided I couldn't face the nightfall alone, so I sneaked out. I followed her all the way to the portal and then through it into the Timeless Kingdom."

"How much trouble were you in?" Arcana asked, her eyes wide. In her own youth, she'd been painfully shy and would never have dreamt of getting out of bed, let alone following her mother through a portal.

"In theory, an awful lot - but my mother had been called away to assist with a birth, which as I have already mentioned is a dangerous and rare thing for the deerken." Fenris hesitated, then winked. "I was strategically placed and leapt out of the bushes to catch the fawn when my mother would have dropped it. So I was in trouble, but I also had a bit of room to wriggle. It's hard to be angry at your son when the mother deerken is fawning all over him."

"You sound like you were a handful," Arcana laughed.

Fenris considered, his gaze far off. "I suppose I was. My mother took me to the Weaver when it was done - instead of scolding me, she told me I was born to be a Warden and offered me the position immediately. My mother never said a word and I never asked but I wonder now, looking back, if she knew all along that would be my fate."

"She wasn't angry?" Arcana asked.

"My mother grew up in the Unseelie Court - so no, she wasn't angry," Fenris chuckled. "She has a strong sense of honour, and is staunchly loyal to the Weaver for saving her life, but she is an unseelie fey, and they have an odd sense of humour. My father was often frustrated by my headstrong nature, but mother never questioned or scolded."

"So you became a Warden, moved to the Kingdom and lived happily ever after?" Arcana made a little heart shape by pressing the tips of her thumbs together and curling her knuckles over. She couldn't pinpoint the moment she'd become invested in the story but Fenris' past intrigued her; it was refreshing to analyse the history of someone else for a change.

"It's not as simple as it sounds. The Timeless Kingdom is exactly that - a place out of time. Nobody is inducted into true timelessness before they are fully grown and I was still technically a child, though I resented the idea at the time. The Weaver decreed that I would wait until I was matured and then return." Fenris frowned, his shoulders hunching. "I went back to my old life but nothing was ever the same. My mother commenced my training immediately and I spent most of my time with her. I stood apart even more than before."

"You never really fitted in to begin with." Arcana reached out to touch his shoulder in comfort, his skin pleasantly warm beneath the thin knit of his tunic. Fenris met her gaze and smiled.

"No, I didn't. When I was finally old enough to return to the Timeless Kingdom, my father went, too." Fenris' lip quirked in one corner and he shook his head. "He had been a Guardian all along in his own right and never told me."

"And you?"

"As much as I was a Warden first, I had no wish to lose my physical edge. I sparred and trained with the Guardians by choice and eventually the Weaver allowed me to ascend into their ranks as well. When the Over-lord position became vacant, I was an obvious choice." Fenris shrugged, as though it made all the sense in the world to grow from a misfit child into one of the highest positions his adopted kingdom had to offer. The supe-rior attitude which had grated Arcana's nerves suddenly made sense; Fenris didn't simply believe he was better than others, he knew it with every fibre of his being - because he'd worked hard to achieve it. And he was looking at her, she realised; a long, slow look with his lips curved at the edges. A look that made her wrack her brain for whatever it was he'd said that she had missed.

Fighting her body's urge to blush, Arcana blinked rapidly and attempted a smile. "So being timeless... Does that mean you're immortal?" It was a stupid question, really, just the first thing that tumbled out of her mouth - but Fenris uncrossed his ankles and leant forward, reducing the distance between them to mere inches.

"No, I am not immortal. I can be killed, as can any other living creature - as you well know." his fingers curled around the tunic at his chest, an unconscious movement that Arcana forced herself not to watch. "I am just... Timeless. Ageless, if you will."

Arcana frowned, unnerved by the strange intensity in his voice. "Let me get this straight - if nobody kills you, what happens then?"

"I would live forever." Fenris hesitated and leant a little closer, his eyes seeking hers. "Just like you."

"I'm not timeless," Arcana scoffed, fidgeting uncomfortably in her chair.

"Arcana -" Fenris flicked a glance at Caelum, chewing on his lower lip. When he spoke again, his voice was infinitely gentle, a velvety purr so soft Arcana had to strain to hear it. "You know you are. I can feel it, even if you won't admit it. Caelum is a deerken and all children of the Weaver are born timeless. Your bond with him is symbiotic - one does not exist without the other. He is timeless and so are you."

"It's not true," Arcana whispered. She blinked back sudden tears and clamped her teeth together, staring blindly out of the blackened canopy of the sled. "It can't be."

Fenris seemed to be holding his breath, eyes searching her face. One hand twitched as though to reach for her, before curling around the opposite wrist and gripping tightly. "You said you preferred a hard truth to a pretty lie - and this is the truth. I would not say such a thing lightly, not when I can see it is causing you upset."

"You think I want to live on endlessly?" Arcana hissed, her hands curling into fists. "It might be all right for you, with your family also living on, but my relatives aren't timeless. Caelum and I will go on forever, whilst they eventually return to the soil. What joy is there in such a curse?"

Fenris flinched as though he'd been slapped. "I see."

"Do you?" Arcana demanded. She turned away, forcing the air into her lungs. *'You know you are.'* His voice echoed in the back of her head, clattering down the aisles of her brain and shouting from the balconies. The worst part of it was that he was right - again. "You say you understand how I feel. Do you *really*?"

"I do. Timelessness was a boon for me, but..." He ran both hands through his curly hair, causing it to stick up at odd angles. "After I watched many mortal friends pass and die, I began to ensure such friendships didn't bloom as often or become as deep. I should have thought before I pursued the topic so bluntly. I am sorry." His voice trembled and she looked across to see his face drawn.

128

"I think that's the first genuine apology I've gotten from you," Arcana mused. Fenris just stared at her, face pale in the artificial light of the sled's interior. The sight of such a human emotion on his face calmed her as nothing else would have, and Arcana found her mind ticking slowly over what little she knew of his life. When she spoke again, her voice was soft and steady. "Were your parents in the kingdom when it was attacked?"

"No, they were abroad - but that does not guarantee their safety." Fenris rubbed a hand over his face and sighed. "My parents are skilled warriors but the warg are a formidable adversary, particularly when they swarm in large numbers. I will know nothing until I can get back to the Timeless Kingdom."

"There is always hope," Arcana told him.

Fenris flicked a glance up at her from underneath his brows, his face stripped of all pretence. Vulnerability was written in the lines of his shoulders, the curve of his back. "I am just one man," he said, and in those few words she felt the essence of his doubt, the understanding that he was pitted wholly against interminable odds, completely and utterly alone.

"Even one man can accomplish great things." Arcana thought of him in the Council chamber, his face peaceful as he helped Caelum access the dreambank. She thought of him aboard the cruiser, blood spattering his torn body as he impaled the warg standing over him. She thought of him pale and motionless on the floor in Lesce's lounge, completely spent, clinging to life by a thread. And lastly, she saw Caelum, staring at Fenris as though he were an oasis in a desert. Her heart squeezed. "We'll help you," she said.

Fenris froze, his fingers curling around the edge of the chair. "You'll help me?" He repeated.

"Yeah." Arcana leant back and tried to look calmer than she felt. "I'll make you an offer - we'll help you get back to the Timeless Kingdom if you take us to meet the Weaver."

"You want to fight the warg and free a kingdom you've never even *seen?*" Fenris demanded, his voice hitching uncertainly at the last.

He hadn't moved, but his eyes burned with an intensity that caused Arcana to shuffle nervously on her chair. Part of her, the cautious part of her, shrieked in terror, but she squashed it resolutely down - the words were out and there was no going back now. "Yes," she said simply.

"But... why?" Fenris was mystified, truly and utterly flabbergasted. In any other situation, Arcana would have laughed to see someone normally so composed taken by surprise, but she only swallowed heavily, drawing a deep breath to reply.

"Because Caelum is right - somehow, and I don't know how or why, but somehow, we're a part of this. It can't be coincidence that we found you, bleeding and dying, on the floor of that temple. It can't be. As much as I hate to admit it, we were sent there to get you." Arcana paused, her hands trembling as she voiced the thoughts which had been haunting her since they arrived on Sorcen. "After fifty years, scouring the galaxy, looking for - well, for the Timeless Kingdom, I suppose - and finding nothing, I refuse to believe we stumbled across a man with answers by pure accident."

Fenris tilted his head to one side, expression thoughtful behind his veil of hair. "I theorised that the Weaver led you to my side earlier. Why wait until now to change your mind?"

Because you're terrifying for a whole host of other personal reasons but running away just because you're unfairly attractive would be both cowardly and selfish, Arcana thought, but she forged on. "I don't like being thrust into situations against my will, but here we are. And Caelum *is* a deerken. He wants to meet other deerken and do deerken things. You can help him - and we can help you."

"True." Fenris' voice dropped an octave, took on a thrumming, velvety quality that had Arcana fighting a shiver. "But I thought you didn't trust me?"

"I don't trust you," Arcana answered, waving an admonitory finger under his nose. "I don't trust your pretty accent, your magic eyes or your fey blood. I don't trust the way Caelum stares at you with shiny eyes and I certainly don't trust the idea that an entity I've never even met marched me halfway across the galaxy to rescue your skinny ass. I am not, however, stupid - and I need to look past the inner voice that says you're still keeping secrets and that I'd be better off staying the hell away from you." Reining in her traitorous tongue, Arcana levelled the Guardian with her best no-nonsense glare. "I'll help you if you help Caelum - but I'll also be keeping you right where I can see you."

Rather than look intimidated or offended by her implicit threat, Fenris' face broke into a slow, predatory smile. "I believe I am left with little option but to accept your offer," he murmured, his voice, if anything, more full of midnight promises than it had been before. "It will be my utmost pleasure to stay exactly where you can see me."

Shit. Arcana flushed and swung towards the sled's nightmap but there was nothing to provide her with a distraction - they were still soaring swiftly above the inland lake. Fenris reached across the moments between them and enfolded her trembling hands in his, thumbs warm as they stroked across the back of her knuckles. It should have been a soothing gesture but it made Arcana jump, drawing her back to look at him when she would much rather have leapt out of the moving sled. "What are you doing?" She managed, tossing a look over her shoulder for moral support. Both Flare and Caelum were still, their bodies relaxed in the rhythms of sleep. Traitors.

"My touch is intimidating you." Fenris frowned but his face was perplexed rather than irritated, his voice losing none of that velvet quality which wanted to creep inside her very bones. He peered at her as if she were a particularly intriguing puzzle. "Why?"

"I am *not* intimidated," Arcana hissed, tugging at her hands - it was like trying to break free of plascrete.

Fenris raised an eyebrow and repeated the stroking of his thumb, eliciting yet another involuntary start. "I can smell it," he said quietly. "I have no wish to harm you."

"I know that." And she did. For all his unusual effect on her, Arcana knew beyond doubt Fenris was a man of honour, that his heart was kind - though that very certainty was yet another thing that frightened her. She swallowed heavily, caught in the glow of his eyes, the warmth of his hands upon her own. "It's just that..."

"Yes?" Fenris prompted, ducking his head to look into her face.

Arcana shook her head, her eyes dropping to their interlinked fingers, his flesh like a brand across hers. "I can't."

"I see." Fenris released her hands and Arcana clutched them to her chest, clenching her teeth together lest anything else foolish tumble from her lips. He was still watching her, his face calculating.

"I'm not like Flare," Arcana said at last. It was a paltry explanation, she knew, and if he was half as perceptive as he seemed, Fenris would immediately grasp there were plenty of words she didn't - couldn't - say.

Those burning eyes settled firmly on her face. "Neither am I."

"Oh. Well, excellent," she squeaked.

"That was intended as reassurance, but I am still making you uncomfortable. You are an enigma," Fenris tilted his head to one side, frowning - but she noticed his hands, cradled in his lap, were trembling. "I must confess, I am at a loss."

"She likes tea." Flare's voice floated up from the back of the sled, full of barely contained laughter.

"Then I shall make you a cup of tea." Fenris nodded, rolled out of his chair and moved to the sled's small refreshment station.

Arcana turned to find her brother watching her, grinning

mischievously. "I thought you were *asleep*," she accused, hoping her voice conveyed the gravity of his betrayal.

"Black, medium strength, no sugar. Extra hot," Flare instructed. He winked unrepentantly at Arcana and rolled away, his shoulders shaking in silent amusement.

Arcana turned back to the front of the sled, rubbing her forehead. Were they all mad? She barely knew Fenris, certainly didn't trust him, and here he was... What, exactly? Being nice to her? Making her a cup of tea? And as for Flare - Arcana shook her head. That man was definitely the wrong kind of crazy. Although, considering she'd just agreed to accompany Fenris on a rescue mission she still didn't entirely understand, it was more likely *she* was the crazy one. Arcana stared out into the inky night until her eyes watered, unclenching her fists when she realised her nails were digging painful grooves in her palms. She was the one who had offered her assistance and Fenris had done nothing overtly threatening or unto-ward. In fact, if they *were* going to traipse through space together, it wouldn't hurt to be friendly - and making tea was, in and of itself, no crime. Arcana rubbed at her palms until the marks from her nails faded, listening absently to the clatter of teaspoons and the slosh of boiled water. When Fenris at last returned with a steaming mug, Arcana forced herself to smile as she accepted it.

"How is it?" Fenris asked, watching as she sipped.

Arcana closed her eyes a moment, savouring the distinct balance of flavours. "Perfect, thank you."

"The hot water doesn't burn you?" Fenris cradled his own steaming mug carefully as he relaxed back into his chair.

"No." Arcana waggled her fingers in the air. "Magic."

Fenris nodded. "Of course. You absorb the heat."

"Sure do - not that tea magic is good for much," Arcana snorted, sipping again.

"My mother always said to me that tea was a source of magic unto itself," Fenris replied, the corners of his lips twitching in a smile that invited Arcana to join in.

She allowed her eyes to crinkle in agreement, sipping again. The sled's display beeped abruptly, and Arcana turned to check the instruments. "Huh. That came up fast."

"Is that a collision alarm?" Fenris asked, squinting out the window.

"Yeah. We're across the lake and the sensors detected a range of low hills," Arcana murmured, setting her tea down and flipping a switch to raise the steering yoke. She prodded at the command screen and scratched behind one ear." According to this, we've shaved a good hour off the original estimated time. I must have overcharged the sled."

"Does that happen often?"

"More often than you'd think." Arcana slipped her hands into the yoke and banked gently, guiding the sled to one side of the range. "Thankfully the crystal arrays can take a fair bit of power. Other engines aren't so forgiving - the old combustion styles, for example, are definitely a bad idea."

"Oh?" Fenris sagged back in the chair, curling his legs beneath him and balancing the steaming mug on his chest. "I take it you've had some less than favourable outcomes in the past."

"I blew up a couple of engines, if that's what you're asking," Arcana admitted.

He tried - unsuccessfully - to hide a wicked grin behind his mug. "How did the owners of those engines react?"

"About as well as you'd imagine." Arcana grinned in return as she leant forward, sipped her tea, and set it back in the cradle. "Powering an engine or recharging a battery with magic is a fickle and dangerous task, but it's saved our skins more than once."

"I can imagine. Your ability to absorb and reflect the energy around you is more versatile than I at first assumed." Fenris took a long draught from his mug and pointed through the windscreen, where the first hints of pink were visible across the horizon. "Look - the sun is rising."

"Morning already? I slept longer than I thought." Caelum's sleepy voice drew Arcana's attention briefly to the back of the sled, where the groggy looking deerken was dragging himself upright. "We're a lot closer now. Keep going east." The sun's first rays crept across the ground, illuminating pools of shadow with brilliant shafts of gold. Frost kissed the grasses and icicles dripped from the trees, a sure sign that winter was fast approaching. Caelum crowded to the front of the sled, his antlers whizzing by Arcana's face as he ducked around the pilot's seat to try and get a better view. "Up ahead, a crook in the hills, where there's a little pool. Still in the shade... Can you see it?"

Arcana squinted. "Behind that overhang?"

"Yes, that's it." Caelum pushed forward until his knees knocked against the front of the sled, his downy tail flicking back and forth in anticipation.

"If you don't stop that and back up, we're going to have an accident," Arcana said, elbowing him firmly in the hindquarters.

"Sorry." Caelum slunk backwards, his antler rack thunking against a bulkhead as Arcana angled the sled towards the ground. "Next time, we're renting something bigger."

"We could always file those antlers down to make them fit." Flare's tease was followed by a squeak of surprise and a thump as Caelum used those very antlers to sweep the fire sorcerer onto the floor and sit on him.

Arcana circled the sled, looking for a place to land. The area Caelum had indicated was on the side of a gentle slope, where a pool of water was fed by a thin waterfall which trickled more than tumbled off the side of the hill above. The sled was too bulky to fit in the cradling arms of the hillside but there was a smooth, clear area of grass a short way down the slope on the banks of a shallow lake. Arcana switched the sled into hover mode and lowered the craft onto the ground, running through the landing checks and powering down the engine.

Fenris palmed the main door open and leant backwards with a chuckle as Caelum scrambled to fit his bulk through the opening, leaving Flare to grumble good-naturedly as he moved to follow. Chill autumn air flooded into the cabin and Arcana shivered, draining her tea and setting the empty mug back on the refreshment station.

"Winter is almost upon us," Fenris remarked, tilting his chin towards the frost-touched grass.

"Yeah. Here - you'll need this." Arcana handed him a hooded cloak. "Winter comes earlier out here."

Fenris swung the cloak over his shoulders with a murmur of gratitude, the fur lining giving his features a more feral appeal. "Snow?"

"Not for another couple of weeks." Arcana pulled her coat on, looped a scarf around her neck and ushered Fenris out into the daylight.

Flare stood with his head tipped back to the sky, stretching languorously. "That sunlight is glorious," he announced. "Looks like it's going to be a clear day."

Fenris eyed Flare's light robes dubiously. "You don't need a coat?"

"Nah." Flare waved his hand dismissively. "I'm a fire sorcerer - we cool down when we're dead. Where now, Caelum?"

"This way." The deerken began to ascend the gentle slope, ears flickering in a gesture to follow.

Arcana palmed the sled door controls and jogged to catch up, welcoming the exercise after sitting for so long. Fenris strode easily alongside, his long legs having no trouble keeping up with the brisk pace. The greatsword was barely visible, poking out from beneath the hem of his cloak in another makeshift rope harness. "Don't need the walking stick anymore?" Arcana asked, eyeing the shimmering edge of the blade.

"Not really. My fatigue is almost entirely gone." He spread both arms in smiling emphasis. "My weapon can return to its' primary function."

"You know, in a universe full of lasers, I'm surprised to see you carrying a sword," Flare remarked, squinting up the hill. The rising sun cast a sharp glare off the frosted grass, rendering everything in front of them a mix of glittering sunbeams and bruised shadows.

Fenris raised one hand to shade his face and smiled. "I prefer something that cannot be jammed, run out of ammunition, require reloading or backfire on me when I least expect it. The greatsword is more versatile than it appears."

"It's bloody heavy," Arcana grunted, recalling how she and Flare had struggled to lift it between them.

"So I am told." Fenris shot her a quick grin. "I trained long and hard to gain mastery over this blade but I have never regretted it."

"Not even when it sliced you from nip to hip?" Flare asked, drawing a line down his torso with one thumb.

Fenris laughed. "No, not even then. In fact, it was my opponent's inexperience with the greatsword that saved my life. If I had been carrying an ordinary sword, I would not be standing here now."

"It's comments like that which make me glad to be a sorcerer." Flare snorted, shaking his head. "Ain't nobody setting me on fire with my own magic."

"Are you not weapon trained?" Fenris sounded surprised.

"Of course I am - training and preference are two different things, though, brother," Flare replied, grinning.

Fenris nodded sagely. "On that, we are agreed. Arcana?"

"Pfft, don't look at me." Arcana held up both hands in benediction. "I'm useless at hand to hand combat, both with and without a weapon. Just ask Flare."

"It's true. She's a glass cannon in every sense of the word, that one," Flare nodded. "Don't downplay your own skills though, sis. You know your magic better than anyone and you fight dirty."

"I'll take that as a compliment," Arcana said dryly.

"You should." Flare's tone was airy, but he flicked Fenris a meaningful glance. "I'd think twice before taking you on."

Arcana stiffened but if Fenris noted the warning he gave no sign, simply continued to hike uphill with carefully measured strides. They crested the hill as a group, looking down upon the small pool Caelum had indicated from the air. Moss covered cliffs cradled the water, providing an almost sheer surface for the thin waterfall which dribbled down one side.

The scene seemed entirely unremarkable but Caelum stared intently into the navy water, his eyes whirling softly.

"What am I not seeing?" Arcana asked, trying to follow his gaze.

One black-tipped ear flickered. "We need to go down."

"Into the water?" Arcana winced. Small and well sheltered, she had no doubt the water would be icy.

Caelum nodded. "Yes. It's under the hill."

"*Under* the hill?" Flare repeated. "Where in the name of Firius are you taking us?"

"I don't know but I'm pretty sure the god of the flame won't be able to help you underwater," Caelum turned to Fenris. "Any ideas?"

"No." Fenris shook his head, bewildered. "My people would never put a portal underwater. The structure would survive, but the gateway..."

"Yeah, water stuffs up the magic. We know," Arcana muttered, frowning at the pool. Her gaze wandered upwards, around the cradling hillside and stopped on the waterfall, watching it drip and trickle into the water below. "Flare - are you seeing this? The cliffs are almost a perfect semicircle and the pool, too."

"Terraformed, perhaps?" Flare's gaze sharpened as he inspected the cul de sac. "If you're right, that's a lot of magic. A *lot.* Several very powerful sorcerers and their lackeys."

"Are you saying this pool is made with magic?" Fenris asked, twisting his head this way and that to get a better look at their surroundings.

"Not just the pool - the cul de sac in the hillside, even the flat grassy area below us." Arcana waved a hand around them. "This entire area has been completely remodelled with magic."

"Why wouldn't the Elders say something?" Fenris frowned.

Arcana shrugged. "They said they had no knowledge of a portal on Sorcen. My best guess is that this was done a long time ago, before our culture was unified and history was recorded. Back then, we lived in clans and had a rather... medieval approach to things." She crouched at the edge of the water and dipped a finger in. "Wow."

"Cold?" Caelum asked.

"Very," Arcana answered, dropping to her knees so she could immerse both hands. The echoes of long forgotten magic whispered around her wrists and she closed her eyes, attuning herself to the essence of the water. "And deep. Deep, deep, deep."

"There's only one issue with your theory, you know." Flare's buttery voice was speculative. "At that point in our history, sorcerers from different schools of magic didn't work together. Think about what needed to be done here - there's multiple types of sorcery involved. It doesn't make any sense."

"Are you sure the portal is down there?" Fenris asked.

"Positive," Caelum answered.

The Guardian's confusion was palpable. "Then why...?"

"One way to find out. Now stand back or get wet," Arcana warned, pushing to her feet. She opened her eyes and raised both arms, bringing with her a cascade of water from the pool. Up and up it rose, a towering pillar of navy that undulated like a great serpent as it stretched down the hill to connect with the lake below. The water level in the pool began to drop, revealing a smooth-sided pit with a narrow staircase cut into the edge.

"Don't sink the grav sled." Flare's face pinched with worry as he watched the waterline surge towards the grassed area where the sled was parked.

"Don't worry - It's almost done now." Arcana clenched her teeth as she muscled the last of the pool up into the air. The tail end of the watery serpent flicked back and forth as it arced over their heads to disappear into the lake below without so much as a ripple. Arcana released the magic with a sigh, rubbing a damp hand over her face. "Okay, we're good. That was quite a workout."

"I will never, ever tire of watching you work," Flare announced. His grin was huge and full of brotherly pride. "Look at that pit! You're incredible."

Arcana turned her head towards the now waterless pool. An impressively deep sheer-sided pit dropped away from her feet, the bottom of which was cloaked in darkness. The narrow staircase she had glimpsed earlier wound around the edge, disappearing ominously into the shadows. "Huh. It looks like a giant well."

"I was thinking the same thing." Fenris toed the edge of the pit and nodded as the stone side held firm. "How many water sorcerers would it normally take to handle such a large body of fluid?"

"You're assuming more than one," Arcana said, raising an eyebrow.

"Judging by Flare's reaction to the feat we just witnessed, I am *definitely* assuming more than one," Fenris replied, turning his luminous green eyes on her.

Arcana shrugged. "I don't know. A couple, I guess."

"Four solid Class Ones, each stationed at a cardinal point around the well, supported by as many Class Twos. Potentially with a few minor assistants - don't look at me like that, sis, it was a lot of water," Flare pointed down at the lake, where the grav sled's landing gear was partially submerged.

"You sound certain of those numbers," Fenris said.

"I am. Look around the perimeter of the well - four evenly spaced raised areas perfectly sized for standing on," Flare said, waving a hand at the hillside. "Considering the entire area was terraformed to disguise this pit, those are no accident. Whoever made this commanded a number of powerful sorcerers." He moved to the staircase, bumping Fenris aside to wipe a finger across the top step. "Fire and smoke, Arcana! The stairs are completely dry - not even a slimy residue. Did you disappear the waterfall, too?"

"No. It's only a trickle, so there didn't seem any point," Arcana said, joining him at the top of the stairs. She pointed up the wall, where a soak of water could be seen dribbling slowly down the mossy rock face. "See?"

Neither of them answered and Arcana turned to find Fenris and Flare exchanging a loaded glance. At last it was Fenris who said, "So you're saying you *could* have dried up the waterfall if you had wanted to? At the same time as emptying the pool into the lake?"

"It's only a trickle," Arcana repeated, feeling suddenly defensive. They were still staring at her, so she frowned to cover a wave of embarrassment and turned back to the pit. "Whatever. Shall we?"

"After you." Flare gestured ahead and she stepped swiftly past him, Caelum on her tail.

The steps were narrow but not uncomfortably so, each one well moulded and sturdy. Arcana trailed one hand along the wall as she descended, trading her lingering water magic for the strength of the earth. Caelum was close enough that his chest bumped her shoulders, his head shading her face from the morning sun. When they descended into the shadows, Flare muttered under his breath and the air around them was illuminated by tiny, floating flames.

Arcana grinned, pausing for a moment to admire the sparkling display. "Neat trick."

"Thanks," Flare grunted. "It's harder than it looks though, so keep walking."

"I'll bet. How long did it take you to get this one right?" Arcana asked, resuming her forward progress.

"A few months and a lot of burnt spellbooks," Flare admitted. "It was Gravella's idea."

Caelum snorted. "The Earth Elder inspired you to create floating fire?"

"Less talking, more walking! I'll explain later," Flare gasped.

Concerned by the tension in his voice, Arcana picked up speed. She could see the floor of the well below, as smooth and flawless as the walls around them. A minute later they reached the bottom and the flames abruptly extinguished, plunging the area into darkness. Arcana cleared her throat. "Flare?"

"Yeah, hang on." He was panting heavily, his voice no more than an exhalation. A single light flared to life, nestled in the palm of Flare's hand - the first spell he'd ever learnt, Arcana knew, and one of the simplest. Flare was drenched in sweat and partially bent over but his face was alight with triumph. "That's a new record!"

"You look exhausted," Fenris pointed out.

"You try lighting a bunch of tiny fires from nothing and then keep them all afloat in mid-air," Flare returned, wiping his brow with the back of one hand. "And I'll be fine - A few minutes and the recharge will start."

"Look." Arcana followed the curve of the well to a dark recess in the wall.

Flare trailed along behind, his light revealing a stone door with a rune carved into the surface. "Wow. It looks like a derivative of ancient Sorcen."

Arcana shook her head. "Not one I can read."

"No," said Flare slowly, "The ancient Sorcen we know was after the formation of the clans into a single people and the written word was formalised. Before that, each clan had their own variations on the runic dialect."

"Can you read it?" Fenris asked.

"Maybe." Flare squeezed into the recess, bending his head to examine the markings. "The shapes are a little strange and I've never seen runes overlaid like this before." He flexed his fingers, then began to draw the three runes carefully on the rock wall with one finger. Flare's fingertip left sweeping lines the colour of ash, and once he was finished he took a half step back and gestured Arcana to join him. "Can you see it?"

"No. I'm not as fluent as you are."

"Bullshit - just think outside the box a little. If this first one was missing those extra strokes and I change the shape a little like this..." Flare wrote a different, but remarkably similar rune underneath the first symbol.

"Repel," Arcana gasped. "Yes, I see it."

"Right." Flare moved his hand to redraw the next. "And here, this part, is outside, or exterior. And then -"

"Death," Arcana whispered. "The last rune is death."

"Keep out on pain of death," Fenris translated, his expression filled with horror. "Caelum? Are you sure this is the right place?"

"The portal is through that door," Caelum confirmed. "I can feel it."

"Someone went to great pains to seal your portal away inside a hill, with a lovely warning on the front, at the bottom of a well full of water," Flare said, looking at Fenris over one shoulder. "Are you sure about this?"

Fenris hesitated, licking his lips. "Not at all. But if the portal is active... Whatever else is in there, I need to check it."

"Well then." Arcana laid her hands flat on the stone and called her magic. "In that case, shall we go inside?"

CHAPTER
NINE

THE STONE DOOR SLID FORWARD WITH A GROAN, SPILLING STALE AIR AND THICK silence through the dark opening beyond. Arcana stepped back with a gagging cough, fanning one hand over her nose. "Whatever's in there has been shut away for an awfully long time," she wheezed. "Give it a minute for some clean air to cycle through."

"Bah, it's not so bad." Flare stepped into the inky black, tossing his flickering flame aloft. It pulsed overhead like a miniature sun, then split into several smaller fires and whistled off into the gloom. A heartbeat later the darkness lifted, revealing an immense cavern.

"I guess that's our cue." Arcana tugged the end of her scarf across her face and ducked through the doorway. Her feet slithered through a thick, loose layer of sand and she stumbled almost immediately, balancing herself with a hand on Caelum's shoulder. He pranced beside her, eyes wide and staring down at the gritty floor, which Arcana realised was littered not just with rubble but skeletal human remains. "What *is* this place?"

"Some sort of shrine, maybe?" Flare pointed at the raised dais in the centre of the room. "There's the portal - or what's left of it. Looks like there was a bit of a tussle."

"More than a bit," Arcana stared up at the crumbling ruin of stone atop the dais and then around her at the mess of bodies and broken masonry. "I count at least fifty dead."

"Whatever happened, it was long ago. The flesh has rotted clean away." Fenris poked at a skull with the toe of his boot. "None of my people are among these dead."

"How can you tell?" Caelum lowered his head towards a pile of bones and sneezed, stirring up a great cloud of sand from which he promptly retreated. "They all look the same."

Fenris hesitated, then tapped the side of his head. "All Guardians and Wardens swear a blood oath to the Weaver upon entering her service. It connects us on a subliminal level, helps us to locate fallen comrades and seek out allies in dangerous situations. If one of my people died here, I would be able to sense it."

"Hmm." Arcana scuffed at the sand beneath her feet, revealing an intricately laid stone mosaic in shades of burgundy and purple. She followed it towards the dais, kicking sand aside as she went. "More runes."

"What do they say?" Caelum asked.

"Dunno. I've never seen that one before - but it's important, judging by the repetition in the design." Flare crouched down, brushing the sand aside to get a better view of the mosaic. "Whatever this place was, it was important to somebody."

"Important enough to die for," Arcana agreed. She pointed at the cavern walls, where the roughened edges of natural stone cut a sharp contrast to the smooth, conjured work of a sorcerer. "Look at the scorch marks on the walls - they're only on the back half, the natural formation. This cavern was created after the battle and given the layout of the land up above, I'm willing to bet that the portal was once outside."

"Meaning that your terraformation theory may indeed be correct." Fenris ascended the stone steps and stood atop the dais, frowning down at the jagged masonry. "Would that the destruction had not been so final."

Caelum hopped up to stand beside the Guardian, nudging a hefty stone block with one cloven hoof. "It's ruined, then?"

"Essentially, yes." Fenris used his hands to map out where the circular structure should have been. "Portals are powered by a trilogy of crystals set inside a stone ring at specific points. The energy of the gateway itself is still here, but without the crystals to attune it or the framework to support them, the portal cannot be activated."

"Our portals are made entirely by magic. I've never seen one that runs on crystals." Flare clambered onto the dais, blowing dust off a scarred brick. "Could we replace the stones with new ones?"

"Broken crystals can be replaced, yes - but I cannot attain them without visiting the Timeless Kingdom and without a portal to do so, that is impossible." Fenris frowned. "As for the methodology, the Weaver places her energy into the stones and specially trained Guardians set and tune them."

"What if the crystals are still around here somewhere?" Caelum asked. "Could we put them back in and get it working?"

Fenris shook his head. "Look at this mess, brother. The portal is a ruin. I know enough to be able to set and tune the stones but this amount of damage is beyond me."

Arcana laid a hand on the jutting edge of the portal, feeling the whispers of an ancient energy tickling the base of her palm. What was it Fenris had said? *'The energy of the gateway itself is still here...'* The image of a tall, circular structure rose in her mind's eye, silvered by moonlight. Alien symbols marched across the surface of the stone and a swirling blue light roiled in the centre. Arcana's senses curled inwards and suddenly she knew, completely and intimately, how the portal was made. "If the crystals are still intact, I can rebuild the rest of the portal."

"Rebuild the portal?" Fenris repeated, his face blank with shock.

"The stones remember." Arcana lifted her hand from the portal and turned it back and forth as though she might see inside, where the soft, whispering memories still bubbled. "I saw... I guess it was a blueprint, stored inside the energy of the gateway. If we find the crystals, I can use earth magic to reconstruct whatever else was once here."

Fenris stared at the stones as though waiting for them to grow teeth. "How often do you experience such visions?"

"Never." Arcana shrugged, then blushed beneath his astonished regard. "Usually Caelum's the one seeing things."

"Hmmmm." Fenris took her hand in his, turning it over as though he, too, could look inside. "Perhaps those instructions were left specifically for you to find, in the same way you were deliberately led to the temple on that frozen planetoid. The Weaver's situation must be dire indeed if she is forced into such subtle ways of communication." Fenris released her hand but his expression was no less intense as he bent to look into her face. "We are bound together in multiple ways, it seems. Are you certain you can replicate what you saw?"

Arcana nodded. "Completely certain. If we can find the stones, I can do the rest."

"I dunno, sis. Creepily invasive memories aside, finding the stones is a pretty big 'if'." Flare clicked his tongue between his teeth, the noise echoing back from the vaulted ceiling. "Surely the crystals would have been destroyed, or taken elsewhere. The chances of finding them here are next to none."

"Only one way to know for sure." Arcana jumped down onto the floor behind the dais and crossed to the closest corpse - a pair of skeletons who lay partially intertwined.

"So... what's the plan?" Flare asked, crossing his arms over his chest. "Are you going to inspect every single body?"

"If that's what it takes." Arcana bent to brush her fingers over the pale curve of a rib. The bone was silken to the touch, without so much as the barest film of dust or grime. "There's no flesh, no clothing - so looking for a bunch of round crystals shouldn't be difficult." She met Flare's twisted expression with a firm one of her own. "Is this the point where I remind you that you volunteered for this trip?"

"Fine!" Flare threw his arms up in the air and jumped down into the sand, moving out at a different angle to Arcana. He was none too gentle with the first body he encountered, kicking the bones aside with a loud clatter. "Huh. They're sturdier than I expected - not brittle at all."

"Show a little respect. They were people once," Arcana scolded, pushing to her feet and moving to the next corpse. This one was alone, face down, arms reaching. She scuffed the sand around the body, sending up a cloud of fine grit which set her coughing and revealed only more sand beneath. Turning away, she spied a trio of skeletons at the back of the cavern. One was propped in a sitting position against the wall, the other two collapsed in front. Guards, perhaps? Guards of what? Arcana edged up to the bodies, looking down at the two in front. No signs of trying to run, and both facing away from the skeleton propped against the wall, protecting their charge even in death.

"Anything?" Flare's voice echoed in the cavern and Arcana jumped. He stood beside Caelum at the foot of the dais, hands on hips. "I've done my quarter. Not so many people - and none of them with anything other than regrets."

"I'm still looking. It was quite a fight," she answered.

"No arguments here." Flare grimaced and ran one hand through his hair. "I guess I'll help Fenris on the other side. Yell if anything turns up."

"Sure." Arcana turned to examine the vacant grin of the third and final skeleton, skull positioned awkwardly atop the cradling curve of his ribcage. Vertebrae littered the sand, mingling with arms and fingers and... something that glittered in the light when she tilted her head for a better look. Arcana stepped over the fallen guards and crouched down, splaying her fingers in the sand for balance. Half-hidden beneath an ivory leg lay a shard of pale blue crystal, one edge smooth and the rest a jagged mess of angles and hollows. Gently nudging the ancient femur aside, Arcana wrapped her fingers around the crystal. A shock of energy frissoned up her arm, tingling and burning across the back of her neck. Arcana gasped and dropped the shard, falling to her knees in the sand and shaking her hand to be rid of the sensation. Fool, she scolded herself. Fenris had warned her the stones were charged with energy - she should have known better.

Setting her jaw, Arcana wrapped the end of her scarf over one hand and reached in for the crystal, breathing a sigh of relief when the fabric prevented a second shock. The stone's surface was faintly clouded, soft tendrils of white amongst a clear, pale blue. One side was smooth and rounded, the other rough but not sharp and the entire piece fit comfortably in the palm of her hand. Arcana tumbled the stone into her pocket and carefully repositioned the skeleton's leg, feeling a strange sense of dishonour for thieving something it had clearly gone to great pains to protect. She sifted carefully through the sand but found nothing else, leaning back with a sweaty brow and a frustrated sigh. A section of the stone was better than nothing, but Arcana didn't need Fenris to tell her that a shattered crystal would not be able to power the portal. She dug both hands listlessly into the sand, allowing the soft breeze to sweep her hair back from her face and -

A breeze? *Inside?*

Arcana leapt to her feet and gagged on the scent of rotting meat and charred flesh, carried on the wings of the ever-strengthening air current. She burrowed her face into her scarf and turned against the wind only to realise the skeleton beside her was now covered in a thin film of dried meat. Bones which had been scattered across the floor began to wriggle and twitch, inching their way back to those who had once owned them.

Flare appeared around the edge of the dais, holding his nose between finger and thumb. "Can anyone else smell -" he cut off abruptly as a half formed skeleton began to raise up on its' singular arm. "Holy shit, these things are coming to life!"

Fenris dropped from the top of the ruined portal, slicing the skeleton in half with a single, fluid swing of the greatsword. "I think we've worn out our welcome," he announced, kicking the bones aside.

"No shit," Flare agreed. "Time to head for the - Arcana, watch out!"

A heavy weight cannoned into Arcana from behind, knocking the breath from her lungs and slamming her onto the ground. A half-formed corpse lay across her knees, yellow eyes glaring from pitted sockets. Withered lips peeled back from cracked teeth and the body - a man, once - hissed and moaned as he dragged at her clothes with grisly fingers.

Arcana kicked at the creature but his grip was too strong, wiry hands dragging him closer to her face an inch at a time. She scrabbled for purchase in the loose sand, showering her attacker in clouds of fine grit. It sifted over and *through* the holes in his ribcage, dropping back onto her clothes in ichor coated clots. Inspiration struck and Arcana called her magic, gathering those tiny grains of sand and twisting - until the ghastly body shredded into a cloud of sticky black mist.

Arcana scrambled upright and lunged towards the door, blinded by what had quickly become a howling sandstorm. She staggered into a malformed silhouette, glimpsing lank clumps of hair and a withered, vaguely female face in the midst of hissing a spell. Arcana flung up one arm and the floor heaved underfoot, extruding a thin stone barrier which clipped the woman under the chin and sent her reeling backwards. Arcana flattened herself against the stone, feeling a tug on one arm as a hail of primitive wooden arrows shot by. Nature magic? She pulled an errant sliver from the now-shredded sleeve of her winter coat and threw it on the floor, grimacing at the blood trickling down her arm. Great, resurrected sorcerers who could actually cast spells. Arcana peered around the edge of her impromptu barrier and narrowly dodged the grisly hand which swiped for her face. She shrank backwards, using her magic to topple the giant stone onto the revenant with a sickening crunch.

Now where was the door? Arcana struggled to keep her feet beneath her, disoriented by the flying sand and howling, choking wind. She'd barely pushed upright when another desiccated body cannoned into her side, words of power hissing in his malformed mouth. A sharp pain lanced through Arcana's shoulder as the man slammed them both into the cavern wall, spindly fingers closing around the column of her throat. Arcana summoned her magic, calling the nearby sand particles to scour flesh from bone but unlike a living opponent, the undead creature simply ignored her efforts, fingers squeezing mercilessly as his wretched lips worked to finish his own spell.

Then Caelum was there, blinking into existence with a popping noise that echoed in the space behind Arcana's ears. He buried his antler rack in the man's chest and swept him aside with a great heave of his head. Arcana wrapped her good hand in the deerken's fur and swung astride, clinging with her legs. "Go," she shouted.

"Where? I can't see a thing," Caelum retorted, prancing sideways as a sand-blurred projectile smashed into the wall behind them.

Right. Of course. Arcana sent her magic into the storm, calling to each and every flying grain of sand. It pelted her face and grazed her flesh, sweeping and whipping through the cavern with such wild abandon the magic struggled to take hold. Arcana's senses bowed beneath the weight of the elements and she clenched both hands to fists as she worked to extricate the singular grains from the grasp of the air, the water, the nature and fire magic that also flowed through the unnatural storm. Slowly, so slowly, the sands began to coalesce into a singular, serpentine entity which ignored the screeching winds and fizzing spells. The air cleared, revealing a room teeming with shambling, moaning corpses - and far beyond, Flare and Fenris waiting by the door, a streak of charred and dismembered bodies in their wake. Caelum lowered his head and charged, catching shambling revenants in the razor sharp cradle of his antlers and flinging them aside. Arcana sent her sandy creation ahead, scouring flesh from bone and bowling unstable enemies out of Caelum's path.

"Duck!" Flare's shout barely prefaced a fireball as it whizzed past one ear, warming Arcana's face and leaving behind the faintest odour of singed hair. The doorway loomed ahead and Arcana tucked her arms and legs in as Caelum shot out into the bottom of the pit. He shortened stride, propped and swung, skidding to a halt on his haunches so that Arcana could slide off. She sprinted back to where Fenris stood guard by the door, watching over Flare as the fire sorcerer loosed wave after wave of fire spells into the cavern.

"We need to seal the chamber," Fenris said, leaning around Flare to hack at an unseen enemy. Thick black ichor dripped down the length of the greatsword and splattered across one wrist but he didn't so much as blink. "Can you do it?"

"That's why I'm here." Arcana slapped her hands against the stone door and poured magic into it, willing it closed. "Both of you, outside."

Flare backed out into the pit, positioning himself opposite Arcana so that he could continue to lob fireballs through the doorway. "Make it quick!"

"Trying," Arcana grunted, leaning her weight against the stone slab and shoving harder with her magic. The door began to shift, slowly at first and then with gathering speed. Fenris lifted the greatsword as a hail of wooden splinters shot by, deflecting the leading edge with the flat of the blade. Flare summoned a wave of flames that swept into the cavern and the atmosphere filled with the scent of burning flesh. Arcana gagged on the scent, staring up at her brother and wondering how much fuel he had left in his tank - and the stone door slammed into place with an echoing boom.

"Thank the Weaver," Fenris muttered, dropping the greatsword and throwing his weight against the door to hold it in place.

"Save it for after she's sealed them in, brother," Flare replied, adding his own bulk to the stone. "We're not out of the woods if they can just open the gate anytime they like."

"Shut up, both of you." Arcana slid her hands over the seams of the doorway, using her magic to fuse the stone together. Was it only her imagination, or did she hear the wet thump of flesh on the other side? When the door was totally sealed and the sickly yellow runes once again glowed with power, Arcana allowed her hands to relax and rested her forehead against the stone.

"Well... that was gross and terrifying." Flare sagged back against the wall. His face was a mask of soot and sweat, his robes torn open down one side, but he grinned across the bottom of the well at Arcana. "We make a good team."

"Yeah," she gave him a half-hearted smile in response. "I guess so."

"Not to be a party pooper, but can they open that door?" Caelum nudged Arcana's ear with his soft nose. "I mean, if there are earth sorcerers in there..."

"I think we're safe." Arcana sank to her knees, tangled hair tumbling around her face. Now that the adrenaline had begun to fade, her shoulder shrieked and the slashes in her arm felt like firebrands. She looked down to see blood trickling out from the remains of her sleeve and grimaced. Damned nature magic. Caelum nudged her again and she butted her head against his nose in response. "I mean it. Did you see how the wood dissolved? Whatever magic brought those creepy things to life ends about two paces from the stone door. Even if they do open it - which I don't think they can - they'd dissolve in the bottom of the pit."

Caelum sighed in relief, his breath ruffling her hair. "Good."

"Arcana?" Fenris' hand was gentle on her back whilst the other tipped her chin up. "You're bleeding. Are you all right?"

"Of course," she lied. "I just need to rest a minute. What happened in there?"

Fenris frowned, his eyes sweeping down her body in a way that said he did not buy her story for a second, but he allowed himself to be distracted. "It was a time flux, most likely created when the portal was destroyed. Something triggered it whilst we were inside, bringing those people back to life - such as it was."

"Ah. That might have been me." Arcana reached into her pocket and withdrew the shard of blue crystal. "I found this. All hell broke loose shortly after I touched it."

Fenris took the fragment, rolling it over in his fingers. "This is a piece of a portal stone. They focus a lot of time and power into one place. Destroying them would be... Unpleasant for anyone involved." He closed his eyes, the shadow of despair flickering over his features. "It is likely the smashing of these crystals which caused the flux, and the ensuing horror is most likely why the survivors chose to seal the portal away."

"I'm sorry," Arcana murmured.

"No matter. It was a slim chance from the beginning." Fenris sighed, clenching the stone in his fist. "Now, and more importantly, you are bleeding. What has happened? And no more prevarication," he added, raising a stern finger.

"One of those sorcerers got me," Arcana's eyes dipped to her torn sleeve. "It's just a scratch."

A single brow winged skyward. "And yet you are slumped wholly on the ground."

"Magic takes a toll," Flare pushed off the wall and gave himself a shake. "Imagine how you'd feel after a hard run - she'll be fine in a minute. Although, sis, those scratches do look pretty nasty." He cocked his head and grinned. "Getting slow in your old age?"

Arcana flipped him a vulgar gesture. "You're older than me, you cretin!"

"Prove it," Flare leered.

Arcana repeated the gesture and earnt a sharp laugh from her older brother. Fenris exhaled loudly, muttering to himself about the negative qualities of sorcerers as he tucked the crystal away in the recesses of his clothing. He pushed to his feet, secured the greatsword across his shoulders - and scooped Arcana up in his arms. "I said nothing major," she squeaked, eyes rounding. "My legs aren't broken!"

"Enough. I can smell the pain rolling off you in waves." Fenris' lip curled back from his teeth, revealing a healthy amount of fang. His tone was smooth and calm but his heart thundered in his chest and Arcana laid her hand atop it, belatedly realising that both his cloak and borrowed shirt were gone. Fenris' breath caught at her touch, his body turning rigid and his arms tightening convulsively.

"Sorry," Arcana murmured, dragging her gaze to his face and blinking through the velvet caress of his glamour. "My hands are probably freezing."

Fenris' jaw clenched so hard a muscle twitched up beneath his ear and, if anything, his arms clenched tighter around her body. "That is entirely secondary to your wellbeing." Arcana's fingers twitched against his warm skin and the Guardian shivered. "Caelum, will you carry Arcana back to the sled? The environment here is too hostile for me to treat her."

"Of course," Caelum trotted over and Fenris arranged Arcana carefully on his back.

"I'm *fine*," Arcana began, twisting her good hand into Caelum's fur. "It's really not-"

"Behave," Fenris growled, baring his teeth for real this time. "Accepting assistance is not a sign of weakness."

Arcana rolled her eyes skyward and huffed loudly. "Fine."

Flare, who had been watching the entire exchange with a ridiculous grin plastered over his face, turned to frown up at the dark cornflower sky. "Where's the sun? It was barely dawn when we came down here."

"Time fluxes are unpredictable - an hour in that tomb could easily be several out here," Fenris replied. He flicked a glance back at Arcana, looked as though he was about to speak, then shut his mouth firmly and strode to the narrow staircase.

"So you're saying it's... what? Late afternoon?" Flare whistled between his teeth, strolling over to Caelum. "This whole thing has been too weird for words. You okay, sis?"

"I'll survive," Arcana watched Fenris climb the stairs ahead of them, muscles shifting in his back and shoulders. "You?"

"Yeah, not even a scratch." Flare shrugged, somehow managing to look adorably dishevelled. "But I didn't get jumped by a posse of zombies."

Arcana snorted. "A posse of zombies?"

"Well, what would *you* call them? 'Reanimated sorcerers' seems a little tame for what happened back there, don't you think?" Flare said.

"I guess," Arcana frowned down at her grazed knuckles. "Zombies just sounds ridiculous."

"Yeah? Who's going to argue with us?" Flare grinned and then sighed, his face sobering. "Shame about the portal. We came all that way for nothing."

"Not nothing," Fenris cast a quick glance over his shoulder. "The journey answers many questions - the least of which being why the portal was so difficult to find."

Arcana looked back the way they'd come but the recessed doorway of the tomb was already hidden in shadow. She shivered, the movement sending a swift lance of pain through her shoulder. It didn't feel broken, but the solid clout of the wall meant the joint was already stiffening.

Arcana clenched her fingers tighter in Caelum's fur, wishing suddenly for a shower and a hot cup of tea.

"I know you're tired but I should probably remind you that the sled is almost underwater," Caelum said as they crested the stairs. "I'd also feel safer if the well was filled up again."

"Ugh," Arcana slumped against his neck, squinting down the hill. She thought about pointing out that the undead didn't need to breathe and that, therefore, the deep pool of water wouldn't really be a deterrent - but instead, she slipped off his back and limped over to put her hand against the cliff, into the tiny soak of a waterfall.

The trickle of water was like ice across her skin and Arcana shuddered as she waited for her body to absorb the magic and adjust her temperature accordingly. When the soak sang in her veins, she turned towards the lake at the bottom of the hill and raised both hands in silent command. The surface of the water began to crease, swirling and rising into a long, amorphous protrusion. Arcana set her teeth and dragged upwards, curving the probe into the pit from whence they'd come. Water gurgled and sloshed against the sides, echoing back upon itself until it sounded like a thousand voices whispered their secrets into the oncoming dark. When the waterline lapped at Caelum's hooves Arcana released the magic and rubbed at her face with damp, trembling fingers. "There we go. Now nobody will ever know we were here."

"I'll know we were here," Flare shuddered, making a face. "The sooner we're gone, the happier I'll be."

"I second that - Arcana needs to rest. She hasn't slept since yesterday," Caelum announced, picking his way down the slope on neat hooves. "If she burns any more magic it won't be pretty."

Arcana rolled her eyes. "I'm not going to spontaneously combust, mother hen."

"Perhaps we should return to your family home?" Fenris suggested. His breath clouded in the air and goosebumps marred his bare chest and arms. "Spontaneous combustion or not, I will be glad of an excuse to get indoors."

"I'm not surprised, Captain Fripple-me-sideways." Caelum snorted. "What happened to your clothes?"

Flare coughed delicately. "I may have set him on fire."

"You *what*?" Arcana's jaw dropped.

"Your brother shot a particularly persistent revenant which leapt onto my back. I wasn't fast enough to remove it before the fire spread." Fenris shrugged, as though losing his shirt to a flammable corpse was part of his normal daily routine.

"Sneaky bastard needed a lesson in manners." Flare grinned, skipping over a heap of small boulders. "Besides, nothing wrong with showing a little skin every now and then."

Fenris' cheeks darkened. "I usually prefer to keep my clothes on, if it's all the same to you," he snapped. "Not all of us have an internal heating system as good as a fire sorcerer."

"It *is* rather convenient, isn't it?" Flare tipped his head back, arms spread wide, and awarded Fenris a broad wink. "My snuggles are very popular during winter time."

Arcana regarded her brother through narrowed eyes. "Flare Veritax, did you actually *enjoy* that battle?"

Flare raised an eyebrow. "Don't act so surprised, sis. I'm a warrior. This," and he waved back at the tomb behind them, "Is what I'm good at. Fighting and... other things starting with F."

Arcana turned to Fenris, who only shrugged and offered a lopsided smile. "He makes an excellent case with which I cannot argue."

"But they were... those... *things*," she protested.

Fenris nodded. "Yes. And you fought them, too."

"Not because I thought it was fun!" Arcana shook her head. "Fighting for fun and fighting because you have to are two different things."

"Of course they are. We're all born with a talent, Arcana - mine is just different to yours." Flare spread his hands and gave her his best roguish grin, the one which always got him what he wanted. "I fight because I need to test my edge, to push, to be *more*. And afterwards... I tumble someone into bed to wash it all away. To celebrate not only the lives I saved but the one I've been given; this gift of seeing both the worst and best of another person." His grin turned a little bitter around the edges. "*You* are a protector. *I* am a blade - and a damned good one."

Arcana turned away, her chest tightening. She wanted to argue with him, but... what would she say, when she knew he was right? Flare hadn't become a decorated soldier because of his handsome face, but because of the cutthroat skill behind it. Knowing he'd be expecting a response, she flicked a look back from beneath her lashes. "In that case, I'm glad you came." Flare laughed and threw her a lazy salute as they reached the bottom of the slope.

The sled's hull glowed a faint white in the fading light, the mud which had been splashed across the plasteel washed away by the lake water. Caelum drifted to a halt at the edge of the flattened grass, ears flickering as he assessed the earth. Flare poked gingerly at the ground with his boot before stepping forward, flicking Arcana a guilty grin. "I was expecting a bog," he admitted.

"I'm not that lazy," Arcana returned.

"No, but you are tired." Caelum crossed to the sled, poking the access plate with his nose.

"I guess I can't really argue with that." The door whooshed open and Arcana slithered off his back into the warm interior, stifling a groan. "Tired and sore, that's me."

"Exactly." Caelum nipped gently at her ankle. "I'm going to graze outside for a little while, if there's time."

"Sure, but don't take forever - It's a long flight." Arcana worried at her lower lip, watching the sun as it dipped closer to the horizon. "I don't want to fall asleep in the pilot's chair."

"I can fly the sled," Flare offered. "We'll eat first and then you can catch some beauty sleep."

Arcana raised an eyebrow. "I thought you hated flying the sled?"

"I also hate vegetables, cold showers and the colour brown. Doesn't stop me doing what needs to be done," Flare shrugged, pulling himself through the hatch.

"The colour brown?" Arcana barked a sharp laugh. "And here I was about to say you were finally maturing."

"Yeah, don't get too excited," Flare chuckled, offering an arm to Fenris. "Go enjoy some grass, Caelum. I'll let you know when we're ready to leave."

Arcana dragged herself onto the nearest of the bench seats as Fenris took Flare's hand and hauled himself into the sled. She couldn't help but smile at the green calves hanging out of his borrowed trousers, now torn and filthy from their expedition into the cavern. Fenris followed her gaze and frowned, tugging ineffectually at the fabric before giving up with a grimace. "I will be glad to get my own clothes back."

"I can imagine." Arcana smiled as he palmed the door shut, sealing the cold air outside. "We might need to get you some new clothes."

"That would probably be sensible, but it can wait." Fenris wiped the greatsword down with a rag and propped it against a bulkhead, the muscles in his back rippling in a fantastic display of strength and masculinity.

"What, you prefer borrowed trousers?" Arcana chuckled. Her amusement fled as Fenris dropped to his knees at her feet, giving Arcana a spectacular view of his scarred chest and flat stomach, the aforementioned borrowed trousers riding dangerously low on narrow hips. He leant forward, close enough that Arcana could smell sweat and mud and the mysterious scent of the night-time forest clinging to his skin. "What are you doing?" she squeaked.

"Someone needs to check you over. I am no Lesce, but what little skills I have will do. Off," Fenris added, tugging imperiously at her coat.

"It's not that bad," Arcana prevaricated, her heart thumping overtime. "I can wait."

"Don't be ridiculous - I can smell your pain, remember?" Fenris tapped his nose with one finger, then sat back expectantly. After a long pause, Arcana sighed and wriggled out of her coat, shucked her oversize sweater dress - now ruined, thanks to her sloppy dodging - and sat before him in her leggings and tank top, trying not to blush. Flare appeared with a bowl of hot water and a cloth, dropping Arcana a broad wink before excusing himself on the pretext of making dinner. She bit her tongue to keep from swearing as Fenris dipped the cloth and began cleaning her wounds, fingertips ghosting across the sorest spots and eliciting a shiver from Arcana that she couldn't control. He shot her an apologetic look. "Sorry. I am trying to be gentle."

"I... It's fine." Arcana cleared her throat and forced her hammering heart to calm. "I've spent plenty of time offplanet recovering the old fashioned way, just like anyone else."

A single brow twitched. "Really? I assumed Lesce would take care of most things."

Arcana snorted. "Lesce is an amazing healer, but she's only one person and I certainly don't run to her every time I stub my toe. Besides, there are limits to what healing magic can do. Lesce, as a Class One, can tackle just about everything but not all healers can tend all ailments. More than any other calling, healing magic is... fickle."

"Oh?" Fenris' voice was muffled as he leant around behind her, dabbing carefully with the warm cloth. "I imagined a healer's magic would vary only in strength."

"Most people do, but sorcery doesn't work that way." Arcana looked out to the field, where Caelum was grazing peacefully. "It's why the test for our skill range is so extensive."

"Explain it to me, the testing process," Fenris invited. Arcana turned her head, blinking to find his face so close it filled her entire field of vision. He smiled, hefting a jar of salve and a roll of bandages. "It will help take your mind off the pain."

"Oh. Okay," she took a steadying breath as he set to work. "There's an official set of spell books - the contents are different per Tower, of course, but the idea is the same. Each book is progressively more difficult than the last, and spells vary in type to help isolate particular talents. Sorcerers are classified based upon how many of the spells they can perform in each of the books." Arcana winced as he tugged on the end of the bandage, tying it off with a neat knot.

"So the levels are a reflection of how many books you complete?" Fenris twisted, his chest brushing her arm as he began probing her sore shoulder.

Arcana jumped, wondering how he knew which shoulder to tend, and then dismissing it as a potentially embarrassing answer - for her. She closed her eyes and tried to concentrate on his question. "The levels are actually how many books you did *not* complete," she said. "There are ten spell books in total. Testing starts with the easiest book and continues until the sorcerer can no longer perform the spells within."

Fenris snorted. "That sounds completely backwards."

"Yes and no. A category five water sorcerer - which is what I was, you know, before - means I was unable to complete the fifth book, so that becomes my classification. Flare, being a Class One, only had one book remaining - or rather, he made it to the one book. The last book." Arcana stopped, no longer able to marshal thoughts more coherent than the tingle of Fenris' fingers across her skin. He was careful, so careful, never removing the straps of her top or bra, never lingering more than necessary for a simple evaluation of her health, but still her stomach tied itself in a knot and her cheeks burned.

"How did it change after you met Caelum?" the touch of his fingers disappeared and Arcana opened her eyes to find Fenris' luminous gaze only moments from her own. His glamour whispered on the edges of her hearing, the tickling of feathers brushing the outer edges of her senses. Arcana made to deflect it and then paused. She was immune - why bother? Curious, she brushed her magic against the leading edge of Fenris'. The glamour immediately surrounded her spirit, filling Arcana with heat and wrapping her in Fenris' evergreen and cinnamon scent. The midnight caress of velvet stroked across her skin and she shivered in delight, leaning into the energy as it curled around her like some enormous, ethereal kitten. *This* was what she had been so worried about?

Strong hands gripped her by the elbows and Arcana blinked as the warmth wrenched away. Fenris' face swam into focus, sweaty hair plastered to his temples, jaw slack. "What did you do?" He croaked.

"You mean the glamour? Nothing," Arcana shrugged and his body undulated in response, hands still firm - though with less desperation - on her arms. "I just..." Arcana wrinkled her nose, searching for the right words. Had he truly never made honest, uncomplicated eye contact with another person? Ever? She thought over what Fenris had told her about his glamour and realised it was entirely possible he hadn't. Arcana looked at his face, at the fragile vulnerability there, and felt something inside her crack. "I might be immune to your glamour but I can feel the energy all around me. I wondered what would happen if I accepted it - so I did. That's what you felt."

"But..." Fenris shook his head as if to clear it.

Emboldened by his haggard expression, Arcana tilted his chin up, waiting until his eyes inevitably sought her own. "This is what it's like to see somebody - really see them."

They sat that way for a long moment, Fenris' mobile face displaying a range of emotions, Arcana's index finger propping up his chin. She let him work through it, the warmth of their energies curling together, and wondered if he could feel it the way she could. Eventually Fenris closed his eyes and the connection severed, leaving Arcana feeling oddly exposed. "Thank you." His voice was rough as he leant backwards, hands sliding over her knees to drop listlessly in his lap. "I don't - I'm not sure -"

Arcana smiled. "Relax. It's fine."

"You have given me a great gift," Fenris insisted, eyes still closed. "I require some time to process it. Would you... would you keep talking?"

"I suppose so. What should I talk about?"

"You were talking about Tower testing, and I asked how life changed when Caelum was born." Fenris settled back on the floor, feet tucked beneath him and hands clasped in his lap, as though preparing to meditate. "Please continue."

"Okay. After I met Caelum, I did months and months of testing. I went through every spell book the Towers gave me. All of the official books, for all of the Towers, and then some of the not so official ones." She curled one hand into her hair and tugged gently, gnawing on the memory of days that had seemed endless and terrifying. "There was no spell I could not complete. Before long we realised I didn't need a book at all - I could command my magic however I wished."

Fenris opened his eyes and though they seemed a little haunted, his voice was clear. "That is what earnt you an unclassifiable status," he guessed.

"Yes. Unclassified, Class Zero - however you prefer." She shrugged.

"How's the patient look, doctor?" Flare appeared as if from nowhere, leaning between them to offer two steaming bowls of soup. He turned a mock stern expression on Arcana. "I trust she's behaving."

Fenris snorted, accepting the soup with a nod of thanks. "Some jarring and bruising, but nothing serious. Lesce can better attend those shallow cuts on her arm when we return, but for now, I believe she will live."

"Glad to hear it," Arcana snorted. Her stomach rumbled in anticipation as Flare handed her a bowl and a spoon of her own.

"It's always good to check," Flare produced a third bowl and dropped onto the seat beside her, spooning soup into his mouth. "It's hot, by the way."

"It's delicious," Arcana responded, sipping at the soup on the edge of her spoon. "Bit spicy for Ma's cooking, though. Have you been playing chef?"

"Actually, Gravella made it," Flare answered. "This one's my favourite."

"Gravella... Makes you soup?" Arcana blinked, trying to picture the officious Earth Elder in a kitchen. She made the obvious connection and narrowed her eyes at Flare. "How long have you been sleeping together?"

"Oh, I dunno." Flare tapped his chin in thought. "About twenty years, give or take."

"Twenty years?!" Arcana spat out her soup, sitting bolt upright. Fenris dodged a flying piece of carrot with a twitch of his head, one eyebrow arching as he looked between the two siblings. Arcana, however, had eyes only for her brother. "Flare, do you realise you're in a *relationship* with this woman?"

Flare snorted. "Don't be silly, sis. Just friends with benefits, as per usual."

"Gravella doesn't have friends! She hates everything that breathes. How in the world did she end up making you soup?" Arcana waved her spoon in emphasis. "Tell me everything - and start at the beginning."

"The beginning... Okay, I guess so." Flare frowned. "About twenty five years ago, Gravella asked me over to her place. She was studying you and she wanted some advice."

"She was studying me? Gravella hates me," Arcana protested.

"As you've already pointed out, Gravella hates everyone. You, she loathes with a special sort of passion, because she's jealous. She's devoted her entire life to magic and within a week of her confirmation as Earth Elder, you come along and bond with Caelum." Flare's grin was lopsided. "She was incensed."

"Not planned," Arcana protested.

"I know," Flare held up a placating hand. "But it doesn't change the fact that your unusual ascension quickly eclipsed the recognition Gravella had been receiving for her hard work. She spent a good while being bitter, then decided that by studying you she might be able to improve her own skills."

"Seems reasonable," Fenris nodded.

Arcana shook her head. "No, it doesn't. Magic is innate - our capacity for wielding it is set at birth and then revealed upon imprinting. It can't be changed."

"No?" Flare raised an eyebrow. "Yours certainly was."

"What happened to me is different," Arcana returned. "Sorcerers who try and blow their own roof off either burn out or die. Everyone knows that."

"Gravella believes otherwise and she's set on proving it." Flare shrugged. "If she succeeds, it'll make her not only a better sorcerer, but also a famous one for becoming the first person in history to increase her natural abilities."

"Thereby regaining the recognition she lost to me all those years ago," Arcana muttered, poking at her soup with a spoon. "That's... I don't know whether that's insane, inspired or just sad."

"I thought the same thing at first, but you *did* ask me for the whole story," Flare relied tartly, crossing his arms over his chest.

"I did." Arcana forced herself to sit back and continue eating. "Please continue."

"Right. So about twenty five years after you left Sorcen, Gravella invited me over to her house. She made it painfully clear that there was to be 'no funny business'," Flare hooked his fingers around the words, rolling his eyes. "But I went, because she said it involved you and I... I really missed you. She asked if I'd help with her studies in return for dinner."

"How were *you* going to help?" Arcana frowned.

"Nobody knows you better than me, sis, that's no secret," Flare's smile all but overflowed with brotherly pride. "Gravella believed that if you could change your capacity for magic, perhaps she could too - if she knew enough about you. I was the logical choice."

"Okay, fair call. So you agreed to tattle on me... For food? This is weird, Flare," Arcana laughed.

"I guess it sounds weird but I'm serious. I missed you. I never wanted you to leave and I was lonely. I don't get on well with Lesce and everyone else wants to sleep with me - and while there's nothing wrong with that, sometimes it's nice to have friends *without* benefits." Flare frowned. "It was strange at first because I knew Gravella resented you but I thought maybe if she came to know you as I did, she might change her mind."

"And you never made a move on her? Not once?" Fenris asked.

"No. She said no. I'm not like that," Flare made a face.

"Then how did you go from dinner to..." Arcana gestured expansively. "All the rest?"

Flare grinned, mischief sparking in the depths of his gaze. "We had dinner and chatted once a week. Gravella showed me her library and I helped with her notes. She's really not so bad once she warms up."

"That's pushing it even for you, Flare. The warmest I've ever seen Gravella is when she's not there," Arcana said drily.

"Once upon a time, I'd have said the same," Flare chuckled. "Anyway, years passed with the arrangement never altering - though the visits lasted longer and longer. Then one night, or morning, it was pretty late I guess, we were going through scrolls and she threw hers aside and said 'That's it, Flare! This is ridiculous.' She was so angry. I asked what the matter was and she slapped me, super hard, right in the face," Flare rubbed one hand ruefully along his jaw.

"Sounds like Gravella," Arcana snorted.

"I was surprised, to say the least. And while I sat there looking stunned, she grabbed my head in both hands and kissed me. Properly," he added, then fell silent.

"Do you love her?" Arcana asked.

Flare blinked, then barked a short, bitter laugh. "No, more's the pity. I enjoy our time together, but not so much that I've changed my lifestyle."

Arcana's heart squeezed. "You don't feel anything? At all? I don't believe that, not if you keep seeing her."

"Oh, I like her... the same as anyone else I see or sleep with. People are fascinating - so many layers, so many mysteries. But love? No. I'm not sure if I'm capable. Which is unfair, because I know she's not seeing anyone else," Flare admitted, his face twisted with guilt.

"Surely you've been honest with her," Fenris placed his empty bowl on the floor in front of him, looking at Flare as though he'd never seen him before.

"Of course I have. She knew from the start what she was getting into and she tried to avoid it. But somewhere along the line..." Flare trailed off and shook his head.

"She fell in love with you," Arcana said softly.

He flinched as though slapped. "I'm not sure I'd go that far."

"A woman does not makes you soup - your favourite soup - let you sleep in her bed, or slap you in the face, or any of those other things, if she is not in love with you," Arcana said firmly. "Refusing to acknowledge that disrespects Gravella in a situation that's already borderline."

Flare dropped his head into his hands. "Don't you think I know that? Dammit, Arcana, when did I become an asshole? I *wish* I loved her. I wish I could give back what she's giving to me... But I can't. I've tried talking to her, even tried turning her away - she won't go."

Silence fell, and Arcana put her bowl aside to wrap her arms around Flare's shoulders. He leant into her, causing a line of sweat to break out on her forehead. Arcana ignored it - fire sorcerers always ran a few degrees hotter than average - and stroked the back of his hair with one hand. "Sooner or later you're going to have to make her understand."

"I know," Flare mumbled.

Fenris watched from the floor, his expression heavy with pity. "The Weaver once told me that there is a warp and a weft for everyone within the fabric of the universe. Just as the night is coupled to the day, so are we all paired to another," the Guardian said. Flare peered out between his fingers, and whatever Fenris saw there made him smile. "You are brave, brother of flame. I have no doubt you will meet the right person some day. Fight on a little longer."

"I'm not sure the woman he's been sleeping with for twenty years will like that," Arcana said slowly, tracing gentle circles on Flare's back with one finger. "In fact, if I know Gravella at all, she's likely to rip his balls off."

"Hah! And I'll deserve it, too." Flare snorted.

"Forgive me, but I thought you were..." Fenris winced, waving a hand and muttering under his breath in another language. "Well known for your promiscuity?"

Flare chuckled at that, an empty rattle of a sound, and sat up. "Yes, I am. Soldier and lover, that's me. But I don't normally keep going back - because *this* happens. Fun only, nothing else."

"And what do your other lovers say about Gravella?" Fenris asked.

Flare drew a sharp breath. "Nothing. She's a secret. I mean, I'm a secret." He shook his head and laughed, a soft huff of breath. "What I'm trying to say is, Gravella has expressly ordered me to say nothing."

"Huh. So she knows," Arcana mused, tapping one finger on her chin. "I always thought she was smarter than she let on."

"She's not so bad, sis, really. Anyway, this conversation turned a little more serious than I intended, so if it's all the same to you guys, I'll fly the ship now." Flare's grin lacked his usual lustre as he stood and gathered the empty bowls. Arcana watched him go, her heart heavy.

"I will sit with him," Fenris promised, catching her eye.

"Thanks. I better call Caelum." Arcana rose and limped stiffly to the door, poking her head outside.

"Already?" Caelum asked, his head appearing around the side of the ship.

"How much grass do you need?" Arcana demanded.

"Oh, I finished ages ago. I just don't fancy getting my barge-arse back on the sled," he shook his antlers in frustration. "And if you even *mention* the cargo bay doors, I swear I will gore you."

"Fine. Get in then, barge-arse," Arcana laughed. "I'm going to bed." She settled herself on the rearmost of the bench seats, pulling her coat over her legs. Caelum's hooves scrabbled awkwardly in the confined space and she bit the inside of her cheek as he swore and grunted his way into the empty cargo area beside her.

"Made it," he wheezed, lipping at her hair. "In case you were doubting."

"Never," she replied, her tone as innocent as possible. Caelum nudged her once with his nose and subsided, leaving Arcana to concentrate on steadying her breathing and forcing herself to relax one muscle at a time.

Fenris and Flare spoke in low voices as the sled's engine hummed to life and for a moment Arcana feared she wouldn't sleep for the noise but her body had other ideas and she'd barely finished the thought when her body sunk into the welcoming embrace of oblivion.

CHAPTER
TEN

THE BEDROOM DOOR OPENED WITH LITTLE MORE THAN A SNICK. "HAVE YOU come to lecture me?" Fenris asked, jerking his chin in greeting.

"Lecture? Now, why would I do that?" Flare's voice carried laughter.

Fenris continued his careful study of the greatsword's leather wrappings, fitting his hands to the hilt of the sword and flexing experimentally. "Why, indeed?" He began removing the leather with patient fingers, coiling the excess neatly at his feet. "I saw you watching Arcana and myself on the sled. I am many things, but rarely a fool."

Flare snorted. "Rarely?"

"To say never would imply an infallibility I've yet to encounter." Fenris looked up at last, offering a lopsided smile which felt as alien on his face as the first time Arcana had drawn it out of him.

Flare leant against the foot of the bed, arms crossed over a stack of papers. "Ah, yes. Wouldn't want anyone to assume you're perfect."

"Least of all myself," Fenris agreed, inclining his head. "But considering you paced outside the door for a good ten minutes before entering, I think I'm safe in my assumption that your visit isn't simply for idle chatter."

"Fair enough." Flare dropped the stack of papers - books, Fenris realised - on the small table at the foot of the bed. "I bought you some light reading."

Fenris raised an eyebrow, perusing the stack of literature. "No lecture, then?"

Flare's eyes twinkled. "I never said no lecture."

"I see." Fenris repositioned the leather and began winding it back around the sword's hilt with practised fingers. "So, what have you picked for me to read?"

"History books." Flare tilted his head to one side. "Arcana's history, to be precise."

"There's a history book regarding your sister?" Fenris tucked the final scrap of leather into place and palmed the hilt again. Perfect.

"There are plenty of history books about Arcana," Flare chuckled. "These are just the ones my parents keep on hand for curious guests."

"Curious guests," Fenris repeated, allowing disapproval to lace his tone.

"Weird, isn't it? Still, my parents are proud, in their own way." Flare picked up one of the books, a heavy tome with a picture of a woman on the front. She had soft beige skin, a healthy dusting of dark brown freckles and gently waving hair the colour of aquamarine. The image completely at odds with the picture on the back cover as Flare turned the book over; Arcana as Fenris knew her now, her salt white skin framed with long, straight black hair and bottomless ebony eyes. Flare spun the book in his hands several times before dropping it back on the table. "If you're going to spend any length of time with Arcana, you should familiarise yourself with the circumstances that made her who she is."

"Ah," Fenris pushed out of the chair, leaning the greatsword against one wall. "Is this where you warn me to stay away from your sister?"

"No - this is where I warn you not to chase her unless you mean it. For her sake."

"Oh?" Fenris hooked both thumbs through his belt - *his* belt, which he'd never been so glad to see as when he arrived back here - and leant one hip against the room's narrow desk. "That is a presumptuous choice of words, brother."

Flare merely grinned. "I've seen the way you look at her. She doesn't notice, but I do. I always do. And I don't blame you - she's a bombshell, more so since the transformation, though the gods know she's completely unaware." Flare hesitated, then shrugged. "After Algae... he wasn't kind to her. He left her a shell. A thinking, unfeeling shell."

"Arcana has emotions," Fenris contradicted. "I have seen and scented them."

"Oh, she has emotions. Just don't confuse them with *feelings*," Flare's grin was vicious, and faded as quickly as it had appeared. "Algae... ugh. I can't believe I'm telling you this."

Fenris waited out the silence, his face impassive. Flare's scent was an interesting mixture of affection, guilt, sadness, and a host of other more subtle things that would be impossible to decipher without knowing the fire sorcerer better. Even so, those which he *could* translate were enough to pique his interest, to stave off the instinctive denial that had been forming - albeit politely - in his mind.

Flare exhaled between his teeth. "Algae was always cocky, even young, but he had a rough sort of charm about him. Arcana seemed to like him, so I told myself that was good enough for me. Things were fine until Arcana changed, until she became... better than him."

"Algae didn't like that, I take it."

"No, gods no. Not at all. He's a possessive sort, and insanely jealous. I didn't find out until later, but he started to undermine Arcana's confidence by insinuating she was ugly, making her believe that only *he* would ever be able to put up with her. He undermined her talent, made her believe she wasn't skilled or blessed, but cursed and dangerous. He isolated her, insinuating that family and friends would eventually abandon her and there was nothing, no-one in the world who cared." Flare ground to a halt, his hands clenched to fists.

"Except, presumably, for Algae," Fenris struggled to keep his voice even, to mask the same rage he could see flickering in Flare's eyes. "That is typical behaviour for an emotionally abusive relationship. Did he ever become physical?"

"No," Flare answered and his tone made it clear that he'd certainly investigated the possibility. "Arcana was too soft and vulnerable - he never needed to be violent. Algae loved her in his strange way, he just wanted to control her for his own benefit and nobody realised how bad things were until it was too late."

"You blame yourself," Fenris observed.

Flare nodded, his face pinched with guilt. "I was around a fair bit. I should have seen it. When Arcana found him in bed with those other women, it was a massive wake-up slap. She holoed and told me every-thing he'd ever done - I'll never forget that look on her face, the absolute devastation in her eyes."

"And you went to her," Fenris finished.

"Damned straight I went to her," Flare growled. "I burned Algae's house to the ground and I would've killed him if Arcana hadn't been there."

"Do you regret it?"

"Not killing him? Often," Flare admitted. "Algae's a scumbag - but his death would've been trickier to cover up, and it would have hurt Arcana more than she already was. Sometimes there are more important things than petty revenge." The fire sorcerer tilted his head to one side and Fenris got the impression he was mentally listing each and every one of those reasons.

"After associating with Algae myself, albeit briefly, I feel your deed might have been seen as a public service," Fenris said gravely.

Flare barked a sharp laugh. "I'd be the first to agree with you, brother. I'm sure you also noticed that, despite everything, he's still obsessed with Arcana."

"I did." Now for the dangerous part. Fenris could feel the tension ratcheting up, could see Flare's body tensing in anticipation. He drew on his court training, forcing his voice into complete neutrality as he said; "I'm still not certain why you feel these intimate details of Arcana's past are relevant to me."

It was, in essence, throwing meat in front of a pack of starving lions, but Flare was ready. "I've seen you looking at her," was all he said.

Fenris acknowledged with a sharp nod. "Arcana is breathtakingly beautiful. I would have to be dead not to notice."

"Agreed, but that's not what I meant." Flare grinned, a sharp, pained flashing of teeth. "I've seen you looking at *her*. Beyond the shape, behind the magic and the curiosity of her bond with Caelum is a woman whom you've unequivocally noticed."

"Is there a problem with noticing?" Fenris tried to keep the growl from his voice and failed.

"Not really," said Flare, his voice soft. "But she looks at you, too, and *that's* what has me worried. Arcana hasn't shown interest in another living creature since I reduced Algae's house to ashes."

Fenris' mouth went abruptly dry. Arcana was looking at *him*? All she had expressed so far were fear and disdain, perhaps a grudging tolerance on Caelum's behalf. He coughed lightly to hide his surprise. "I see."

"And so do I," Flare stalked closer, his broad frame intimidating for all he was the shorter. "So I thought I'd say - don't look. Not unless you really, really mean it. Because I like you, I do, but I won't see what precious little of her there is shattered into oblivion." Flare drew to a halt so close that Fenris could feel the static electricity jumping between them. "I've failed Arcana once and I'm not about to do it again - so whatever game you're playing, if it's going to involve your sudden and irrevocable departure, then think twice."

"And if it's not?"

"Then you sure as flaming feathers better know what you're doing," Flare growled, the hostility in his voice no longer hidden.

Fenris stared down his nose at the fire sorcerer, doing his best to summon the words. To tell him there was nothing to worry about, that his attraction to Arcana was no more than a passing interest in a beautiful woman. He opened his mouth to promise he would stay away, that he would keep his thoughts, his hands - his heart - to himself.

He couldn't.

Flare pounced. Fenris narrowly dodged the flaming fist that came sailing through the air towards him, leaping aside on instinct alone. Flare pushed forwards with a series of quick, strong blows that had Fenris ducking and blocking, twisting away from fire and fist and well placed foot. This was a very different warrior to the one who'd put his back to Fenris' in the cavern and defended over a long range with great gouts of flame - *this* Flare was full of righteous fury and dirty, street wise punches that had even Fenris wondering where the next blow would come from.

Flare's fist grazed the side of Fenris jaw, leaving a tingling trail of heat behind. Impressed in spite of himself, Fenris drew on his preternatural speed and took three short strides up the wall, landing neatly behind his opponent. Time to end this before they did any real damage to the room, or woke Arcana from her restorative sleep. Fenris lashed out with a low kick designed to sweep Flare's feet out from under him but the other twisted as he fell, threading his own legs through Fenris until the two of them tumbled to the floor in a confused mess of limbs. Fenris collected his wits enough to land on top, pinning Flare beneath his body and laying a forearm over the fire sorcerer's neck as if it were a sword.

"Satisfied?" He said stiffly.

"Not at all." Flare turned his head to the side, spat blood on the floor, then looked back with a grin. "You're good, brother."

"Why did you attack?"

Flare's eyes flashed. "Because you were going to lie to me."

"And now?"

Another flash. "Tell me the truth."

Fenris considered. The truth? Not even *he* was entirely certain of the truth. In reality, he had sworn an oath to the Weaver and nothing, nobody, should come before it - that was the truth. But Flare wasn't asking about the Weaver and they both knew it. And perhaps he had earnt, through bravado and skill, somewhat of an explanation.

"Arcana is immune to my glamour," Fenris was shocked at the hoarse quality of his own voice. "There has never been anyone immune to it before. I will admit that tempted me to look further beyond the surface than I normally would."

"I knew it," Flare nodded and some of the ire faded from his face. "And your intentions?"

"I don't know. I want to say I'll stay away, but I cannot. There is something about Arcana that draws me." Fenris shook his head, unable to completely describe a thing for which he, himself, still had no name. "She is a uniquely fascinating enigma."

"She sure is," Flare's grin was slow but steady. His hair was flecked with blood and sweat and there was a faint, attractive dusting of freckles across his cheeks and nose that seemed to shine in the light. "But she's also broken."

Fenris sighed. "So am I."

That particularly foolish admission drew Flare's eyebrows up in surprise, but he made no move to follow with a new line of questions. Instead, he simply said; "Good. Lecture over."

"Over? You don't seem in the position to be issuing a lecture at all, brother." Fenris flicked a gaze down to his arm, still pinned against Flare's neck. The fire sorcerer's grin only widened.

"I can get you off any time I like," he purred, and the edge to his voice had Fenris blinking rapidly.

"I am stronger, faster. I fail to see how," the words drew out by themselves and even as they did, Fenris knew he'd said exactly what Flare had set him up to say. Beneath him, Flare's body *shifted*. No longer combative, it became suddenly soft and pliable, welcoming. The fire sorcerer's muscular frame fitted against Fenris' lean lines like the pieces of a jigsaw and before Fenris had a chance to react, Flare caged his face in gentle hands and kissed him.

The slant of lips on lips was soft, inviting, a question and an offer rolled into one. Flare's breath was hot, pitched to stoke dormant embers into a furnace, his body a cradle of delicious planes and sultry curves. The fire sorcerer's tongue flicked out, teasing the corner of their joined mouths - and Fenris was quite suddenly on the other side of the room, lungs heaving and blood singing, clutching at his chest as though it might burst open.

"Told you," Flare made no attempt to disguise the seductive lie of his body on the floor.

"What - why -" Fenris managed, his cheeks burning. Even across the room, he could scent what he had noticed but not identified before. Desire. Rage, sadness, guilt and desire.

Flare's grin was broad and unrepentant, none of his vast undercurrent of emotions visible on that mobile face. "You let me go, didn't you? It never fails."

"How many battles have you won like that?" It was a stupid question and Fenris knew it, but he had to buy time for his body to sort out the rather complex and confusing mixture of sensations he was now experiencing.

"You'd be surprised," Flare chuckled, the sound throaty. Fenris decided he wouldn't be surprised at all, no matter how great the number.

"But I don't - I'm not -"

Flare's grin grew even wider. "I know."

"Then *how* does that work?" Fenris demanded.

A perfect brow skyrocketed. "Well, when Daddy and Daddy love each other *very much*, they -"

"That's not what I meant," Fenris cut in, both hands up in a gesture of peace.

"Oh?" Flare stretched languorously, invitation still writ clean across his face. "You'd better clarify before you get an education, then, Guardian."

Fenris swallowed, trying to gather his wits. "I meant, how do you manage to - change like that. In the middle of a battle, no less."

Flare blinked, a slow, purposeful lowering of lashes - and even Fenris' keen eyes could not track the change as Flare returned to the normal, bubbly warrior with which he was familiar. "Practice," was all he said.

Fenris levelled a trembling finger. "You are a dangerous man."

"Good." Flare rolled to his feet in a single, swift movement. "That's the whole point." He tugged the bedroom door open, flicking a long, intense stare over his shoulder. "Look after my sister, Fenris - or I'll look after you."

And then he was gone.

Fenris stared at the closed door for a very long moment, clenching both hands into fists to hide their shaking. This entire thing was madness. He should gather what little belongings he had and make a dash for the Timeless Kingdom before the situation got any further out of hand - but that would mean breaching the fragile trust between himself and Arcana, a thing he found he was already very reluctant to do.

Fool.

Fenris strode to the stack of books on the bedside table and snatched up the topmost volume. Weaver save him but this was a bad idea. He stared down at the cover, at the face of an Arcana he'd never met, then flipped the book over to the sombre, more familiar visage on the back.

Broken, Flare had said. A thinking, unfeeling shell. Perhaps the two of them had more in common than he'd realised. With that thought still echoing in his mind, Fenris threw himself on the bed and began to read.

———

ARCANA OPENED HER EYES, STUDYING THE FAMILIAR MOSAIC ON THE CEILING, content to ride the wave of pleasant drowsiness pervading her body. The scent of clean cotton and freshly baked bread filled her room and from beyond it, Caelum's velvet baritone, forever etched into her heart. His voice dipped and rose, answered by Flare's hearty laugh and the softer, almost reluctant sound of Fenris' amusement.

Fenris? Arcana rubbed her eyes and stretched, her brain clunking slug-gishly into motion. Fenris. The greatsword. The portal. She sat up, blinking blearily at the bedroom which still felt like home, even after a half century away. Her clothes were neatly folded atop a chair in one corner - Lesce, most likely - and a soft cotton nightgown clung to her body.

Arcana flipped the covers back and slid out of bed, making her way into the ensuite. Her shower was quick, hot and refreshing, filled with thick steam and her mother's wonderful home-made soap. She returned to her room wrapped in a towel, humming under her breath as she moved to inspect the clothing she'd worn the day before. Though neatly folded, they were covered in grime and reeked of dust and death.

"Maybe not," she muttered, poking the shredded sleeve. Arcana dropped the ruined jumper back onto the chair and strode to the wooden armoire her father had carved for her as a child. "Okay, then. Let's see what the past has got to offer."

The clothes inside were both familiar and alien, relics of a life she had left behind. Soft, flowing dresses, elegant knitted shawls and heavy robes had Arcana crinkling her nose in denial. Towards the back of the wardrobe, she found a deep navy dress, so dark as to be almost black. Made out of soft velvet, it boasted long, clinging sleeves and a draping hood. The skirt fell to the floor in a simple gather from the underbust, elegant and flattering without being ostentatious. Once, it had been too dark for her blue and tan complexion, but now - Arcana placed the dress on the bed.

A set of drawers yielded clean underwear, a bra and a warm pair of winter tights. She pulled them on, followed by a simple, clinging shift and then the navy dress. A quick jaunt to the bathroom revealed a brush but nothing else, so Arcana dragged it through her hair and let the long black

169

tresses trail unbound over her shoulders. That done, she studied herself in the mirror, pulling the hood up and twirling in a circle.

"Nice. I might even keep this one," Arcana nodded to her reflection. Navy velvet offset the stark white of her skin and the black eyes she often cursed stared out from the depths of the hood, giving her an ethereal, almost mysterious appearance. She looked - well, good. Arcana tilted her head to one side and the secretive smile tugging at her lips seemed to belong to someone else, someone powerful and brave.

She turned from the mirror, shoving her feet into a pair of well-worn ankle boots whose heels gave her another couple inches of height without being impractical. Arcana grabbed her leather satchel from the bedside table and slid the strap over one shoulder, settling it into place by her hip. After one last glance at the mirror to ensure everything was as it should be, Arcana opened the bedroom door and strode out into the living area.

"You're awake! At last," Lesce grabbed the kettle from the fire, her face creasing with warmth. "Come on, the tea's waiting."

"How long was I out?" Arcana asked, pressing a kiss to her younger sister's cheek. "I'm unbelievably hungry."

"The whole night and then a little more. From what the boys told me, I'd say about fifteen hours," Lesce guessed, tapping her chin in thought.

"Fifteen hours?!"

"Don't give me that look! You used too much magic, even for you." Lesce poked her in the chest with a firm finger. "You're not taking proper care of yourself, running on empty like that."

"I wasn't anticipating a battle," Arcana grumbled, swatting Lesce's hand away. "Besides, I feel fine."

Lesce shook her head, issuing a long suffering sigh. "I'm serious, Arcana. I checked you over - Fenris insisted - and you were dangerously close to burning out."

"You know I can't burn out, not really," Arcana ran a hand over the scratches on her arm and discovered them healed. "If I push too hard things just get a little uncomfortable, that's all - and I'm telling you, I felt fine."

"Fine is how people feel right before they have a heart attack, you know," Lesce groused, rubbing at her furrowed brow. "Look, I'm not about to tell you what to do - but I don't want to get a holo one day saying you've literally been consumed from the inside out by the vast well of energy inside you. *It* may not have limits, but you do."

Arcana draped an arm over Lesce's shoulders and pulled her close. "Stress less, little healer. You can't get rid of me that easily."

Her sister grunted. "Now you sound like Flare."

"Speaking of, I thought I heard his voice earlier," Arcana glanced around the empty living area. "Did he come back to tease you some more?"

"Hah! No, he just returned from Tower duty. Came to see Fenris, actually," Lesce replied. "They're an unlikely pair but they seem to be getting along."

"Partners in crime," Arcana said drily. "Shouldn't you still be up at the Tower, though?"

"Yes but I excused myself on the pretext of checking you over once you awoke," Lesce offered a cheeky smile that made her look ten years younger. "I needed a break from the endless arguing over those blasted pirate ships."

"You're *still* arguing over that? Are you all nuts?" Arcana stood up straight, her heart thumping erratically.

"Hush. I feel the same as you, but it needs to be unanimous before we can contact the Galactic Alliance. Now have some tea and a little breakfast." Lesce pressed a steaming mug into one hand and a berry pastry into the other.

Arcana sighed, leaning back against the bench. "I can't believe it's been several days and the Council is *still* faffing about. I don't envy you, that's for sure."

"Several days?" Lesce laid a gentle hand on Arcana's shoulder. "It's been a week since you were in the Council chamber."

"What? No, that can't be right. You said I slept for -"

"The flux," Lesce interrupted. "You lost the better part of three days to the flux and *then* you slept for fifteen hours."

Arcana blinked at her younger sister in astonishment. "*Really?*"

Lesce nodded, her expression sober. "Fenris said it had something to do with the violent nature of the flux."

Arcana considered the undead sorcerers and shuddered. "I'd believe it. But... are you seriously telling me Vino's been unable to make up his mind in a week? The man's an idiot. I don't know how you do the Elder job, I really don't."

"It can be frustrating," Lesce admitted. "I'm not sure what's more difficult at times - meeting with the Council or running the Healing Tower. Still, it keeps me busy."

"Mmmmm," Arcana managed, her cheeks bulging with delicious berry filling. She swallowed and said; "Speaking of busy, I promised to go with Fenris in exchange for his help with Caelum."

"Fenris mentioned that. I think he was surprised," Lesce looked amused, but her eyes narrowed as she watched Arcana's face. "Do you really think the Weaver sent you to help him?"

"Yeah, I do. You know it's been a long week when the idea of a mythical woman pulling my puppet strings makes sense," Arcana screwed up her face. "Still, this is the best thing for Caelum."

Lesce swirled her teacup. "And what about you?"

"What about me?" Arcana held up a hand when Lesce would have answered. "Closed topic, Lesce. You know that."

For once, it looked like her sister might argue but eventually Lesce just shrugged. "Don't forget you promised to report to the Council before you leave."

"I haven't," Arcana smiled. "Are you heading back to the Tower soon?"

"Any minute now," Lesce confirmed. "Ember's coming by tonight and I refuse to miss my Grandmama time with Lizelle because of a stuffy Council meeting!"

"That's the most animated I've ever heard you," Arcana laughed. "All right, I'll give you time to get back to the Tower and then I'll swing by to make a report."

"Excellent." Lesce smiled, handing Arcana a second pastry before dusting her hands on her apron. "While I think of it, I've arranged to have your clothes cleaned and mended professionally. It shouldn't take long. Would it suit you to have them delivered directly to the ship?"

"Yes please. The smell is awful - and tell the tailor that if it's too difficult, throw them in the bin. That right sleeve is a mess," Arcana made a face.

"I know, which is why I decided someone else could handle it. That dress suits you, though," Lesce smiled, plucking at the edge of Arcana's hood. "Now, if you'll excuse me?"

"Of course," Arcana kissed her sister on the cheek and watched her bustle away. Her chest ached a moment and she sipped her tea slowly. Children were a dream from *before*, along with love, her own bakery and a normal life. She'd tucked those thoughts and longings away once she'd bonded with Caelum and her life had changed, but having seen Lizelle in person - and the love her family had for such a tiny human being - had bought those longings back full force. Arcana sighed, draining the last of her tea and setting the cup in the sink. For now, there were more important things than worrying about what may or may not have been - like making sure the Council got their precious report before Fenris rushed her back into space.

Arcana crossed to the front door and yanked it open; afternoon sunlight poured in and she stood a moment, enjoying the warmth. Fenris and Caelum stood together on the main drive, some ten paces away from where Flare perched on the gate-post. The fire sorcerer raised an arm in greeting as she approached.

"Hey, sleepy head!" He called.

"Hey yourself," Arcana smiled. Caelum nudged at her with his nose and she embraced him at once. "What are you all doing?"

"I've been *trying* to jump," Caelum said, his voice muffled by her clothing.

"No luck, I gather?" She combed her hands through the long winter coat at the base of his throat, enjoying the silky feel between her fingers.

Caelum made a sound halfway between irritation and a purr. "Not yet."

"I thought some basic training would be a good way to pass the time," Fenris said with a shrug. "I taught him a ritual for concentration that other deerken use and with practice, he can now sense the energy. The problem is that Caelum is bound to a singular reality in the way other deerken are not. We are both learning in this venture."

"Were you trying to reach a destination within our maximum range? Because I'm pretty sure the elastic band effect would prevent you jumping any further away," Arcana said.

"Of course," Caelum sighed, frustration edging his tone. "We already know that within the fence line is a safe distance from your room. I was trying to jump to Flare but it's just not working."

"Then we rest and try again another day," Arcana soothed. She turned to Fenris. "Lesce said you were eager to leave, but I promised we'd meet with the Council first."

"I have not forgotten," he acknowledged, inclining his head. "I am also looking forward to receiving my scabbard from the smith. The greatsword is cumbersome to carry around under one arm all the time."

"Not to mention terrifyingly sharp," Arcana snorted, eyeing the blade where it rested against the fence.

"You needn't worry about that," Fenris returned, his lip twitching. "The greatsword is only as sharp as I ask it to be."

"Magic?" Flare asked.

"I suppose that is as good an explanation as any," Fenris rolled his shoulders in an elegant shrug. "The greatsword is a feather in my hand but an anvil to anyone else. It is deadly sharp in my grasp, whilst dull in the grip of another."

"Fancy," Flare whistled between his teeth. "Do all the Weaver's flunkies get cool loot like that?"

"Yes and no. Every Guardian chooses their own weapon and no two bear the same enchantment." Fenris strode to the greatsword, twisting it to reveal the engravings down the flat of the blade. "Taelon sought to disarm and slaughter me whilst my attention was elsewhere but he underestimated the enchantments. If it had been any other weapon, I would not have survived."

"Taelon," Arcana repeated, turning the name over in her mouth. Fenris stiffened, his brow creased, and she shook her head. "Please don't tell me we're still having trust issues. If I wanted you dead, you'd be dead already."

Fenris hesitated and then sighed, dropping his eyes. "Forgive me. Taelon was a Guardian I trusted and respected. I never thought he would betray the Weaver and endanger us all."

"No point taking the weight of Taelon's choices onto your own shoulders, brother. That'll just make you crazy." Flare reached out to give Fenris a hearty slap on the shoulder. "Just hunt the f-" he cut off as a high pitched trilling filled the air.

"Why is that so loud?" Arcana demanded, plugging her ears while Flare dug a communicator out of his pocket.

"Because sometimes I'm so busy I don't always hear it," Flare winked broadly and then jogged away, answering the call as he went.

"You seem better," Fenris said into the silence.

Arcana examined her chipped fingernails, suddenly nervous. "Yeah. Thanks for getting Lesce to check me over."

"I was worried those slash wounds would fester," Fenris shrugged her thanks away and then offered a tentative smile. "That dress suits you."

"Oh," Arcana blushed and smoothed her skirts. "Thanks. I'd forgotten I even owned it, if I'm honest." She looked up at Caelum. "How are you finding the training?"

"Good," the deerken answered, his eyes alight with excitement. "I'm learning tonnes - and I suppose now that you're awake, I should tell you that I can feel your emotions."

Arcana's jaw dropped open. "What?"

"It happened while Fenris was teaching me those basic mental exercises. Something clicked inside my head and now I can feel things that I didn't feel before." Caelum's ears flickered. "It was confusing at first... then I realised I was feeling *your* emotions as well as my own."

"My emotions." Arcana sucked on her teeth a moment, tracing one finger up the stem of his antlers and watching soft white flowers bloom where she touched. "Okay. So, all the time? Or when you feel like it?"

"I'm still trying to work that out." Caelum fell silent, considering. "It was all the time at first but I'm starting to get the hang of filtering - unless it's really strong, in which case, you knock my proverbial socks off."

"Anyone else's emotions?"

"Just yours."

Arcana looked sideways at Fenris. "Care to weigh in on this?"

"It's an unusual phenomenon but I'm assuming it's a characteristic of your soul merge," he answered. "It is not unreasonable to expect that Caelum may garner new skills as his training progresses."

"Sure," Arcana pressed her lips together, feeling suddenly and uncharacteristically exposed. "I think I need to sit down a minute."

"I'll fetch you a cup of tea," Fenris offered, jogging off towards the house. Arcana sagged against the fence, watching him go.

"Are you okay?" Caelum asked, nudging her with his nose.

"Can't you *tell*?"

"Hmmph. This isn't easy for me either, you know. I'm not always sure *whose* feelings I'm feeling," Caelum snapped. "And as for what I *can* tell - I can feel your emotions flip flopping whenever Fenris looks at you."

Arcana froze. "Oh?"

"Don't worry, he's inside. We've got a minute." Caelum tilted his head, no doubt analysing the chaos now roaring inside Arcana's chest. "I know you like Fenris, in spite of your words. I just don't understand your reaction sometimes... As though you're angry, when you're not."

Great gods of Sorcen. Arcana took a deep breath, holding it in for a moment as she considered her answer. It seemed impossible to hide the truth from Caelum - and he was her heart, after all, so she said; "Yes, I like him. Maybe too much."

"Too much?" Caelum's chest rumbled with laughter. Arcana closed her eyes and an image of Fenris rose in her mind's eye, shirtless and dripping with water, his face creased with a sensual smile.

"Definitely too much," she muttered, banishing the image. "We've known him little more than a week. I've made mistakes before and I'm not prepared to do it again."

"I like him," Caelum announced. "I don't think he's insincere."

"I didn't think Algae was insincere either and look how *that* turned out. I don't need another pair of rose coloured glasses," Arcana said.

Caelum snorted. "Just jaded ones, then?"

"Enough," Arcana flicked him on the nose, none too gently.

"Look, just don't write him off because of a bad past experience - that's not fair, either. It's plain as my antlers that he's interested in you," Caelum replied.

"Then he has terrible taste."

Caelum snorted. "I just felt your stomach flippity floppity."

"Well don't," Arcana growled. "It's a terrible idea, Caelum. I don't think I've got it in me to go down that road again."

Across the yard, the door of the house swung open and Fenris stepped out, cradling a thermos in the crook of his elbow. Flare followed, his face uncharacteristically grim.

"We have a situation," Flare said as soon as he was close.

"Dare I ask?" Arcana accepted the thermos from Fenris with a grateful smile. "Thank you."

"Lesce warned me that you are not in the habit of looking after yourself properly," Fenris replied, his face etched with the sort of stubborn determination that said he expected her to argue.

"I don't," said Arcana - at the same time that Flare said; "She doesn't."

The Guardian blinked, then pointed at the thermos. "Perhaps it is time for that to change. Drink, while Flare talks."

"Yes, mother hen." Arcana unscrewed the thermos and sipped dutifully. "Flare?"

"Wind of Fenris duel with Algae got out while we were away. I expected as much, which is why I followed up when we got back." Flare still had his communicator in hand and was looking at the screen, brows furrowed. "Turns out that Algae copped enough flak over his defeat that he disappeared to the pub - where he drink drank drunked, made a massive disgrace of himself and was thrown out."

"And is blaming me for the entire situation, I presume," in spite of his grave words, the corner of Fenris' mouth twitched in amusement.

Flare nodded. "Bingo, brother. Anyway, while Algae was *in* the pub, he was pretty vocal about Arcana and how she's his one true love and Fenris was an evildoer and blah, blah, blah." The fire sorcerer waved a dismissive hand. "Nothing we haven't heard before but vindictive enough that after the bouncers threw him out, they called the Tower to report it."

"Do you think he's a danger?" Fenris' head lifted.

"I know he is," Flare answered. "The angrier Algae gets, the more likely he is to do something stupid. Monumentally stupid. I issued a search order for him the moment I got the report."

"Probably passed out behind the waterfall at Lake Greene," Arcana said, sipping from the thermos again.

"First place they checked, followed by his house and all the other usual haunts, but no dice." Flare clicked his tongue against his teeth. "Apparently Algae was seen meeting with a hooded figure two days ago - about the time we were stuck down the well - and then hasn't been seen since."

"Not even at the Water Tower?" Arcana gasped. Algae might be a pompous ass but he took his duties at the Tower seriously.

"No, he's missed several rounds of duties," Flare replied. "I've just elevated him to wanted status and you, my dear sister, are now officially under my protection."

"What?" Arcana blinked.

"You heard me. If Algae's after anything, it'll be you. As First Flame, this is more my domain than anyone else's - so until you're ready to leave Sorcen, you're stuck with me." Flare pinned Arcana with a hard glare, daring her to argue. When she didn't, the fire sorcerer looked to Fenris. "If the time comes, I expect you to put that blade to use, brother."

"No mercy this time?" Fenris asked, looking not in the least perturbed by the idea.

Flare shook his head. "Not from me." He slipped a hand into his robes and withdrew a round, carved stone the size of his own fist. "Now, it's time to report to the Council."

"What is that?" Fenris asked, leaning over to get a better look.

"A jump stone," Flare clenched his fingers around the rock and the carvings began to glow. "They take a while to recharge, but it'll get us to the Fire Tower instantly - and minimise the amount of time Arcana's out in the open."

"I can't believe we're hiding from Algae," Arcana muttered, pushing off the fence.

"We're not hiding, we're being sensible," Flare returned. "Now, for this to work you all need to be touching me, so grab a handful and let's get out of here."

There was no use in arguing, so Arcana linked elbows with Flare and buried her other hand in the fur at Caelum's shoulder. Fenris tucked the greatsword under one arm and gripped Flare's other wrist.

"Okay, here goes. Next stop, the Fire Tower." Flare rubbed his thumb over the orb and the orange light grew steadily brighter until it shone like a miniature sun. The world dropped away and Arcana tightened her hold on Flare's arm as they fell with stomach lurching swiftness through a veil of howling black. The ground re-formed with a barely audible pop and Arcana staggered, clutching at Caelum for support.

"Urgh," Fenris managed, his face pale. "That was..."

"Yeah, sorry. The more people it has to move, the tougher the trip." Flare pocketed the darkened stone with an apologetic smile and gestured at the small, square room in which they had appeared. An orange sunburst took up most of the floor and afternoon sunlight streamed in through narrow windows. "Welcome to the Fire Tower."

"No guards?" Fenris looked mildly surprised.

"They're on the way - but the chances of Algae getting into any Tower with a search order out are slim," Flare replied. He turned to Arcana and swept a low bow. "After you, Grand Sorceress."

Arcana snorted, striding out into the vaulted foyer. The walls were hung with a variety of vibrant tapestries and set with arched windows. A long strip of vermillion carpet extended from the main doorway to the opposite wall, where a large carving depicted an ecstatic woman surrounded by leaping flames.

Arcana laid a hand against the stone. Flare joined her and their magic flowed free, lighting the carving in shades of bronze and gold. The solid stone dissolved and Arcana raised her face to the cool, tingling energy of the portal, stepping through to the Council chamber beyond. The Elders were already there, clustered around a thick tome that lay open on the large central table.

"Ah! The very sorceress we were waiting on," Vino beckoned with a gnarled hand.

"Good afternoon, your graces." Arcana inclined her head as she crossed the room. "My apologies for the delay. Our journey was a taxing one - I came as soon as I was able."

Vino smiled. "So I understand. Flare visited us earlier and described the unusual situation you faced in the mountains."

"Did he?" Arcana cut a glance at her brother, who shrugged.

"He certainly did - but before we go down that path, I must ask the First Flame if he's any news on our fugitive," Vino said, turning to Flare.

"Nothing yet, your grace," Flare replied. "The team is still searching."

"Really, your graces, I'm sure there's nothing to worry about. I've dealt with Algae before," Arcana held up both hands in a gesture of peace.

"Be that as it may, threats of any sort must be taken seriously," Brook said, her voice smooth and soothing. "Now, Vino - shall we get on with it?"

"Oh, yes. Of course. But first, I need your word that this discussion will remain private. This tome contains a selection of Sorcen history which is... Not in the public record," Vino said, indicating the large book before him.

Arcana frowned. "You have my word, your graces - and Caelum's, of course."

"And mine," Fenris added.

"Excellent. Now tell me, is this the place you saw on your journey?" Vino grasped the edges of the book and swung it around. An ink drawing lay over the vast majority of the two page spread, displaying a familiar crease in the mountains. The tiny waterfall was there, trickling down on the left into a small pool. A haphazard house slouched on the right hand side of the frame, with a winding path leading around the back of it. Clearly visible behind the building was a slight incline with a dais and a circular shaped structure atop it.

"I... Yes, I think so. But this was underground... There was a large, deep lake. The ridge line of the mountains is correct but they were further forward... What is this place?" Arcana trailed one finger across the surface of the page, lips pursed.

"This is the residence of the sorcerer Bering and his wife, Shala. A great many centuries ago, they ruled this locality." Vino tapped the house, the lands beyond. "They were a charismatic pair, from all reports, both strong water sorcerers with good farming land and a stable community."

"I'm waiting for the catch," Arcana said.

Vino smiled without humour. "Indeed. Over time, strange rumours began to emerge: stories of gods and sacrifices and terrible, dark magic." He flipped to the next page. "Is this the portal you were searching for?"

"Yes, that's it," Fenris nodded. "And these portraits... I presume these are the sorcerers in question?"

"Correct. Bering and Shala claimed your portal was a doorway to the heavens and that they alone possessed the keys to speak with the gods on the other side. Gods who had granted them extraordinary powers, and could bestow those powers upon other water sorcerers who made the appropriate sacrifice."

"Sacrifice?" Arcana repeated.

Vino nodded. "Bering and Shala were blood sorcerers."

Arcana covered her mouth with one hand, swallowing against the lump in her throat. Beside her, Flare's fingers flinched on the table top, his face pale.

"What is a blood sorcerer?" Fenris asked.

"Water sorcerers who extract water from the body of a living being. Forcibly," Vino said grimly.

"Water... from a living person?" Fenris' brow wrinkled and he glanced at Arcana. "I presume this is one of those lesser branches of magic you mentioned earlier."

"Yeah," Arcana swallowed heavily. "Water moves in a variety of forms - including blood. It's forbidden, of course, but sometimes there are still people crazy enough to give it a try."

"Yes. Unfortunately so." Vino turned the page to reveal several illustrations featuring grotesquely withered corpses. "Not only had Bering and Shala perfected the art, they were teaching it to other members of their cult. Those that could perform the technique were crowned blood sorcerers, and those that failed... gave their lives to the gods. Thousands of innocents were slaughtered in the process."

"That's just..." Arcana trailed off, her stomach knotting. "Surely they wouldn't have been able to actually power the portal?"

"No. A portal can only be activated by a Warden or Guardian, but it would be a powerful symbol nonetheless." Fenris crossed his arms over his chest, eyes narrowed in thought. "My guess is that these sorcerers used the portal to lend credence to their twisted ideology. Even inactive, the mystery of such an artefact would give untold weight to religious dogma."

"Correct. The blood cult's reliance on the portal was so widely accepted that several neighbouring clans united and determined to destroy the structure, no matter the cost - and it was great, as you've seen. Once it was over and the cult had been eliminated, the allied clans terraformed the site so that nobody else would be tempted to step onto the cursed ground. The first Council of Elders was born on that very soil." Vino's beard quivered, his mouth a thin line. "The people moved, escaping their nightmares and heading west, where they eventually built Sorca City. The Council decreed that the blood cult should be erased from public history lest it ever surface again - the site you discovered and the pages of this book are all that remain of it." Vino grasped the edges of the tome and closed it with a dull thud.

Arcana took a step back from the table, exhaling slowly. "And the flux?"

"Destroying the portal stones would create an explosion with more than enough errant energy to spawn a time flux," Fenris said quietly.

"I pray you understand our confusion when you first asked about the portal's existence," Brook's teeth were white and even as she smiled, her expression was tight. "We would never have thought to equate your gateway with such a dark moment in our history."

"Of course," Fenris inclined his head. Arcana glared at the raw-edged pages as Blaze slid the enormous book to the edge of the table and began buckling thick leather straps around the circumference. Once finished, the Fire Elder laid his hands across the closure, muttering under his breath.

"Oaths of secrecy and wards on the book... Just how much of our history is hidden away in there?" Arcana asked.

Gravella tossed her slate coloured braid over one shoulder. "That's not relevant to this discussion."

"Isn't it? I can understand the delicate nature of certain information but you play a dangerous game hiding it away." Arcana jerked her chin at the book. "The more forbidden a thing, the more desirable it becomes."

"Do you *really* think everyone should have access to such morbid tales?" Brook's face was white. "You were a water sorcerer once. Surely you understand the level of perversion required to perform such spells."

"Unless the Water Tower has seen fit to throw me out, I believe I am still on the register," Arcana hissed. "And I resent the idea that I *would* understand that level of perversion. Powerful magic has nothing to do with the forbidden arts, your grace. Morality is a choice."

The Water Elder recoiled, one hand on her chest. "My apologies. I only meant that you had ascended beyond, to..."

"To what?" Arcana asked, propping one fist on her hip. "Someone capable of blood sorcery if the wrong book were left lying around?"

"No! No, Arcana, of course not," Brook gushed, beseeching her with trembling hands. Arcana took a small but perceptible step backwards and those pale hands dropped. Brook swallowed. "The Water Tower would never throw you out - I only meant to reference that you no longer owe allegiance to a singular Tower and are your own classification."

Arcana blinked, her temper momentarily arrested by the odd phrasing. "What do you mean, I don't owe allegiance to a singular Tower?"

"Oh," Brook looked suddenly panicked. "I'm sure it's not really relevant to the discussion."

"Indulge me," Arcana commanded, crossing her arms over her chest.

Brook looked around for moral support and Arcana was not at all surprised when Gravella cut in. "According to the records, one Spring Lurien is registered to the Water Tower - and her status is suspended due to transformation."

"Suspended?" Arcana repeated.

"Yes." Gravella's sandstone eyes gleamed. "After much discussion, it was decided that it would be politically incorrect for you to show favour to any one Tower, so the Water Tower were asked to release you from your contract of service. If you bothered to visit more often, you would have known that."

Arcana pressed her lips together in what rapidly became an uncomfortable silence. "You couldn't have just registered me to *all* the Towers?" She said at last.

"That would have required your presence," Gravella's smile was vicious. "Barring that, there was no other choice but to remove you. I'm sure you understand."

"Arcana's Tower status is not the topic of discussion here, Elder Gravella," Lesce's tone was sharp with disapproval. "Let us remain focussed, please."

"Oh yes, the book of dirty secrets," Arcana's voice was hoarse with emotion - enough rage that the Council leant back as one, with the exception, perhaps, of Gravella and her thin-lipped smile. Arcana prodded the spine of the book. "Is this information hidden to protect the people, or to cover the shame of the Water Tower?"

"Shame?" Blaze hooked both thumbs through his belt and shook his head. "Are you mad? These people are long dead."

"Try telling *them* that," Arcana snapped. The Fire Elder's throat bobbed and he shuddered. She planted both palms on the edge of the table and leant towards them. "I understand that the actions of the blood cult were reprehensible, but we wasted several days and almost died because the facts were hidden away. Beyond that, surely the heroic actions of the sorcerers who prevailed are worth remembering. Do you really think those families who lost loved ones have forgotten, just because you told them to?"

"The decision on what gets told to whom is not up to you," Gravella snapped.

Arcana barked a sharp laugh. "No, it isn't, is it? That blame lies squarely on your shoulders... your grace."

Gravella's face purpled with rage but Vino laid a cautioning hand on her arm. "May I remind you, Grand Sorceress, that you gave your word on this matter before we began?"

"I did," Arcana nodded. "And you needn't worry, I won't break it. But hiding things from the people - our history, the pirate ships in the solar system - those things are wrong. This is a treacherous path that borders on tyranny at best and treason at worst."

"How dare you!" Gravella spat, shaking free from Vino's grasp. "We are the *Council*. You have no right to question us!"

"I am a citizen of Sorcen and I care for my people," Arcana hissed. "I'll question whatever I damned well like."

"I could have you thrown in prison," Gravella growled, leaning over the table with her teeth bared.

Arcana spread her arms wide. "Try it and see what happens."

"Please, ladies, that is quite enough." Vino held up an intervening hand. "Arcana, whilst I appreciate your enthusiasm, these laws were set into place by that first Council, centuries ago, for our people's protection. Your unique classification within our society does not give you the authority to wade in and change those laws, or to throw around baseless accusations. I must ask you to stand down."

"With all due respect, your grace, I won't. As the Council of Elders, you have a moral responsibility to our people *and* the authority to carry it through. Are you so tightly chained to the fears of long dead Elders that you've lost your own sense of reason?" Arcana held out her hands to Lesce, pleading with her sister. "These are your people, too. They deserve honesty and respect."

"I agree," Lesce said and beside her, Blaze nodded. "But without the unanimous vote of the Council, this law can't be undone and at the moment, there are far greater issues that require our attention."

"There always are," Arcana's lips twisted bitterly. "I find it entirely strange that you can vote so swiftly to have my name stricken from the register of the Water Tower, yet after several weeks, still haven't contacted the Galactic Alliance."

Vino's face darkened, his brows beetling. Before he had a chance to respond, Lesce placed a gentle hand on the Nature Elder's shoulder. "That matter is still under discussion." She locked eyes with Arcana, her stern voice full of warning. "Fenris - I have received word from the blacksmith that your commission is ready. Perhaps now would be a good time to collect it."

Fenris stepped smoothly in front of Arcana, cool fingers brushing her wrist. "An excellent suggestion, Elder Lesce. If it please you, we shall take this opportunity to bid farewell. Arcana and Caelum have volunteered to escort me to the Timeless Kingdom and as such, we will be leaving as soon as our preparations are made."

"How convenient - say your piece and scuttle off with your tail between your legs." Gravella leant back in her chair, lips pinched into a supercilious sneer.

"As you have so carefully pointed out, these issues are none of Arcana's concern." Fenris' tone was smooth but his words were so clipped Arcana could see fangs flashing in her mind's eye. "So unless you would prefer Arcana to continue challenging your misguided authority, I'd sit back and let us go."

The Earth Elder regarded them down the length of her nose, dismissing Fenris with little more than a flaring of her nostrils. It was to Arcana she looked, those slate coloured eyes measuring her length with a lazy contempt Gravella didn't bother to hide. When she spoke, her voice hissed through the room like a viper's. "Too bad, really, that you don't owe allegiance to any of the Towers. Such a sudden rise to power, only to be cast out by absolutely every single person you ever knew. Forged and forgotten - I wonder what that must be like." Her lips pursed, cherry red in the sunlight. "Without even the claim of your native Tower, you have less rights than the cattle on our farms. No wonder you hide in that flea-bitten starship; it's certainly better than the understanding that you are, now and always, *nothing*."

Arcana's breath caught in her throat; the Council stared open-mouthed. But it was Flare who leant forward, placing both hands flat on the Council table, his lips peeled back in a snarl of unadulterated fury. "How *dare* you," he spat.

Gravella blinked, her superior facade fracturing. "Flare-"

"Arcana has given more to this planet than any one person ever should, and you all know it." Flare pinned Gravella with his stare, smoke curling from beneath his palms. "You are a disgrace to the Council."

"That will be quite enough, First Flame," Brook's voice was breathless but she gathered herself up, literally fisting her hands in her robes for fortitude. "Show some respect."

"Show some respect?" Flare's breathing came ragged, tongue flicking over dry lips. He lifted one hand, revealing a perfect handprint scorched into the table beneath. Arcana was not the only one to gasp in surprise; involuntary displays of magic were so rare as to be considered almost impossible. But Flare was oblivious - he spat into the palm of his hand, the saliva sizzling on contact. "Respect is earnt; on the battlefield, in the Council chamber, before the kitchen hearth - by deed or word to defend the rights and honour of others." Flare strode toward Arcana, spit-soaked hand extended. He was already growling, the spell building in clean, bright lines across the veins in his hand. She swallowed heavily as Gravella's words hissed through her mind. *Nothing, nothing, nothing. Forged and forgotten.* Flare halted in front of her, throwing a cutting glance over his shoulder as he mouthed the final syllables of his spell. Gravella paled as his lips twisted in fury. "Respect *this*."

Arcana spat in her hand and clapped it into Flare's waiting palm.

Light flashed through the room, blinding and brilliantly white - so bright Arcana closed her eyes against it, so bright that the other occupants were hidden from view. When it faded, her hand glowed where it joined with Flare's, ringed in threads of spiralling runes that bound them as surely as if a rope had been wrapped around both wrists. It was a simple spell, a rarely used declaration of allegiance and honour that had once been reserved for royalty. Arcana's heart swelled and she thought that she had never loved her brother so much as she did in that moment. And Flare? His face was wreathed in unholy light, jaw clenched as he sought a now trembling Gravella, silver tears rimming her eyes.

He opened his mouth.

"Don't," Arcana said simply. Flare paused. "Enough."

He dragged his fierce gaze to hers. "You are my *sister.*"

"And I'm asking you to stand down." She cupped his cheek with her free hand. "You've made your point. Let it go."

For a moment she thought he wouldn't listen; that he'd fall prey to the fierce temper she had seen only once before - the night he'd reduced Algae's house to ashes. But Flare inhaled, his broad chest inflating until Arcana wondered if he might burst. He held it for a second, two, and then exhaled in a great gust, the tension bleeding out of him. Arcana leant in and pressed a soft kiss to his cheek; Flare bowed his head as though to a queen. Their hands slipped free, runes vanishing in a puff of smoke. In a single moment, Flare had turned the tables of the argument and it was clear the Council knew it, each one regarding Arcana with varying degrees of distress - bar Gravella, whose horrified expression was still fixed on Flare.

Arcana drew herself up. "As I owe no allegiance to *any* of the Towers, none of you have the ability to detain me - though as I said before, you are certainly welcome to try."

Silence. Absolute, horrified silence.

"Excellent. In that case, I'll take my leave. Good luck with your government," Arcana bowed stiffly from the waist, then turned and marched towards the nearest portal, flanked by both Fenris and Flare, Caelum ghosting silently along behind.

"I'm sorry," Flare murmured as they laid their hands against the stone carving and began pouring magic in. Bright orange runes shimmered beneath the surface of his skin - they'd fade with distance, but whilst he and Arcana were together, their oath to each other would be clear for all to see. Flare stared at the runes and then back up at Arcana. "I can't believe she said that."

Arcana offered a half smile. "Gravella never liked me; not even before the change. It's nothing new, Flare."

"Yes, but-" he checked himself, worrying his lower lip. "I'm proud of you. Someone needs to put those idiots in their place."

"I don't think it worked, but thanks anyway." Arcana squeezed his fingers for a moment and then let go, looking for Fenris. He was already there, lips quirked in an odd sort of smile that allowed the tips of his fangs to poke at his lower lip.

"My lady," Fenris purred, his voice pitched perfectly to carry back to the Council behind them. He swept a low, flourishing bow and gestured her to precede him. "I am at your service."

Arcana couldn't help the wicked grin which spread across her face as she looked from one male to the other, each unwavering in their support. Any lingering hurt the Council had caused faded as she drew herself up, lifted her chin, and stepped through the portal without so much as a backwards glance.

CHAPTER
ELEVEN

Sorca City's streets passed by in a blur. The citizens drew back as usual but Arcana was so deeply entrenched in her own fury she barely noticed. Fenris and Caelum stalked on either side of her, the latter uncharacteristically silent and the former doing an impressive - and probably well practiced - show of looking dangerous. Flare trailed a few paces behind, his voice low as he answered a call from his communicator, the device affording him a rare moment of peace from the usually enthusiastic citizens of the city.

Arcana paused beside the green, inviting pathway which led to the smithy's front door, flattening her hand against the cool brickwork and taking several deep, slow breaths. Flare finished his call and stepped up beside her with a frown. "I'm going to have to run," he said by way of opening. "There's been a potential Algae sighting that I need to follow up."

"Want backup?" Arcana asked.

"Nah," he shook his head. "You get that scabbard and I'll meet you afterwards. I want to try and sort this out before the Council reach a unanimous decision to fire my ass."

"They won't fire you," Arcana teased, forcing a smile onto her face. "You're too pretty."

Flare's answering grin was slow and tight. "We'll see." His smile faded and he shook his head. "Not the way I wanted to end things with Gravella but maybe this is for the best. I can't believe she said that to you."

"Did you know they cut me off the rosters completely?" Arcana asked.

"Of course not - I'd have lost my shit at them," Flare growled. "I might be in charge of the armies but I'm not involved in every discussion the Council has. I'll wager Lesce was outvoted and didn't want me to make a fuss."

"Mmmm." Arcana nodded, trying to smother the sting.

"Hey," Flare stepped in and gave her a quick, fierce hug. "I know you feel cut out but remember I'm here."

"Thanks, Flare." Arcana pressed a kiss to her brother's cheek. "Now go before Algae disappears. I'll catch you later, I promise."

"All right." Flare stepped back and gave Fenris a hard look. "I'm counting on you to watch her while I'm gone. This could be a ruse to catch us off guard."

"I will defend Arcana with my life," Fenris promised, clicking his heels together and offering Flare a half bow.

"Excuse me, egos one and two? I'm right here," Arcana waved a hand between them and both men laughed.

"I know, I know - I'm paranoid. But I've got a feeling." Flare frowned. "Look after each other."

"We will," Arcana replied. Flare tossed a little wave over his shoulder and blended back into the crowd with a trail of fluttering eyelashes and giggling fans following in his wake.

"Are you all right?" Fenris asked, his voice pitched low.

"I will be," Arcana returned, closing her eyes and trying to exhale the tension she'd carried from the Council chamber. "I just need a moment. Wright and Briolette don't deserve my bad temper."

"Do you realise the Council are afraid of you?" Fenris reached out a gentle finger and tilted her head up.

Arcana blinked. "I beg your pardon?"

"You heard me," Fenris' grin was slow and wicked. "You really didn't know?"

"I - don't be ridiculous." Arcana jerked her chin away and glared up at him. "The Council are many things, but afraid of me is certainly not one of them."

"Are you sure?" Fenris paused, a long, drawn out moment, and then tapped his nose with a slender finger. "Because I could smell it."

Arcana stared at him, her jaw working. "Why would they be afraid of *me*?"

"Power," he shrugged, picking at the leather wrappings on the greatsword's hilt. "They feed you titbits of information, let you into their inner sanctum, make you feel special - and in return, they give you the illusion of control. Today, you broke that illusion."

"Control isn't an illusion. You either have it or you don't - and as evidenced by Gravella's timely reminder, I don't."

"You *think* you don't, but you are wrong. Flare is one of the most beloved and powerful sorcerers on the planet, is he not? And who did he just swear to?" Fenris asked. Arcana growled low in her throat and his lips twitched. "Very well then, let me ask you this - could you defeat them?"

"What?"

"If it came to a fight, a true test of strength," Fenris clarified. "Could you defeat the Council?"

Arcana sucked on her teeth, her mind grinding reluctantly into motion. "Lesce is non-combative, so she's no threat. Blaze and Brook never work well together, would be easy to separate - or to catch in each other's crossfire. Vino is crafty, he'd be the challenge... Gravella's the most powerful on paper but she burns through her magic too quickly. If I took her out first, kept out of Vino's way long enough to disable Brook and Blaze..." she shrugged. "I suppose it's possible. Difficult, but possible."

"You suppose..." Fenris shook his head, blinking rapidly. "I actually meant one on one, but you have just admitted you may be capable of defeating them *all at once* - the five most powerful sorcerers on your planet - and you wonder that they're afraid of you?"

"I wouldn't be alone," Arcana protested, temper vanishing as she backed up a step. "Caelum would be there."

"And Flare," Caelum added.

"Oh yes. Flare would set fire to the universe in your name and dance in the ashes as you fashioned it anew," Fenris' eyes sparkled with wicked glee. "That much was obvious even before the... spit shake."

Arcana frowned, momentarily diverted. "It was more than a spit shake. It was a binding spell - an oath of allegiance." Fenris remained silent, waiting, so she elaborated; "They're archaic, a relic of the time when all our people were split into clans and allegiances were worn like Tower colours."

"The ultimate signal of loyalty and respect," Fenris nodded.

"Yes. They fell into disuse when our people were united under the Council, but - the symbolism speaks for itself."

"So I saw," Fenris took hold of Arcana's wrist, turning it back and forth. She clenched her fist and the runes activated, glowing like embers just below the surface of her skin. He rubbed a thumb over one of the characters and said; "For something that hasn't been utilised for centuries, you both seemed remarkably familiar with the practice."

Arcana shrugged. "We've talked about it, just never done it. When the Council had me... under observation, I pretty much read and attempted every spell in written history. Flare's a bit of a history buff and is always researching old spells and languages in his spare time."

"So you both knew the spell in advance." Fenris released Arcana's wrist, a rogue's grin tugging at the corners of his mouth. "Do you truly still doubt your influence when Flare swore allegiance to you over and above the Council?"

"Oh, please." Arcana threw both hands up in the air. "Flare's statement was for Gravella, and Gravella alone - I would never challenge the Council."

There was a long silence, into which Fenris' smile said more than any words he could have offered. "I dare say Gravella got the point. Nevertheless, the source of your frustration with the Council is born from their fear. If you can understand that, then *you* will control *them* - without ever having to lift a magical finger."

"I'm not sure how I feel about that, but thanks anyway." Arcana straightened and cut a glance at Caelum. "I notice you didn't have much to say."

He gave her a look that was half-wild with anxiety. "Your emotions too, remember? Bit hard to think when I'm drowning in your rage."

"I'm sorry." Arcana stroked her hands along his jaw, immediately contrite. "I forgot."

"Don't worry about it." He nudged her with his nose and then, when she did start worrying about it, nipped swiftly at one ear. "I'm serious. Give a poor guy a break, will you?"

Arcana blushed. "Right. Sorry. Let's go in, shall we?" Caelum nodded, stepping back to allow her around the corner and into the clanking, steaming chaos of the smithy.

Wright looked up as they entered, his sweaty face breaking into a broad grin. "Welcome, welcome," He dropped his tools on a scarred bench and crossed the room in three easy strides, crushing Arcana to his chest.

"Hello, Wright." She plastered a smile on her face, returning the embrace with an awkward pat to the other man's burly shoulders.

"I was starting to think you'd forgotten me," Wright's ochre eyes twinkled as he set her back on her feet.

"Of course not! I got caught up with some official business," Arcana waved a vague hand. "Now, what have you got for me?"

Nothing! But for him? Oh, I think you'll like it." Wright snatched a wrapped bundle from a nearby rack and handed it to Fenris.

"Thank you." Fenris propped the greatsword against a bench and carefully unwrapped the bundle. The scabbard's silver housing shimmered in the light of the forge, an intricate pattern of twists and swirls that mimicked the etching on the greatsword's blade. Dark brown leather was visible beneath, tooled in a subtler pattern to match.

"This is excellent craftsmanship." Fenris hefted the greatsword in one hand and slid it slowly into the scabbard, settling the leather rim snug against the hilt. "And a true fit."

Wright nodded. "It suits you."

Fenris swung the scabbard over his shoulder and adjusted the chest strap. "You have my gratitude; it is perfect. And so light," he added, jumping up and down on the spot.

"Don't thank me for that, Briolette's the one who does all the mumbo jumbo," Wright laughed, wiggling his fingers in the air around him. "Ah, I forgot! She also made this for you. A gift." The smith produced a small leather pouch and set it into Fenris' open hands.

"Oh?" Fenris flicked a glance at Arcana, who shrugged.

"It can attach to a belt if you prefer, or to the strap of the scabbard, which should sit it near your hip. Bigger than it looks, of course," Wright grinned.

"How much bigger?" Fenris asked, flipping the pouch open and peering inside.

"Big enough for your basics - a few days' worth of food, water, clothes. May not fit that giant blade of yours, but definitely smaller tools or spare weapons." The smith scratched his head and shrugged. "You'll work out the limits soon enough."

"Thank you." Fenris offered his forearm, which Wright pumped enthusiastically.

"It's no problem! A friend of Arcana's is a friend of ours. Your sister already set up the payment, by the way," Wright said over his shoulder.

Arcana rolled her eyes. "Of course she did. Well, that saves me doing it, I guess. Is Briolette in? I'd like to thank her."

"She was having a nap, but she'd be annoyed if you didn't wake her," Wright waved a hand towards the house. "Go on in."

"Thanks." Arcana smiled, moving to the door and sliding it open. Beyond was not the spacious interior of the house she'd expected, but a pair of flat, amber eyes bordered by dirty grey fur.

Warg.

Fenris shouted a warning but Arcana had already lurched backwards, sweeping her magic through the smithy and collecting the giant, blasting heat of the forge. The warg's face drew into a snarl, lips peeling back to reveal rows of dripping fangs, a growl issuing from the depths of his muscular chest. The creature lunged and Arcana ducked between his reaching arms, thrusting her fist deep into the warg's gaping mouth and pouring fire down his throat. She leapt aside as the corpse toppled onto the floor of the smithy, leaving her arm streaked with blood and soot.

"What is *that*?" Wright leapt back with a gasp, eyes wide.

"A warg."

"But - but I thought the warg were just giant wolves," Wright managed.

Arcana reached out to poke one of the warg's legs with the toe of her boot, making sure it was truly dead. "No. Not wolves, not human - somewhere in between. They walk on two legs, they can fly ships, wield swords and bake bread. They have the intelligence of humanity, the vicious nature of a wild beast. The head and fur and claws of wolves, on human shaped bodies."

Wright stared white faced at the distinctly male body, broad chest and narrow hips visible even beneath the thick coat of fur. Atop the shoulders, those lupine jaws still gaped wide, displaying scimitar fangs and a lolling, soot blackened tongue. "I... I never knew."

"Most people don't - they usually just die." Screams echoed out in the street and Arcana cursed under her breath. "He wasn't alone. Where's the bedroom? We need to get Briolette to safety."

The air in the smith flickered as if in a heat haze, and three more warg appeared. Fenris drew the greatsword and decapitated one of the creatures in a flash, whirling and driving the blade deep into the belly of the second. Caelum lowered his head and skewered the third with his antlers, tossing the twitching corpse out into the street. Fenris set his feet and turned to Arcana. "There will be more. Go and fetch Briolette - I'll guard the door."

"Wright?" Arcana turned to her companion.

The blacksmith snatched a short sword from a nearby rack. "Third door on the left."

Arcana threw herself into the house with Caelum close behind, ducking the swiping claws of another warg as it materialised out of thin air. Arcana rolled both wrists and her hands burst into flame, forcing the creature - a female, judging by her curves and slighter stature - to retreat or catch alight. Arcana lobbed a fireball and the warg leapt aside, ducking behind the island bench amidst the stench of singed fur. Arcana sidestepped to the bedroom door, flaming hands clenched into fists. "Get to Briolette. Wait inside until I say it's safe." The smith dipped his chin once and disappeared.

Caelum circled the outer edge of the kitchen, the bladed edges of his antlers shimmering in the muted light from the windows. The warg's rhythmic growl paced the length of the bench and back again but not so much as a hair showed. Arcana hesitated, listening to the sound and weighing her options. She dared not throw too much fire around, lest the house go up in smoke - but it wouldn't take long for the warg to figure that out. Better, then, to strike first. She dumped her fire magic, flattening one hand against the wall and absorbing the essence of the stone house.

Motioning to Caelum to wait, Arcana focussed on the warg's rhythmic growling, trying to judge the speed at which it paced. She curled one hand into a fist and the floor fractured, expelling a sharp stone spike which caught the warg through one leg and hoisted her high in the air.

The creature curled her body upwards, tugging to be free of the stone which had impaled her leg but to no avail. With a howl of fury, the warg began tearing into her own flesh with claws and teeth. Caelum lowered his head and charged but the warg wrenched away at the last moment, dropping to the floor in a pool of blood and gore. She knuckled both hands and her one remaining leg into the tiles and pounced with a blood curdling howl. Caelum twisted, catching the creature with his antlers only to topple in a grunting tangle of bloodied limbs.

The warg snapped at Caelum's face while his blades tore great gashes in her furred flesh and Arcana began to fear the creature would dismember herself just to land a blow. With a monumental heave, Caelum got his feet beneath him and flung the warg aside. She hit the ground hard and Arcana summoned a rain of stone shards. Several drilled into the warg's bleeding body but she dodged the one meant for her head, spitting and hissing in impotent rage. Arcana strode across the room, a final stone spike materialising in the palm of her hand. The warg snarled and snapped, straining to reach her enemy even though she was pinned, her body ruined and bleeding. Murmuring a blessing for the lost, Arcana braced her feet and buried her stone weapon deep in the creature's skull. The warg stiffened, then sagged back against the carpet, still at last.

"Wright?" Arcana called, turning to watch the bedroom door open. The blacksmith emerged sword-first, his other arm wrapped around the shoulders of his pregnant wife. "Are you hurt?"

"No," Wright replied. Briolette took one look at the mangled body on the floor and began retching violently.

"I got this." Caelum scooped up the warg and flung her body over the bench and out of sight. He was covered in blood, fur matted and antlers dripping, but Arcana wrapped her arms around his neck and squeezed nonetheless. Caelum nuzzled at her ear. "We need to get Briolette to safety."

"We will. Where's Fenris?" Arcana craned her head to look over Caelum's shoulder.

"Here." Fenris appeared in the smithy doorway, the greatsword in one hand. Blood splashed up one arm and across his chest but a cursory glance assured Arcana that none of it was his own.

"How many?" She asked as he jogged to her side.

"Hundreds. Maybe thousands. All over the city," he replied, his face grim.

"Gods *dammit*," Arcana growled. She sucked on her teeth. "Okay, first we get Wright and Briolette to safety, then we see about this mess. Stand firm now." She dropped to one knee and flattened both hands against the floor. Carpet buckled and tore as the ground split and dropped away, revealing a slanted tunnel leading into the earth.

"Under the floor?" Fenris asked, stepping out of the way as Caelum urged Wright and Briolette down the slope.

"In the event of an invasion, earth sorcerers open entrances to the underground tunnel network. The tunnels join to a series of safe chambers deep beneath the surface. It means the city can be evacuated swiftly and everyone is easier to protect until the danger has passed." Arcana cast a final look over the blood spattered kitchen and then waved him after Caelum.

"A clever defence," Fenris nodded, sheathing the greatsword as he passed her by.

"As long as we can hold the entrances," Arcana flicked her fingers as she followed him down, drawing the floor closed and plunging the tunnel into darkness.

"Anyone got a light?" Caelum asked, his shoulder bumping hers. There was a long silence, into which he sighed gustily. "Thought not."

"I might be able to help." Fenris stepped forward, the fire in his eyes casting a soft jade glow over the planes of his face. The illumination was barely more than an alleviation of true darkness but it was a light none-theless - enough to see his fangs glisten as he smiled. "I can see in the dark. If you hold on to me, I will guide us safely."

"Neat party trick," Caelum observed.

"Thank you." Fenris offered his other arm to Briolette, whose green-tinged face was set with determination.

"There will be torches once we hit the main network; stay close until then." Arcana moved forward with her arms outstretched, feeling her way to the front wall of the tunnel. The rock was cool and smooth, buckling beneath her fingertips as she flexed them experimentally. Magic flowed from her hands, spreading through the earth in search of the tunnels that wound beneath Sorca City. Arcana stepped forward, pushing with the flat of her hands and the wall retreated with a shuddering groan.

"What's happening?" Briolette's voice hitched in panic.

"It's all right, I'm just forming the tunnel. We don't have far to go." Arcana clenched her teeth, a line of sweat breaking out across her brow as she pushed again. Moving the wall was like walking through thick molasses - though perhaps less delicious, she reflected, and wished suddenly for the restorative powers of a honey and lemon tea.

"Has Arcana no limits?" Fenris murmured, his voice almost lost beneath the roar of the earth around them.

"Given we're walking by the glow of your eyeballs, I'd say you can answer your own question," Caelum returned. "Can't make fire from stone, can you?"

"Even so, the amount of strength required to open the earth in this way is incredible," Fenris said, his tone light and conversational. "She's barely breaking a sweat."

Arcana blushed in spite of herself, pausing to scrub her forehead on the sleeve of her dress. Sweating from hard work was one thing, but knowing he was *looking* was another entirely. Was that a throaty chuckle she heard, or just the grinding of stone on stone? "I have plenty of limits," she said, trying not to sound testy. "I just don't talk about them often. Particularly while I'm sweating."

"Fenris can... you really see?" Briolette gasped. The panicked edge to her voice subsided into curiosity.

"I am naturally nocturnal. So yes, I can see quite clearly - as well as you see in the daylight."

"Is that... Why your eyes..." Briolette trailed off, panting heavily.

"Why they glow?" He chuckled again and Arcana narrowed her eyes. He *had* been laughing earlier. "Correct. Unfortunately it's not bright enough for everyone to see their way."

"It's nice... Just to see... Something," Briolette managed.

"Are you okay, plumapple?" Wright asked.

"Yes," Briolette grunted. "Just pregnant."

"You're not..."

"No," she returned. "The baby's fine. Just very heavy."

"Are you sure?"

"Wright!"

"Okay." The smith subsided with a grumble and Arcana bit her lip to stop a laugh escaping. They pushed on for another few minutes in silence - or at least, as silent as it was possible to be with the rumbling walls and Briolette's laboured breathing - before Arcana drew to a halt, leaning her forehead against the rock for a few precious moments of rest.

"Arcana?" Fenris' query was calm but she knew he could see her and wondered how drawn her face was. Her body ached but she pushed the discomfort aside and straightened.

"We're here. Stand ready." Arcana slid her hands across the stone wall as though opening a curtain. The veil of rock hissed and shuddered as it split apart, revealing a wide, well-lit corridor. There was nobody in sight but the hum of voices echoed from further up the tunnel. She turned back to find Fenris watching her and studiously avoided his gaze. Oblivious to her discomfort, Wright and Briolette stepped blinking into the light, their faces wreathed in relief.

"Thank the Gods for you, Arcana," Briolette breathed, delivering a worshipful smile which made Arcana fidget. "We made it."

"Almost. Head that way." Arcana pointed in the direction of the voices. "I need to close our tunnel, so I'll catch up." Wright gripped his wife's arm and she smiled in thanks when Fenris moved to support her other side. Arcana brought her hands together as though to pray and the gap in the wall ground shut, the tunnel through which they had walked now no more than memory.

"Done?" Caelum waited alone in the torchlight, his fur a sticky mess of blood and grime. The blades on his antlers had retracted, leaving a macabre display of whorled velvet and warg gobbets. "The others are well out of sight."

"Done," Arcana nodded, wrapping one hand in his fur and swinging onto his back - where Caelum's coat was just as sticky with blood as his chest and flanks. She winced. "I'm going to have to set fire to this dress after today."

"At least you *can* burn your dress." Caelum set off up the tunnel at a brisk trot. "I'll never get my fur clean."

"So dramatic." Arcana rolled her eyes. "I can set us both on fire if you want, but I think you'll regret it more than my dress will. And I liked this dress."

"Eh, it was already ruined." Caelum's mouth dropped open in a grin. "Wait until you see yourself in the mirror."

"Thanks. I think," she snorted and shook her head. The echoing voices grew steadily louder and they rounded a bend to discover Fenris and his charges hesitating at the mouth of a large chamber.

"There you are." Fenris looked relieved. "I was starting to think you had been ambushed."

"No, I'm fine. Just tired." She offered him a wan smile, which he returned. "Let's find Briolette somewhere to rest."

"Arcana, is that you?" A sharp voice cut across the hubbub and the crowd inside the cavern immediately parted. Arcana slid to the ground as Gravella stepped out, her face grim.

"Earth Elder." It was impossible to keep the ice from her voice, but Arcana managed a brusque nod and then motioned to Briolette. "Are there healers here?"

"Of course. You there! Help these people," Gravella snapped over her shoulder. Two sorcerers immediately detached themselves from the throng and ushered Briolette away.

"Thank you." Wright grasped Arcana's arm, heedless of the blood on her sleeve.

"Take care of her," Arcana returned. He nodded, then hurried after his wife.

Gravella opened her mouth to speak but Fenris stepped deftly in front of her. "We should keep moving. The longer the warg are allowed to rampage, the greater their damage," he murmured.

"I know." Arcana frowned, accepting a glass of fruit juice from a nearby water sorcerer and downing it in three large gulps. "But it means talking to the Earth Elder."

Fenris raised an eyebrow. "For permission?"

Arcana fought the urge to slap that scathing look off his face and said; "For information. Only a fool would barrel above ground unprepared."

"You wound me with such implications." Fenris gave her a roguish grin and stepped aside, revealing a red-faced Gravella who, wisely, had kept her silence.

Arcana swept a critical glance over the other woman, noting that whilst her clothing was dishevelled she appeared otherwise unharmed. "What's the situation?"

Gravella's face twisted momentarily into the superior sneer she saved for Arcana alone but Fenris cleared his throat in warning and the Earth Elder's expression smoothed. "There are warg everywhere. They appeared simultaneously all over the city. As per Sorcen lore, the military has assumed protective control of the city while the battle is in progress."

"I thought as much." Arcana sucked on her teeth. "Are all the non-combatants here?"

"Hard to tell," Gravella turned both hands palm upward. "There are a few chambers like this one. We're trying to catalogue everybody but it's a lengthy process."

"Any warg in the tunnels?"

"Some; they've been repelled so far. We have guards at both the chamber and tunnel entrances. I wanted to close some of the tunnels completely but it would mean nobody can get in," Gravella sighed, rubbing at one temple. She hesitated, then in a voice that sounded a lot like she were in pain, said; "You know more about the warg than I do. What would you advise?"

Wondering how much those words had cost the Elder's pride, Arcana cast a quick, assessing look around the cavern. "Leave the tunnels open but guard them well. Find anyone who can fight - regardless of age or classification - and station them with the guards who are already there. Set up shifts so they don't get too tired." She waited as Gravella relayed the order to a nearby earth sorcerer, then pointed at the roof. "I need to return to the surface to assist in the battle."

"I'll go with you," Gravella said quickly.

"No," Arcana shook her head. "Protocol dictates that when control is handed to the military, the Elders stay here in safety with the people."

"I know what protocol dictates," Gravella returned, her eyes flashing. "But Flare's up there somewhere."

"Yes, leading the fight - that's his job," Arcana said firmly. "Yours is to stay here and look after our people."

Gravella's jaw flexed and her hands curled into fists. After a cursory glance at the people around her, she stepped in until she was so close to Arcana that their noses almost touched. "You listen here, you trumped-up excuse for a magician. I love that man, and I know you're going to find him," Gravella murmured, her breath a soft caress against Arcana's cheek. "If you don't take me with you, I'll go alone - and I'm sure everyone will simply adore hearing about the way you deserted an Elder in her hour of need."

Arcana was silent for a moment, considering. The Earth Elder was trouble but refusing to take her would result in chaos, particularly if she went alone, which Arcana had no doubt she would. There was no choice, not really - and Gravella knew it, from the sneer of her lips to the triumphant set of her shoulders. Arcana raised a finger and prodded the other woman in the chest, lips twisting into a snarl. "If I do this, you have to agree to follow every order I give you. Lives are at stake here and I'm not risking them just so you can lick Flare's face like a puppy - particularly when he made his position more than clear in the Council chambers."

"You know nothing -"

"I know everything," Arcana cut her off, words no more than a breathy growl. "I know all of it, every slimy detail, and you know what? *He still chose me*." It was a low blow and Arcana knew it but she refused to let up, pushing into Gravella's personal space. "I am *not* taking responsibility for you unless you agree to follow my orders. That's the deal; take it or I leave."

Gravella's eyes were like cut diamonds, sharp and glittering, her breathing ragged with rage. For a moment Arcana thought the Earth Elder might actually attack her, so brutal was the fury contorting her features; and then it was gone beneath a cool veneer of disdain which Gravella slipped on like a coat. "Very well," she muttered. "I will behave."

Arcana wound one hand around Gravella's long braid and gave a warning tug, lips close to the other's ear. "You better. Because you so much as breathe wrong out there and I'll feed you to the gods-damned warg myself." This time Gravella's face paled but Arcana didn't allow herself time to enjoy it as she looked out over the crowd, raising her voice. "Right, I'm going topside and I'm taking Elder Gravella with me. Who's next in charge?"

"I am." A sturdy looking water sorcerer stepped forward, his navy hair flecked with white. "Class Two water sorcerer Whorl, adviser to Elder Brook, reporting for duty."

"Right. If warg come, kill them quickly. They're fast, so you need to be accurate - don't waste time with a chest shot unless you have to and take off the head, even if you think the creature is dead." She paused while Whorl absorbed the information and nodded his understanding, then looked out at the pale faced citizens of Sorcen. "You have never seen anything like these beasts before. They will not stop until you're dead - or they are. Military or no, we must all fight together to survive."

"It will be done, ma'am." Whorl accorded a half bow and hurried away.

Arcana turned to the Earth Elder, who was doing her best not to look uncomfortable. "Which tunnel is the shortest route to the surface?"

"That one - but it's where the warg have been filtering in," Gravella pointed to the central tunnel.

"Forget that. If we see one, we'll kill it." Arcana waved a dismissive hand. "Caelum, can you carry everyone?"

"Of course." Caelum dropped to his knees and the surrounding crowd murmured and drifted back a step.

Gravella's face paled. "I can walk."

"While we dither, people are dying. Get on or stay behind." Arcana slid onto Caelum's back and waited. The Earth Elder bit her lip a moment, then nodded and slipped into place. Fenris settled himself behind them both, his slender fingers gentle as they caught at Arcana's hips, sandwiching the Earth Elder between them.

Caelum surged to his feet, eliciting a startled squeak from Gravella, and trotted to the cavern's entrance. Arcana nodded to the guards and then they were through, picking up speed, heading silently towards the surface. Warg corpses dotted the tunnel at irregular intervals, some alone and others with Sorcen bodies beside them. Arcana hardened her heart and focussed forward, where the light from the outside world grew ever brighter and the sounds of battle drew closer.

They crested the lip of the tunnel and Caelum slowed, dancing around a jumble of bloodied rocks. The scent of burning flesh filled the air and a small, ragged group of fire sorcerers stood back to back at the entrance, blasting warg that seemed to rain from the sky around them. Arcana flung an arm outward and giant stone spikes shot out of the ground, slicing through the warg in a giant wave and peppering the area with their corpses.

"Thanks," one of the sorcerers said, his face drawn with exhaustion.

"Any time." Arcana glanced around as Caelum slipped out of the tunnel into what had once been some sort of large building. "The warg know this is the way to our people - they'll be back."

"We're not going anywhere," a sorceress replied, cracking her knuckles.

"Good. I'll make the entrance smaller so it's easier to guard. Stand inside and make them come at you one at a time," Arcana instructed, clenching one hand into a fist. Behind them, the tunnel's mouth began to pucker and pinch, folding inwards until it was no more than a slit in the rock.

"Thank you, Grand Sorceress," the first man replied, bowing deeply.

"You're welcome. Have any of you seen Flare?"

"He was at the Fire Tower when the warg appeared. I've not seen him since but I'd wager he's nearby." The fire sorcerer tapped his chin in thought. "If I had to guess, I'd say he was overseeing the evacuation."

Arcana nodded. "Thanks, we'll head that way. Keep an eye out for stray survivors."

"We will." the man tossed a salute then jogged to the narrowed entrance, following his companions through.

Caelum turned away from the tunnel, picking his way through the building until they emerged in the middle of the city. Many of the houses were already reduced to rubble and those still standing were scorched and scarred. Greenery littered the streets, peppering both Sorcen and warg corpses and turning the ground into a treacherous maze - made worse by the water dribbling down walls or pooling in gutters.

Arcana turned her eyes skyward, where the silhouette of the five Towers was visible above the pitted roofs. "Take it slow. Head for the Healing Tower," she murmured. Caelum flickered an ear in acknowledgement, picking his way across the street and into the lee of a gutted house.

"The guards said Flare was at the Fire Tower," Gravella hissed.

Arcana spared her a brief, hard look. "Did you receive any training *at all* when you ascended?"

"Of course," Gravella bit back, her words low and vicious.

"Then you should know that in the event of an emergency, the Healing Tower takes the longest to evacuate," Arcana snapped. "You should also know that once the other four Towers are safely emptied, remaining forces converge on the Healing Tower to lend aid."

Gravella's jaw worked, her face visibly torn between defending her status as an Elder and admitting she'd forgotten in the face of her own fear. Eventually, she settled on: "So?"

"So if Flare is anywhere, that's where he'll be. He knows how the warg work and he'll be trying to draw them out into the most open, well-lit area. If it was me, I'd set the main defence at the base of the Healing Tower and wait," Arcana said.

Gravella hesitated. "Why not retreat to the caverns? Defend the tunnel entrances?"

"Because you don't want to lure the enemy to where the children are hiding," Fenris supplied. "You want the battlefield to be as far as possible from those in the most danger - especially when the warg are involved. It is already bad enough that the warnings were ignored."

"They came from nowhere," Gravella protested.

"Really?" Fenris' tone thickened with scorn. "You mean to tell me you haven't made the connection between anonymous ships raiding the outlying edges of your system and this convenient invasion?"

"Those were pirate raids," she snapped.

"Do you know anyone who trades willingly with the warg?"

Gravella stiffened against Arcana's spine. "Of course not."

"Then how do you expect they accumulate food and other supplies if not through piracy?" Fenris asked. The Earth Elder said nothing.

"More concerning than that is *how* they managed to get close enough to teleport planetside." Arcana pointed at one of the bodies, a male warg clad in tattered shorts and little else. "Look - no personal units, meaning that someone transported them en masse. The sheer numbers alone mean several starships are involved. Where were our early warning systems?"

"Disabled, I'd assume," Fenris replied.

"They have to be." Arcana frowned. "The only thing in our favour is the invasion clearly isn't going as planned."

Gravella shivered, her body pressing closer as Caelum skirted a tangled mass of limbs. "How can you know that?"

"The warg attack in large numbers and swarm mindlessly over their prey, heedless of the cost. Most planets fall quickly and completely but the people of Sorcen are not as squishy as we appear." Arcana's smile was vicious. "If you look closely, you'll see there are more warg corpses than sorcerers."

"I don't want to look at any of them," Gravella admitted.

"Which is one of many reasons why you should have stayed in the cavern," Fenris replied, his tone sharp with reprimand. "If you cannot act when the need calls for it, you are a danger to all of us."

"How dare you? I've had my basic combat training!"

"Then look and learn and be ready," Fenris commanded, his tone so supercilious that Gravella wilted and fell silent. Caelum paused at the corner of a ruined shop, ears flickering. Beyond him was the wide, main strip of cobbles that led directly to the Towers.

"It's very quiet," he muttered.

"Which means they're waiting for something." Arcana tilted her head. "Or someone. I sense a trap."

"Trap or no, we're as close to the Healing Tower as we can get without stepping into the open." Caelum pawed at the ground with a forehoof, the velvet on his antlers fading into sharp, shimmering blades. "Might be time for a mad dash."

"A mad dash?" Arcana spluttered. "Have you lost your mind? We may as well hand ourselves over to be the next meal and save them the time of actually chasing us."

"Give me a better idea and I'll gladly follow through," Caelum answered grimly. "The warg might not be visible but I can smell them all around us. If we stay here, they'll eventually find us."

"How about another tunnel?" Fenris suggested.

Arcana shook her head. "The emergency tunnels are directly below us, so heading back underground risks the people we're supposed to be protecting."

"And I can't jump, so running is the only option," Caelum added.

Gravella's eyes glittered with malice and the corner of her lip quirked. "You're all powerful, Arcana; do some massive spell and tear the earth open, or rain meteors down from the sky. Perhaps flood the warg out?"

"Assuming I have access to the energy I need to get those elements on hand, what do you think happens to everyone else when I cast a spell like that?" Arcana asked quietly.

"They'd be saved," Gravella said at once.

"Would they?" Arcana began ticking items off on her fingers. "Opening the earth will collapse all five Towers and the tunnel network, killing everyone. Raining meteors from the sky would demolish the Towers and even possibly cause the spaceships to crash, killing everyone. Flooding the city would fill the lower levels of the buildings and the tunnel network, which would - wait for it - kill everyone." She shrugged, flicking her hands palm up. "The warg would be gone of course, but so would everyone else who lives in Sorca City and looks to us for safety."

"Oh." Gravella swallowed heavily. "Maybe not, then."

"Maybe not," Arcana agreed, baring her teeth in a snarl. "One of the first rules of magic any sorcerer learns, Earth Elder - cause and effect. Unless genocide's your aim for today?" When the other woman shook her head, Arcana sighed and rubbed her face. "Okay. This is stupid - but a mad dash it is. Hold on, everyone." She leant over Caelum's neck again, wrapping one arm around his chest so that the other was free. "Be careful, my heart."

"Forget careful. Be ready." Caelum sprang out from the cover of the building, the ground already a blur beneath him. Arcana squinted towards the Towers, her eyes streaming from the speed of his movement. Howls rose around them, punctuated by flashes of brown and grey as warg took their chances with wild leaps from nearby buildings. Several landed in a tumbled mess behind them, snapping and snarling at Caelum's heels. One landed squarely in front but had barely touched the ground when he was swept aside with a flick of bladed antlers. The Healing Tower loomed ahead, a giant black monolith surrounded by an earthen barrier comprised of spikes and deep pits. Arcana gathered her magic, preparing to temporarily disband the defences - and Caelum staggered, screaming as he toppled to the left.

"Caelum!" Arcana leapt clear as he fell, dragging Gravella with her. The Earth Elder flopped heavily onto the ground, rolling unceremoniously to a stop in the mud. Arcana landed in a crouch beside her, looking up to see Caelum skidding across the grass, a warg clinging to his flank and Fenris nowhere to be seen. The deerken kicked and bucked, trying with no avail to reach the creature with his antlers, blood streaming from long gashes in his flank. Arcana's heart leapt into her throat and she yanked at Gravella's arm, trying to twist between the warg flickering into existence around them without success. Caelum disappeared from view behind a wall of fur and Arcana released her hold on Gravella to raise both arms, a long stone spear materialising in each hand. The warg in front of her fell instantly, impaled though the eye; Arcana cocked her arm and threw her second spear directly into the flank of a second warg, pinning his body to the ground.

Something flickered in the air above Caelum and Arcana cried out in horror but it was Fenris who appeared, slashing downwards with the greatsword and taking the head of the warg who tormented her companion. He kicked the body aside and knelt next to Caelum, checking the wound with steady hands even as more warg, more and more and *more*, flickered into being around them. Arcana jerked suddenly as someone shoved her aside. A dead warg rolled in front of her, its head crushed with a rock.

"Don't just stand there! I don't know what I'm doing," Gravella shouted, her face white.

"We have to get to Caelum." Arcana scooped up the rock, stepping around Gravella to intercept the next attacker. The stone slimmed, lengthened - and buried itself in the leaping warg's neck with a terrible squelching sound. Arcana spun with the beast's movement, letting the body stumble past and topple onto the bloodied grass.

"We're cut off and he's not moving," Gravella panted. Arcana flicked a glance back to Caelum, her heart wrenching. Fenris stood over the deerken, the greatsword flashing in a trail of silver and red as he fought off waves of snapping teeth and slicing claws.

"You're right. He can't go anywhere like that." Arcana drew a deep breath, dragging the pieces of her heart together, and looked at Gravella. "New plan. We need to get to the Tower."

Gravella blanched as a warg materialised in front of them; Arcana summoned a stone dagger and slit the creature's throat. The Earth Elder stared wild-eyed at the body, then back up at Arcana. "What?"

"We need to cut through the warg and get to the Tower. We're going to run and kill and run some more. Move as fast as you can and don't cast any spells that will mess with the structural integrity of the Towers. Got it?" Arcana asked. Gravella nodded and began chanting out loud, her hands moving in an intricate, elegant dance.

Arcana cast a look at Fenris but he was beyond her reach. Hoping he would understand, she set her eyes on the Tower - on the waves of warg before it - and began to run. Gravella kept pace alongside, shouting the last few words of her spell in a rush. The ground before them erupted, boulders flying into the air in a long line towards the tower's base. Some warg went flying whilst others merely stumbled, shambling aside as the earth buckled and warped. Arcana focussed on the debris, turning the haphazard shower of rubble into deadly missiles that chased down any warg in their path, crushing and grinding with relentless abandon.

As they got closer, the earthen barrier surrounding the Healing Tower began to split and a hail of fireballs shot out through the gap. Arcana yanked Gravella aside as one of the spells slammed into the ground where the Earth Elder had been running - then they were through the barrier, with sorcerers shouting all around them.

"We're in," Gravella gasped.

"Not far enough!" Arcana sprinted for the entrance to the Tower, praying her gamble would work. As she approached, the tall, white door swung open and Flare stepped out. Arcana cannoned into him, spinning and staggering through the doorway and into the Tower itself.

With a loud *pop!* Caelum and Fenris appeared on the floor at her feet. The Guardian's eyes were wild and he was covered in blood and grime, half crouched, one hand twisted in Caelum's fur and the greatsword's dripping blade bared in the other. Arcana threw herself on the floor beside Caelum, dragging his head into her lap. His eyes opened at her touch, the galaxies within swirling far too slowly.

"Get the healers!" Fenris shouted. The greatsword clattered to the floor as he pressed both hands over the wounds in Caelum's side.

"What can I do?" Flare appeared beside them, heedless of the blood he knelt in.

"Seal his wounds," Fenris commanded, pulling the edges of the largest gash together. "Now."

"Are you -"

"Do it, or he dies and your sister with him," Fenris snapped, his face set. Flare laid his hand over the edge of the wound and the air was immediately filled with the smell of burning hair and flesh. Caelum screamed and thrashed but his movements were sluggish and Arcana held him fast, murmuring soothingly in his ear.

"That's all I can do." Flare leant backwards and Caelum sagged listlessly into Arcana's lap. Strong arms wrapped around her shoulders and she was surprised to hear Gravella's voice promising the healers were coming.

"Stay with me," Arcana whispered, stroking one hand across the fluttering pulse in his neck. "It doesn't end this way. Hold on to me. Hold on, Caelum, please." She struggled for air - or was that him - their heads swimming with pain and panic. Caelum's heart beat within her own chest, a stuttering, frantic rhythm that threatened to overwhelm, to drag them both down.

"The healers are here," Fenris said.

The healers are here. *The healers are here.* Arcana clung to Caelum, her eyes squeezed shut against waves of dizziness. She sought her own steady heartbeat and commanded his to emulate, exerting her will as though casting a spell. But what magic could soothe a failing heart? She was no healer - her only weapon was the love they shared, the bond which had been forged so many years previously. Arcana tugged at the threads which bound them, seeking refuge, offering protection, begging for a moment more. Then another. Slowly, Caelum's heartbeat began to reflect her own, weak and fluttering though it was. The cool, soothing flow of healing magic washed over them, bolstering flagging energies. Arcana forced herself to take slow, steady breaths; commanded his lungs to follow. Caelum responded quickly this time and at last she was able to differentiate something other than the vast, sparkling darkness within which they were connected.

The soothing balm faded, taking with it the remaining pain. Caelum shifted beneath her hands and Arcana sat up, blinking as she saw her own face, tear streaked and bloody. Then the sensation was gone and Caelum lifted his nose to rub against hers. "Arcana," he croaked. Someone sobbed with relief - was it her? Arcana didn't care; she was too busy kissing his nose, his furry cheeks, tears streaming down her face.

"He needs rest," one healer said.

"He will have it," Fenris promised. His hand was warm on Arcana's cheek. "Are you all right?"

She looked up, swallowing her tears. "Yes. Just a little dizzy. You?"

"Fine. Quick thinking out there," Fenris added.

"I was worried you'd think I was leaving," Arcana admitted, rubbing her cheek along Caelum's.

One corner of Fenris' mouth twitched in a smile. "For the barest moment. Then I remembered the elastic band effect and realised what you were doing."

"Thank you," Arcana whispered, her breath hitching. "For keeping him safe." Fenris inclined his head, his face grave.

"I'm fine, really," Caelum said, his voice croaky. Arcana leant backwards as he rolled to get his hooves beneath him.

"You're too slow, is what you are," she managed, lightheaded with relief.

"I was carrying three people and a sword bigger than Flare's ego. Of course I was too slow," Caelum grunted as he pushed upright, legs wobbling unsteadily.

"You knew," Arcana realised, taking Flare's hand and allowing him to haul her to her feet. "You knew the warg would catch us."

"Yeah." Caelum shook himself thoroughly. "I knew if they were on the other Towers, there would be a moment of danger when they could reach us. But what else could we do?" He touched noses with each of the healers and butted his head against Flare.

"Sorry about that," Flare's hand strayed to the singed patch of fur on Caelum's flank.

"You saved my life. Don't apologise," Caelum answered. "Next time there's a cold snap, that fur will grow right back."

"What about the warg?" Gravella asked, stepping forward. Her clothes were torn and bloody, her hair in disarray - but her eyes were clear and hard.

"They were repelled at the barrier. The dead litter Tower Field and the survivors teleported away." Flare's brows beetled and he flexed his left hand, the runes of his oath glowing. "Care to explain what *you're* doing here?"

"What I..." Gravella set her jaw and flicked a glance at the other sorcerers in the room, silent for a long moment. Then she stepped into Flare, pressing her body against his, and kissed him with such passion that Arcana blushed and averted her eyes.

"I see." Flare braced his hands on Gravella's waist and gently pushed her away. She stared up at him in surprise, clearly not expecting such indifference, and opened her mouth to speak. Flare was quicker, shaking his head as he said; "Now is not the time or place for this."

"How can you say that?" Gravella demanded. "I risked my life to come here and apologise."

"To who?" Flare asked, propping one fist on his hip.

Gravella's brow furrowed and she licked nervous lips. "To you, of course."

"Wrong answer," Flare returned equably. "All those years I spent helping with your research, sharing personal thoughts and feelings and the first opportunity you get, you spit on all of it. Not only did you ruin any bond we may ever have shared, you did it at the expense of the person you know I love the most - and knowing me the way you do, you think the apology needs to go to *me*?"

"But..." Gravella trailed off, her eyes darting to Arcana and back again. "But I'm the Earth Elder!"

Flare raised an eyebrow, his expression cool. "All the more reason you should be setting a better example. I won't stand by and let you use me for information, no matter who you are. If you're more interested in pursuing childhood pettiness - which by the way, you instigated even back then - than you are in being a mature adult, then I have no wish to be involved with you on anything but a professional level."

"You're turning me away," Gravella whispered, her face stricken with horror.

"I'm sorry," Flare shook his head, reaching out to tuck a stray strand of hair behind her ear. "I told you this wasn't the time or place and I meant it, but I'm also not going to pretend for the benefit of your pride." He leant forward and pressed a gentle kiss to her forehead. "Goodbye, Gravella."

"Flare," Gravella choked out, her voice thick with emotion. "Wait."

But Flare had already turned away and was dusting his hands on torn and dirty robes. "Right," he said to Arcana, his voice brisk. "I'm glad you're here, sis - I could use your help."

"That's why I came," Arcana flicked a glance in Gravella's direction, feeling a pang of pity even though the Earth Elder had sealed her own fate. "What's the situation?"

"We're killing more of them than they are of us, but it's pretty nasty." Flare jerked his chin over one shoulder. "The last of the sick were moved just before you arrived and there are a few earth sorcerers down below sealing the tunnel entrance in case we're overrun."

"You mean *when* we're overrun," Arcana corrected. "Once the warg get over the initial shock of our retaliation they'll be teleporting directly into the Tower."

"Yeah, I know. We need to figure out how to get rid of them before that happens," Flare sighed and scratched his head. "Oh, and Blaze is dead."

"The Fire Elder?" Gravella gasped, edging closer.

"He died defending Brook." Flare crossed his arms and stepped away, thwarting Gravella's less than subtle attempt to slide into position at his side. "They fought well but Blaze and two other water sorcerers died. Last I saw, Brook wasn't in great shape but the healers had her."

"Lesce?" Arcana whispered, her heart hammering.

"Fine. Took the first party of critically ill down the tunnels," Flare assured her. Arcana breathed a sigh of relief and nodded.

"So how do we get rid of the warg?" Gravella asked.

Arcana gave the Earth Elder a hard look. "You shouldn't be doing anything, like I told you - but the only way the warg will leave is if they are dead."

Gravella flinched. "Surely -"

"No, Arcana's right," Flare affirmed. "We gotta kill 'em. The warg don't talk, they destroy."

"First Flame?" A battered looking sorcerer in nature green jogged up to Flare, her face pale.

Flare straightened his shoulders. "Yes, Veinne?"

"There's... There's a man outside with a group of nine warg." Veinne flicked a nervous glance towards the Tower's tall doors. "He's asking for you."

"A man?" Flare frowned. "Care to be a little more specific?"

"Ah." Veinne cleared her throat.

"*Veinne!*"

She flinched. "It's Class Three water sorcerer Algae, sir."

"Algae?!" Arcana exploded. "What in the name of - wait, is he a prisoner? Because they can have him."

"He is not restrained, Grand Sorceress," Veinne murmured, biting her lip. "He, ah... He appears to be in charge of the warg."

A fist of ice clenched around Arcana's heart. She looked up at Flare, knowing his expression mirrored her own. "Great Gods of Sorcen," she whispered. "He's doing this because of me."

"No! Arcana, no," Flare shook his head, his face set. "No."

"You know he is," she snapped. "Asshole thinks he owns me and no matter what I do, he can't get it through his thick skull that I'm not some sort of trophy - and now he's put the whole planet in danger, just to prove a point."

Fenris took a half step forward. "Arcana, wait-"

"No." Arcana whirled away, her booted heels echoing through the silence which had fallen across the Healing Tower. "Algae is a curse on everyone he touches. This ends now."

Footsteps hurried after her; Fenris and Flare appeared on either side, the former stalking in silence and the latter spluttering indignantly. "Arcana, you can't - there's an entire pack of warg - *think*."

"Think? All I've done is think. For fifty godsforsaken years, all I've done is *think*. I've lain awake at night, thinking - remembering, reliving it all. Every single, aching, awful *second*, Flare." Arcana whirled at the door, her eyes brimming with tears of rage. "Look around you. What good has thinking done? I don't have a home anymore, because he haunts it. I can't have a normal life, because he prevents it. I can't even rescue a dying stranger," she jabbed a finger in Fenris' direction, "Without Algae Enrien sticking his nose in - no, without him inviting a host of invading warg along and murdering half of the city!"

"Arcana," Flare's voice hitched and broke.

"What is the point of having power beyond imagining if I am a prisoner inside of myself, Flare? Answer me that, and I'll stay inside," she was panting, trembling.

Flare growled incoherently, both hands clenching to fists. "I can't, but this is *not* your fault. You didn't start this - he did."

"It doesn't matter. I'm going to end it," Arcana growled, holding up a hand when Caelum made to join her. "No. You stay here."

"I'm fine," the deerken protested.

"The healers said you need to rest. Stay and look after Gravella," Arcana spun on her heel and strode outside, where a contingent of sorcerers waited below one of the earthen barriers. Flare cursed and hurried after her - Fenris, with his preternatural speed, was already by her side.

Arcana shouldered past the guards and clambered up the slope, striding brazenly over the crest. As Veinne had promised, nine warg lurked some distance from the foot of the Tower. Algae stood in the centre of the group, clothing untouched and hair immaculate. The grass around him was trampled and bloody, littered with the corpses of the warg who had ambushed Caelum.

"Algae! You filthy, useless pig." Arcana crossed her arms over her chest, twisting her face into a sneer. "This is low, even for you."

"Hello, my sweet angel." Algae blew a kiss in her direction. "I'm glad to see you're unharmed. How is that filthy deer, by the way?"

"You'll be disappointed to learn he survived the attack," Arcana returned, drawing calm from the icy fist around her heart. She stared down her nose at Algae and said; "It takes more than that to kill him."

"Well, that is a shame. Nevertheless, there will be other opportunities." Algae waved a many-ringed hand negligently. "Now, where is that odious brother of yours? Much as I enjoy your sweet voice, *he's* the one currently in charge."

Flare appeared immediately, his face cool. "I'm here, you lecherous son of a bitch. What do you want?"

"I've come to negotiate terms." Algae puffed his chest out, the sunlight glinting off his shimmering gold tunic.

"Terms?" Flare laughed. "*You?*"

Algae picked casually at his nails. "If I were you, First Flame, I'd take this seriously. Unless you want more dead on your hands, of course."

Flare snorted. "I've never been one to bow to idle threats before, and I'm not about to start now. Speak, and do it quickly."

"The terms are simple - Hand over that barbarian Fenris, the stinking deer and my darling Arcana." Algae smiled, his teeth too white in his taupe face. "Once they're safely in our custody, my friends and I will be on our way."

Arcana's body flushed with rage and she opened her mouth but Flare reached out and squeezed her hand. "What makes you think I would hand my sister and her companions over to anyone, let alone a traitor?"

"Because if you don't, your people will die," Algae returned. "You've seen the damage these few warg have caused - and we have many, many more. What is the value of three lives when weighed against those of an entire planet?"

"You snivelling weasel," Arcana pushed Flare's hand aside, taking a shaking step forward. "How dare you?"

Algae barked a sharp laugh. "How dare *I*? You've had multiple opportunities to return peacefully, my love. It was only after my humiliation at the hands of your off-world pet that I realised the time for talking is long past." His eyes narrowed to slits. "A few drinks with my new associate, a quick shake of hands - and I finally had a method with which to make you see sense."

"And what interest does your *associate* have with me?" Arcana snapped.

"Nothing. He wants Fenris, I want you - and in exchange for my help getting the warg past our defences, we both get what we're after." Algae grinned, the sunlight glinting off his teeth. "A savvy business deal."

For once, the insult bounced straight off as the implication of his words sank in. Arcana blinked down at the warg, her stomach twisting as she said; "Fenris?"

The Guardian in question stepped up beside Arcana, his eyes roaming the empty field. "Show yourself, Taelon. I know you're down there."

"Your nose is better than I credited." One of the warg in the pack straightened, the top of its head falling backwards to reveal the man beneath. Taelon was tall, standing at eye level with the warg who were head and shoulders above Arcana. His skin was the colour of rust, his matted hair a ruddy brown. A dirty orange glow seeped from his eyes, casting a harsh light over cruel features. Taelon shared Fenris' pointed teeth and glowing eyes, hazarding Arcana to guess they had originated from the same people - at least in part. Unlike Fenris, however, Taelon was a hulking brute. His neck was thicker than his ears, his body a hideous cording of muscle on muscle, his legs short and squat against longer, tree trunk arms and stumpy, thick fingers. Taelon looked up at Fenris and his eyes flickered with a hatred so strong it made her shiver. "I should have followed you through that portal and torn your throat out with my teeth."

"You should have." Fenris, by quiet contrast, was calm. Compared to any male, he was tall, cultured, beautiful. Next to Taelon? Breath-taking. Arcana wondered, as she looked between the two of them, if Fenris had suffered at the hands of his people not because they thought him inferior but because they were jealous. Fenris, oblivious to her musings, hooked his thumbs into his belt and shrugged. "You didn't. And now here I stand, whole and hearty, while you stoop to stealing warg skins and tricking desperate fools. How the mighty have fallen."

Taelon laughed, lips drawing back to reveal not only fangs but an entire mouth full of pointed teeth. "Ah, but tricking desperate fools has ever been a favourite game of mine. The only mistake I made was in assuming you'd fight - but you fled like a coward. Must be your mother's blood."

Fenris stiffened, his face like plascrete. "The people of Sorcen have nothing to do with this, Taelon. You had no right to come here."

"Indeed?" Taelon laughed, jabbing a thick finger at Fenris. "*You* made them part of this. You. Nobody else."

"What is he talking about?" Arcana murmured, flicking a glance up at Fenris. He shook his head slightly, a muscle working in his jaw, but Taelon laughed.

"I've been tracking Fenris since the moment he leapt through that portal," Taelon sneered. "He's been a walking time bomb since the moment he arrived. He's been blocking me, of course, but that only delays the inevitable - and leaves him blinder than a newborn babe. Did he forget to tell you that? Oh my," Taelon laughed, his face crinkling. "What a naughty boy he is."

Arcana bit her lip to keep from speaking; from making the situation worse than it already was. She longed to wallop Fenris but it would only show Taelon he'd made a mark - and that would never do. So she summoned a deep, meditative breath, her magic curling close, and said; "It's time for you to leave, Taelon. Take the warg and go."

Taelon's lips curved into a cruel smile. "Oh, I will - as soon as you agree to my offer. Come quietly, bring the deerken and his Warden, and we will leave your planet and its innocents alone. You, madame sorceress, have the power to end the bloodshed here and now. Refuse, and everyone you have ever loved will be torn asunder."

"Your promises are meaningless," Fenris snarled. "You seek only to treat with these people because they are *beating you*."

Taelon's face flushed a darker shade of rust. "I seek to honour the pledge I made in the Weaver's chamber and no more than that," he hissed. "And I will see it through, Fenris - if not today, then another. You were clever to hide so long but all you buy yourself is time. There is nowhere you can go to hide from me and nothing anyone can do to protect you. Not even your precious Weaver."

Flare stepped forward with a lazy yawn. "Threats and promises will get you nowhere, I'm afraid, and I'm getting rather bored of all this talking in circles." He balanced both fists on his hips and glared at Taelon. "Fenris is under Sorcen's protection. Now leave this place or die."

"A shame," Taelon tutted, shaking his head regretfully. "You leave me no choice but to remove Fenris and his deerken by force." Taelon raised a hand to the teleporter on his chest. "I will ensure you watch your people die wretched deaths before you join them."

"Now!" Flare shouted, fire crackling to life in his hands. Arcana raised one arm and the earth rose up, slamming together like two giant hands clapping. The impact rippled underfoot and several nearby sorcerers staggered.

"I don't think I got them," Arcana murmured, loosening her fist. The ground opened in response but as she'd predicted, the earthen trap was empty.

"Shit." Flare shook his fire out and thrust both hands into his hair. "Flaming, stinking, Godsbedamned *shit*."

"I am sorry this has happened," Fenris said. "It was not my intention."

"Don't worry, brother, I know. We've got you." Flare clapped Fenris on the shoulder and offered a tight smile. "Now if you'll excuse me, I need to go word up the warriors. I've got a feeling they're going to be back with friends real soon." Flare began slithering down the slope, checked halfway and looked back at Arcana. "Take a moment. Channel it - all that anger and hate. Then meet me inside and let's teach these bastards a lesson."

Arcana opened her mouth to respond but he was already gone, leaving her shivering in the sudden breeze. Flare wanted her to channel her rage, but she only felt cold - cold and empty. All this death, all this destruction, because of *her*, because she refused to be cowed by that arrogant, possessive jerk.

"Are you all right?" Fenris laid a hand on Arcana's arm and she jumped in surprise. No - not all because of her. Not entirely.

"Keep your hands to yourself," Arcana hissed, wrenching free of his grasp. "How dare you lie to me?"

"I never lied to you, Arcana." Fenris' voice was soft and regret flickered in the depths of those flaming eyes - an emotion she ruthlessly ignored. "I only sought to keep you safe."

"Look around you, Guardian," she snarled, baring her teeth. "Secrecy only puts people in danger. It's a betrayal of trust as thorough as any lie."

Fenris frowned. "I did not set out to betray your trust. I know you've been through a lot-"

"You know *nothing*," she spat. "Not a single godsforsaken thing."

"Is that so?" His eyes narrowed. "I know Algae charmed you when you were young and impressionable. I know the Council kept you isolated and hidden away for over a year following your transformation. I know the gruelling schedule you were forced to keep, the insane hours, the workload, the demands." He took a step closer. "I know they wouldn't release you without someone to supervise, and that Algae took you home, took you in. That he shared custody of you - *custody* - with Flare."

Arcana's breathing came short and sharp. "Congratulations. You've learnt how to read."

Fenris pushed closer, invading her personal space, lips peeling back in a snarl. "I also know how he spoke to you. How he treated you. What he said, what he did, how he turned you inside out and made you doubt the very ground you walked on. I know how he took you apart, tore you down, tried to rebuild you into something weaker, more submissive. A tool, a weapon -"

"Stop!" A loud crack echoed through the cooling afternoon air - it took Arcana a moment to realise she had slapped Fenris, hard. She shuddered with rage, tears boiling in her eyes and burning down her cheeks. Fenris watched her from beneath lowered brows, his face cool, hands slack by his sides. Arcana closed the few inches between them, fisting both hands in his tunic and shaking - for all the good it did, because he was immovable as the stone walls of the Tower. "I trusted you. I *trusted you* and you betrayed me."

Fenris sighed. "All Guardians and Wardens share a blood bond. It enables us to find each other in times of need, even if we are unconscious or deceased. Taelon is using that bond to track us down, one by one. I attempted to block him, to seal it off, at the expense of my own ability to keep track of *his* location. I knew it would only slow him down, that eventually Taelon would find his way to face me - but I did not think he would appear so quickly. I only sensed his presence when he appeared on the field," he said softly, his face begging her understanding. "I swear on the Weaver's life that I did not intend to hurt you. I made a mistake."

Arcana stared into those eyes, tracing the lines of his cheeks, the sweep of his nose, the regretful twist of his full lips. She *had* trusted him. When? Why? A lock of dark, curling green hair had fallen over Fenris' face, softening the curve of a jaw clenched too tightly. She'd known not to trust him. She'd known - and done it anyway. And now he offered her truth; she was not imagining the desperation burning in those eyes, the way his breathing came ragged. He knew he'd screwed up and he *was* sorry. Whatever his initial intentions, somewhere during his convalescence Fenris had taken more of an interest in her than he ought and now his caution had come back to bite them both. Arcana swallowed heavily, slowly becoming aware that their bodies were pressed together, her fists still twisted in his tunic. Fenris made no move to bridge the gap between them but even so, their faces were only inches apart, his breath tickling her cheek. Arcana ducked her head, trying to think around the cascade of emotion, of reaction, to block out the heat of his body and the way hers had begun to tremble.

"So, what was the plan?" Her voice was hoarse; she licked her lips and tried again. "Just keep running across the galaxy and hoping he wouldn't catch you?"

"Until I was able to formulate a better solution, yes." Was that a wobble she detected in his voice?

"And when were you going to tell *me*?" Arcana forced herself to look up at him, to meet those burning eyes with her own flat black ones - knowing, as his glamour rose around them like a curtain, that the eye contact would cut Fenris to the very depths of his soul and drag the truth out of him like a fish on a line.

"I wanted to wait until we were offplanet, where I could control the amount of people who might potentially overhear." His voice dropped lower, so low it vibrated with a velvety intensity that slid along her bones. "I thought I would have a chance to talk to you alone before Taelon found us."

"But you didn't."

The corner of Fenris' lip twitched, ever so slightly. "I have never claimed infallibility."

No. He hadn't. And he was only human - or as near as an approximation as anyone could get these days. Arcana loosed her grip on his tunic and immediately stumbled, the ground sliding beneath her. Fenris' arm slid around her waist and for a moment, he crushed her against him without the barrier of her fists - her rage - to separate them. His eyes burned, his skin burned, and worse, she burned with him.

Arcana cleared her throat and pushed away. "You better believe this isn't over."

"I understand - I only ask for another chance to prove I am not as dishonest as you believe," he said quietly.

Arcana sucked on her teeth for a long moment. "I don't know. I'll need to think about it."

"Of course."

"Arcana!" Flare's voice rang out from below. "Are you coming? We've got warg to kill, dammit."

"He's right." Arcana raised her eyes to Fenris'. "Truce, for now."

"As you wish, Grand Sorceress."

"Oh, shut up, you trumped up excuse for a hobgoblin. Come on, Flare's waiting." Arcana could have sworn she heard him chuckle as she slithered precariously down the slope and raced after Flare.

CHAPTER
TWELVE

ARCANA STORMED THROUGH THE CENTRE OF THE HEALING TOWER WITH HER hands clenched tightly into fists. Sorcerers in battle dress ran hither and thither in a flurry of activity, shouting to one another as they moved to carry out whatever orders they'd been given. Caelum stepped out of the crowd, ears laid flat against his head. "I can't believe Algae sold out the entire planet to the warg," he muttered, rubbing his face against her cheek. "Are you okay?"

"I'm not sure," Arcana growled, burying her face in the soft fur of his neck. "I don't know if I'm angrier at Fenris for lying by omission, or at missing a perfectly good opportunity to squash Algae like the pond scum he is."

"Oh, you're definitely more angry with Fenris," Caelum answered with such certainty that, in spite of the situation, Arcana felt her cheeks heating with a blush. "Don't write him off just yet, though. A mistake is not the same as a deliberate decision to destroy someone from the inside out."

Arcana ground her teeth, words and feelings tumbling over themselves in an effort to be heard. Caelum watched her with such calm that she said, "Are you feeling all of this right now or not?"

"Yes," he nodded, a spark of laughter glimmering in his eyes. "But whatever happened when you connected us before... I saw what to do. How to filter, how to feel without drowning and how to turn it off."

"I don't know what I did," Arcana admitted. "I thought it was you."

Caelum's jaw dropped open in the deerken equivalent of a grin. "Well, it was one of us - and I meant what I said about Fenris, too. Either way, I feel better than I have in days."

"You almost died," Arcana ran her fingers through the fur at his jaw, breaking up sections of dried blood and scattering a cloud of rust into the air. "And I'm not making any promises about Fenris. I knew I shouldn't have trusted him and all he did was prove me right."

"No," Caelum murmured; "All you did was watch until Fenris slipped up and gave you something to hold against him, because you're afraid to trust someone and get hurt again."

"Ouch," Arcana grunted, tipping her head back. Sunlight streamed in through the stained glass windows above, coating whitewashed walls with shimmering rainbows of light. She watched the play of colour, carefully considering Caelum's words. "I don't know if I like this new, perceptive side of you. Particularly when you're right."

"You'll get used to it." Caelum frowned, his head also tipping back to look upwards. "Did you hear that?"

"Hear wha-" Arcana cut off as a muffled explosion tore through the Tower and the stones buckled beneath her feet. Glass shattered and people screamed; she summoned her magic and sent it out into the smooth, black brickwork, feeling other earth sorcerers doing the same thing as they worked instinctively to steady the building lest it collapse around their ears. When it was done and the tremors faded, Arcana grabbed at the nearest sorceress, a woman in water blue. "Where's the First Flame?"

"He went down to the bunker to see about the planetary defences," the woman answered. "With the Earth Elder."

Arcana nodded, looking up to where a haggard-faced fire sorcerer was half hanging over a balcony, frantically waving to get her attention. "What?"

"Warg, Grand Sorceress! On the roof."

Another explosion rocked the building - this one further away, the shockwave easier for Arcana and the other earth sorcerers to dissipate. "Fenris!"

"They're firing on us from space," Fenris supplied, appearing by her side from seemingly nowhere.

"I know that," Arcana grit out. "I need you to come with me. And you," she turned back to the water sorceress. "Pull everyone back to the caverns. Keep the earth sorcerers at the rear to keep the Tower stable until everyone's safe, then seal the exit."

"Yes, Grand Sorceress," the woman inclined her head and rushed off.

Arcana swung onto Caelum's back and offered an arm to Fenris. He swept his gaze down the length of her body and back again. "Are you-"

"Later," Arcana snapped, "Or I'll turn your favourite parts to stone and watch you waddle everywhere from now on."

Blinking in surprise, Fenris gripped her salt-white hand in his teal one and swung up behind her. Caelum set off through the Tower at a trot, threading his way through weapons and supplies in the opposite direction to the many rushing bodies. Fenris clamped one arm around Arcana's waist, his chest a hard wall against her back. She bit back the urge to tell him to let go, well aware he was putting function over modesty, moulding their bodies together to make Caelum's life easier while keeping a hand free for the greatsword should he need it.

It took mere moments for Caelum to fade back against the walls, circumnavigating the cavernous foyer until he reached a small stairwell in the back corner. Ducking his antlered head, the deerken took them down beneath the very foundations of the Healing Tower, where a small bunker housed Flare, Gravella, and a pair of sorcerers whom Arcana was unfamiliar with.

Flare was deep in conversation with the male, a stocky fire sorcerer with pale blond hair and a capable air about him while the female, a petite nature sorcerer with eyes and a long braid in deep bottle green, hunched over a console display, tapping frantically at the keys. She looked up as Arcana slid down from Caelum's back, Fenris hard on her heels. "Grand Sorceress," she gasped.

"Please - call me Arcana." Arcana extended her arm.

"Verdure," the woman replied, returning the forearm grip. She swallowed and jerked her chin at the man. "My husband, Pytch."

"A pleasure," Pytch offered his own forearm grip and then they both looked at Fenris and paled slightly. "Is he…"

"With me," Arcana returned. "This is Fenris." Without bothering to give Fenris time to add anything of his own, she turned to Flare. "They're firing from above. I say we have minutes before Taelon starts dismantling the Towers in an effort to flush us out. I've ordered the bulk of the defence to retreat into the tunnels but we can't go there - Taelon will use Fenris like a beacon and teleport the warg in."

"Good call." Flare ran both hands through his orange hair, exhaling in a long gust. "I hate to ask you this, sis, but Algae's locked us out of the defence systems and changed the password. I don't suppose you want to take any wild guesses as to what it might be?"

"Me?" Arcana blinked. "Why would I know?" There was a short, awkward silence. "Great Gods of Sorcen - Flare, I left him over fifty years ago!"

"Battleships are firing on the Tower and Verdure's been trying to guess for over an hour," Flare growled - and promptly staggered as the earth shook around them in emphasis. "I'm sorry but I've gotta ask."

Arcana turned to Verdure. "Try 'Flare is an asshole.' That might work."

"Come on, sis, you'd do the same," Flare growled. His communicator beeped and he cursed, ducking partway into the stairwell to take the call.

"Any idea where Taelon is now?" Arcana turned to Fenris with a raised brow. The Guardian's eyes immediately unfocussed and Arcana admired his ability to simply shelve whatever personal issues lay between them to focus on the task at hand - while she, meanwhile, was caught between wanting to smooth the tension building in his jaw, or punch his perfect nose.

Fenris blinked and cleared his throat. "Taelon is offplanet. I thought I might be able to get a fix on the location of his ship but it is difficult to pinpoint." He sighed, fists clenching and relaxing as though he longed for something to throttle. "Our only option for victory will be to decimate Taelon's forces enough that he must retreat to gather more."

Arcana hugged her arms to her chest, nails biting into her biceps. How many sorcerers would die scrambling for a victory that wasn't really a victory? She shivered. "At least we know he won't level the place immediately - not on purpose, at any rate."

"Why not?" Verdure asked, her brow pinching prettily.

"Because he wants Fenris, Arcana and I alive," said Caelum from the doorway. "He's more likely to send warg into the Tower to extract us first."

Flare came bustling back into the room, his lips pressed into a thin line. "There are warg in the upper reaches of the Tower."

"Told you," Caelum shrugged, rubbing his blood-stained shoulder against a darkened console. "Fenris is right. We need to kill 'em all somehow."

"Surely you've got a plan," Gravella said, her face pale as she turned beseeching eyes on Flare. "This can't be it."

"I don't -" he began.

"I do," Arcana cut him off. She looked back at Fenris. "He'll be tracking your location. If we can get back to the cruiser, we can lead Taelon away from Sorcen."

"The cruiser? Think about how close the spaceport is to the city - that's a suicide mission," Flare protested.

The Tower rumbled around them, masonry groaning in such a way that Arcana blocked out the conversation to brace the building, aware of Gravella doing the same beside her. She washed her magic over the black bricks in a gentle wave, finding the places where the other earth sorcerers were struggling and lending her strength to theirs. When the Tower's shuddering settled, Arcana threaded a subtle magical support throughout the structure and retreated into her body again. "If someone can give me a working jump stone, the three of us can commandeer a sled and lure Taelon *away* from the city; then after he follows, use the stone to portal back in, run for the cruiser and high tail it into space."

"And then what? He just chases you across the galaxy forever?"

Arcana shot Fenris a look. "That was the original plan, wasn't it?"

"Until I came up with a more suitable one, yes," the Guardian allowed. "Our ultimate goal is returning to the Timeless Kingdom and freeing the Weaver - but I had already anticipated such a journey would be done with the warg snapping at my heels."

"I don't like it, but okay." Flare frowned, then turned to Gravella. "My stone's flat. Where's yours?"

"In my office," the Earth Elder mumbled, then flinched when Flare cursed loudly.

"There'll be spares up in Lesce's office, surely," Arcana cut in. "We'll go get one."

Flare rubbed at his temples and then nodded. "All right. Pytch, Verdure - escort the Earth Elder straight to the tunnels and make sure everyone gets inside. Seal it behind you. I'm going with Arcana."

"You can't," Gravella gasped. "It's too dangerous."

Flare blinked, long and slow, his face closing over. "You gave up the right to comment on my actions in the Council chamber, sugar. You've shown your true colours; it's too late to go back now."

"But -"

Flare turned such a frozen look on Gravella that, for a fraction of a second, Arcana almost pitied her. "I told you at the beginning I don't do feelings or relationships. You were warned and you tried to take advantage of me anyway - used me for information on my sister. There's no way you can swing that where you come out on top, so don't even try."

Tears gathered in the corners of Gravella's eyes but she set her teeth. "I am an *Elder*. I command you to do as I say."

"Tsk tsk. Martial law, remember?" Flare clenched his fist, igniting the fire orange runes of his oath. "I can - and I will - do as I please. For now, Earth Elder, you may consider yourself outranked."

"How dare you?" Gravella clenched her hands into fists, slate eyes flashing. "I can have you removed from your position for such insolence."

"Sure you can, your gracelessness - but not until this is over." Flare winked, his smile a razor's edge, then looked out to the room at large. "Well? I'm pretty sure I issued some orders."

"I hear and obey, First Flame." Pytch clicked his heels together and snapped off a smart salute. "I will guard the Earth Elder with my life."

"Excellent," Flare nodded, dismissing Gravella with a turned shoulder. She stared after him in shock and disbelief, one hand partially raised in blatant denial - but it was too late. Flare's voice was clipped, every inch the First Flame as he said; "We move out together, cut a path through any warg that are already in the Tower. Once you've entered the tunnels, the rest of us will head to Lesce's office."

"Yes, sir." Pytch snapped off a crisp salute and moved to join his wife by Gravella's side. "Stay by me, your grace."

Flare strode past them to the door, peering up the staircase with a fireball crackling in one hand. Arcana moved towards him and froze as the air began to shimmer in front of her. Fenris drew the greatsword in a silken motion - and there was a strangled sound as the lone warg misjudged its teleport, materialising with the top three quarters of its body inside the roof. Arcana watched in fascinated horror as flesh fought stone and inevitably lost, sealing the crushed torso inside. Moments later a pair of monstrous, furred feet dropped to the floor of the bunker, leaving behind a steaming trail of blood.

"Well, that's going to give me nightmares," Caelum announced.

Arcana blinked down at the severed feet and then up at the ceiling, where a pair of bloody smears was the only evidence anything had ever happened. "We're out of time. Come on."

Caelum led the way back up the narrow stairs, the blades on his antlers shimmering in the artificial light. They emerged into the Tower's foyer to a sea of warg, with yet more teleporting in by the moment. Shouts echoed from the opposite side of the Tower, where a group of sorcerers was frantically defending the entrance to the kitchens - and beyond it, the tunnels below. One of the warg spotted Arcana and tipped his head back, loosing an eerie, blood curdling howl. Another joined it, and another, until the air vibrated with the battle symphony of the warg, their attention now firmly divided between the two fronts.

"Shit," Flare breathed. "That's a lot of warg. We'll never cut through to the tunnels."

"Then we find another way to get your Elder to safety." Fenris took a slow, purposeful step forward, fingers flexing on the greatsword. "Tell your people to retreat, Flare. I will buy them the time they need."

"Wait," Arcana grabbed his arm and stared up into those flaming eyes as Flare began barking orders into his communicator. "What are you doing?"

The Guardian's smile was heartbreakingly gentle. "Whatever I must. When the time comes, bar the door so the warg cannot gain access to your children." And then Fenris was gone, no more than mist and shadow as he launched his body straight upward, the leap augmented by his extraordinary strength and speed. He landed squarely in the midst of the warg, the greatsword a humming blur. Several heads thumped to the floor before the creatures even registered his presence and by then, Fenris was already gone, ducking beneath falling bodies to reappear further into the throng.

A new set of howls went up, these ones ululating with bloodlust as the warg began to claw at each other in their desperate attempts to reach the spinning, slashing Guardian in their midst. Fenris moved like nothing Arcana had ever seen, his body barely corporeal as he ducked and spun and leapt, the greatsword flashing silver in the light filtering down from the Healing Tower's enormous, stained glass windows.

Across the foyer Arcana saw the other sorcerers begin to retreat and she called her magic, dragging several stone blocks from the Tower's grand staircase and using them to barricade the door. She felt the gradual withdrawal of earth magic as the sorcerers slowly drew out of range and threw an extra layer of her own power into the bricks, feeling Gravella doing the same alongside her.

"Can you feel the cracks down low?" Gravella asked quietly.

"Yeah," Arcana nodded. "I don't know how many more blows the Tower can take."

Gravella grunted. "Not many - if any." She traced a rune in the air which would have her spell circling back on itself, repeating the pattern of support without requiring a constant stream of power.

Arcana felt the last of her people's magic slip out of range and prayed they would be safe in the caverns. "They're out," she said to Flare as he stepped up beside her.

"Good. Now it's our turn - if you want Lesce's office, it's upstairs." Flare pointed upward, where wave upon wave of warg were materialising on the wide staircase and flinging themselves down into the room at large. "Where's Fenris?"

As though in answer, a cloud of warg parts flew into the air and Fenris appeared, leaping straight upwards to land neatly on the second floor banister. He braced himself with one arm and then barrelled head first into a new group of warg, cleaving a path onto the landing. Arcana clenched her fists, crumbling the section of stairs behind Fenris so that the warg at his back tumbled unceremoniously to the floor below - where Caelum was waiting with his scimitar antlers at the ready.

A warmth against Arcana's spine revealed itself to be Flare, shoulder to shoulder with Pytch as the two sent fire spells into a pack of warg trying to sneak around from behind. Verdure's fingers tugged Arcana's sleeve, enough to gain attention without distracting her completely. "I don't think we're going to make it to Elder Lesce's office."

"No. We need to get Gravella out and then re-evaluate," Arcana responded, her eyes darting around the foyer. "I think the closest option is probably the portal to the Council chamber."

Verdure looked to the left, where the Healing Tower's carved plinth stood in pride of place beneath the largest of the stained glass windows. Her fingers flexed and she whispered under her breath; a long, thin sliver of wood appeared in each hand. Palming the makeshift projectiles with the familiarity of long practice, she sent her splinters flying - straight into the eye sockets of two separate warg. "This is going to take time."

"We could make a barricade," Gravella said suddenly, her voice by Arcana's other shoulder. "Push them back. You still have the earth magic?"

"I do but -" An explosion rocked the Tower, throwing Arcana to her knees and leaving her ears ringing. Masonry roared around them and glass shattered, peppering her with sharp shards that left bleeding trails in their wake. The floor shuddered and groaned and Arcana felt the rein-forcements she and Gravella had set into the bricks begin to crumble. She flung out her magic to help steady the building, feeling the Earth Elder doing the same, their powers whispering against one another as they fought desperately to keep the sixty-seven floors of the Healing Tower in one piece.

"I can't keep this up," Gravella spoke through gritted teeth, her eyes squeezed shut. Powerful but lacking in stamina had always been the other woman's curse and it seemed the last fifty years hadn't changed that.

"Give it all to me." Arcana braced both hands on the floor, spreading her magic up through the walls of the Healing Tower. The monolith was cool and soothing, as though years of love and dedication had sunk into the very foundations. As her energy swept upwards, so too did the Tower reach down, wrapping Arcana in a mother's warm embrace, murmuring gentle comforts in her ear. It didn't make sense but Arcana had long learnt to push aside such mundane concepts as logic and reason where magic was concerned. And so she breathed in that gentle comfort, allowed herself to bathe in those voices. Magic flowed, invisible threads that bound each brick and tile and pane of glass to her will. Gravella's magic slowly subsided and Arcana gasped as the full weight of the Tower settled onto her shoulders.

"Do you have it?" Sandy eyes peered into hers, filled with concern.

"For now - don't help me!" Arcana gasped as a breath of magic brushed back against her own. "If I fail, you're the only one with a chance to save everyone else. Reserve whatever strength you've got left." Gravella hesitated and Arcana gnashed her teeth in frustration. "Gods above us, will you just trust me for once? We're wasting time!"

"Okay." Gravella crawled to Flare's side and began shaking his shoulder. "Flare! Arcana's holding the Tower alone - we need to get out!"

He stirred with a groan. "What did you say?"

Gravella repeated herself while Arcana merged her consciousness fully with that of the enormous edifice still shuddering and quaking around them. Outside, a stiff breeze caressed the upper reaches of the Tower, tickling across roof tiles and shivering down Arcana's spine. Their hearts beat together, lungs moving as one - and the stones did breathe, shifting and flexing beneath the fading sunlight, exhaling those beautiful, soothing voices directly into her heart.

Flare leapt to his feet and began shouting, an explosion of light and movement that cut through even Arcana's addled thoughts. The warg were already recovering, some crushed by rubble but others - far too many to count - taking up an ominous, growling chorus. Arcana weighed her own strength against the sheer volume of warg and began to panic. They'd have a very limited time to escape before she could no longer hold the crushing weight at bay and there was still no sign of Caelum or Fenris. Her eyes watered as she tried to search the room but even attempting to reclaim such a tiny portion of her senses from the Tower made the building sway unsteadily. Arcana gasped and re-routed her power, pushing it back into the bricks. Where were the others? They hadn't been far before the shuddering building had forced her to her knees. Flare shouted a second time and then Fenris was there, and Caelum, the deerken's energy reaching up to bolster Arcana's rapidly flagging reserves.

"How long have we got?" Fenris' hand brushed her shoulder but Arcana couldn't muster the words to answer. Her muscles strained, her bones shrieked - she was the Tower, tall and strong, basking in the final rays of the afternoon. She was stained glass, silver accents, river sand and slick, black brick. And heavy. So, so heavy. No matter what those siren, soothing voices said, no matter how hard she tried, Arcana knew - she was going to fail.

"She's losing it," Caelum answered where Arcana could not. "We need to get out of here."

It was easier said than done - warg continued teleporting into the foyer as Taelon pressed his advantage, oblivious to the danger hanging over-head. Arcana would have laughed if she'd had the energy; in his attempts to capture them alive, the ex-Guardian was only increasing the chance of their deaths.

"Gravella - make a tunnel!" Flare shouted. "If we can get outside, we might stand a chance."

The Earth Elder's voice was full of frustration. "I haven't got enough magic left for something like that. But if we go back to the bunker, I might be able to brace it when the Tower falls; deflect the worst of the impact elsewhere."

Fenris scooped Arcana up as though she weighed no more than a feather and slid her limp body onto Caelum's back. "I will carve a path. Follow me."

"Hurry," Arcana managed, tears slipping down her face. Fenris' greatsword flashed, gleaming red in the glow of Flare's endless rain of fiery wrath as he led them back to the narrow stairwell. Caelum lunged, lowering his head to fit inside the narrow space, the others close behind. Fenris stood guard by the door, slicing apart the warg who attempted to follow.

"Give me a minute," Gravella grunted. She began muttering under her breath, her magic whispering against Arcana's as it moved to brace the stone and earth around them, setting in place a domed shield which wouldn't absorb the shockwave of the falling building so much as send it elsewhere.

"Don't spend it all," Flare warned - and indeed, the Earth Elder's magic was already flickering. "We need to seal the door so the warg can't get in."

"I know that," Gravella spoke through gritted teeth, signing a rune in the air to seal the spell so that it would hold without needing her continual attention. The magic glowed a sandy yellow before fading to nothing, leaving the Earth Elder to slump to the floor. She raised tired eyes to Arcana. "You can let go now."

With a silent apology to the black monolith above, Arcana used the last of her control to command the bricks to crumble inward. Agony wracked her body as she withdrew her magic, muscles seizing with strain and exhaustion and a scream tearing from her throat. A tremendous *crack!* filled the air as the weight of the Tower bore down on the roof of the bunker but Gravella's magic held firm.

The Earth Elder struggled to her feet. "Get back; I'll seal us in."

"Hurry." Fenris retreated from his position by the door, sheathing the greatsword in a fluid movement. Of everyone in the room, he alone came to Arcana's side, his hand - sticky with blood - cool on her forehead. "Is she injured?"

"No - just totally spent," Caelum murmured. "If Gravella's spell doesn't hold, we're all dead meat." As though it heard the deerken's words, a great roaring filled the air as the Healing Tower began to crumble, folding in upon itself from the top down.

Fenris glanced up at the roof. "Is it likely to break?"

"She put a seal on it so, in theory, the spell should keep cycling until the end of time." Caelum shifted beneath Arcana, his fur a silken caress across her cheek. "If the Tower's heavier than the magic, however, it'll shatter and there will be nothing Arcana can do to catch it. If you've got gods, I'd start praying to them."

Fenris' murmured reply was lost as the Tower groaned again, a steadily increasing rumble of masonry and shattering glass. The air inside the bunker shimmered and Gravella screamed as a warg appeared, tackling the Earth Elder's legs out from under her. Flare leapt forward to intercept, fire crackling to life in both hands but the warg tumbled both himself and Gravella out into the narrow stairwell, turning to use her body as a shield. Snuffing out his flames mid-leap, Flare caught the Earth Elder's reaching arms with his own as the warg began dragging her up the stairs. Oblivious to the destruction about to rain down on their heads, the creature roared in fury and tugged, his claws digging deep into the ribcage of his prey.

"Flare!" Gravella cried, her face white with agony. "I'm sorry."

"Forget that now. I've got you." He set his feet but the warg snarled and *pulled* - and Flare gave a step. Another. There was no way he could free his hands to cast a spell without losing his grip on Gravella and though the fire sorcerer was fast, he wouldn't be fast enough to save her.

Fenris raced to help but Flare's broad frame was braced in the doorway, blocking both the greatsword and any magical assistance Pytch and Verdure could have offered. Arcana reached for her own magic but pain flooded her body, stealing her breath in a star-flecked gasp that rendered her utterly useless. And above them, the steady roar and crash of the Tower's collapse drew ever closer.

The greatsword flashed as Fenris drove it into the floor, the giant blade cleaving easily into solid rock. The Guardian wrapped one hand around the leather-bound hilt and the other around Flare's waist, muscles straining as he gathered his preternatural strength and pulled back - but a second warg sank fangs into Gravella's legs, followed by a third, growling and tugging like angry dogs while the Earth Elder screamed in agony. Cracks appeared in the ceiling of the bunker and Arcana saw Fenris glance upward, saw in his posture that they were out of time.

Gravella's eyes sought Flare's, love written in bold lines across her face. Her lips framed words that, Arcana realised quickly, were not of love but of power. The last of Gravella's magic rose in a tide, shredded remains of energy dragged from the Earth Elder's soul by a will so iron strong that not even the rending warg could smother it. With a twisting motion so smooth Arcana knew Flare must have taught it to her, Gravella wrenched her arms from her ex-lover's grasp. Flare tumbled backwards into the bunker, cannoning into Fenris and sending them both tumbling beneath the safety of Gravella's shield. Arcana felt the final, whispering touch of the Earth Elder's power as a stone barrier shot up over the doorway of the bunker, sealing them inside - and Gravella outside with the warg.

The walls shuddered and buckled as the full force of the collapsing Tower at last bore down on the bunker. Caelum stumbled and strong arms caught Arcana's limp form as she slid from his back, helpless to save herself. The earth groaned and rumbled and pitched for what seemed an eternity but was likely less than a minute before settling into the silence of a tomb.

"Arcana?" Flare's voice hitched and a flame flickered to life in the palm of his hand. He stared around the bunker - now crumbled around them until it was dome shaped, supported only by Gravella's spell. "Holy shit. Please be alive."

"She's here," Fenris' voice rumbled against Arcana's spine and a moment later his weight lifted as he rolled off her.

"Thank the Gods." Flare's eyes were lined with silver tears but he drew a steadying breath, looking around at the rest of their group. "Did we lose anyone else?"

"No, just Gravella." Caelum's voice, his antlers casting sharp shadows on the walls. "We're just lucky she looped that shield or we'd have been crushed the minute her light winked out."

"Dammit." Flare passed a hand over his face, turning his eyes skyward. "She should never have been here in the first place."

Pytch gripped Flare's shoulder, one warrior to another. "She made her own choices, First Flame. The Earth Elder saved our lives."

Flare nodded, hands clenched into fists. Arcana tried to speak to reassure him but her lips didn't work. As though sensing her distress - and indeed, with that nose, he likely could - Fenris' warm arms tightened, cradling her against his leanly muscled chest. She closed her eyes a long moment and breathed in the night and the forest, glad her face was hidden so that Fenris couldn't see how much she needed his strength in that moment.

"Flare," the Guardian's voice was calm but his heart thundered against her cheek, a sure sign of distress. "I do not mean to interrupt but Arcana is not responsive."

"It's all right, she's just exhausted." Flare rummaged in his robe, withdrawing a battered leather water-skin and a foil wrapped package. He uncorked the skin and pushed the neck between Arcana's lips. "Drink."

It wasn't water - it was firewhiskey.

Arcana choked as it flowed down her throat but Flare was ruthless, refusing to remove the skin until she'd had several solid swigs. Warmth began to spread as the firewhiskey set in, fuelling her battered body, giving Arcana the strength to chew as Flare jammed dried fruit into her mouth and commanded her to eat. While she obeyed, her brother sat back on his heels and looked up at Fenris. "Arcana's magic never runs out but if the strain is too great, her body gives up. Being a channel for all that power requires a lot of energy; in case you've not noticed, she eats a lot."

"I've not had an opportunity to pay close attention yet." Fenris' tone made it clear that, from now on, he would. "I am still learning how this all works."

"Imagine lifting the greatsword - easy, right? Then do it a million times. The sword doesn't get any heavier but it becomes more difficult to wield. With training and practice you grow stronger but there's still a limit." Flare set his tiny flame floating in the air overhead then leant forward to peer into Arcana's face. "It's been a long time since I've seen you this bad, sis."

Arcana fought hard to swallow her latest mouthful of fruit and commanded her vocal chords to obey. "*You* try lifting a sixty-seven story Tower and then tell me how you feel afterwards."

Flare's grin was tight but genuine. "There she is. See, Fenris? Told you she'd be okay."

"I am monumentally relieved," the Guardian replied and for once, his emotions were fully present in that velvety voice.

Flare gave Fenris a long, measuring look, his face unreadable in the strange lighting. "I hope you know what you're doing."

Fenris stiffened for a fraction of a second and then let out the most inelegant sound Arcana had yet heard him make. "I think it is safe to say that by this stage in the proceedings, I am - how would you say it? Flying blind." He sighed, the movement brushing his chest against Arcana's cheek. "I believe the first order of business is deciding what to do next."

Arcana forced her tired mouth into a nasty smile. "Algae and Taelon are still out there. I say we make those bastards regret the day they were ever born."

Flare swept her body with a critical eye, one perfect brow arching. "You're going to extract vengeance like that?"

"Fenris could throw me at them." She tried to shrug, but her body still didn't want to do as it was told. "It might work."

Fenris' hands tightened, fingers digging into her ribs. "I would never throw you."

"You're a better man than me, then." Flare's haggard face cracked into a smile and he flopped backwards on the floor. "Do you think we got all the warg?"

"With the Tower?" Fenris asked, the muscles in his chest shifting as he, too, looked upward. "It is hard to tell but I would imagine so. Taelon is a cunning enemy but he would not have expected the Tower to fall in such a fashion. If I were to make a wager, it would be that he sent the vast majority of his forces in here to retrieve us with my signal as a guide. When Arcana collapsed the Tower, it would have crushed them almost instantly."

Arcana grimaced. "I didn't collapse the Tower - it was hit by the laser batteries from one of the orbiting ships. I told Gravella to save her strength for an escape and tried to hold the Tower up until everyone could get to safety."

For the first time since the collapse, Verdure cleared her throat. "You mean to say you supported the entire Tower all those minutes... alone?"

"Yes," Arcana responded, too tired to flinch away from the awe on the other woman's face. "As you can see, I failed miserably. It fell anyway and killed the Earth Elder in the process."

"You didn't fail," Pytch said stoutly. "If not for you, Grand Sorceress, a great many more of our people would have died."

Arcana sighed, allowing herself the forbidden pleasure of rubbing her cheek ever so slightly against the rough linen of Fenris' shirt, deliberately ignoring the fact that she was still angry at him and that the gesture was wildly inappropriate. None of her companions noticed the motion but Fenris stiffened beneath her, arms going rigid and Arcana knew that he, at least, was not blind to the action - which was likely going to cause all sorts of trouble later.

Caelum shifted beside her, shaking dust from his fur. "I think our more immediate concern is going to be getting out of here."

Flare barked a sharp laugh. "We've got an entire Tower on top of us, fuzzbutt. How exactly do you think we're getting out when Arcana's fried? We don't have any other earth sorcerers handy."

Silence, as the implications of his words sank in. Arcana sighed. "I'll do it."

"You need to rest," Fenris contradicted.

"I do - but if I sleep now I'll be asleep for days, and our air won't last that long." She tilted her head back to look at him. "Can you carry me to the wall?"

Arcana could feel the protest rising in Fenris' throat but he unfolded anyway, carrying her to the back of the chamber so that she could flatten one hand against the wall. She tried to call her magic but the burn inside her veins was so intense that stars sparkled in front of her eyes.

"Stop." Fenris yanked her half a step backwards, his voice a low hiss of anger. "I won't let you kill yourself for this - you've done enough."

Arcana waited for the pain to recede, panting in his arms. "There's nobody else," she managed at last, staring up into those brilliant jade eyes and begging him to understand. "If I don't do this, we suffocate."

Fenris' jaw clenched and while his face remained impassive, Arcana was fascinated by the inner struggle she glimpsed in his eyes. The Guardian's body heat leaked into her skin, breath tickling her ear as he lowered his head. "What do you need?"

"A boost." Something to take away the pain in her body, to mask the burn of having lifted an entire Tower. Something to numb the shriek of her muscles, just long enough to find the surface. Arcana swallowed. "I'm screwed - but there is a way. It's stupid and dangerous but it's possible."

"If what you said before about our air supply was correct, then I feel stupid and dangerous are probably our only options." Fenris' tone was light but his lips moved against her cheek, as though the situation were dire enough that he no longer felt a need to keep himself as tightly under control as he normally would. "Tell me."

Arcana drew a deep breath. "I need the firewhiskey."

Flare appeared as though summoned, leather skin in one hand, and crackling flame in the other. "Are you sure?"

"No," Arcana gave him a nervous smile. "If you have a better idea, I'm open to it."

Fenris growled, frustration edging his tone. "Yet again, I do not understand."

"If we can numb Arcana's body enough that she doesn't feel the pain, she'll be able to over-reach and gain access to her magic again." Flare weighed the skin of liquor in his hand. "Problem is, if we make Arcana *too* drunk, she could kill us all by accident instead."

"Or not drunk enough and her heart explodes," said Caelum gravely from the other side of the room. "I for one vote not that avenue, thank you."

Fenris was silent a long, long moment. Then, "That's the answer? We get Arcana drunk?"

"It's a temporary solution but it should work," Arcana said softly, glancing up at the hard lines of Fenris' jaw. "But when I crash, I'll crash hard. And if I get out of hand…"

"I won't let that happen," Flare promised, offering the skin.

Arcana accepted the liquor with shaky hands. "Good." She fumbled with the stopper, almost dropping the skin twice before Fenris growled low in his throat, a curiously feline sound.

"Here." He shifted his grip on her body, long fingers sliding like silk against her own as he popped the stopper free.

"Thanks." Arcana immediately tipped her head back and slugged the firewhiskey. Warmth spread through her body, a tide of effervescence that coated tired nerves in a layer of sticky, soothing honey. Fenris steadied her arm with one hand, his eyes tracing the way Arcana's throat worked to swallow. When the skin was empty he drew it away, returning it to Flare, whose face was grim as he replaced the stopper and slid it back inside his robe. Arcana swallowed a giggle, lightheaded with relief as the awful, choking exhaustion dissolved. She wriggled against Fenris for a fraction of a second, swallowing a second giggle as he stiffened in surprise - and then carefully lowered her to the ground.

"Steady," Caelum warned, his voice cutting in the small chamber.

Steady, steady, steady, Arcana wanted to chant - and snorted an inelegant laugh. Her hands *were* steady as she splayed them over the wall, magic leaping to her fingertips with wild enthusiasm. Her body burned but it was a peripheral awareness, a discomfort not even worth acknowledging. She pushed away from Fenris and began to walk through the shattered stone, humming and sniggering to herself as she went. The tunnel lacked the grace and finesse of her normal work, with a jagged roof and slight deviations whenever she stumbled - but it was a functioning tunnel none-theless, slowly curving upwards towards the surface. Not that the shape of the tunnel mattered, Arcana reflected, as long as they lived. And with that thought shining in her sparkling mind, she opened the earth and stepped into the purple shadows of twilight.

The remains of the Healing Tower jutted out of the ground, the field around them littered with enormous black bricks, shards of glass and jagged sections of tiling. The Tower's base was mostly intact, Arcana's final command meaning it had collapsed inwards upon itself rather than tipping sideways and causing even more destruction. The ground was scorched and gouged by laser fire, with many of the nearby bricks melted into piles of glittering black slag. Arcana swayed gently in the silence of impending night, glad to expel the scent of blood and death from her lungs - and then giggled, staggering sideways into Caelum.

"Are you okay?" The deerken twisted his head backwards to sniff at her face. "I can carry you, if you like."

"I'm fine," Arcana returned in her best stage whisper.

Flare snorted, tipping his head to the sky to fill his lungs. "You have a funny definition of the word 'fine', sis. Nevertheless, I'm glad we're out."

"Are you..." Fenris trailed off as Arcana grinned wildly at him. He flicked a glance at Flare. "How long before she crashes?"

It was Caelum who answered - Caelum, who could feel everything she felt, who knew her better than she knew herself. "Not long."

"We need to make sure the invasion is really over before we can get Arcana to safety," Flare said. He turned to Pytch and Verdure. "You both did well in there. Are you strong enough to continue?"

"Yes, First Flame," Pytch returned. "I won't rest easily until I know the w-"

"Quiet," Fenris held up a hand for silence and got it, even if Arcana had to shove her fist into her mouth. He swung his head to the left. "I hear someone talking." He drew the greatsword and padded off, blending into the hushed, rippling shadows as though he were a part of them.

Arcana staggered after him, Flare supporting her with one solid arm when it became apparent she couldn't walk in a straight line by herself. Fenris set his back against the wall of the ruined Tower and Arcana thumped into the stones beside him, breath leaving her lungs in a whoosh. Fenris extended a single, warning finger, heedless of the fact that it was waving almost beneath her nose as he strained to see around the corner. Arcana stared at his finger until her eyes crossed, examining elegant knuckles, sections of bone and flesh that were so long as to be almost spindly, giving Fenris an elegance that would have been more at home in a music room or perhaps even an art studio. His soft skin was almost blue in the twilight and Arcana leant slowly closer, fascinated by the sweep and swirl of Fenris' skin, the tiny etched design of his fingerprint. Somewhere in the back of her mind, a sensible woman demanded her stop and think - but considering Arcana was operating largely on firewhiskey, all she knew was the overwhelming temptation to taste the Guardian in front of her. He vexed her completely, alternately cool and charming with his dark hair and smooth, unfairly masculine body. Surely, just this once, it wouldn't be so bad to let her body do as it wished? Testing her lips with a tongue, Arcana swallowed heavily, so close now she could scent evergreen forest and the softest hints of cinnamon. Good enough to eat. With that thought foremost in her mind, she opened her mouth and bit down on Fenris' finger.

Fenris jumped as if - well, as if he had been bitten - and turned wide eyed to stare. Arcana's teeth gripped his index finger like a dog with a bone; tight enough that escape was impossible yet not so deep as to hurt. With the Guardians' astonished green gaze locked firmly on Arcana's face, she flicked out her tongue and tasted his silken skin.

Someone choked on a laugh and Flare's face appeared in the gloom. "Stop it," he mouthed, and flicked her in the centre of the forehead. "Listen."

Arcana released her grip so that she could snap her teeth at Flare instead. He shook his head and leant away, giving Arcana a close up view of Fenris, who was staring down at his finger as though he'd never seen it before. His face flickered, seemingly unable to decide if he was scandalised or amused by the display. Then the sound of someone kicking through rubble caught Arcana's attention and she frowned, Fenris and his intriguing digits immediately forgotten. Digging her fingertips into the Tower for balance, Arcana strained her ears until the faint murmur of conversation carried through the cool air.

"I see nothing... No, my lord. It's... I can't explain it. Dropped," the male voice said.

"I know that voice," Arcana breathed. She leant around Fenris to see better, clutching at his clothing lest she topple. A familiar silhouette stood just inside the ruined Tower, his shimmering gold tunic almost luminous in the twilight.

"Floors, walls... It's all collapsed inwards. Packed solid," the silhouette kicked viciously at a block of stone. "Yes, my lord. I understand, my lord. I will find them. Over and out." A click in the dark; a communicator snapping shut. Arcana clenched one hand into a fist and the figure yelped in surprise, dropping his communicator as the stone beneath his feet melted and reformed, burying him up to the ankles.

Arcana lurched out into the open, kicking the smashed communicator aside by luck rather than intention. Gathering herself up in what she hoped was an excellent imitation of a sober person, she said; "Algae Enrien. You were a fool to come here."

"Arcana? You're alive!" Algae's face lit up with relief. "Thank the waters for that. I've never been so glad to see you, baby."

"You actually mean that," Arcana giggled, cocking her head at him like a bird. "I suppose it *would* be ironic if you gave up our entire planet and I got squashed at the last minute."

"Are you feeling all right?" Algae asked, brows furrowed as he watched her wobble unsteadily. "Wait a minute - sweet lips, are you *drunk*?"

"None of your business," Arcana snapped. So much for the illusion of sobriety - she'd never been much good at it. Instead, she allowed her temper to provide the strength she needed to keep her feet. "Do you realise how many people died today because of you?"

Algae snorted and rolled his eyes. "Oh, please. Always so sanctimonious. Not nearly so many sorcerers died today as warg - Taelon's forces are decimated."

"How reassuring." Fenris materialised by Arcana's side, sliding one arm around her waist as she swayed in an invisible wind. "Do you normally give out the tactical information of your allies?"

Algae's eyes flashed. "Oh, you're alive too. I must say, I'm much less excited about that. Who else have you got with you?" He squinted as the rest of the little group stepped out of the shadows. "Oh yes, the filthy deer... And the First Flame, no less! Well now, this is an exciting turn of events."

"I wouldn't be laughing, if I were you," Flare said quietly. "You're single-handedly responsible for hundreds of Sorcen deaths, up to and including the Fire and Earth Elders. There's no running this time."

"You think this is *my* fault?" Algae barked a laugh. "If Arcana had done what she was told from the beginning, this would never have happened."

"I'm not a pet, Algae," Arcana waved an admonitory finger, glad that Fenris' silent support kept her upright during the motion. "I'm a person - something you never quite understood. And with every betrayal, you only make me hate you more and more."

"Oh my. Drunk *and* cross. Cute," Algae's lip twitched and Arcana fought the greasy shiver that tracked up her spine. "I have powerful friends, as you've seen. It's only a matter of time before you'll belong to me, sugar pie." He reached into his pocket to pull out a small teleportation unit - and yelped as it flew from his hand, clattering off into the gloom.

"Nice shot," Fenris nodded to Verdure, whose hand was still raised.

The nature sorcerer nodded, a second splinter already in hand. "I practice for moments just like this. Should I put one through his eye, Grand Sorceress?"

"You think Arcana's going to order my death?" Algae let out a loud, braying laugh. "Don't be ridiculous - she's too soft for murder. Or am I wrong, sweetness? Maybe fifty years off-planet has changed you. Go on, do it," Algae crooned, his eyes dark with desire. "Let me remember the curves of that body while you're at it. Scream for me, one last time."

Arcana stilled, blood roaring in her ears and breath catching in her throat. He was baiting her intentionally, she knew, trying to find a weakness to exploit - but damn if she couldn't move, or think, or breathe for the humiliation colouring her cheeks. "No," she managed, her voice little more than a rasp. Fenris splayed a steadying hand across her back, his body once more a pillar of strength beside hers. In a way she would never have done whilst sober, Arcana leant into him, yielding her soft lines to his hard ones. "No, Algae," she repeated, stronger this time. "You can't buy a coward's death at my expense - I'll rot before I let you manipulate me again. It's over."

Algae merely laughed, his sharp eyes savouring Arcana's reaction as though it were a fine wine. "I knew you couldn't do it, luscious. You're too good for murder."

"You're right." Flare's robes billowed as he flowed over the cracked cobbles, folding Algae in half with a quick, vicious punch to the stomach. He spread one hand over the water sorcerer's face, fingers digging in either side of Algae's jaw. "Arcana *is* too good for murder. But I'm not."

Flare spoke a single, damning word of power. Algae's eyes went wide, terror written in their depths - and then disappeared as a brilliant flash of white lit the night. There was no noise, no shockwave in the wake of the spell; just searing silence. Arcana blinked frantically as the light faded, certain she must have misheard her brother - until Algae's headless body slumped to the ground, the cauterised stump of his neck giving off a thin curl of smoke.

"Flare!" Arcana gasped, slapping both hands across her mouth in horror. "What have you done?"

Her brother stared down at Algae's corpse, his face unreadable. "As First Flame of Sorcen, I, Flare Veritax, charge Algae Enrien with high treason and sentence him to death. Anyone who wishes to object may do so now," he added, raising his eyes to those assembled.

Pytch stepped into the silence and spat on Algae's singed chest. "I stand witness. May he burn in the depths of Craddagh's cauldron."

"I stand witness," Caelum said.

"And I." Verdure emerged from the darkness and handed Flare the teleportation unit. "I think you should handle this, First Flame."

"Oh, yes." Flare bent and tucked the unit into Algae's tunic, flicking the switch to power it on. "Thank you, Verdure. Remind me to promote you later."

Arcana stared at the space which, until moments ago, had been occupied by Algae's head, her heart beating a staccato rhythm of disbelief. She'd have fallen to her knees by now, she was certain of it - except that Fenris' arm around her waist was like satin over steel. His lean strength was such that if she decided to lift her legs, Arcana was almost certain her body wouldn't shift as much as an inch. A tiny, warning stab of pain had her blinking tears back from her eyes, the firewhiskey lifting enough for her to say; "What are you doing?"

"Sending a message," Flare responded, weaving his fingers over the unit. An orange rune glowed for a moment, sinking into the plasteel. "Does Taelon enjoy singing telegrams?"

"I think he's more partial to wine and flowers," Fenris said quietly.

"Well then, he might be a little disappointed." Flare's teeth flashed in the night. "What a shame." The light on the teleporter flickered blue. Flare made another set of quick gestures with his hands, watched a second rune sink into the device, then leant over and pressed the button. Algae's body disappeared, taking a section of the Tower's melted stone with it. "Those spells will detonate in about two seconds, splattering what's left of that asshat all over his master." Flare's face lit up with a vicious grin. "I think that would officially be the most useful Algae has ever been."

"He's really dead," Arcana managed, the liquor shifting enough that her head was suddenly light and her limbs far too heavy.

Flare nodded, cupping her cheeks. "Yes. It's over, Arcana. He's gone."

Years of pent up grief and rage clawed at Arcana's chest and she burst into tears. Flare pulled her close, wrapping his arms tightly around her as only a brother knew how. And though Fenris released Arcana into her brother's care, she was well aware of his constant heat at her back, waiting to catch her should she fall. The comparison to Algae - who would have gleefully tripped her and laughed while she sprawled - was so vivid that not even Arcana's exhausted, drink-addled mind could have missed it.

"He was a traitor to our people," Arcana whispered at last, drawing back to catch Flare's burnt orange gaze. "But was it really worth an eye for an eye?"

"I didn't do it for them." Flare tilted his head, face strangely calm. "I did it for you."

Arcana swallowed heavily, barely managing to smother a second, stronger frisson of pain behind her eyes. Sobriety was returning and with it, pain that would ultimately lead to unconsciousness. "You can't go around incinerating people's heads in my name, Flare."

"Actually, I can." Flare raised an eyebrow. "In a state of military rule, I'm literally the beginning, the middle and the end. Algae needed justice - I simply dispensed it."

Arcana didn't know what to say, so she pressed a gentle kiss to her brother's cheek and allowed him to release her - only to have Fenris catch her yet again as she stumbled. "Taelon is leaving," the Guardian said, his face turned up to the stars. "Your planet is safe for now."

"For now?" Verdure repeated.

"As long as I stand upon Sorcen's earth, I endanger it," Fenris sighed. "The sooner we leave, the better for everyone."

"We can't just leave," Arcana protested. Another sharp pain lanced into her head and this time she winced, rubbing her eyes with trembling fingers. "We need to stay and help."

Fenris bent to stare into Arcana's face, his jade eyes wide and pleading. "Your city is in ruins. Many of your people have died and your government is decimated. If Taelon returns - and he will, when he has attained reinforcements - your people may not survive."

"Much as I hate to send you away, Fenris has a point," Flare murmured, shoving both hands into the pockets in his robe. "I can see how wrecked you are right now. When you crash you're going to be out for days - you said so yourself. Secondly, if you hang around you'll be drawn into the political debate. Two of the Elders are dead; the Healing Tower is rubble. And yes, your strength during the clean-up would be invaluable but I believe Fenris when he says Taelon will return. We can't afford for that to happen."

Fenris' face tightened. "I am sorry for the pain I have caused you, brother."

"Don't apologise." Flare gripped Fenris' arm firmly. "Taelon might be an unknown quantity but the warg are everybody's problem. Sorcen stands with you, and with the Weaver. You are always welcome."

"You don't even know the Weaver," Arcana frowned, her head swimming. The horizon dipped alarmingly and she sagged against Fenris, whose arm slid further around her ribs to compensate.

"No, but I've met Taelon, and the enemy of my enemy is my friend," Flare's lips twitched and he summoned his tiny flame again, peering at Arcana in the flickering glow. "You look like shit."

Arcana blinked slowly, owlishly. Flare's face was streaked with soot and blood and even as she tried to focus, those familiar features blurred. Her bones groaned in warning, her thoughts turned sluggish. "You vaporised a man's head," she said dreamily. Her knees buckled but it didn't matter - Fenris, as per usual, was right there, sweeping her up into his arms.

"I did," Flare's expression was fierce, his eyes gentle. "And I'd do it again." He flicked a look at Caelum. "Go now, while you can. I'll send a message when I get the chance."

"You don't want to come?" Caelum asked.

"I do - maybe too much." Flare hesitated, then leant in to press a brotherly kiss to Arcana's brow. "I'm furious with Gravella, with the Council, with everything - but I'm also currently in charge. And much as I hate the idea, I'm now the Fire Elder. Temporarily, anyway."

"You're stronger than Blaze was. They'll want to keep you," Caelum warned.

He nodded. "Something I've had nightmares about ever since Blaze offered to abdicate all those years ago. I know he's got me listed as his successor - and I don't want the job - but I can't just leave, either."

"You're a good man, Flare," Fenris said into the ensuing silence. "Be safe."

"Always. Until next time, brother. Take care of her," Flare thumped Fenris soundly on the shoulder and received a grunt in return.

Arcana gathered her wits, forced her tongue to move even as her body went limp in Fenris' arms. "Flare... Gravella deserves... to be recognised for her sacrifice."

He huffed a laugh. "And that, right there, is why I love you, sis. Be safe." Flare's voice drifted into the darkness and Arcana wasn't sure if it was because Fenris had begun walking, or she had fallen asleep.

~ THE END ~

Thanks for reading!

Can't wait for the next instalment?

Keep up to date with all the latest shenanigans at:
www.sliceofsammy.com

ACKNOWLEDGMENTS

To my mum Helen, for always being my number one fan, for staying up late reading my drafts over and over, and for listening to me drone on endlessly during long car drives.

To Glen, whose creative input revived me before I was ready but right when it was needed. It seems like only yesterday that a glib conversation became an idea for a novel – now here we are, at the other end.

To Bron, for harassing me to get it finished, pointing out all the things that were Fenris Green, and for being so dreadfully excited that I had no option but to finish this book so you could read it.

To Erin, for always being my other unicorn, for 28 years' worth of incredible friendship, and for volunteering to be a part of this. Here's to the next chapter.

IF YOU LOVED THIS ONE...

Please leave a review!

Reviews really help authors; it directs our books into the right kind of hands, which in turn allows me to keep writing more books for you to enjoy.

So, if you had a blast reading this story, I'd be ever so grateful if you left a review wherever you can.

Thank you!
🤍

ALSO BY SAMANTHA STORMFURY

Prince of Storms. Lady of Shadows.

God of Chaos.

Bound in eternal servitude to the Atlantean royal family, dark fairy Liria Atlannon spends her days bending to the whims of her mistress. When Atlantis' youngest Princess announces her betrothal to the great Pharaoh Taos of Egypt, Liria has no choice but to follow her Princess across the sea to a kingdom - and a life - unlike anything she has known before.

As Commander of the Pharoah's honour guard, it is Prince Raiden Horushood's duty to defend his brother at all costs. He's never met a foe he couldn't conquer - until Set the Anarchist, god of war and chaos, attempts to steal the Pharaoh's fiancee from her own welcome banquet. While Raiden rages helplessly in the thrall of Set's magic, Liria, the softly spoken handmaiden who spends most of her time staring at the floor, not only turns Set away but injures him in the process.

With the threat of an unpredictable god hanging overhead, Raiden begs Liria to join the Pharoah's honour guard. Though Liria aches to become part of something greater, self preservation dictates she stay away from the vital, strong, and irritatingly handsome Prince Raiden. For if the warrior angel gets too close, he'll discover that the biggest threat to Merged Egypt is not Set at all – it is Liria Atlannon, damned by the magic which shackles her soul, steals her free will and shapes her actions... until all that remains is a shadow.

———————

Read on for a sneak preview of Chapter One!

HEARTH AND HOME

Liria Atlannon looked around at the cool marble pillars of Princess Ione's quarters and knew she wouldn't miss it for even a moment. There was something to be said for the elegance of gold-shot marble which glowed in the light of the noonday sun, and perhaps even something to be said for the open, breezy architecture and gauzy drapes in Atlantean aqua - but for her, the paradise island of Atlantis had only ever been a prison.

Moving quietly to the edge of the balcony, Liria set delicate hands on the railing and cast her gaze out over the cheery city which glittered in the sun, shimmering marble and deep gold sandstone broken up by swathes of cloth in all the shades of the ocean. Beyond that, the azure sea lapped lazily at a pristine shore of pale sand that sparkled with hints of silver silica. A pair of Atlantean Dreadnaughts bobbed offshore, one with her steel decks unfurled like a silvered ocean lily, and the other curled in tight upon itself in preparation for an underwater journey.

"Beautiful, and yet I don't see that I will miss it."

Liria lowered her head as the Princess Ione came up beside her, lest the other woman see the way her face set into an involuntary grimace. The motion shifted her focus to her fingers, gripping tight to the balcony rail. Her skin had begun to turn the mottled blue-grey of a storm-tossed sky, her emotions slipping their leash and causing the truth of her nature to creep through. Drawing deep of the salt-laden air, Liria forced her face into smooth lines and exerted just enough power to shift her skin back to the blemish-free cream her mistress preferred.

"You won't miss it?" she asked, her voice carefully modulated to be soft and submissive. "Surely Atlantis is in your bones, your highness."

Princess Ione tossed her head. She was beautiful - exquisite, even, with long black hair that hung in perfect curls midway down her back, softly tanned skin and deep, dark blue eyes - yet there was a glitter in her gaze, an edge to her cultured smile that spoke of bitter hunger.

"No," Ione said, her lip curling. "I am meant for greater things than to be the fifth child of the ruling family of Atlantis. I am meant to be a queen."

"And so you will be," Liria answered, bowing slightly from the waist. "Your marriage to the Pharaoh of Egypt will ensure such."

An arranged marriage sounded like the worst kind of torture to Liria, but Princess Ione had been the driving force behind the entire affair. In fact, Liria's eavesdropping around the palace had her safe in the certainty that the King and Queen of Atlantis had only acquiesced to keep Ione happy; no-one had actually expected Pharaoh Taos to accept.

"Yes. Soon, I will be Queen of Egypt," Ione breathed, spreading her arms wide and tipping her head back to stare at the sky. "Soon, I will witness the technological marvel of Egypt's great airships, and view their crystal-topped pyramids with my own eyes. I shall rule over the country which stands at the forefront of science and magic, sip wine with the most powerful of gods and be bathed in the adoring praise of my subjects – while Atlantis will become but a faded memory, a pale imitation to be laughed at and forgotten." The Princess clasped her hands at the base of her throat, gleaming midnight eyes locking on Liria's face. "Are you ready, my shadow, to follow me on this path to greatness?"

It wasn't like she had any other choice, but Liria knew better than to say such things aloud. Instead, she bowed deeply, locking her gaze on the embroidered hem of Ione's gown. "Of course, your highness."

Princess Ione ran her slender fingers across the shimmering surface of Liria's wings, the sensation akin to hot knives slashing her wide open. Her breath caught in her throat, the urge to protest becoming the very thing that ensured her silence as the magical chains which bound her to her mistress snapped into full effect.

"Such flawless mystery in you, Liria. The subtlety of twilight, of hidden, magical things. You are well suited to accompany a jewel such as I." Another caress of Ione's fingers, her movements flicking away the long layers of trailing gauze that served to shield Liria's wings from view. "I wonder if Pharaoh Taos' wings are as magnificent as yours?"

"He's of the blood of Horus, your highness, and thus carries the wings of the falcon - whereas I am but a lowly fairy. I'm sure my wings are as nothing in comparison to the strong, feathered pinions of the angels."

"Hmmm. I suppose we shall see, soon enough." Ione tapped Liria's spine, silent permission for her to straighten. "I've heard the angels can even carry passengers, should the need arise."

So had Liria, but she didn't say as such, lest the Princess ask where she'd come across the knowledge. Instead, she adjusted the many layers of gauze which hung from her shoulders so that they once more protected her wings from casual view and said, "Perhaps, once you are wed, you can convince the Pharaoh to take you flying."

"Oh, yes." Ione clasped her hands to her full breasts, dark blue eyes shining. She blinked a few moments later, a crease forming between her brows. "And you will follow us, my shadow, will you not?"

Liria inclined her head again, glad of the way her hair swung forward to hide her face. "Such is my duty, your highness."

Want to find out what happens next?

Grab your copy here:

https://sliceofsammy.com

LOVE A FREE BOOK?

LEARN TO LET GO... OR BURN.

Dating Noah Acheson has always been gentle, predictable and above all, safe – but when the softly spoken foxkin breaks the rules of their carefully crafted relationship, Deanna cuts him off, retreating to her private sanctuary deep in the Australian bush.

Stinging from Deanna's rejection, Noah returns from a brief stint fighting fires in New South Wales to face an infinitely more vicious fire front in Victoria. Though his broken heart still very much belongs to Deanna Schellponte, he's determined not to chase her – until the wind changes, turning the fires towards pack land, and Deanna is reported missing.

With fire raging all around, Noah races into the bush to find the wolfkin he loves. To survive, Deanna and Noah must confront not only the fury of Mother Nature… but the ghost whose memory tore them apart.

Get your FREE copy here:

https://sliceofsammy.com/contact

OTHER TALES BY SAMANTHA STORMFURY

Sorcery and Stardust

A sweeping science fiction series following the adventures of Arcana, Fenris, Caelum and Flare as they work to save time and space from the bestial warg and their vicious leader.

The Kin Chronicles

A paranormal romance series featuring the Kin, a race of people who can shift into animals and live alongside humanity in an alternate contemporary reality.

The Merged Worlds

A fantasy and paranormal romance series that starts in a time before our written history, when gods roamed the Earth, technology was crazily advanced and humanity shared their space with angels, vampires, fairies and a host of other magical creatures.

A Perfectly Paranormal Anthologies

A collection of paranormal romance anthologies in conjunction with several other wonderful authors.

To find out more about any of these, visit my website:

www.sliceofsammy.com

WANT TO KEEP IN TOUCH?

I love to hear from, and hang out with, like minded people (yes, that's you!) and expand my tribe. Whilst I'm most active in my newsletter, you can also find me in other places from time to time! If you've already joined my mailing list and are still looking for more, then check out the following:

BLOG - www.sliceofsammy.com/blog

INSTAGRAM - @sliceofsammy

Or send me an email at -

samwrites@sliceofsammy.com

I love hearing from readers and authors alike!

See you there ^_^

Love,
    Sammy
    XOXO

ABOUT THE AUTHOR

Hi, I'm Sam!

I've been writing my whole life, scribbling stories on anything close to hand – from the shopping list to napkins to post-it notes.

I grew up reading fantasy of the likes of Anne McCaffrey, Terry Pratchett, and their peers. I'm also a lifelong vampire fan, along with all things spooky. In my late teens I was introduced to paranormal romance and discovered a whole new layer of storytelling with a bit of a spicy edge! Taking what I learnt from all of the above, I devoted myself to creating full-bodied characters, meaty plots, epic adventure, and a little bit of naughty sauce on the side.

I completed a Diploma of Professional Writing and Editing after high school and spent the next several years in my writing cave, working on a novel that is now in a drawer somewhere, followed by a couple of others who shared the same fate. (What can I say? I'm a recovering perfectionist.)

I came close to debuting my novel career in 2009, then ended up pregnant and took some time off to have kids. I debuted for real in 2019 with *Sorcery and Stardust* and won ARRA's Favourite Debut Romance Author for 2019, which was extremely cool!

I write speculative fiction that is a fusion of multiple sub-genres and therefore doesn't fit particularly well into any of them, but after many years and a lot of angst, I'm okay with that. I love all my characters and their stories for different reasons, but have a soft spot for an excellent villain and a tortured protagonist.

I had an attack of the Real Life in the early 2020s which resulted in a long hiatus, followed by a gradual rebuild into the Samantha Stormfury you know today. I learnt that sometimes, there is nothing you can do but hold on, even if it feels like there's nothing left to hold onto - and in doing so, I had a strength I never realised I was capable of.

I believe in unicorns, dragons, and true love. I'm passionate about great writing, interesting characters, chai tea - and, until the stars burn out of the sky, holding on for happily ever afters.

www.ingramcontent.com/pod-product-compliance
Lightning Source LLC
Chambersburg PA
CBHW020127120726
47903CB00007B/2136